Praise for the novels of

THE GERMAN WIFE

"Skillfully researched and powerfully written, *The German Wife* will capture you from the first page. Kelly Rimmer always delivers a poignant story—this book is no exception."

—Madeline Martin, *New York Times* bestselling author of *The Last Bookshop in London*

"*The German Wife* is a heart-wrenching, uplifting story about love and family and the choices people make in impossible situations. An unforgettable historical novel that explores important questions highly relevant to the world today."

—Christine Wells, author of *Sisters of the Resistance*

"Once again, Kelly Rimmer has turned my emotions upside down. With every book of hers I read, I become a more thoughtful and empathetic person, but *The German Wife* is, without a doubt, the jewel in her crown."

—Sally Hepworth, *New York Times* bestselling author of *The Younger Wife*

"*The German Wife* moves beyond the better-known stories to uncover the hidden horrors of the Second World War and what it was like for the women—and the men they loved—during that time. A must-read."

—Jane Cockram, author of *The Way from Here*

THE WARSAW ORPHAN

"Rimmer's heart-stopping rendering of the war in Nazi-occupied Poland will captivate readers page-by-page. Elżbieta's tale offers a carefully researched portrayal of history's darkest hours."

—Lisa Wingate, *New York Times* bestselling author of *Before We Were Yours*

"What a fantastic book! Intensely moving, [this story] is also a wonderful, ultimately life-affirming love story. I'm going to be recommending this book to everyone I know."

—Karen Robards, *New York Times* bestselling author of *The Black Swan of Paris*

Also by Kelly Rimmer

THE PARIS AGENT
THE GERMAN WIFE
THE WARSAW ORPHAN
TRUTHS I NEVER TOLD YOU
THE THINGS WE CANNOT SAY
BEFORE I LET YOU GO

KELLY RIMMER

THE

PARIS

AGENT

GRAYDON
HOUSE

GRAYDON HOUSE®

ISBN-13: 978-1-525-82668-9

The Paris Agent

Graydon House
22 Adelaide St. West, 41st Floor
Toronto, Ontario M5H 4E3, Canada
www.GraydonHouseBooks.com
www.BookClubbish.com

Printed in U.S.A.

If the multiverse is real, there's probably a world where I dedicated this book to the memory of my mother. As I was working on revisions to this story, she had a series of sudden health emergencies—a major heart attack, a series of strokes, COVID. We came close to losing her time and time again.

But she's still here.

Our family and her friends get more glorious days to enjoy her company, her wise advice and support, her pathological inability to *not* spoil her grandkids, the way she shows her love through good food and generosity, and a kindness that comes from her very soul.

Every extra hour we get to spend with her is because of the skilled intervention of those who choose to spend their lives working in health care. Cleaning staff kept the hospital sanitized; administration staff kept the paperwork moving; paramedics, specialists, doctors and nurses and allied health care workers went to work in a system under strain and did their best for their patients.

I publish this story in honor of the staff of the NSW Ambulance and Orange Health Service who saved my mother's life, but also for health care workers everywhere. At its heart, this is a book about sacrifice and courage, and in that sense, and after these last few difficult years, there is no more fitting dedication.

Thank you, thank you, thank you.

THE

PARIS

AGENT

PROLOGUE

Perhaps at first glance, we might have looked like ordinary passengers: four women in civilian clothes, sitting in pairs facing one another, the private carriage of the passenger train illuminated by the golden light of a cloudless late-summer sunrise. Only upon closer inspection would a passerby have seen the handcuffs that secured us, our wrists resting at our sides, between us not because we meant to hide them but because we were exhausted, and they were too heavy to rest on our bony thighs. Only at a second glance would they have noticed the emaciated frames or the clothes that didn't quite fit, or the scars and healing wounds each of us bore after months of torture and imprisonment.

I was handcuffed to a petite woman I knew first as Chloe, although in recent weeks, we had finally shared our real names with one another. It was entirely possible that she was the best friend I'd ever known—not that there was much competition for that title, given friendship had never come easy to me. Two British women, Mary and Wendy, sat opposite us. They had trained together, as Chloe and I had trained together, and like us, they had been "lucky enough" to recently find themselves imprisoned together too. Mary and Wendy appeared just as shell-shocked as Chloe and I were by the events of that morning.

As our captors had reminded us often since our arrests, we were plainclothes assassins and as such, not even entitled to the basic protections of the Geneva Convention. So why on earth had we been allowed the luxury of a shower that morning, and why had we been given clean civilian clothes to wear after months in the filthy outfits we'd been wearing since our capture? Why were they transporting us by passenger train, and in a luxurious private carriage, no less? This wasn't my first time transferring between prisons since my capture. I knew from bitter personal experience that the usual travel arrangement was, at best, the crowded, stuffy back end of a covered truck or at worst, a putrid, overcrowded boxcar.

But this carriage was modern and spacious, comfortable and relaxed. The leather seats were soft beneath me and the air was clean and light in a way I'd forgotten air should be after months confined to filthy cells.

"This could be a good sign," I whispered suddenly. Chloe eyed me warily, but my optimism was picking up steam now, and I turned to face her as I thought aloud. "I bet Baker Street has negotiated better conditions for us! Maybe this transfer is a step toward our release. Maybe that's why..." I nodded toward our only companions in the carriage, seated on the other side of the aisle. "Maybe that's why *she's* here. Could it be that she's been told to keep us safe and comfortable?"

Chloe and I had had little to do with the secretary at Karlsruhe Prison, but I had seen her in the hallway outside of our cell many times, always scurrying after the terrifyingly hostile warden. It made little sense for a secretary to accompany us on a transfer, but there she was, dressed in her typical tweed suit, her blond hair constrained in a thick bun at the back of her skull. The secretary sat facing against the direction of travel, opposite the two armed guards who earlier had marched me and Chloe onto the covered truck at the prison, then from the covered truck onto the platform to join the train. The men had not introduced themselves, but like all agents with the British Special Operations Executive, I'd spent weeks memorizing German uniforms and insignias. I knew at a glance that these were low-ranking *Sicherheitsdienst* officers—members of the SD. The Nazi intelligence agency.

The secretary spoke to the guards, her voice low but her tone playful. She held a suitcase on her lap, and she winked as she tapped it. The men both brightened, surprised smiles transforming their stern expressions, then she theatrically popped the suitcase lid to reveal a shockingly generous bounty of thick slices of sausages and chunks of cheese, a large loaf of sliced rye bread and…was that butter? The scent of the food flooded the carriage as the secretary and the guards used the suitcase as a table for their breakfast.

It was far too much food for three people but I knew they'd never share it with us. My stomach rumbled violently, but after months surviving on scant prison rations, I was desperate enough that I felt lucky to be in the mere presence of such a feast.

"I heard the announcement as we came onto the carriage— this train goes to Strasbourg, doesn't it? Do you have any idea what's waiting for us there? This is all a bit…" Wendy paused, gnawing her lip anxiously. "None of it makes sense. Why are they treating us so well?"

"This is the Strasbourg train," Chloe confirmed cautiously. There was a subtle undertone to those words—something hesitant, concerned. I frowned, watching her closely, but just then the secretary leaned toward the aisle. She spoke to us in rapid German and pointed to the suitcase in her lap.

Had we done something wrong? More German words—

but it may as well have been Latin to me, because I spoke only French and English. Just then, the secretary huffed impatiently and pushed the suitcase onto the empty seat beside her as she stood. She held a plate toward me, and when I stared at it blankly, she waved impatiently toward Chloe and spoke again in German.

"What…"

"She wants you to take it," Chloe translated for me, and I took the plate with my one free hand, bewildered. Chloe passed it to Wendy, and so on, until we all held plates in our hands. The secretary then passed us fat slices of sausage and cheese and several slices of bread each. Soon, our plates were filled with the food, each of us holding a meal likely more plentiful than we'd experienced since our arrival in France.

"She's toying with us," Mary whispered urgently. "She'll take it back. She won't let us eat it so don't get your hopes up."

I nodded subtly—I'd assumed the same. And so, I tried to ignore the treasure sitting right beneath my nose. I tried not to notice how garlicky and rich that sausage smelled, how creamy the cheese looked, or how the butter was so thick on the bread that it might also have been cheese. I told myself the increasing pangs in my stomach were just part of the torture and the smartest thing I could do was to ignore them altogether, but the longer I held the plate, the harder it was to refocus my mind on anything but the pain in my stomach and the feast in my hands that would bring instant and lasting relief.

When all the remaining food had been divided between us prisoners, the secretary waved impatiently toward the plates on our laps, then motioned toward her mouth.

"Eat!" she said, in impatient but heavily accented English.

Chloe and I exchanged shocked glances. Conditions in Karlsruhe Prison were not the worst we'd seen since our respective captures, but even so, we'd been hungry for so long. The starvation was worse for Chloe than me. She had a particularly sensitive constitution and ate a narrow range of foods in order to avoid gastric distress. Since our reunion at the prison, we'd developed a system of sharing our rations so she could avoid the foods which made her ill but even so, she remained so thin I had sometimes worried I'd wake up one morning to find she'd died in her sleep.

"What can you eat?" I asked her urgently.

She looked at our plates then blurted, "Sausage. I'll eat the sausage."

For the next ten minutes we prisoners fell into silence except for the occasional, muffled moan of pleasure and relief as we devoured the food. I was trying to find the perfect compromise between shoving it all into my mouth as fast as I could in case the secretary changed her mind and savoring every bite with the respect a meal like that commanded. By the time my plate was empty and my surroundings came back to me, the guards and the secretary were having a lovely time, laughing amongst themselves and chatting as if they didn't have a care in the world.

For a long while, we prisoners traveled in silence, holding our plates on our laps at first, then after Wendy set the precedent, lifting them to our mouths to lick them clean. Still, the guards chatted and laughed and if I judged their tones correctly, even flirted with the secretary? It gradually dawned on me that they were paying us very little attention.

"How far is Strasbourg? Does anyone know?" I asked. Wendy and Mary shook their heads as they shrugged, but Chloe informed me it was hundreds of miles. Her shoulders had slumped again despite the gift of the food, and I nudged her gently and offered a soft smile. "We have a long journey ahead. Good. That means we have time for a pleasant chat while our bellies are full."

By unspoken agreement, we didn't discuss our work with the Special Operations Executive (SOE). It was obvious to me that each of the other women had been badly beaten at some point—Wendy was missing a front tooth, Mary held her left hand at an odd angle as if a fractured wrist had healed badly, and Chloe… God, even if she hadn't explained to me already, I'd have known just looking at her that Chloe had been to hell and back. It seemed safe to assume we had all been interrogated literally almost to death at some point, but there was still too much at stake to risk giving away anything the Germans had not gleaned from us already. So instead of talking about our work or our peculiar circumstances on that train, we talked as though we weren't wearing handcuffs. As though we weren't on our way to, at the very best, some slightly less horrific form of imprisonment.

We acted as though we were two sets of friends on a casual jaunt through the countryside. We talked about interesting features outside our window—the lush green trees in the tall forests, the cultivated patches of farmland, the charming facades of cottages and apartments on the streets outside. Mary cooed over a group of adorable children walking to school, and Wendy talked about little shops we passed in the picturesque villages. Chloe shared longing descriptions of the foods she missed the most—fresh fruit and crisp vegetables, eggs cooked all manner of ways, herbs and spices and salt. I lamented my various aches and pains and soon everyone joined in and we talked as if we were elderly people reflecting on the cruelty of aging, not four twenty-somethings who had been viciously, repeatedly beaten by hateful men.

I felt the warmth of the sunshine on my face through the window of the carriage and closed my eyes, reveling in the simple pleasures of fresh air and warm skin and the company of the best friend I'd ever known. I even let myself think about the secretary and that picnic, and feel the relief that I was, for the first time in months, in the company of a stranger who had shown kindness toward me. I'd almost forgotten that was something people did for one another.

I'd never been an especially cheerful sort of woman and I'd never been an optimist, but those past months had forced me to stare long and hard at the worst aspects of the human condition and I'd come to accept a certain hopelessness even when it came to my own future. But on that train, bathed in early morning sunlight and basking in a full stomach and pleasant company, my spirits lifted until they soared toward something like hope.

For the first time in months, I even let myself dream that I'd survive to embrace my son Hughie again. Maybe, even after all I'd seen and done, the world could still be good. Maybe, even after everything, I could find reason to have faith.

CHAPTER 1

CHARLOTTE
Liverpool
May, 1970

Dad and I sit side by side on a picnic blanket on Formby Beach, gazing across the blue-gold gradient of the sunset reflecting off the Irish Sea. A red thermos full of hot tea is propped into the sand in front of my legs, and between me and Dad, our golden retriever Wrigley lies flat on the checkered rug, staring longingly at the newspaper on Dad's lap. There's only a handful of chips left, but the scent of salt and fat and vinegar seems to be driving poor Wrigley mad.

If Dad wasn't here, I'd let Wrigley tear into that newspaper. I always did find it hard to say no to that dog, but since my mother's death, I don't even try.

Today should have been Mum's fifty-fourth birthday. Christmas was miserable, but this, the first of her birthdays since her death, is somehow an equally confronting milestone. Mum always liked to make a fuss of birthdays, and we always did the same for her. This should have been *her* day, so now that she's gone, it's a day when her absence is all I can think about. Even Wrigley seemed miserable this morning, sulking around the house as if he knew the date as well as we did. That's when I decided we had to get out of the house this evening. Yes, this feels stiff and awkward, but this pathetic, depressing picnic is at least some attempt to mark the day.

Geraldine Ainsworth would never have tolerated sulking.

"I've been worried about you, Lottie," Dad says suddenly. His words are slow and careful, ever-so-slightly slurred as they always are—the unusual pattern of his speech the lasting result of a traumatic brain injury from a car accident when he was young. But I have no trouble understanding him, and I turn to look at him in disbelief. He's worried about *me*? That's rich, coming from him. Even the new notches he's punched into his belt aren't enough to keep his trousers from sagging off his hips these days. He's a shriveled version of his old self but even as my defensiveness rises, I note the deep concern in his eyes. That gives me pause. Dad clears his throat and says hesitantly, "You don't seem yourself since—" He breaks off, obviously searching for words, then settles on a muttered "Well. Since your mum left us."

"She didn't leave us, Dad," I snap. "She was *taken* from us."

I wince, immediately regretting my sharp tone, but Dad doesn't react. He stares right into my eyes and waits, almost as if he'd wanted to generate a reaction in me.

Well, he got one. And now I feel awful for it.

If it had been a friend or colleague who died, I'd have gone to Dad for support. I'd have cried all over him and blubbered about the injustice of it all. I've always known Noah Ainsworth as a man who could do a passable impersonation of an extrovert when the situation commands it, but who's truly most comfortable listening one-on-one. And given I have always been someone who loves to talk, this suited me just fine right up until my mother died. I've had so many words I wanted to say since then. I still have no idea if my father will ever be ready to hear them.

The problem is this: I lost my mother, but Dad lost the love of his life. He's been my emotional rock since I was a child, but I can't burden him with my pain when his is even greater.

It hits me suddenly now that Dad has seemed every bit as broken and furious about her death as I have, until the last week or so. Flashes of memory cycle through my mind—things I noticed but didn't pause to be curious about at the time, lost in my own fog of sadness. Dad up early last Saturday, making himself eggs for breakfast. Dad ironing his clothes for the week on Sunday night, just as he always used to. Dad smiling as he walked out the door to go to work on Monday.

And the most telling of all—how did I miss it? Every night this week, Dad waiting for me in the evening with robust, hearty meals—rich beef stews and pastas and baked chicken. He's eat   well again! He's been quiet, but it's the old kind of quiet—   ind that allows space for me to talk, not the kind of tense   erable silence that told me he was too bereaved to listen. And now, after months of introspection, he's prompting me to share.

"You're doing a little better," I blurt. He tilts his head a little, thoughtful.

"I will miss your mother every minute until I join her on the other side, Lottie," he says quietly. "But she wouldn't want me to spend the rest of my life bitter." He paused, then added with a wry chuckle, "She wouldn't have allowed it, actually, and I know that for a fact."

There are unspoken words at the end of that sentence. About me. About my bitterness and the ferocious anger that still burns so fiercely in me, every bit as destructive as it was when I found out she was gone. And that's too bad, because I'm still not ready to let any of that go. I'm curious about the change in Dad though, because now that I've acknowledged it to myself, I start to wonder.

He isn't just calmer, he's focused. Steady. So much more his old self.

As for me, I haven't missed a day at work, but I haven't been fully present in that classroom since I returned from my bereavement leave. I'm with those five-year-olds all day long and I spend every second of my work hours pretending I'm the woman I used to be. My heart isn't in it anymore. The loss of my mother has changed me in a way I'm not sure I can come back from.

"What's the secret, Dad?" I whisper, throat tight. "How do I stop feeling like this?" Some days, the students in my class do something I *know* is funny or adorable but I have to force myself to smile. Last week, little Aoife Byrne finally mastered the letters of her name. It's a feat that's taken a year of concentrated effort because of her developmental challenges, but I felt no spark of pride or relief. Instead, I am numb or sad or angry all the time, no longer capable of the joy I once took for granted in my life and my job.

"I lived such a wonderful life with your mother, you know," Dad says. "Truly, we shared so many wonderful years—"

"But she was only fifty-three," I interrupt him sharply. "You were meant to have more time. Don't you feel cheated?"

"Cheated?" He considers the word, then gives me a soft look. "There would never have been enough years, love. I'd never have had my fill of that woman! And think of all we shared. You...your brother...a beautiful granddaughter. We built a marvelous home, and we supported one another in our careers and we spent all of those lovely Saturdays in the garden and honestly, when I look back, it feels like a glorious dream." When Dad becomes emotional, his speech slows even more, the slur becoming more and more pronounced. He pauses now, collecting himself, then adds roughly, "I've felt stuck since she died."

"That's how I feel."

"A few weeks ago, I was looking at our old photo albums and I found one of us standing together outside of her family home in 1941. Just a few weeks before that day, I'd learned that my family was gone and the look on my face… I was still in shock when that photo was taken." He pauses, overcome with emotion again, and my heart aches at the pain in his voice. He was the eldest of five children, but his parents and siblings were killed during the Liverpool Blitz when their home was destroyed in an air raid. "I could barely drag myself out of bed but your mother told me I needed to find a way to move forward. She had much the same advice for me in the dying days of the war when I was confronted by a whole other kind of grief. She used to tell me 'Noah, you will not bring any one of your loved ones back for even a moment by refusing to live your own life.'" I look out to the water, my eyes stinging with tears. I hear those words as if she's whispering them to me herself, but I still don't have a *clue* how to apply them. "Twice already she brought me back to life by pointing me to look beyond the immediacy of my loss. This time it was the mere memory of that advice that woke me up. I need something to focus on so I've decided to take on a new project."

"At work?"

Mum was a schoolteacher, just as I am, but Dad owns a small chain of auto mechanic shops—his pride and joy, second only to those of us lucky enough to be his family. He reaches down into the newspaper to withdraw a fat but likely cold chip. Wrigley watches hopefully as Dad raises the chip to his mouth, then slumps again when Dad chews the whole thing in one bite.

"The idea came to me when I looked at that photo, actually," he says. "It got me thinking about those days again. You know I served."

He rarely talks about the war, but I've seen photos of him as a young man in uniform, and in one, I recall he was holding a spanner.

"You worked as an army mechanic, right?"

"Well, no," he says carefully. I glance at him in surprise. "I left school at sixteen to enlist."

"Sixteen," I breathe, shaking my head. "Dad, that's so young."

"Yes, I was young enough that they'd only take me with my parents' permission, but my mum and dad were thrilled to give it. I'd never been good at school, but I was good with my hands, so it made sense for me to enlist and learn a trade. They were so proud when I qualified..." Dad trails off, draws in a deep breath, then finishes slowly, "...as a flight mechanic."

A flight mechanic? I turn to Dad, eyebrows high.

"Wait. Are you telling me you trained on planes before cars? Why don't I know this already?"

"It was always my dream to work on airplanes, right from when I was a little boy," Dad says wistfully. "And it was incredible work. I loved the problem-solving and the challenge of it—I mean, honestly Lottie, it was just so bloody cool. I spent my whole school years feeling stupid, but I felt like the smartest man in the world once I knew how to make a plane work."

Dad's always shown a vague interest in planes, but he's never seemed especially passionate about aviation. Not like this. Even as he's speaking, there's a wondrous glint in his eye.

"But you work on cars," I say stupidly, as if he might have forgotten. "You always have." Dad glances at me, and I add weakly, "At least, as long as I've been alive."

"I came out of the war a changed man. I knew I needed to reinvent myself and to be completely frank, my mind wasn't up to the challenge of resuming aviation work. I mean, cars are still plenty complex. Still challenging. But given my..." He waves toward his head, and my eyes widen.

"The car accident? I thought you said that happened when you were a kid."

"Well, I *was* a kid. I was only in my twenties. And it probably was a car accident but..."

"But what?"

"My memories of that day aren't perfect, that's all. Anyway, after the war, it was helpful for me to go back to basics and learn a new trade. So, I went right back to the start of an apprenticeship, this time with cars."

"You never told me any of this," I say. Dad and I are close and I thought I knew his life well. It stings a little that this is a part of his past he's never shared with me.

"There's a lot I never told you, love," he says gently.

"Well? What else?"

"When the war started, I had a promotion of sorts, and I ended up working as a flight engineer. It was marvelous fun at first, soaring into the sky with a crew that soon enough felt like brothers to me. But...everything changed in 1940 with the Battle of France. Me and the boys were so proud to be defending our neighbor—we knew England was at risk too and we wanted to do for France what we hoped the world would do for us if the Germans came to our shores. But one day, on a mission over Northern France, my plane took a brutal hit." I gasp in shock, and Dad nods slowly, still staring out at the water, but his gaze is distant now and his voice drops. "We had no choice but to bail out and it was terrifying. Ian Owens' chute didn't open. No chance he could have survived a fall like that. The rest of the crew were captured pretty much right away."

"And you?" I ask, stunned.

"Ah, I was the lucky one that day," Dad says softly. "By some miracle a gust of wind caught my chute, and I was blown away from the others, right into the backyard of a sympathetic French farmer. He hid me for months while the area was lousy with Germans. He put me to work with his sons—fixing their cars, working on the fields—hiding in plain sight as it were. Not an uncommon thing for helpful Frenchmen to do for downed airmen at the time. Once that initial phase of the occupation had settled into something calmer—still awful, mind, but not quite as chaotic—the farmer sought out a local resistance group and in time, they took me into their network of safe houses. Your mum and I weren't married yet, but we were dating, and she had no idea if I was alive or dead for over a year." He shakes his head as he exhales. "I suspect that just about drove her crazy."

"But...*what*?" The slight sting that Dad had been keeping secrets from me is now a soul-deep ache and confusion. "Dad." He doesn't react, so I say again, this time more urgently, "That's how you learned French, isn't it? You told me you learned at school..."

"Like I said, love," he says quietly, "I didn't want to lie to you and your brother, but it was easiest to give you both simpler explanations for these things at first. Then time got away from me. Some things are easier to forget than to confront."

"Wow," I breathe, shaking my head. "Dad! This is incredible."

"They were wild times. Everyone my age has a story to tell about the war years."

"But...but *you*?" I suppose any daughter would be shocked to hear a parent had lived through such an ordeal, but my father is so quiet—at times, bordering on shy. I don't think of Dad as weak but even so, I just can't picture him living under such danger.

"And then, after I escaped France—"

"How did you *'escape France'*?"

"There was really only one way out and that was the escape lines operated by resistance volunteers. They made up false papers for me, then smuggled me through a series of safe houses, from Lille to Paris, where they paired me up with a girl...a resistance operative, of sorts. She also needed to get out, so we escaped via the Pyrenees."

"But—the French–Spanish border is...what...500 miles from Paris?"

He gives a little shrug.

"Thereabouts."

"So, you and some British girl just...what? Drove from Paris to Spain?"

Dad shakes his head.

"Oh no. We caught a train together to St. Jean de Luz, then a guide took us onward from there by foot through the mountains. I mean, it wasn't as simple as a leisurely hike. Those mountains were riddled with people who wanted to stop evaders like me. First there was the German Gestapo, and the Milice Française, and of course, even the Spanish in the Guardia Civil wanted to stop us. It was an impossibly difficult twenty-four hours." He glances down at his feet and mutters, "My God, by the time we reached the safe house in Oiarzun, even my blisters had blisters. Every step was agony."

"You *walked* out of occupied France. You just walked out through the mountains into Spain," I whisper incredulously.

"I needed to get home and that was the only way to do so."

I pinch the bridge of my nose and squeeze my eyes closed for a moment, trying to piece it all together. "When were you shot down?"

"June 19, 1940."

"But...when did your family die?"

"August 29, 1940."

"Oh, Dad..." I croak, eyes filling with tears. "When did you find out they were...gone...?"

"The day I arrived back here to Liverpool. July 27, 1941," he whispers unevenly. "When I left, my parents and brothers were alive and well in our beautiful home. When I came back, our house had been leveled. The bomb caused a fire, so everything we owned had been burnt so even the rubble was cleared. The only thing I had left of my family was their graves and my memories. That was it."

"My God, Dad. I'm sorry."

"It was tough," he says, but I catch a glimpse of the stoic father I'm used to as he clears his throat and straightens his spine. "Plenty of people had difficult stories through those years. Mine isn't special. My family was gone, and your mother was right—I couldn't bring them back by sitting in my misery. So I guess that's where the story really gets interesting, because—"

He pauses for a moment, and when he speaks again, his tone has changed. It's darker now—heavier, somehow. He stares out at the ocean, his shoulders slumped forward as he speaks.

"The Special Operations Executive approached me and invited me to try out to train as an agent to return to France. I owed my life to the French, and I wanted to do more to help the war effort after what had happened to my family. That invitation to join the SOE felt like an answer to my prayers."

I'm aware of the work of the SOE. I've seen those old films about beautiful women acting as spies behind enemy lines, courageous and dashing British men working alongside them too. My father is nothing like those characters. He's not physically imposing or courageous or especially handsome, or brilliant and charismatic like the actors in those films. Or maybe he is, and I've just never seen it, because to me, he's always just been Dad—a dreadfully uncool, slightly shy man with a heart as big as the world itself.

He's staring out at the water now, the wind tousling his faded brown hair, his gaze distant and somber. And for the very first time in my life, I wonder if I know my father at all.

"I just don't understand why you would keep any of this a secret from us," I say. Has Dad lied to us? Maybe not openly, maybe not directly, but even so, there's a deception here. I try to ease the pain of that by staring into his kind eyes as he turns to me, but I can't shake the sense of hurt.

"I never intended to lie to you and Archie. Your mother and I married right after the war ended and you were born ten months later. It all happened very quickly, Charlotte, so I wasn't close to ready to explain when you were little, but even as you grew older..." He exhales, his eyes growing cloudy. "The truth is that my SOE days were very complicated, love. Not easy to reflect upon, even now. To be completely frank, I've spent a lot of my life trying *not* to think about those times. Speaking about it like this was out of the question for most of my life."

Dad opens the thermos and pours out some tea, steam rising from the black liquid and dissipating into the cool air. He pours a second mug for me and when he passes it to me, I warm my hands around the metal. When he's still again, I ask hesitantly, "This new project...it's related to the SOE?"

"I almost died, you see. Something went awry on a mission, I think. There was the head injury and...well, I was shot—" He rubs his left shoulder absentmindedly.

"You always said that scar was from the car accident..."

"You first asked me about that scar when we were swimming at this very beach when you were three or four years old. Exactly how truthful do you think I should have been, even if I was ready to talk about it at the time, which I was not? Besides, from what I remember, there *was* some kind of car accident. I just happened to be shot at the same time. I think."

I'm trying to appear calm now because it's clear this isn't easy for Dad to talk about, but my heart is racing and it's increasingly difficult to contain my shock. "I can't *believe* you never told us this."

"It was complicated. It *is* complicated," he says hesitantly. "I woke up in a hospital bed. I had a hole in my shoulder and a skull fracture—my brain was all but scrambled. I had a sense that I was British, and I knew the war was raging, but I had no idea why I was in France. All the nurses could tell me was that my 'friend' Remy brought me in and saved my life."

"Who was Remy?"

"That's just the thing—I had no idea at first. I didn't even know my own name right at the start. Many memories returned eventually, but even now, I look back at the war years through a thick mental fog. In time, I became reasonably certain Remy was an agent like me. But if I'm right about that, there's a good chance I never knew his real name."

"You're going to try to track this Remy down?"

"Everything I've enjoyed in this life in the years since then—marrying your mum, the honor of being her husband for decades, being Dad to you and Archie, even being little Poppy's grandfather... I'd have missed *all* of it but for this Remy. You and Archie and even Poppy might never have been born. Isn't that strange to think of it like that? This man's actions changed the course of all of our lives and I have no idea who he was. After so many years, maybe the best I can do is lay some flowers on his grave, or make sure his family knows what he did for me. But I need to do it. I need to try to find him."

"But...why now, Dad?"

"It's like I said: life moved on so quickly after the war. First I had to focus on my recovery from that head injury and that really was a full-time job. Even once I found my feet, it was better...so much easier...to avoid examining those years too closely. The downside is that there are things about my own past I don't know and plenty of things I don't understand. I'd like to change that and I just have an inkling that Remy is the key to it all. I've set myself a real challenge because I'm not even sure where to start, but having a goal has left me feeling much more myself, even if I'm not sure how to achieve it."

"I'm glad, Dad. Maybe I need to find a project of my own," I say, but then slump. Even *thinking* about finding a new project is too exhausting for me. The way Dad glances at me tells me he understands.

"Only when you're ready, Lottie. I'm sorry to tell you that grief is forever, but the acute phase does ease—in its own time. I just wanted to remind you today that your mother knew we all adored her. She wouldn't have needed us to stay miserable to prove it."

I look down at Wrigley and my gaze sticks on the scar on his left front shoulder—where his leg used to connect to his torso.

I always feel a pinch in my chest when I see that scar. Wrigley lost more than a limb that morning.

The dog looks up at me then rises, pushing himself effortlessly onto his three paws. He bends to stretch, wobbling just a little on that single front leg, then sprints down to the water's edge, where he splashes his front foot in the water and gives a bark of joy.

"Hi, Aunt Kathleen. It's Charlotte."

I'm home from the beach, and Dad has retired to his study to start work on his project, but I have one last task left to do before I turn in myself. I invited Mum's sister, my aunt Kathleen, to join us for the picnic. She said she was too busy with end-of-year work at the girls' college where she's headmistress and maybe there's some truth in that, but it's not the *whole* truth. Since Mum died, Aunt Kathleen is busy just about every time I invite her somewhere unless I make it clear the invitation is just for the two of us. She and Dad have always had an odd relationship and I suspect she doesn't want me to be put in the position of buffer, as Mum so often was.

"How was your picnic?" she asks me now. She sounds miserable, and I wonder if I should have made the effort to visit her alone after the picnic instead of calling. She and Mum were so close. Kathleen is as heartbroken over Mum's loss as Dad and I am.

The whole reason I chose Formby Beach for the picnic today was that many of my happiest childhood memories of Mum are from Saturdays there. We'd throw the family dog into the car and we'd drive, the radio blaring and the windows down, wind in our hair and smiles on our faces, to meet Aunt Kathleen in the parking lot. She and Mum would often walk so they could gossip or brainstorm some school issue in privacy, while Dad supervised me and Archie as we paddled in the water or played in the sand. Afterward, we'd sit on a blanket together and share fish and chips, just as Dad and I did today. Despite the ever-present hint of friction between her and Dad, Kathleen is a branch of our family and the distance between us now just feels wrong.

"How are you holding up?" I ask her gently.

"I should be asking you that question, Charlotte," she sighs. I can't answer her honestly, so I lie and tell her what she needs to hear.

"I'm okay," I say, then I force a positivity I don't feel. "The 'firsts' are hard, but we've survived her first birthday without her now. Next year will be easier."

"Hmm," she says noncommittally. "And Noah?"

"He's doing a little better, actually." It strikes me that Kathleen has known Dad for as long as Mum did. "Did you know Dad was in the SOE, Aunt Kathleen?"

She sucks in a breath and seems startled as she says, "I...well, yes. I did." There's a pause before she adds cautiously, "Why do you ask?"

"He never told me and Archie."

"I know that. I'm curious how you know now."

"Dad told me he's starting a project to try to find some man who helped him when he was in France—" I say, but I've barely finished the sentence when Kathleen says abruptly, "Your mother would have *hated* that."

My eyebrows lift in surprise.

"Dad just says he wants to focus on something else. Something other than his grief for Mum."

"Geraldine was always adamant that the war years were best left forgotten," Kathleen says stiffly. "She was a wise woman, Charlotte."

"You think I should discourage him?"

Aunt Kathleen doesn't answer me at first. There's a long, strained silence before she sighs.

"I really don't know, darling. But the timing of this is awfully strange, isn't it? Your mother dies and Noah starts dredging up the past like this? What good could possibly come of that?"

Despite her abrupt tone and how certain she sounds, it seems to me that something good already has come of Dad looking back.

"He's struggled so much since Mum died. We all have. But now, he seems relieved to have something else to focus on. Isn't *that* a good thing?"

"Your father was a completely different man during the war years," Kathleen says. "It's a blessing that you never knew that version of him, Charlotte. That's all I'm saying."

The coolness in Aunt Kathleen's tone sends a chill down my spine. She's never been fond of Dad, but she's never been openly hostile toward him—at least not within my earshot. It's clear there's still more history here that I've never been privy to. Once upon a time I'd have laughed at the idea that my father might have some darkness hidden in his past. Not *my* dad, who cries in sad movies and who catches spiders and releases them outside rather than squishing them.

He's a soft man. A kind man.

But is he an honest man? Dad's involvement with the SOE is no small thing to hide, and even *he* has questions about those days.

"Have you ever talked to Dad about the war years, Aunt Kathleen?" I ask uneasily.

"You know he and I have never been close," she says heavily. "But I do care about Noah. I want what's best for him. And trust me when I say that looking back at those years now is *not* what's best for him."

That strange, unfamiliar chill runs down my spine once more at the gravity in Aunt Kathleen's tone. Whatever's buried in Dad's past has been hidden for a very long time and he *is* so vulnerable right now. Maybe I need to put aside my own curiosity and encourage him to think twice before he embarks upon this project.

★ ★ ★

"Dad," I begin carefully, as I sit down to breakfast the next morning. He's up early again and there's a steaming plate of scrambled eggs waiting for each of us. Dad pours himself a cup of tea and sits opposite me.

"Yes, love?"

"This project...your SOE project."

"Yes?"

It's the softness in his gaze that gets me. Dad doesn't look happy—not exactly—but he does seem at ease, and just like that, I'm second-guessing myself again.

God, I wish my mother were here. She'd have sat me down with a pot of tea and some scones. She'd have folded her hands on the table and sat up straight and tall as she looked me in the eye and said, "Listen, Lottie, here's what you need to do..."

"Are you sure this is a good idea?" I blurt uncertainly now. Dad picks up the table salt and shakes some over his eggs, then stirs sugar into his tea, considering my question.

"Not at all, Charlotte," he sighs. "But it's time. In fact, it's probably past time. This is something I *need* to do."

How can I argue with that? Dad is an adult, and he knows his own mind. If he's sure he needs to do this, I have to let him try.

CHAPTER 2

JOSIE
Montbeliard, France
October, 1943

"Are you alright back there?"

I'd been sitting in the cramped rear cockpit of the Lysander for several hours when the kindly pilot's voice crackled over my headset. I couldn't remember his name and I felt bad for that, but in my defense, my mind was completely full of details I could not afford to forget.

"As well as can be expected," I replied, but he did not respond. I'd only been shown quickly how to use the headset and I'd forgotten most of those instructions too, so it was possible he didn't even hear me.

It was the polite response, but it wasn't the truth. My whole body was humming with nervous tension and the past twenty-four hours had been so surreal, I'd wondered more than once if I were dreaming. Now in the plane, every time I looked down and saw just how close the ground was, my body would spin back into a panic. Flying was nerve-wracking at the best of times but we had to fly low to avoid radar detection and that meant flying as slowly as the plane would allow, right over enemy-occupied territory. It was sheer madness and I'd been sitting in that violent anxiety for hours.

What was I even *doing* there? I was just an ordinary woman—someone sheltered and slight and sometimes even frail. I wasn't ready to die and I was not nearly courageous enough to face capture. I hadn't even landed yet and already I felt paralyzed by terror—painfully aware that I was completely out of my depth. I couldn't even pray for help or salvation. I didn't really know how to, given I'd been raised by a woman who abhorred religion. And just like that, my thoughts were back to my mother and that awful, awkward farewell.

I was startled out of my regret when the plane's wheels collided with the ground, pitched forward without warning as the vehicle slowed, then thrown back when it came to an abrupt stop. As I scrambled to find my bearings, the pilot shouted,

"Out! Run into the bushes!"

It wasn't uncommon at all for an SOE agent to have their mission cut short by a bullet or handcuffs at the moment of landing. I did not need to be told twice to take cover.

I pushed the latch to open the roof above me then checked the ground. Two men were scurrying toward the plane, carrying a woman on a makeshift stretcher. The field right below me was clear, so I tossed my suitcases out and then scrambled down the ladder against the fuselage. Case in each hand, I sprinted as fast as I could to hide in a nearby thatch of trees and shrubs. From there, I watched the men struggle to lift the moaning, wailing woman from the stretcher into the plane. They shut the hatch and within seconds, the Lysander did a sharp U-turn and began to accelerate. The men crouched low and ran back toward me as the tiny plane bounced back across the short field to lift sharply into the air.

The Lysander had been on the ground for only a minute or two. Now, it leveled off above us and quickly disappeared from sight.

I was finally back in France—finally home. This was far from the homecoming I'd dreamed of, but it was *something*. I breathed in deeply and blinked away tears of relief that filled my eyes. Even under such trying conditions, it was good to be back where I belonged.

"You must be—" a familiar voice started to say as the men approached me, but he broke off in shock when I offered him a shy wave.

"Yes, I am *Chloe*," I whispered pointedly. "And you must be *Marcel*." These were our operational names—the names by which other agents, and our local contacts, would refer to us.

Noah Ainsworth held up a hand in stunned acknowledgment, but then ran the last few steps toward me and lifted me, spinning me around in an embrace. The moonlit countryside around me blended into a whirlpool of cool blues and grays and silvery white, and I laughed as he spun me, almost carefree for a moment, despite the absurd danger we were in for our reunion.

"My God! I had no idea it was you coming to join us. What a marvelous surprise!" he exclaimed, squeezing me tight. I slapped him gently to put me back down, and once my feet were on the ground, he said cautiously, "But...why did they... you and I *do* know one another—"

"Extenuating circumstances," I explained lightly. Our arrangement was unusual—SOE agents were generally never posted with friends—but there was no alternative this time. Noah and I would just need to be very careful that our existing relationship did not compromise our work. "The agent they wanted to send injured her ankle on her final test jump last night and is out of action. I was ready for deployment and given your 'wife' was 'arriving from Paris this week'..." I shrugged ruefully. "Well. Here I am."

"I suppose you heard what happened to the first agent they dropped in," Noah murmured, wincing. I nodded. The previous agent had mistimed her drop from the belly of a bomber and managed to hit the side of the plane as she fell, briefly knocking herself unconscious. Her parachute deployed automatically thanks to the static line attached to the bomber, but she landed as dead weight and shattered the bones in one of her legs in the process. Her emergency medevac was the reason I had the privilege of climbing down from the Lysander onto solid ground instead of dropping down through the hole in the body of a bomber myself.

"I'm Adrien and I'll be your pianist," the other agent introduced himself, extending his hand to shake mine. The "pianist"—our casual SOE term for Wireless Telegraphy officer, also known as w/t operator—was the person who operated the telegraphy unit that was our only method of communication back to the SOE's Baker Street headquarters in London. Adrien took one suitcase, and Noah took the other, and I automatically fell into step beside them as they started to walk. The field still appeared peaceful and quiet, but even so, we couldn't linger. Once we'd started down a winding dirt road, Adrien asked pleasantly, "How do you know one another, then?"

"We met in Paris in 1941," I explained. "I occasionally let the escape line hide airmen in my apartment for a night or two. Marcel here just happened to come along right when I needed to leave France myself, so we traveled the line together."

"I couldn't have made it without her," Noah said.

I wanted to point out that he had helped me as much as I helped him on that fraught journey, but Noah's confidence in me was part of the reason I'd dared to come back to France in the first place, so I forced myself to accept the praise instead of protesting it.

"And now here you are. Happily 'married,'" Adrien said wryly. I glanced at Noah, and he offered me a cautious smile.

"That's right," he said earnestly. "Welcome to France, Mrs. Béatrice Martel." That was the name on my falsified identity papers. Noah's papers would say *Jean-Baptiste Martel*.

I wasn't at all anxious about living with Noah. We had traveled together under difficult circumstances once upon a time and he'd seen me at my very worst. But despite the emotional intimacy we'd shared, our relationship had always been strictly platonic, so I was surprised by the flutter in my chest when I thought about what lay ahead of us. We had to give a convincing performance of man and wife. Even if we had a second bedroom, which I expected we would not, it would be far too risky for us to maintain separate sleeping quarters in case someone peeked in a window or made a late-night visit.

"*Marcel*, your French," I said, clearing my throat. "It's..."

"Passable at long last, surely?" he teased, and he and Adrien chuckled. Noah's accent was still there, but it was faint. He was fluent and fluid enough in French now that I'd never have suspected him to be British. "Keep in mind, I've been here for almost a year—they deployed me a few weeks after I came to see you in that hospital, actually. And if I hadn't worked to improve my fluency, I'd have failed the program anyway."

"You've done very well," I said.

I shouldn't have been surprised. Noah had long shown himself to be a determined and capable man. I'd been hiding airmen in my spare bedrooms periodically for months when we met, reluctantly drawn into resistance work by a friend who was mixed up in it up to her eyeballs. When she was captured and killed, I decided I was going to have to get out of France myself at any cost and by any means.

Just a few weeks later, when escape line operatives brought Noah to my terrace seeking refuge for him, I told them I wouldn't just host him for the night, I'd accompany him on the whole journey back to the UK. We were together every minute from then until we landed in London three weeks later. When the ticket inspector on our first train tried to strike up a conversation with us, I chatted up a storm so that Noah could answer in monosyllables to hide his then-stilted French. When we reached St. Jean de Luz and the guide assigned to walk us through the Pyrenees told me in no uncertain terms I could not bring the bag of food I'd packed for the journey, Noah offered to carry it for me instead.

And on that long, torturous journey through the Pyrenees, whenever I faltered, he pushed me forward, and when he stumbled, I helped him up. As we were smuggled behind bales of hay in a cart from Oiarzun to the British Embassy in San Sebastian, then hidden beneath a stack of blankets on the back seat of a car from San Sebastian to Madrid, then in the back of a truck filled with hundreds of chickens from Madrid to a safe house on the River Guadalquivir, and then finally, locked in the body of a Norwegian collier all the way to the RAF base in Gibraltar, Noah Ainsworth and I ate, slept, walked, hid and even wept, side by side. It was no wonder we stayed in touch. Since our return to the UK, Noah and I communicated by letter, weekly like clockwork, and even managed a handful of face-to-face catch-ups. At the last of these, when I was stuck in a hospital recovering from surgery, he told me he'd been recruited to a top secret agency and would be out of contact indefinitely.

For well over a year, I had no idea where he was or even what that agency was. And then one day at the secretarial job at Westminster my mother lined up for me, I was called into a meeting with two stern-looking officials who introduced themselves as Miss Elwood and Mr. Turner. Just two weeks later, I started SOE training.

I did wonder if the SOE was the "secret agency" Noah had disappeared into, but those suspicions were only confirmed the night before I landed there in that field near Montbeliard. Miss Elwood was a senior SOE official tasked with completing my final checks at the airport before we departed. She spent thirty seconds explaining that I'd be working with Noah, and thirty very long minutes lecturing me about how unorthodox this situation was and how important it was that our friendship not get in the way of our work.

"It's vital that you both maintain a professional distance, even if you're pretending to be spouses, even living in the same house and working on the same circuit," she told me grimly. A circuit was our term for a local network—often comprised of a team of three SOE agents, a circuit leader like Noah, a courier like myself, a w/t operator like Adrien—plus as many local contacts as we could recruit. "Frankly, Chloe, I'm worried about this situation, but we need to send someone tomorrow and you're the only agent available who is even close to ready."

"I won't let you down," I promised her, and as we walked along that dirt road, back toward the township, there was no doubt in my mind that I'd keep that promise.

Adrien returned to his own apartment, and Noah and I were soon alone at our little place in Montbeliard. Our temporary home was charming, almost romantic—a former garden shed that had been converted into a tiny apartment. French doors led to a small courtyard off the kitchen, and a wooden ladder hung from the ceiling, adorned with well-used cooking utensils. But the apartment was even smaller than I'd expected—just a studio space without so much as a separate bedroom, the double bed jammed in beside the small circular dining table where Noah and I sat now nursing cups of tea. Given how intimate the space was, it was a strange blessing that the toilet was an outhouse, and we'd have to bathe in the laundry room beside it.

"This mission," I said quietly. "I understand Baker Street is concerned about a large factory near here?"

"That's right. It's owned by a local family and run by its patriarch, Fernand Sauvage. By all accounts he's a reasonable fellow stuck in a very bad position," Noah told me. "The factory has always manufactured the Sauvage line of cars but since the Nazis took control of it in 1941 it has been churning out tanks.

THE PARIS AGENT 39

While that's bad enough, there are growing whispers that the factory is being retooled. Within months, it will be producing munitions and perhaps even a new range of rockets. Something called the 'V1.' Have you heard of it?"

"Yes." I nodded. "No one has seen them in action yet, but intelligence suggests they're some kind of pilot-less flying bomb. Baker Street isn't sure of the range of the things or how accurate they will be, but they know enough to be nervous."

"They want us to destroy the factory, and that's no small task given the size of the thing. Tens of thousands of locals come from all over the region to work there every day—the facility is the size of a town itself. It even has its own power plant, for God's sake."

"So the plan is for me to work for the factory's accountant?" I asked, motioning toward a very large house a few doors down from our humble little studio.

"His name is Jullien Travers. His wife Mégane has some health issues, and their nanny recently left to have a child of her own."

"And you—we—won't move around much? We'll stay in this apartment?"

"Yes, setting up the circuit in the region from scratch has been more challenging than I'd anticipated." Much like the operational names of individual agents, SOE circuits were each assigned a code name. The circuit Noah had established was called *Postmaster*. "When I landed here, I didn't have any secure contacts, let alone a network of safe houses to move between. I needed to stay close enough to scope out the factory, so I decided to rent a place longer-term. As the circuit leader I'd have tried to remain a step removed from the local contacts but starting from scratch, it hasn't been possible to stay anonymous. I managed to recruit a mechanic shortly after I arrived and the locals think I work with him."

"And this 'job' you've lined up for me. I'll be working with the Travers children?"

"I've been looking for a way to determine if Jullien and his wife might be sympathetic to the cause, so when I saw him out taking his girls for a walk last week, I stopped for a chat. He told me their nanny had recently left and they've struggled to replace her. I told him my wife would be arriving soon and would be looking for work."

"Well done for thinking on your feet."

"Even if we can't recruit him, it seemed like an incredible opportunity to get someone into that house," Noah said. "You'll try to form a good rapport with them, see if they're receptive at least to assisting us. Plus, you can search Jullien's home office if and when the opportunity arises. I've watched him come and go so I know he does carry a briefcase to and from work, so it's possible there is documentation in his study that might confirm our fears about the retooling. We have our work cut out for us, but I'm certain that we can do something to throw a spanner into the works of that damned factory."

"Good," I said, even as my stomach buzzed with nerves. Noah's face was suddenly transformed by a wide smile as he stared at me. "What?"

"We've always worked so well together. This is going to be brilliant."

"Yes," I agreed, but I looked down at my tea, avoiding his gaze as the nerves in my stomach shifted suddenly toward butterflies.

"My only concern is…" I looked back at him, alarmed, and he winked at me. "Chloe, do tell me you like children? It's one of the few things I don't know about you."

I had always avoided the topic of my childhood when Noah and I spoke, despite the endless, rambling conversations we'd shared on our journey and over the course of our correspondence since then. I was diagnosed with Coeliac Sprue as an infant and had suffered from its ill effects my entire life. Too poorly for school for much of my childhood, I was instead schooled at home by a series of nannies, and spending so much time on my own, I learned to be content with my own company. Even when I was well enough for school, I found the carefree, playful ways of other children baffling.

And now, as an adult, I didn't have children of my own or even siblings to give me nieces or nephews. I had never so much as changed a diaper.

But despite all of that I loved children, and desperately wanted some of my own one day. I didn't begrudge a single decision my mother had made along the way, but I wanted a different life for myself—a house full of laughter and contentment, a loving husband, as many children as my body would allow me to have.

From the moment I heard about this mission, I decided I would use the nannying aspect as an opportunity to learn. I'd use my experiences with the Travers children as fuel for my own dreams for a future after the war.

"I don't have much experience with children, but I'll find a way to manage," I assured Noah.

"I didn't doubt that for a second," he said, raising an eyebrow. "I've seen firsthand how capable you are. I can't imagine you failing at anything."

That warm rush once again returned to my belly at his quiet, unfailing confidence in me. I liked a lot of things about Noah, but perhaps I liked this best—he always saw me as endlessly competent, and endlessly capable.

CHAPTER 3

ELOISE
Paris, France
February, 1944

There were virtually no motorcars on Parisian streets in those days, and the buses no longer ran at all, so I had planned to walk from my temporary accommodation in an apartment in the Rue St. Peres to the Gare St. Lazare, but I woke to threatening skies. My hostess, a quiet Parisian woman named Célestine, suggested I rethink my walk.

"Best not to be boarding the train sopping wet when you have such a long journey ahead or you'll catch your death of cold. A bicycle taxi will get you to the station quickly and on a day like today the sidecar will be covered so you'll stay dry."

Madame Célestine reminded me of the new, softer version of my mother, the one I had come to know since her latest marriage broke down and she came to live with me. Célestine, just like Maman in recent years, had mastered the perfect balance between offering support and smothering. I took her advice and flagged down the taxi almost as soon as I left her apartment.

At first, I was pleased with my decision. The clouds above me grew heavier even as the bicycle taxi swifted me through the streets. I watched the buildings pass, and found myself almost fixated on the Germans, visible in every conceivable public space—Wehrmacht and SS and SD officers in their uniforms, countless ordinary German citizens, unmistakable in their starkly utilitarian clothing, especially alongside our more ornate French fashions. I knew those German civilians were probably in France to conduct business, and once upon a time they would not have seemed at all a threatening presence, but the war had changed everything. I was getting a glimpse of the future the Nazis wanted, one where France was more theirs than ours.

I was so distracted thinking about this that it took me some time to begin to suspect that the bicycle driver was not going directly to the station. I left Paris for London as an impoverished fifteen-year-old and even then, I'd never spent much time in the 7th Arrondissement. But I had familiarized myself with maps of the city when I was planning my mission back at the SOE's Baker Street offices in London, and something about our direction seemed off. When I caught a glimpse of Les Invalides I finally understood that the driver had veered west at some point instead of traveling north.

"Sir," I said, alarmed. "You are supposed to be taking me to Gare St. Lazare!"

"This is the way," he called back to me, his tone calm but firm. I grasped the sides of the sidecar and shook the thing until he cried out in protest. "Easy, mademoiselle! I mean you no harm. This is just the fastest way to the station!"

"You take me for a fool, sir. You're going to tell me the ride took longer than you anticipated, and you'll demand more money."

"How dare you insult my integrity!" he said, but he sounded defensive and guilty, and I was sure now that I'd caught him out in the scam. "You are a visitor to this city so you'll have to trust me. I have lived in Paris my whole life and I know all of the shortcuts."

"What do you mean... I'm a visitor to the city?" I frowned, momentarily distracted from my outrage at the scam. "I'm every bit as Parisian as you are."

The driver rattled off a short string of German words, and panic raced through my body even though I had no clue what he was saying. Was this man a collaborator? Were the Germans already onto me? But when I had no response, the driver glanced back at me and chuckled.

"Just as I suspected," he said smugly. "You're British."

"I assure you; I am not!"

"With that accent, you are either from Alsace Lorraine—in which case you'd speak German—or you're British." At my stunned silence, he chuckled again. "Your accent is very subtle, mademoiselle, but it is obvious to a native Frenchman."

This wasn't the first time I'd misjudged my linguistic abilities. I was convinced my English was flawless when I boarded that ferry to the UK at fifteen. I had just run away from home, intending to reconnect with the British father I hadn't seen in more than ten years. It was quite a shock to me to arrive in London only to find that he had married a woman who had no idea I existed and my father, determined to keep it that way, wanted nothing to do with me. I was also stunned to discover that while I understood English, I did not speak the language nearly as well as I'd assumed. I worked so hard in those first few years to refine my English until I could live and work in the UK easily.

It had not occurred to me once that eight years in Britain might have left a mark on my accent. No one had mentioned it when I was speaking French twenty-four hours a day during my training with the SOE—but then again, I trained in a cohort that was almost entirely Brits speaking French as a second language. It was likely that, in a group like that, no one would even notice.

My heart sank. Baker Street had gone to great lengths to ensure there was no way I could be identified as anything other than a Frenchwoman. The clothes I was wearing had been specifically designed by French seamstresses to ensure that the seams and buttons and techniques and fittings were all authentic. My makeup brands were French, smuggled across the Channel, and my bags were exact replicas of French brands. Every square inch of my pockets had been searched for ticket stubs or cigarettes or scraps of paper that might give me away if I were detained.

After all of that, it was heartbreaking to think that within two days of my arrival, a stranger on the streets had identified me as a visitor simply from a handful of words. I told myself to be grateful—that this wasn't a failure but a blessing. Now that I knew about my accent, I could be careful how I spoke, and even *when* I spoke.

"You are wrong," I fiercely told the bicycle driver, this time being careful to enunciate each word precisely. "Stop the bike this instant. I'll walk the rest of the way."

"I believe they call that cutting off your nose to spite your face, mademoiselle," the driver said, still pedaling furiously, continuing stubbornly on his trajectory away from the train station. "It will rain any minute and you have a train to make. No?"

"Stop *immediately*!" I cried, shaking the basket again, and at this, he shrugged and slowed. I hauled my bags and briefcase from the covered sidecar and set off on foot, ignoring the sound of his laughter as he cycled past me.

I walked halfway to Gare St. Lazare before I managed to flag down another bicycle taxi—this time, a helpful, honest driver got me to the station just as the heavens opened and a steady rain began to fall. Thanks to my long detour, I was running so late that my planned breakfast before departure was no longer possible and I had to sprint to buy my ticket then sprint onward to the platform where I discovered that the train had already arrived. A swarm of passengers pushed forward, impatient to board as the rain fell heavier.

I passed several public compartments but found every seat taken in each. Even the designated military compartments were all bursting with German soldiers. Some men had resorted to standing in the aisles.

A German officer suddenly swung out from a door and waved his arm at me. Gold braiding on his uniform, two pips. I clocked him instantly as a Wehrmacht colonel and my rapid footsteps came to an immediate halt.

"Mademoiselle," he said politely, as I struggled to keep my expression neutral. "Please, follow me." Sheer frustration shot through my body as I once again wondered if my cover had already been blown. Before I could even formulate a plan, he added quietly, "The train is oversold. You won't find a seat on any of the public carriages, but I'll make room for you in ours."

The all-stops train would take three hours to reach Rouen in the *zone interdite,* the highly restricted "forbidden zone" that ran along the Nazi Atlantic wall. My SOE trainers would pitch a fit if they found out I had already stumbled into a situation where I would have to spend hours in a compartment full of enemy soldiers, but the minute the colonel made the offer, I had no way to refuse it without arousing suspicion.

Dozens of men stared at me as I followed the colonel into the compartment. As I stepped into the aisle, almost all rose to offer me their seat, in a move so sudden and coordinated it might almost have been rehearsed. I stared back at them, completely lost for words.

"The young lady will sit with me," the colonel said firmly, and I could not miss the disappointment in the eyes of other men. My mind had been clouded by the frustration of the situation I'd stumbled into, but a realization punched through the fog. The colonel wasn't suspicious of me at all. He was bored already ahead of the long journey and probably lonely, eager for the company of a pretty girl, and maybe the desperation in the eyes of these soldiers meant they were lonely too.

Sometimes I wondered if there was something wrong with me because I very rarely felt fear, not the way other people seemed to. Instead, I tended to default to anger, and a wave of it surged within me as I looked around that train carriage. I wanted to rail at every one of those men. *Look what you've been a part of! Look what you've done to France! To Europe!*

But the SOE had invited me to train as an agent months earlier not because of my skill set or my intelligence or even my courage, but simply because I was a pretty young thing who spoke French and knew France and who would likely never attract much suspicion, even if I did attract attention like this. Apparently I was going to test that theory right off the bat.

Releasing my rage this early in the mission was not an option. I drew some deep breaths to try to calm my racing thoughts.

There was some shuffling around the colonel's seat as the other men made room on the luggage racks above their heads for my bags. One reached to take my leather shoulder bag, and I pretended not to notice as I quickly sat down and tucked it between my shoulder and the window. As the train left the platform, the men in the seats closest to me turned to face me. In painfully stilted French, a young man of only eighteen or nineteen years old asked me shyly, "What is your name?"

My every sense was on high alert as I tried to articulate each sound carefully to hide an accent I hadn't been aware of even an hour earlier.

"Felice Leroy," I said politely, giving him my cover name. This was the name on the set of identity papers I was carrying, but I had spare papers buried in the bottom of my bag, and I could adopt a new cover name if my circumstances changed— even if I simply became anxious that I might have been exposed. My operational name, Fleur, was known only to those within the SOE or the resistance and would not change unless my cover was completely blown at some point.

"This is…you to…be visit to Rouen today?" another asked me in broken French, which meant it was time to trot out my cover story for the first time.

"I spent a lovely Easter with my aunt in Paris, and now I will go spend a few days in Rouen before I go home to Le Havre."

"Are you seeing boyfriend in Rouen, perhaps?"

A fictional boyfriend might end their apparent fascination with me, but would that be a good thing? This polite chitchat was harmless enough. It was probably better to bat my eyelashes and play along.

"No boyfriend," I said lightly. "I'm stopping in Rouen to see if I can find an uncle who disappeared on a business trip some weeks ago. The British have bombed the city so much that my aunt is convinced he's been injured or…" I tried to feign some combination of concern and dismay. "…well. Or worse."

There was sudden movement beside me. The colonel had reached into his jacket and now passed a small white business card toward me.

"What a concerning situation that is for your family, mademoiselle," he said gravely. "I'm staying at this hotel in Rouen for a week. If you need help, please contact me."

I murmured my thanks and forced a shy smile as I took the card and slipped it into my shoulder bag, right beside the hidden compartment stuffed with forged currency and identity papers.

I'd expected my mission in France to be wild—exciting, dangerous, meaningful—but *this?* This was utterly surreal. Over the next few hours, I chatted with the young soldiers as they talked about the brief reprieve from the war they'd enjoyed on leave in Paris. I was careful not to speak too much myself, but did gradually relax as I realized that my slight accent was not likely obvious to these men—the young soldiers' French was so woeful the conversation was half chit-chat, half French lesson, and the colonel himself spoke fluently but had such a thick German accent that at times, I had to strain to make sense of him.

The younger men seemed to share a strange delight at conversing with me—as if my presence on that carriage extended their leave by a few more precious hours. There was an innocence to the conversation that might almost have blinded me to their uniforms for a moment or two along the way. Most were junior Wehrmacht soldiers—by that point in the war, almost certainly conscripted. Perhaps they were reluctant players in this battle, just as, I supposed, most of us were—drawn into the war if not by conscription, then by circumstance, just as I had been.

During my training I had learned that when it came to a cover story, revealing less was always the best strategy, so I tried to deflect the focus back onto the men as we talked. I asked about their lives back home, and some flashed me faded, well-worn photographs of young wives or tiny children. Others had photos of beloved pets. The colonel carried a well-loved photograph of himself, seated in a leather armchair with an enormous cat in each arm.

But if, for even a second, I had felt a shred of empathy for those men given how polite and respectful they had been toward me, the reminder that some had wives waiting at home was like a slap to the face. *I* was once a wife sitting at home waiting for the return of my husband away at war, and *he* had been taken from me, by men likely wearing uniforms not dissimilar to these. It made no difference if the man who shot down my husband's plane at El Alamein was young or respectful or even conscripted against his will. Giles was still dead. The world would offer no justice for that so I had to eke it out myself.

But I could not afford to become distracted by thoughts like this. I knew when I left Britain I would need to stop my mind from wandering to my grief for Giles, or longing to be with my son Hughie, who was back home in Bexley with my mother.

My boys would never be far from my mind, nor could they be front and center. I could not afford to lose focus. Distraction meant carelessness. Carelessness could be catastrophic.

So I maintained my polite facade by reminding myself that I was playing along with the charade so that later, I could wreak havoc upon these men and everything they stood for.

CHAPTER 4

CHARLOTTE
Liverpool
May, 1970

At first, Dad is so cheerful as he goes about his project to find Remy that I feel certain I'm right to ignore Aunt Kathleen's warning. I don't mind that my skirts are soon snug from the endless stream of rich meals he's cooking for us, I'm just pleased to see he's filling out in the face a little too. He clams right up when I try to talk to him about the project or ask questions about his war days, but I remind myself that Dad told me about the SOE when he was good and ready, and he'll tell me more when the right time comes, too.

He was semiretired before Mum died. He still worked five or even six days a week, but they were short days, focused on oversight of his managers at each of his six workshops rather than business specifics. He had reached a point where he was financially secure and didn't need to continue expanding the company so instead, he delighted in extra time for family, golf and gardening.

Right after Mum's death, Dad went back to working full-time and then some, but now for the first time in months, I'm leaving the house before him and returning to find him already home. He's in his study most waking hours around his work, on the phone or reading or pecking away at a typewriter. Letters come in the post with return addresses from all manner of government agencies across the UK and even France.

But his mood slowly drops again. First, he starts leaving for work earlier, and then I come home a few nights in a row to find he's still at the office and the kitchen is dark and still. Within a week or two, the light has faded in Dad's eyes. He once again looks on the outside as I feel on the inside—frustrated, depressed, angry.

Has he found Remy? Does he have any answers about that wartime accident? I'm curious about what he's discovered that's caused such a change in his mood. I'm also starting to think I should have listened to Aunt Kathleen, because Dad does not look happy. He doesn't even look well.

One night, he comes home from work late and sits down to the subpar sausages and mashed potato I've prepared for us. The bags under his eyes are shadowed and heavy. He sits slumped and weary at the dining room table and my heart aches as he shovels my terrible food into his mouth.

"How's the SOE project going?" I ask gently.

"Ah, that." He swallows the last chunk of potato on his plate, then dismisses me with a limp wave of his hand. "I never thought it would be easy to find Remy but I assumed I'd at least be able to confirm that he was an agent. It turns out even that is just about impossible. I've gotten nowhere."

This surprises me. I foolishly assumed he learned something upsetting or was finding it challenging to confront the past. It didn't occur to me that he isn't finding answers at all.

"Have you given up?" I ask him. I'm equal parts relieved and concerned by the thought.

"I think I'm running out of people to approach, to be honest." He pauses, then laughs self-consciously. "I'm a silly old fool, Lottie."

"You're none of those things—" I start to say, but it's clear Dad is ready to change the subject, because he stands and forces a smile.

"You cooked. I'll do the dishes," he says, even though most nights recently he's been doing both. Wrigley, who had been asleep by my feet as I worked at the kitchen table, stands and follows Dad toward the sink, shooting me a doleful look.

Dad is gone when I wake up the next morning. I dress early and plan the school day in my mind, groaning as I ponder the long list of things I have to do before I can crawl back into bed—end of the school year is a brutal time for teachers. I pass Dad's study on my way out but pause, staring inside. When Mum was alive, Dad was perpetually untidy but now, he keeps most of the house pristine, just as she preferred. The only place he allows his own standard of cleanliness to stand is this study, which is in its usual state of chaos.

I glance back down the hallway, double-checking that Dad has really left the house, then step into the room. The rubbish bin is overflowing and one of the cabinets where he keeps his business paperwork is half-open, overstuffed files peeking out the top. I straighten the folders then push the drawer closed before I wander to his desk. There's a leather folio beside the phone and I pull it toward me, then open the front cover to find dozens of pages of handwritten notes. Each page is a long list of times, dates, phone numbers and remarks. Every entry has been crossed out. Some of those lines are drawn with a heavy hand, the page almost torn with the force of the slash. I flick across a few more pages and find more of the same.

Poor Dad. No wonder his optimism is fading. As far as I can tell, he's contacted just about every government department and military organization in existence but if this list is anything to go by, he really is getting nowhere. On the corner of one page, he's scrawled a note diagonally in letters so heavy I can picture the confusion and disbelief on his face as he wrote them.

The SOE ceased to exist in January 1946?

My heart aches for him, but right off the bat, I can't help but wonder if he's approaching this the wrong way. Maybe to my dad, the war is a living thing—active in his mind even across the decades, even though he's kept all of that to himself until now. To the rest of the world, the war has been consigned to the history books. For all of these calls my dad has made and for all the letters he's sent, he hasn't contacted a single historian.

On my lunch break, I pick up a pen and write to the professor who taught the handful of history classes I took at university. I don't tell Professor Berrara much about my father's quest. The details don't really matter. I just ask what advice he'd give to someone looking into the history of the SOE. To my surprise, less than a week later and on the last day of my school year before summer break, a letter lands in our postbox.

Dear Charlotte,
It is true that increasingly I forget the students who pass through these halls, but I do remember you as a diligent student who did not miss a lecture and could be relied upon to deliver essays of the highest quality. I expect that by now you're married to that nice young chap of yours and hope life is treating you well.

I cringe at the reference and the memories that rise with it. Billy and I met on the first day of university and we were inseparable throughout our studies—so much so that he would often swap subjects so we could attend the same lectures. That seemed romantic at the time, but now it just seems pitiful.

There is much secrecy around the SOE even to this day, but even so, in some ways you are fortunate that this is the area of study that has piqued your curiosity. There are several historians with a special area of focus on the SOE, most notably Prof. Harry Read of Manchester University. He is official historian to

the British government and I understand he is trying to write a
book on this very subject. If it's the SOE you want to research,
he's the first person you should reach out to.

As my father reads the letter that night, he beams with such pride and excitement that my cheeks flush.

"Clever Lottie," he says, shaking his head in wonder. "It didn't even occur to me that what I really need is a historian, not a bureaucrat! Look what you have done with one attempt after those fruitless weeks this old fool has spent barking up the wrong tree..." He scratches the back of his neck, then looks at me hesitantly. "I'm not smart like you are, love."

"Dad!" I protest. "You're plenty smart—"

"You know what I mean," he interrupts, but he's cringing awkwardly. "I'm just a simple man and I don't know how to research like you do. I really don't have a clue how to talk to..." He motions toward the letter. "You know. Professors and such."

Dad's a successful, accomplished man—but I've seen people treat him as though he were lacking in intellect once they hear him speak. He's always been especially intimidated by the academic world. Dad was bursting with pride for me at my graduation, but when he thought I was looking elsewhere, his sparkling gaze would drop until he was staring at the ground while he scratched the back of his head or adjusted the collar of his shirt, over and over again. Archie's graduation twelve months later was no better.

I only pause for a single moment to consider Aunt Kathleen's concerns before I dismiss them once again.

"Okay, Dad," I say, as his eyes brighten with hope. "It looks like we have a father-daughter summer project ahead of us."

I enjoy a long lie-in on Monday, the first day of summer break. Dad is long gone by 10:00 a.m. when I finally drag myself out of bed to call Professor Read's office. I'm disappointed and a little alarmed when the call rings out. I thought the timing of Professor Berrara's letter was fortunate—arriving when it did as my school year ended. But what if Professor Read is one of those lecturers who disappears to Spain or France or the countryside for the entire summer, totally out of reach until the new academic year? I try again several times in the hours that follow and as every call rings out and I become increasingly alarmed, I start to hope that Professor Berrara has accidentally given me the wrong number. I call the university's main switchboard to check.

"Professor Read works all year round but he doesn't *ever* answer his own phone. I expect his secretary Mrs. White will be in sooner or later but you'll have to keep trying until you reach her."

I drag an armchair into the hallway and sit by the phone to read my novel. I try the number again at the end of every chapter. By late afternoon I've just about given up hope of getting through today and I'm startled when the call connects.

"Manchester University History Department. This is Professor Read's office."

The woman's voice is husky and rough, almost as if I have just woken her up, but then she gives a hacking cough and I hear a purposeful inhalation. This is a woman who enjoys a cigarette.

"Hello there," I say politely. "Who am I speaking with?"

"This is Mrs. White. Professor Read's secretary," the woman says before she gives another cough.

"Good afternoon, Mrs. White. My name is Charlotte Ainsworth. I've heard that Professor Read is something of an expert in the history of the SOE and—"

Mrs. White interrupts me, her tone sharp. "Young lady, Professor Read is not 'something of an expert' in the SOE. He's the only sanctioned SOE military historian for the British government."

"Of course," I say hastily, wincing. I'm caught off guard, first that someone has finally answered the damned phone, secondly by the mild hostility.

I draw a breath and try to refocus.

"The thing is, my father was involved with the SOE at some point—"

"Are you calling to schedule an interview for him with the graduate students for next academic year?"

"An interview?"

"Your father will have received letters inviting him to participate in Professor Read's archival program if he is of significance to the historic record."

"No, I don't think he has." Surely Dad would have mentioned if he had.

"Well, the most likely explanation for that is that he is not of interest to Professor Read's work. Thank you for your call—"

"Wait, don't go," I say hastily. "He doesn't want to be interviewed—he just wants to find someone—"

"Professor Read is a very busy *historian*," Mrs. White scoffs. "He's not a missing persons expert."

"Of course I appreciate that but we don't really know how else to proceed without Professor Read's help. This man we are seeking was probably an SOE agent and he saved my father's life."

"So this is an amateur history project?"

"I suppose you could say that?"

"Professor Read is too busy to help with amateur history projects." She sounds exasperated now, and there's instant heat on my cheeks. "He is a professional historian, for heaven's sakes."

"Mrs. White, I don't mean to waste your time and I certainly don't intend to waste Professor Read's time but we don't know where else to turn," I say.

"There is a group of amateur historians who meet at St. Barnabas Church. It's run by one of the professor's former students—a very capable young man. That group may be a more appropriate resource for your father. Good day."

The harsh click in my ear tells me that Mrs. White has already hung up. I hang up too, and stare at the receiver warily as I try to process the conversation. I didn't necessarily expect that the professor or his staff would drop everything to assist us, but by the same token, I was not anticipating a flat refusal to even entertain a conversation with Dad.

I glance down at the folio on the desk and realize that I've been doodling as I spoke with her. I've written snippets from our conversation.

interview

oral history?

amateur history project?

St. Barnabas' church

I reach for the phonebook and quickly find the number for the church in Manchester. A much more helpful receptionist there advises me that the history group is headed up by one Theo Sinclair. I hear the rustle of papers as she finds a copy of the parish timetable and informs me the group meets every second Thursday at 6:00 p.m. in the church hall.

It's only thirty miles from Liverpool to Manchester. When my father arrives home from work Thursday afternoon, we climb into his periwinkle-blue Peugeot 404 and start the journey. It's drizzling, and the sky above is depressingly heavy.

"I'm still a bit confused why the university sent us to a church history group," Dad says. "You really think this is going to help us find this Remy?"

"Honestly, Dad, I have no idea." I don't want to discourage Dad, so I haven't told him how unhelpful Professor Read's secretary was. Hopefully, this group can help us and I won't need to call her again.

We pass several other meetings in various rooms of the

church—a choir; what looks a lot like a support group; three ministers sitting around a desk. When we finally reach the hall, we push open a door and step into an expansive but somewhat musty space, with thin red carpet on the floor and wood-paneled walls. No less than a dozen chairs are arranged in a semicircle, each one already occupied. I look down at my watch. We aren't late, but the group has started anyway.

The man seated at the front of the room looks up at us expectantly. His silver-framed glasses sit slightly askew on his face. His checkered shirt is poorly ironed and covered by a knitted vest that has possibly been attacked by moths at some point. He gives a polite smile even as he greets us dismissively.

"Sorry, this is the family history group. Who were you looking for?"

I scan my gaze around the circle and hesitate. The young man in the vest is probably only in his late twenties, but everyone else appears to be at least forty or fifty years older. I count two walking sticks and one Zimmer frame.

"*Family* history group?" I repeat in confusion. I glance at Dad, who shrugs and gives me a bewildered look. "I suppose we're in the right place. I thought it started at six o'clock?"

The young man blinks at me from behind the thick lenses of his glasses.

"Well, no. Not anymore. It starts at five thirty now."

The convener seems visibly flustered and confused—as am I—but he rises to his feet and begins to motion for the rest of the semicircle to expand. The group's members all begin to shuffle, making way for two more chairs. We're soon seated between the convener and a man at least twice his age who is clutching an aggressively large box of paperwork.

"Okay. Um," the young man mumbles. He scrubs a hand through his unruly sandy hair and clears his throat. "I—yes. Well. Hello. I'm Theo Sinclair, I'm the group's coordinator. Sorry—we don't often have visitors to the group, that's all. I'll just allow Mrs. Lowe to finish telling us about her progress this week and then perhaps you can tell us why you're here."

It turns out family history meeting has moved the start time earlier because its membership has a *lot* to say and some tire early. Mrs. Lowe has now traced her family history back to 1723, when one of her ancestors was in the court of George I. This week, she spent a great deal of time at the library researching the cemetery where he was buried. Midway through her story, Mr. McTavish interrupts to give a tenuously linked but startlingly detailed account of the American Revolutionary War battle which cost his grandfather his life.

When I glance to my right, I see Theo Sinclair is utterly enthralled by these discoveries, but when I glance to my left, I see my father is staring at me in confusion, as if he cannot understand why we're staying. As Mrs. Lowe once again takes the floor and her next library anecdote drags on until it devolves into an analysis of the politics of the 1950s, I start to wonder that myself.

Just when I'm thinking about the politest way to excuse myself, Mrs. Lowe finally runs out of steam and all eyes turn to me and Dad. Theo smiles expectantly.

"Would you like to introduce yourselves?"

"I am Noah Ainsworth, and this is my daughter Charlotte," my father says. "We are... You see, it is because... I just think that we—" He looks to me helplessly, then trails off with a confused "I really do think we're in the wrong room or something."

I wince as I explain. "To be completely honest, we aren't looking to complete our family history."

"Oh, you should," one of the men in the group says. "Our family history teaches us so much about ourselves, young lady. How can you know who you are if you don't know where you came from?"

"Absolutely," I agree hastily. "But the thing is, we are actually looking for a specific man that my father probably knew during the war. Right, Dad?"

"Right," Dad says.

"We've tried several routes to find him which led us to Professor Read's office and his secretary suggested that this group might be able to assist us better."

"Mrs. White sent you here?" Theo says, surprised, but his tone is resigned as he adds, "Ah. I see." There's an awkward pause. I rush to fill the silence.

"It's just...she said that this was an amateur history group and I thought—"

"Amateur!" someone exclaims, outraged. Theo winces, then shoots the woman a placating glance.

"Now, now, Ms. Peters, that's not an insult at all. I'm sure Mrs. White just meant that in the sense that none of us are paid in a professional capacity to work with history, we are *technically* amateurs."

I recognize that tone. I use it myself every day in the classroom when one child or another becomes upset by something that seems bewilderingly insignificant to me. Theo turns his bright blue gaze on me and Dad and I feel myself inexplicably blushing.

"Mr. Ainsworth." He glances down at my left hand then adds, "Miss Ainsworth?" I nod. "This group generally does exist to help people find their ancestors and trace their family tree so it's not really a fit for what you're trying to do. However, it *is* true that some of the people in this room have research skills to rival any academic I've ever worked with so if you stick around and listen, I know you'll learn a thing or two. And perhaps if you hang back at the end I can hear a little more about what it is you're trying to achieve."

I glance at Dad, and he shrugs, so I stay seated and the group continues on around us. By 7:30, some of the participants are yawning, others look half-asleep, and Theo draws the meeting to a close. The men begin to pack up the chairs and I rise automatically to help them—it only seems right given I'm the youngest person in the room. Theo walks the women to their cars, and then he and Dad gravitate toward a small kitchenette at the back of the hall.

I leave three chairs out. Dad brings me a tea and sits beside me with his own. Theo's instant coffee is strong enough that I can smell it when he sits beside me.

"So you're looking for someone you knew in the war, and I'm guessing since you found your way to Professor Read, you or they worked with the SOE?"

"I was an agent," Dad confirms, then he points to the scar on the side of his head. "I was injured in the field, you see. I woke up in a hospital and a nurse told me a man named Remy brought me in."

"Remy was his operational name?"

"I think so, but I'm not entirely certain. I had a terrible concussion and haven't recovered all of my memories from around that time, but I do feel as though he was an agent."

"Remarkable," Theo murmurs. "Where was this? And what year?"

"The hospital clinic was in Brive-La-Galliarde. And it was 1944, probably June, but I'm guessing that because I have a sense that the mission was just after D-Day."

"And you say you were an agent. Did you complete the finishing school at Beaulieu?" Theo asks, leaning forward, his gaze intently fixed my on dad's face as he nods. "Did you work with Colonel Maxwell?"

"Not closely, but of course, yes. I knew of him," Dad says.

"Helen Elwood? Freddie Booth? Gerard Turner?"

"Yes," Dad says, eyebrows lifting. He gives me a surprised, pleased look. "Yes, I knew all of them. You really know your stuff, Theo."

"I'm guessing they were the only real names you ever knew."

"Maybe that's part of the problem," Dad admits. "Secrecy was paramount. Everyone had a code name and we weren't ever allowed to share personal details. It's hard to recall information now when the main thing I do remember from my training is that we tried so hard to make sure we didn't know much in case we were captured and interrogated."

"Who are those people?" I ask. Theo glances at me.

"Colonel Maxwell was right at the top—agency director. The others I mentioned hovered just beneath him."

"And how do you know about all of this?"

"I completed my Master's degree with Professor Read," Theo tells us. "He holds the lion's share of knowledge about the SOE and is the only person who has access to the most confidential information but I do know the basic, commonly known details." Theo's gaze slides back to Dad. "I'm a little confused, Mr. Ainsworth. *Have* you spoken with Professor Read's team?"

"Charlotte tried, but they said they couldn't help us."

Theo frowns.

"No actually... I meant, have you sat down with the professor or his students for an official interview. That's a key part of his role—recording the histories of those who witnessed these events firsthand. It's an immense job and for about ten years he's been permitted to delegate some of this to his graduate students, which is what I spent much of my Master's degree doing. You would surely have received letters over the years." At Dad's blank look, Theo clarifies, "Letters inviting you to join the project."

"The receptionist on the phone asked me the same," I tell Dad. He frowns and shakes his head. Theo sits back in his chair and stares into space, pondering this.

"It's rare, but not unheard-of for people to be missed," he says thoughtfully. "There were extensive records kept at the headquarters in Baker Street, but many were destroyed at the end of the war—some intentionally because the administration staff didn't understand how important they'd be in the future, although most were destroyed accidentally. I suppose if other agents only knew you by your code name *and* your file was destroyed, it's possible Harry Read has been trying to contact you but didn't know who he was looking for."

"These files at Baker Street contained our real names?" Dad asks.

"As a general rule, yes."

Dad and I share a hopeful look.

"So all we need to do is find the file for Remy."

"Ah, that's the thing, Mr. Ainsworth." Noah winces. "What remains is still, for the most part, highly classified."

Dad deflates, sagging forward over his tea. I feel myself do the same.

"Surely there is some way…" I say.

"The only person who has access to the remaining files is Professor Read but I can assure you he takes that privilege very seriously. And it's not like there's one great big list of everyone's code names or their real names, or even a directory of contact information for the agents who survived. The remaining records are complex and fragmented and require expert interpretation. So… Perhaps Professor Read does know of an agent code-named Remy, but he couldn't tell you even if he does." Theo offers a gentle smile. "Noah, even the fact that he has never tracked *you* down should tell you how patchy those surviving records are."

"This archival interview," Dad asks cautiously. "What would that be like, then?"

"It's just a conversation about your memories, usually recorded or at least transcribed. Nothing too threatening." I can tell from the pinched expression on my father's face that to him this sounds plenty threatening. Theo smiles again. "Mr. Ainsworth, I spoke to quite a few agents when I was completing my Master's degree. Not one of those stories was ordinary, and that's how I know you must have a remarkable story, too."

A strange shiver runs through my body as I'm reminded of the courage Dad must have shown in those days and the strength it must have taken to build the life I've shared with him when it was all over. Dad shifts uncomfortably on his chair.

"There has to be a way to find this man," I say firmly. "How many agents were there? Surely this isn't that difficult."

"Hundreds," Dad tells me grimly and Theo nods. *Hundreds?* I'd almost imagined we might find a list of a dozen or so names somewhere and we could investigate them one by one.

"I hope you understand," Theo says, dropping his voice. "It's not that Harry—Professor Read—won't want to help. He's a good man and I know he would understand your dilemma. But he takes this work very seriously, and so he should. If he were to use his privileged access to those records for any purposes outside of the commission he's been given as the official historian, it would be the end of his career—he may even face jail time. But this isn't a dead end forever. One day, the government will declassify enough of those records to allow Harry to publish a book on the subject. He may help you then, or you may be able to find some answers yourself just by reading it."

"Is this book likely to happen soon, Mr. Sinclair?" I ask.

"Please, call me Theo. There really is no way to tell. Harry has been in the process of seeking permission to publish such a piece of work for well over a decade."

Elsewhere in the church I can hear the other groups, the sounds of a distant choir and children playing, even the murmur of voices as people share their souls. I wonder what happens to my father if this really is a dead end to his quest before it's even really begun. Does he go back to working long hours and losing weight and feeling every bit as miserable as I feel every day. Is that just who he is now that Mum is gone? I hate the very idea of that.

I can hear the finality in Theo's voice and I know he's trying to wind this discussion to a close, but I can't accept that. I reach across and place my hand on his forearm and drop my voice to a plea as I say, "Theo. Please. There has to be something you can do. This means so much to Dad."

"It's okay, Lottie—" Dad starts to say, but I see a softening in Theo's face as he looks from my hand back to my eyes. A spark of hope flares to life in my chest.

"The best I could offer would be to try to speak to Harry on your behalf," Theo says hesitantly, but when Dad and I immediately brighten, he hastens to add, "I don't know that it will do us any good, but I could make a call for you." Then he sighs and adds, "At the very least I know Mrs. White will be more helpful if I'm on the other end of the line."

Dad and I exchange numbers with Theo then start the drive back to Liverpool. The rain is pelting down now as I stare out the window, watching the blurred lights inside the houses passing by. I think about the families putting their children into bed, parents sitting before a television to relax at last after a long day. All I can remember about the night before Mum died is that it rained just like this. I can't help but wonder how many people innocently going about their lives tonight have no idea that it is the last time they are sitting with someone they love.

"He seemed very smart. Knowledgeable and helpful," Dad says, startling me out of my reverie.

"He also seemed pessimistic, Dad," I say reluctantly.

"Perhaps it was foolish for me to think I could find a man I've not seen for twenty-six years when I don't know the first thing about him."

I don't know what to say to that. I'd have to lie to say I'm not having the same concerns.

"Dad, you must have seen things…done things…" I break off uncertainly. "It must have been very difficult for you during the war. Is that why…why you never…" God, it's hard for me to even ask him about it. No wonder he's never spoken freely about that time.

"Right after the war, I put all of that era into a box in my mind and closed the lid so I could marry your mother and build a life with her. But this is exactly why I am so determined to at least try to look back now. It's overdue, love. I need to try to find Remy and I need…" Dad breaks off, then sucks in a breath. "I need to make some sense of it all. My memories of that time are so muddled, and sometimes when I think about those days, feelings float by me and they don't make much sense out of context. It's hard to look back, but I've run long enough. I need to make peace with whatever happened back then." Dad reaches forward and turns the radio on, but he keeps the volume low. His voice is barely a whisper as he adds, "If you have questions, and I imagine you do, I will try to answer them. But as you've probably already noticed, there's a lot I'm not sure of. A lot I don't *know*."

We fall into silence after that—a space held by my father for me to probe and question, and yet, I don't.

It's not that I'm not curious. I am, desperately so.

It's simply that I can hear the tension in his voice even as he offers to share his past with me. My father has been through more than enough in this past year without me digging around in what's left of his darkest memories. Perhaps Aunt Kathleen is right and there are a few skeletons buried in the closet of my father's past, but surely that only makes it more difficult for him to embark upon this project.

For the very first time, I wonder if the gaps in his memory aren't just from his injury…but maybe from trauma too. And maybe that's why my mother was so determined that Dad should just look forward, never back.

CHAPTER 5

ELOISE
Rouen, France
February, 1944

By lunchtime, the train had reached the outskirts of Rouen. I stared out the window as we passed through the southwest of the town, the industrial district, or what was left of it after the sustained Allied bombing raids in recent months.

"Such savage bombing, no?" the colonel beside me said sadly, leaning forward as he followed my gaze to the rubble. I bit my tongue—suppressing an irrational urge to point out that the Allies were hardly unprovoked in trying to ensure the town's infrastructure remained useless to her occupiers. "I do hope your uncle is found safe and well. Please be in touch if I can help."

Soon enough the train had stopped at Gare Saint-Sever. The soldiers around me said goodbye as they passed me my bags, but when one saw me struggling to make my way out of the seat, he insisted on carrying the two suitcases that had been stored above his seat. When he lowered them to the ground outside of the station, I heard the colonel calling me.

"Miss Leroy?" I had been about to walk away—so close to escaping unscathed! Now, my spine stiffened despite my best efforts to hide my frustration, and I turned back to him, trying to force a calm but questioning smile on my face. "I have a car waiting. Could I offer you a lift to your hotel?"

I would be staying the night in a lodging house, but I was never going to reveal the details of that to the colonel. Still, this was an offer I did not want to refuse—I didn't want to offend him, or even to have to explain why I didn't want to get into his car. Besides, a chauffeur-driven car ride across a bridge to the right bank of the Seine would likely mean avoiding the military checkpoint on the bridge, and although this would only be a temporary reprieve from that test, it was a welcome one. Basile had warned me the city was filled with Gestapo and the French Milice and I'd be showing my papers to various guards constantly.

Only local residents were allowed to be within the forbidden zone, which was why my cover story and papers listed an address in Le Havre as my home and I would need to register my visit to secure a *permis de sejour,* a visitor's permit.

The SOE had arranged the finest forger to create my papers so they *should* pass review, but I was not at all disappointed about orienting myself in the town before I tested that theory.

"Thank you," I said, feigning surprise and relief. "But I do hate to be a burden to you."

"It's no trouble. Where are you staying?"

"Well, first I'll store my luggage with the *consigne* at the Gare Rive Droite. My uncle has friends in business I can check in with nearby, you see."

"Of course. I'll have the driver drop me to the Hotel De Ville first and he can take you wherever you like after that."

As we traveled into the town, I felt a pang of grief at the endless rubble. It was clear that the Allies targeted the blocks around the Seine again and again, destroying the historical bridges, then the temporary pontoons the Germans constructed in their place, and so on. And in Rouen, like Paris, German soldiers and the Milicens held a very visible presence on the street.

My gut was a churning mix of emotions I didn't want to acknowledge and couldn't afford to name. To focus on them would be to show them on my face.

"All the best, Miss Leroy," the colonel said as he left the car to go into his hotel. I thanked him profusely and wished him well too, and several minutes later, his driver deposited me at the Gare Rive Droite. I went into the station, waited a few moments, then came back out onto the street to find the car gone, so I continued on foot to my lodgings.

By lunchtime, I was alone in my newly rented room, ready for the first test of my mission. I would move around constantly while in Rouen, but selected that first night's accommodation based on the directions of my commanding officer, Basile, during our final briefing before I left Paris. His agents had long used a void behind a loose brick in the laneway opposite my room as a "drop box"—a place where the members of the circuit could pass information to one another.

"The first task of your mission is simple: just hide behind the drapes in your room and watch that laneway," Basile told me.

He had been evacuated to London for a debrief two months earlier, leaving the SOE's proud Normandy region network, the *Janitor* network, in the hands of his trusted w/t operator, Jérémie.

Jérémie was a loyal, dedicated agent, but he tended to prioritize speed over accuracy when it came to signaling. A team of highly trained secretaries at Baker Street did most of the decoding for the rest of the SOE, but Jérémie's signals tended to be so muddled they required Freddie Booth, architect of the SOE's cryptography procedure, to detangle each message.

Then, a few weeks after Basile's evacuation, Jérémie's accuracy abruptly improved. No longer was each message littered with mistakes—now every letter of every word was perfectly accurate, raising suspicions. Then when an agent returned from a mission to the south of France to report vague but troubling rumors of resistance arrests near Rouen, SOE officials became anxious about sending Basile back into the region.

The stakes could not be higher when it came to the *Janitor* circuit. Although only those closest to Churchill himself knew the precise details of the D-Day operation, we all knew the Allies were planning a landing on the continent and we all suspected the Normandy region would play a vital role. Basile built the *Janitor* network so his knowledge of the SOE's operations in the region was simply too great to risk his exposure.

It was decided that he would return to France but would remain in hiding in Paris until conditions in Rouen could be confirmed. That's where I came in. Baker Street had signaled Jérémie, instructing him to check the drop box between 13:00 and 13:30 hours. My first task was to watch to see who turned up. If Jérémie arrived, I'd make contact with him to request a comprehensive briefing on the circuit's status. If all went well from there, I would go back to Paris to tell Basile that his return to Rouen would be a relatively safe prospect.

By 12:50, I had positioned myself behind the drapes in my room so that I could watch the laneway. I'd done my best to memorize Jérémie's features from the photograph in his personnel file back in London. He was baby-faced and eager, grinning into the camera as if he was on his way somewhere exciting, not headed to a risky mission in occupied territory.

Right on cue, at 13:35, a figure walked casually into the laneway. He felt around for the brick, checked behind it, then continued on his way. The man was in his forties or fifties—portly and slovenly. He looked nothing at all like the sweet young man I'd been sent to find.

I recalled Basile's warning to me the previous night.

"If anyone *other* than Jérémie arrives to check that drop box, that likely means Baker Street has been communicating directly with the Germans for over a month. It probably means the rumors are true about arrests, and Jérémie has been captured. You'll find yourself in a tenuous situation."

"I've done the same training you have, Basile," I reminded him. "I'm ready for this."

"If a stranger arrives to check that drop box tomorrow, you'll have to figure out what happened to that network all on your own. You'll be entirely alone in one of the most contentious regions in the occupied territories, with no way to know who to trust, no easy access to weapons, not even a way to call for help. If it all goes horribly wrong, you'll have to figure out how to get yourself to Spain without any assistance at all. You've had less than three months training. Even hardened soldiers with years of experience would be terrified in a scenario like that."

I'd completed all of the SOE's intensive training—weeks spent at SOE "schools" in various manor houses all over England and Scotland. I'd studied everything from demolitions to "silent killing," close combat designed to disarm men much stronger than me with just a knife, or even my bare hands. I'd mastered the art of fashioning makeshift disguises, and eventually, managed proficiency with the complex cryptography we relied upon. I knew by heart the structure and ranks of each wing of each German and collaborating French military organization. I'd endured mock interrogations and survived psychological and physical tests that lasted for days at a time. I could tail someone undetected and knew how to tell when someone was tailing me. I could assemble a Sten gun even with my eyes closed, and I was a better shot than most of the men I trained with, even though it was clear at the outset that many were already familiar with munitions.

In the end, my active training time totaled somewhere in the order of eleven weeks. Perhaps an unfathomably short period of time to acquire such a skill set, but Basile knew as well as I did that the SOE training program was designed to be the most challenging, intensive immersion imaginable.

"I'll be fine," I assured him, and even now that the worst-case scenario had transpired right before my very eyes, I knew I would be. I watched the stranger walk away from the drop box. It would do me no good to follow him—my focus now had to be on finding the remains of our network, not hunting down those who had infiltrated it.

I was alert but unafraid. If anything, the sight of that stranger had only left me more determined to get to the bottom of the problems in Rouen.

And the sooner I completed my mission, the sooner I could return to my son.

CHAPTER 6

The moon was full and the air was still that night. We could not have asked for more perfect conditions for the factory sabotage operation Marcel and I had spent two months planning. After a busy day playing the role of nanny with the Travers children, I was abuzz with nerves as I rode my bicycle through the fields.

I had gone right from work that afternoon to a meeting with our radio transmitter Adrien at a safe house. He'd received a transmission from Baker Street and I now had to deliver that message to Noah, who was waiting at a farm just out of the city, owned by a local resistance operative.

Just as Noah hoped, my presence in Jullien Travers's household opened the family up to us in a whole new way. I quickly learned that his wife Mégane was chronically ill with unexplained seizures, and the phenytoin her doctor had prescribed her caused such intense fatigue she tended to sleep for hours every afternoon. Her sweet toddlers, Sévère and Aimé, were a delight, but had mysterious health challenges of their own— both girls had unusual facial features and misshapen fingers and toes. Aimé's vision was so poor she was almost blind. I quickly came to adore those girls, and Mégane and I bonded over a shared understanding of what it was like to inhabit a body that was periodically unreliable. But it was also immediately clear to me that although Jullien despised the Germans, he would not risk his family's safety. Their lives were complicated enough already.

As it turned out, we didn't need to recruit him. When Jullien was at the factory, I had access to his home office and I was often alone with the children for hours at a time as Mégane slept. Only a few weeks after my arrival I found paperwork in Jullien's desk which confirmed that a factory retooling operation was well underway and the factory would soon be building bombs. That was all Noah and I needed to begin planning a sabotage operation, and tonight, a Pathfinder target-marking plane would drop flares to mark out the factory for dozens of bombers to carpet-bomb the site.

"Do you have news?" Noah greeted me when I dumped my bicycle at the back door of the farmhouse. He was seated at a small wooden table with Clément Masson, the farm's owner and a member of the local resistance network. Both men were drinking cognac from glass tumblers. Clément seemed calm, and on the surface so did Noah—but I knew him well enough to see beyond his façade. My "husband" was every bit as anxious as I was.

"The planes left exactly on time. The operation is proceeding as planned," I said breathlessly.

Noah was concerned that Baker Street had agreed to a plan with the RAF that was more brute force than precision, and I'd been ferrying messages from him to Adrien over the past few weeks raising this concern over and over again. But the message from London was clear: an air raid was the only course of action. Over the past week, Noah and I camped out in the forest near the factory several nights in a row to confirm it was mostly empty overnight, other than a handful of security guards who would hopefully hear the flares as they landed and flee. Now, he briefly closed his eyes.

"God, I hope this works," he whispered.

Clément pushed his chair back and gave me a smile.

"Are you hungry, Chloe? Modestine can cook you some potatoes."

"Yes please," I said gratefully. "I'd so appreciate that."

I'd worried about finding food I could tolerate on this return to France, but I underestimated the kindness of the French country folk. Once I explained my limited diet to Mégane, she had taken to procuring extra meat and vegetables for me. It felt as though hardly a day went by when one of our contacts, particularly the farmers, didn't offer me fresh produce. Clément left the room to find his wife, and I took his chair opposite Noah.

"We've done everything we could," I reminded him.

"We've done a remarkable job," he agreed. He sipped at the cognac, then looked me right in the eye. "*You* have done a remarkable job. My God. I couldn't have done any of this without you."

"Nonsense," I said dismissively. "You had the *Postmaster* circuit well and truly established when I arrived."

"It was an ad hoc collection of people largely untrained with no system of coordination. The difference between that and the well-oiled machine we have ready to go now is all thanks to you."

The farmhouse did not have electricity—it was lit only by oil lamp and, at night, the fire in an open stonewalled fireplace, owing to the chill in the air with the clear skies and the full moon. It was a rustic home that spoke to the harsh lives the Masson family lived, and in that regard, it was the least romantic place in the world. But as Noah and I worked together over those months, I'd learned that any room could seem romantic to me if he and I were alone in it.

He was wrong about our circuit—the credit truly did belong

to him. But I had slowly come to the realization that Noah had always unlocked the very best in me, and maybe I did the same for him. We had been entirely focused on the factory operation since my arrival and I didn't dare admit my growing feelings for him even to myself. But in the back of my mind, I knew a reckoning was coming.

We were focused on the most important work of our lives—work that could well impact the lives of countless others throughout Europe—and so the undertone to our relationship remained unacknowledged and unspoken, a distraction we could not afford. But we were not strangers to these feelings—a hint of something deeper had been there between us even in the earliest days of our friendship. Back then, we suppressed our attraction not for the sake of a mission, but because it was the right thing to do. Noah was then committed to someone else back in England, and while that was the case, we would only ever have been friends.

But now, on this second stint together in France, Noah's relationship with Geraldine was over. As soon as that factory was destroyed, I was determined to finally put words to all that lay between us.

At the sound of the plane, Noah and I both ran outside, the wood-framed screen door slamming behind us. We took our position at the top of Clément's garden and stared in the direction of the factory. The engine's drone grew louder but even as I looked this way and that, I couldn't find the plane.

"It's got to be the Pathfinder," I said uncertainly. "But…"

"Yes. The moon is full. We should be able to see it by now…" Noah frowned. He pointed in the distance to a narrow tower. "There. You can see the factory chimneys on the north side. That's the whole reason I asked Clément if we could watch from here tonight."

"Yes, but…" I said, but then I paused and turned. We were high on a hill, looking down at the valley where the factory was situated, but on the other side of that hill was a series of small villages. From the air, would they look the same? "Noah— God. Is that sound coming from—"

He took off at a sprint before I could even finish, racing around to the other side of the farmhouse. I followed, but I wasn't running—I was stumbling forward, sicker and shakier with every step until…there it was. A glint of moonlight, reflecting off the wings of the Pathfinder as it streaked across the sky in entirely the wrong place. I whimpered in shock and fear as the first flares began to fall, but Noah cried, his fists in the air above his head.

"No! No! *Stop! Please stop!*"

Our only lifeline from Montbeliard was Adrien's wireless set, and it was no use to us in that moment—the pilots would have no way to listen for the signal, no clue how to decrypt our message. Besides, the set was likely miles away, hidden in a secure spot known only to Adrien.

It did us no good to shout, but Noah and I shouted anyway, screaming until our voices were hoarse and our throats ached. It did us no good to cry, but I wept tears of despair and frustration, and Noah's cheeks were soon shiny with moisture too.

We were entirely powerless, but even though we had no idea how such a mix-up could have occurred, we did not feel blameless—in fact, I felt the guilt might crush me, and as Noah's trembling hand finally reached for mine, I knew he was feeling the same.

I wanted so badly to turn away from the carnage, to hide from it, but all I could do was to face it. I clutched Noah's hand like a lifeline as right before my eyes, dozens of bombers swarmed to carpet-bomb the homes of innocent villagers.

The next few days passed in a furious blur. I spent them rushing messages from Noah to Adrien, who would encode them and transmit them to Baker Street, then ferrying messages back again. Everyone was bewildered by the mix-up. News of the disaster had horrified even the highest levels of operation in the SOE and it seemed all of the senior folk were tripping over one another finding someone to blame. Eventually an announcement came over the transmission: Gerard Turner had been tasked with the job of straightening it all out.

I asked Mégane and Jullien for some time off, ostensibly so I could offer first aid and help search for survivors in the village. There was some truth in that. But Baker Street had a whole other reason to send me to the village. They needed to account for each death and to report on each injury. I was there not just as a nurse, not even just as an agent. I was there, among the wreckage and the blood and the broken bones and the bodies, as Colonel Maxwell's eyes and ears. I was there to bear witness to our catastrophic mistake.

I could have handled the stress of the nursing, but the guilt weighed on me, even though, as far as I could tell, Noah and I had done everything right. Even so, I dragged myself home each night on curfew to crawl into bed beside Noah to weep.

"I'm so sorry," he whispered thickly one night.

"None of this is our fault," I whispered back, between sobs. "It doesn't make any sense at all."

"We'll make sense of it," he choked, rubbing soothing circles along my back. "We can't fix it, but...we'll figure out what went wrong. I promise."

A week after the incident, I was exhausted in a way I'd never experienced before—physically drained by my efforts to help the injured, emotionally drained from standing, virtually powerless, among so much suffering. There were funerals every day and when I wasn't needed at the hospital, I tried to attend as many as I could. None of the mourners would ever know who I really was, but it felt important to me that someone from the SOE attended those funerals. Our agency was ultimately responsible for every lost life, even if we still had no idea why the bombers had targeted the wrong area.

The immediate crisis was finally passing, but there was no time to rest and recuperate because I had to return to my "job" with the Travers family. As tired as I was, I couldn't sleep the night before my return to child-minding, and beside me, Noah was tossing and turning too. I knew he was still awake—his breathing was shallow, but we'd been lying in silence for hours, and he startled me when he said suddenly, "You know all about my family, so you know why this is so personal for me."

"Yes," I whispered, after a stunned pause. Over that difficult week, we had not mentioned it once directly, but I'd been thinking about his parents...his brothers. I'd been thinking about that fraught trip from Paris to London via the escape line in 1941, and the way he kept talking about seeing his family again with such longing in his voice. I remembered the shock of the heartbroken letter he sent me a week after our return.

They are gone, Josie. It's all gone—even the house, even their things. I left and they were fine and it didn't occur to me for a minute that might change while I was away. My family was my whole world, and I have nothing at all left of them.

"I know next to nothing about your family, you know," he said. "Only that your mother lived in Paris until just before the invasion, and now she lives in London. Why don't you ever talk about her?"

"We're not supposed to talk about—"

"Josie," he interrupted me, his tone almost as sharp as I'd ever heard it. "You already knew everything about me when you arrived here. If you don't want to talk to me about your family, you don't have to, but at least be honest about it."

"It's just me and Maman. And it's not that I don't want to tell you about her," I whispered. "We were once close, but that's changed in the last few years, and we parted on bad terms the morning before I came here."

Over the course of the awful week since the bombing, I'd wished so fervently that she was there with me in France—a calm, skilled physician like Maman was just what we needed, not someone like me, a woman who took a nursing job once-upon-a-time because that's all that she could find and the war had disrupted her plans to train as a translator. But now, lying in the dark beside Noah, I pictured my mother's face and despite everything, a wave of homesickness crashed through me.

"My relationship with Maman is complicated," I said. "That's all. It's just so complicated."

"Every relationship is complicated. Even ours."

"Ours is simple," I protested and Noah chuckled.

"Sure it is, if you consider a relationship between two-friends-now-spies-pretending-to-be-spouses to be *simple*."

"She calls me *Jocelyn*," I blurted.

"Isn't that your name?" he said, laughing in surprise.

"Yes! But when I was small—maybe five or six—there was this terrible child a few apartments down from us who used to tease me because his grandfather's name was *Joscelin*. I discovered that in France *Joscelin* was historically a male name, so I decided that since France was to be our home, I'd have to be known as Josie. Everyone else in my life—my doctors, my nannies, the few friends I managed to make—just quietly agreed and started calling me Josie. Not Maman. To this day, I am Jocelyn to her."

"Jocelyn is a beautiful name."

"The name isn't the point," I said, sighing. "It's her stubbornness! But...I miss her. I love her so much and I just want her to be proud of me."

"She will be," Noah whispered back. "One day, she'll understand."

"Here am I complaining to you about my complicated relationship with my mother when you lost your entire family three years ago," I said, turning to face him at last.

"I asked, remember? I want—" He broke off suddenly. His voice was little more than a whisper when he admitted, "All I can think about these days is how short life is. We are here in such danger and every minute of the day I'm conscious that *anything* could happen. I just feel like we have to make the most of every minute we share. Even this week, when *everything* feels so out of control, just having you here beside me gives me hope for the future."

It was the one bright spot in a week that was, in every other way, one of the worst. That was the night I realized two things: I was in love with Noah Ainsworth, and he was in love with me too.

CHAPTER 7

ELOISE
Rouen, France
February, 1944

On my second day in Rouen, I crossed one of the temporary pontoons the Germans had constructed across the Seine, returning to the left bank of the river. I joined the queue to have my papers checked and found myself standing behind a young French family. The mother had a wide, angry scar down the back of her arm, as if she'd suffered a terrible burn. The father leaned heavily on a crutch with a foot so misshapen it hung useless and bare beneath his pant leg. The two children seemed well, except that both were so thin their cheekbones jutted out, and both stood silent and subdued in line, staring down at the water beside them.

I had no way of knowing what that family had lost—other members? Their home? But I did know that something had been taken from them. I could see it in the dullness in their eyes. I could see it in the way that they all stood, shoulders slumped and eyes downcast, as the guard stared at the father's foot with visible revulsion.

"What happened?"

"I was born like this, sir."

"How do you work…support your family?"

"My wife works. We are getting by."

"A man who cannot work is of no use to his family. His community. A man who cannot work is not a *man* at all." At this, the father did not speak. He simply slumped further, as though the guard's very words were causing him to shrink. "Cover it up next time you leave your house. People should not have to see a thing like that."

A wave of frustration and anger surged through me. The spring sun was suddenly unbearably hot on my scalp and shoulders, and the gentle sway of the pontoon beneath my feet seemed violent, even though the river was still. There were only two guards on this pontoon—the one checking papers, and the other, sitting at the edge with his rifle against his back, staring down at the river. Maybe he was taking a break, or maybe he was watching, ready to shoot anyone who tried to cross by boat. The guard closest to me, the cruel guard who mocked the disabled father, also had a rifle on his shoulder.

I'd excelled in close-combat training and I was an accurate shot. I could take that rifle and shoot both guards dead in an instant. I pictured it in my mind—how I'd disarm him, how I'd quickly aim, how I'd feel nothing but relief as I pulled that trigger, even knowing that somewhere else, probably on the riverbank, another guard would be aiming his sights at me in return. The scene playing out in my mind only sent my fury surging higher and for a moment I was nothing but a ball of pure hatred and rage, ready to explode.

Why on earth did the good people of Rouen—the good people of France and Europe—have to endure this ordeal? All because of power-mad men, so determined to foment hate and hoard resources and land that they cared not one jot for the innocent people in their way.

But in a heartbeat, I could do something small to restore some balance of justice. My mission would be over in an instant and before it even really began but oh, how good it would feel to let my rage loose on those guards.

The family shuffled forward past the guard and the next man in line stepped up, but with every fiber of my being I wanted to act before the children walked away. I wanted them to see that guard pay for humiliating their father. They could watch as he was neutralized, and then they would go to bed that night knowing that the next innocent family who came along would not be subject to such needless cruelty.

I had a million reasons to take that gun and shoot those guards, but I would not do it. I couldn't. I had to complete my mission for the sake of the SOE and D-Day and the true liberation of the people of Europe, even for that family, so downcast and humiliated on the pontoon right in front of me.

And further still beyond that, I had a few very important reasons to make it home alive.

I stepped closer to the guard, awaiting my turn now. It wasn't fear that left my palms sweating. It was pure, unadulterated fury. I could not afford to hand over identity papers smudged with sweat.

I had to calm myself down.

During my training, I roomed with a diminutive young woman given the code name Chloe. I thought about her and her quiet wisdom as the guard sent the family on their way. I thought about the times I'd seen the odds stacked against her in training, but she approached each challenge with a cool head and a quiet determination that never failed her. She was likely in the field on a mission too—elsewhere in France, fighting in her own way. Whatever she was doing, wherever she was, I knew what she'd tell me if she saw me on that bridge: *the second they make you angry, they've won.*

"Papers?" the guard said.

My hand was steady as I offered them and I did not flinch as he snatched them away. I refused to so much as glance at the gun slung over his shoulder—to focus on it would be to return to my fury, and then he'd see it in my eyes.

"Visiting from Le Havre?" the soldier asked. I met his gaze calmly.

"Yes, sir."

"Reason for visit?"

"Family, sir."

Just as I'd been taught in SOE training, I kept my answer as close to the truth as possible—in this case, maybe a truer word had never been spoken. I was there for my husband, for the long and happy life he deserved to live—the life that had been taken from him at El Alamein. I was there in Rouen to achieve the justice my Giles deserved.

It had been hard to leave Hughie, but it would have been harder to stay, to take walks in the park and to make him eggs for breakfast and launder his clothes and to pretend the world had not changed forever.

The guard handed me my papers and I stepped away from him.

For Giles, I told myself, and for Hughie. I had to keep my head for my boys.

As I continued on my way, I brought to mind the key data points from my briefing at Baker Street with Mrs. Elwood, Mr. Turner and Basile. We spent days at the Baker Street offices poring over maps and aerial photographs of the region, matching up every detail we could glean from those sources with what Basile knew from recent activity on the ground. If my mission was a success, the first thing I would do when I returned to Baker Street would be a similar extended debrief so I could add my observations to the bank of data the SOE had on Rouen and the Normandy region. I was in the city to confirm the integrity of the circuit, but I was also there to gather intelligence for Colonel Maxwell so he could accurately advise

Churchill and guide planning for a D-Day invasion. That was a responsibility I did not take lightly.

Already, I'd strolled past the *Frontsammelstelle*, the meeting point for newly arrived German recruits, and had been startled by the strangeness of the soldier's ages—almost all of the men milling about were wildly youthful, most no more than fifteen or sixteen, the few adults in the crowd well past middle age. Did this indicate the Germans had exhausted their population of men in their prime? Such an observation might one day underpin a decision which could turn the tide of the war.

I continued on foot toward the first address Basile had me memorize, the home of a Madame Delphine Laurent. She was famous for her wild flair for fashion and rumored to have a secret collection of expensive artwork. Madame Laurent had played hostess to Jérémie many times after the SOE dropped him into France in 1943. He was almost young enough to be her great-grandson, but the two had become good friends, and Basile instructed me to seek her out if Jérémie did not arrive to check the drop box.

"In some ways, Delphine is the worst possible kind of local contact for an agent to make. She attracts attention everywhere she goes—you'll understand when you meet her. But she loathes the Nazis with a passion, has dirt on just about every French official in Rouen, and lives alone in a massive apartment right near the Seine. She was determined to help, but too frail—too visible—to be involved in active resistance. When she offered the circuit the use of her spare bedroom, it was impossible for me to refuse," Basile told me.

The area around Madame Laurent's home had been bombed into oblivion even in the two months since Basile was evacuated. Most of her street had been reduced to rubble, and my eyes watered at the choking dust and the fading smoke that remained heavy in the street. People picked through the ruins of homes, dragging salvageable items down to the sidewalk to be recovered later. A body lay wrapped in a sheet at the curb, awaiting collection. A man sat beside it, covered in dust and blood, his head in his hands. It would be no comfort at all to him that the Allies were pummeling the area to try to destabilize the German stronghold there.

The chances of finding Madame Laurent seemed to grow dimmer with every destroyed home I passed, but right at the end of her street, I found a single apartment block that, other than some blown-out windows and a crack all along the façade, had escaped largely unscathed. God or fate or luck had spared Madame Laurent's building. I made my way immediately to the doorman's office and asked after her.

"Who shall I tell her has come to call?"

"My name is Felice Leroy, but she won't know me by that. I'm the granddaughter of an old school friend of hers, you see. Grand-mère has sent me here to discuss some private business."

"Private business," the concierge repeated, holding the telephone receiver in the air as he stared at me suspiciously.

I leaned toward him and dropped my voice as I said pointedly, "My grandmother is an artist, you see...she tells me Madame Laurent might be interested in her collection?"

Two minutes later, I was on my way up four flights of stairs to Madame Laurent's apartment at the top of the building. She met me at her front door, poking her head out into the hallway as she looked me up and down. Over springy silver curls, she wore a silk scarf in a chaotic swirl of autumnal reds and oranges and yellows, paired with a shade of red-orange lipstick I could only dream to pull off.

"Who is your grandmother?" she asked me without preamble.

"Her name is Viviane Paquet," I said carefully. Whenever Basile sent someone to her doorway, he would give them the code word "Paquet" to indicate she should take them in. Madame Laurent's drawn-on eyebrows lifted sharply, and she stepped back, pulling the door wide open.

"I remember her fondly. Do come in."

Madame Laurent's apartment was expansive but cluttered, full of shelves stacked with dusty books and knickknacks and tables and bureaus buried beneath paint-stained rags and paintbrushes soaking in jars. She took me through to her kitchen and made me coffee—real coffee—and I carried the tray as I followed her through to her sunroom at the front of the building. We sat beside one another in cane chairs, facing large windows overlooking the Seine and the blocks of rubble all around it. Several windows were cracked, and small panes of glass were altogether missing here and there. She caught me staring at the open spaces.

"I won't board my windows up, not even if there's no glassmaker left alive in Rouen to replace them by the time winter comes," she told me flatly. "They've taken my city, but they will not take my view. How long will you be staying with me?"

"Just tonight," I explained. "Basile sent me, but he's instructed me to stay no more than one night in any place."

"Is he safe? I've been so worried. I'm sure you've seen the posters."

"Posters? No! I just arrived from Paris yesterday."

"They are fixed to buildings...electricity posts...all over the place. You'll see them sooner or later," she muttered, scowling. "Basile is a wanted man—quite desperately wanted, I suspect. You must make sure he knows to be careful. They have drawn a likeness of him that is quite good, considering."

It was just as we'd feared. I sent a quick prayer of gratitude that Colonel Maxwell had had the foresight to keep Basile out of the region.

"And Jérémie?" I asked her. "Do you know anything of his fate?"

"That boy was like a grandson to me," she said heavily.

"Was?" I repeated, heart sinking.

"Well, he may well still be alive of course. They arrested him two months ago."

"Then I'm guessing they also found his wireless set and crystals." Jérémie's wireless set was almost certainly camouflaged in a suitcase—most of the SOE sets were. The set required a crystal to be fitted in order to transmit, and it was our practice that these crystals should always be stored separately as an additional security measure.

"I'm sure you know the damned Germans have those vehicles now that detect the signals," she said. The direction-finding vehicles had made w/t operators' lives so much more difficult—they drove up and down the streets searching for a wireless signal and could narrow down the origin point to just a few dozen feet. "Jérémie had been moving all up and down the coast, signaling from fifty-odd locations sometimes dozens of miles away. I never knew when I'd see him, but if he was near Rouen, he usually came back here to rest or just to hide his set here. A few weeks went by and I hadn't seen him, so I started to worry. To contact Basile, I would leave a message with the butcher below his apartment, but when I went to summon him, the butcher told me he was gone."

"He was evacuated to London," I told her.

"The following week, the Gestapo arrested me. God only knows how, but they knew Jérémie had stayed here." The thought of this frail woman being interrogated left me feeling ill. Madame Laurent picked up her coffee cup and cradled it in her trembling hands. "I told them he knocked on my door looking for work. I said he reminded me of my late husband so when he told me he had nowhere to sleep, I did what I could to help him." She grinned. "My Aloïs was short and stout, nothing at all like Jérémie, who is built like a beanpole. But the Gestapo assumed I was telling the truth just as I knew they would. As you've no doubt learned yourself, men are all too quick to believe a beautiful woman runs entirely on sentiment and knows nothing of substance or value." She said this without a hint of irony or self-deprecation, just a calm reflection from a woman in her nineties who had understood herself to be beautiful her entire life. And in that moment, it struck me that she *was* beautiful—that the lines on her face were beautiful, that her silver hair was beautiful...her courage was beautiful. I was probably close to seven decades her junior, but I wanted so much to be like her one day. "And maybe because I am old, they didn't beat me or torture me. I had a few rough nights on an uncomfortable mattress before they sent me home. I learned that Jérémie was also being held at the prison, and after my release, I went back and insisted they let me visit him. I saw him twice before he was moved. I took him food and some fresh clothes but..." She swallowed hard, and her gaze grew distant and her voice faded to a whisper as she said, "...what he really needed was a doctor."

"He'd been beaten."

"Beaten does not describe what that man had been through. He was missing half of his teeth, and that wasn't the worst of it. He was so hysterical, I couldn't get a word of good sense out of him. It almost killed me to see him like that."

Most likely, the Gestapo had beaten and tortured Jérémie until he broke and told them everything—probably the location of his set and crystals, details of his security procedure and encryption key, his transmission windows. Like me, Jérémie was trained by the SOE in ways to withstand such torture, but we all understood that no training in the world could truly prepare a person to resist it for an extended period of time. Sometimes, an agent broke and secrets were betrayed.

The Germans had Jérémie's wireless unit and everything they needed to impersonate him—everything they needed to do a better job of communicating with Baker Street than he'd ever managed himself.

"And Madame Laurent, you say the Germans have moved

Jérémie?" I had to be sure. If there was any chance he was still being held locally, I would try to find local resistance operatives to help rescue him.

"Yes, on my next visit, I learned he was sent on a transport. The butcher told me that the Maquisards were starting to fall too and he was scared he would be next. I went back to see him last week, and his apprentice asked me to leave and not return—the Gestapo took the butcher in the night." Madame Laurent's voice had dropped to a whisper, but she raised her chin now as she told me, "My role in all of this has been small, but I've had a good life. If they come back for me—even if they kill me, I will go to my grave knowing I did my best to help liberate France and that is all I ever wanted. But you, my dear—you are young and you have so much to lose. Do you understand how much danger you are in, coming to the *zone interdite* and asking questions like this?"

"You don't need to worry about me, Madame Laurent," I assured her. "I know exactly what I'm doing."

My life had meaning—*real* meaning, and I was absolutely determined to make it home to Hughie. But no SOE agent went into the field without an awareness that they might not return. We all understood the miserable reality that sometimes, an agent's death could mean every bit as much as their life.

That would not be me. It didn't matter what it took—I was going to make it home.

"I need one more favor from you," I told her quietly.

"Anything," she said.

"Tell me...where will I find this butcher's shop?"

It was one thing to confirm that the circuit had been compromised. Now, I had to confirm exactly what remained intact.

CHAPTER 8

CHARLOTTE
Liverpool
May, 1970

The garden is a chaotic explosion of color this year—sweet peas and roses and lilies and peonies just in this section alone. Closer to the house, masses of sunflowers are stretching higher as they prepare to bloom, and thatches of clematis and creeping thyme border the paved path. Dad planted extra flowers this year, maybe to make up for the ones Mum isn't here to plant herself.

I'm sitting out in my bathing suit enjoying the sunshine. My book is open on my lap, but I've barely read a page all morning. Instead, I've been sipping my tea and watching the bumblebees and butterflies flit from blossom to blossom in Dad's garden.

I'm so relaxed I'm sorely tempted to ignore the phone inside the house when the shrill ring sounds. At the very last minute, I drop my book and sprint through the grass to scoop the receiver up.

"This is Charlotte speaking," I say, slightly out of breath from the sudden burst of activity.

"Charlotte? This is Theo Sinclair." He seems a little hesitant, almost as if he's nervous. That can't be a good sign. "Are you okay? You sound…"

"I just ran to get the phone," I laugh. "It's nice to hear from you, Theo."

"Is it? I mean, yes. I suppose. I...you see, I spoke with Harry. Do you think you could meet me at the History department at Manchester at three p.m. Friday? Professor Read has agreed to meet with your father after all. I know it's business hours, but—"

"I'm a teacher," I interrupt him to explain. "I'm on summer break."

"I'm a teacher too."

"I thought you were a student."

"Ah. No, I was a student—I finished my Master's then did a teaching certificate. I teach high school history classes now. So will this suit Noah?"

"Dad sets his own hours. We'll be there. Thank you."

Theo clears his throat before he mutters, "Yes, well. Let's see how this goes before you thank me."

My father and I arrive at Manchester University at a quarter to three on Friday. We consult a campus map then wander in silence through the grounds admiring the beautiful stonework on the old buildings and the careful gardens around manicured lawns.

When we find the right building, Dad and I sit side by side on a park bench beneath a tree, seeking a reprieve from the summer sun. A groundskeeper is mowing the lawn nearby and the air is flooded with the scent of cut grass. Finding myself at a campus again is making me miss my carefree days as an undergraduate student. Life seemed so simple back then.

Theo greets us as he approaches along the path. Once again, he's dressed as though he slept late and had to rush out the door. I survey his rumpled cords and the misaligned buttons on his collared shirt, the wild way his thick, sandy hair stands this way and that, as if he's yet to discover how to tame it. He's not without his charms—those bright blue eyes chief among them—but it's starting to appear as though last Thursday was no exception and he has a perpetually distracted and disheveled affect. He reminds me of some of the academics I studied under at university but seems nothing like a high school teacher. I wonder if the students make fun of him behind his back. The very thought makes me sad.

Theo leads us up a stairway to a central reception area on the second floor. As soon as he pushes open the door, we're greeted with a wave of cigarette smoke so thick I immediately start to cough.

Behind the desk, surrounded by piles of folders and books and loose yellowed papers, sits a curvy woman with bright red hair. A Dictaphone headset rests over her ears, pressing her wispy bangs down awkwardly onto her forehead, and a cigarette hangs from her mouth as she types furiously with both hands. She looks up and beams at Theo, sending cigarette ash drifting onto her blouse with the movement, but does not break with the rhythm of her typing even as we stand before her desk and wait.

She reaches the end of a sentence and her hands fly off the keyboard. She scoops the cigarette from her mouth and drops it into an overflowing ashtray on the desk, then she rises and swivels around the desk to throw her arms around Theo.

"Theo, love! It is just so good to see you. Why don't you visit more often?"

I recognize this as Mrs. White even if her appearance is nothing at all like I imagined. I was picturing a stern woman well past retirement age—but Mrs. White is probably only in her forties, and at least toward Theo, seems very warm.

"You know I'm very busy with my own job these days, Mrs. White," Theo says, his own voice muffled by the secretary's smothering embrace. When she finally releases him, he has the slightly embarrassed air of a teenager whose mother has just pinched his cheek at the school gate. He makes an attempt at straightening his shirt, before he motions toward me and my father.

"This is Charlotte and Noah Ainsworth," he tells her. "Charlotte, Noah, this is Mrs. White—she is Professor Read's secretary, right-hand woman, all-round mastermind."

"Oh, you," Mrs. White says, and then she giggles like a schoolgirl, a sound so surprising my father and I exchange a wide-eyed glance. But her gaze narrows when she turns her attention to me. "You didn't mention your father's name on the phone, Miss Ainsworth."

"I'm quite certain I did," I say, surprised.

"No. You did not," she says firmly. "Because if you had told me your father is Noah Ainsworth, I'd have put you straight through to the professor." She looks at Dad and smiles. "Mr. Ainsworth, it is a pleasure to meet you at last. I have sent you many a letter over the years."

Dad stares at her blankly.

"I've never received any letters."

"Well," she says, eyebrows rising. "Now that doesn't sound right at all. I know I sent them."

"I… I don't know what to say to you, Mrs. White," Dad says, after shooting me a bewildered look. "I'd never so much as heard of Professor Read until last week."

"Hmm," Mrs. White says, in a tone which suggests she's certain Dad is lying but she can't be bothered arguing with him. She waves to a bank of chairs. "Can I get you some tea?" We obediently take our seats as we all agree tea would be nice, and Mrs. White leaves the room, her cigarette still smoldering in the ashtray, a cloud of cloying perfume lingering in her wake.

"She's not what I expected," I whisper to Theo as he takes the plastic chair beside me.

"She sees it as her role to be Harry's gatekeeper. I'm not surprised you found her unhelpful when you first called, but when

I spoke to Professor Read yesterday he told me he's been try-ing to reach your father for some time."

"Theo," a voice booms from the door, and Theo rises anx-iously as a much older man enters the room. Professor Read is at least eighty years old. His pale blue eyes sit beneath heavy white eyebrows, and there's much sparser white hair curved around a high forehead marked by age spots. He shakes Theo's hand, but his gaze is slightly guarded. "Good to see you, son." Read turns his attention to me and Dad and a broad smile transforms his face. "Well! You must be Noah and Charlotte. Welcome."

"It's a pleasure to meet you," Dad says, standing.

Read clasps the hand Dad extends toward him as he replies, "Truly, Noah, the pleasure is all mine. Please, come join me in my office."

We follow Harry Read down another long corridor, past a long series of tiny, windowless offices, winding toward the front of the building.

"Quite a rabbit warren up here, isn't it?" I remark.

"It's dormant over the summer but a hive of activity during term time. I've lost more than one graduate student up here over the years," Read jokes.

The nameplate on the thick oak door at the end of the cor-ridor tells us that we've finally reached his office. Theo, Dad and I take the three chairs in front of Read's desk and we make small talk. Once Mrs. White has delivered a tea service on a shiny silver tray, Read motions for Theo to close the door be-hind her.

This office is less chaotic than Mrs. White's but no less crowded. Behind Read's desk there are floor-to-ceiling shelves and every single inch of space is filled with books. There's a door to another room behind Professor Read with an impres-sively intimidating lock—possibly the largest lock I've ever seen on an internal door. The window is wide open and framed by white gauze curtains which wave slowly in the slight breeze.

There's not a hint of Mrs. White's cigarette smoke back here—
the room smells exactly like the library at my college. Old books
and leather, a deep note of pervasive dust.

Read pulls a small transcriber from his desk and motions
toward my father.

"Do you mind if I record our conversation, Noah? I'd like
to have one of my students interview you properly at a later
date but if we cover the basics now, I'll be better placed to figure out who that should be."

"I don't need to be interviewed," Dad says stiffly. "I only
wanted to speak to you because I want to find Remy." Dad's
eyes seem locked on that recorder, as if he's willing for it to
disappear. While Read waits in a patient silence, Dad clears his
throat and shifts awkwardly on his chair. "There were many
heroes in the SOE, Professor Read. I'm quite certain I was not
one of them."

"Everyone who served in the SOE is a hero, Mr. Ainsworth,"
Read says, suddenly aghast. But his lips thin and perhaps his
eyes narrow just a little as he adds slowly, "Except the double
agents, of course." My father shifts again, lifts his teacup off
the desk to cradle it in both hands. "We *have* sent you many
letters over the years."

Dad shakes his head.

"So your secretary told me. I'm not sure what address you've
been—"

Read spins a manila folder on his desk toward us. There are
three addresses on the front cover—two have been crossed out,
and our current address—the house we've lived in for more than
fifteen years—is on a typed label beneath them. Read opens
the folder to reveal a stack of copied letters inside.

"We've sent one every few years. Since about 1948," Read
says quietly, flicking through the pile. "You aren't the only
former agent who ignores them but we do keep sending them
unless they specifically ask us to stop."

"I didn't ignore them," Dad says. He reaches forward and picks the top letter up, scans it quickly, then sets it back down. He raises his gaze to Read's, his expression twisted with bewilderment. "I've never seen these before. How did you even know where I lived?"

"We are fortunate to access quality information from other government agencies. And they *are* your addresses, no?"

Dad gives me a bewildered look. The professor closes the folder again and I lean forward to read the addresses for myself.

"The first one was the flat me and Geraldine moved into after we married. The next was our first detached house, and the last house is our home even now," Dad murmurs. Our current house was my mum's dream house. She and Dad saved for years to build it and I know it was a struggle to afford the mortgage at first because Dad's business was still getting off the ground. The house is a single-story bungalow with four bedrooms plus an office. I was ten when we moved in but I vividly remember Aunt Kathleen playfully calling the house "ostentatious" because it had a second bathroom and *two* living areas. It certainly was a step up from the homes most of our friends had at the time.

"I never received these letters," Dad says stiffly. "I might not have agreed to an interview, but I wouldn't have simply ignored you."

"It's perfectly fine if you *did* ignore me," Read says, but it's clear to me that he does not for a second believe my father is telling the truth. "I'm just glad you're here now. And I have of course heard from Theo that you want to track this Remy down. Let's get down to it, then. Tell me what you know of him."

"I don't know much at all," Dad says. It's warm in the office but not unbearably so. There are small beads of sweat over Dad's forehead and I wonder if this is anxiety, rather than the heat. He takes a handkerchief from the pocket of his shirt and mops his brow. "I woke up in a hospital at Brive-La-Galliarde sometime after D-Day. I'd been shot and—" he points to the jagged scar beside his temple. "My skull was fractured. I completely lost my memory at first—all I really knew was that I was British and a fish out of water in occupied France. I couldn't remember my name. I couldn't even figure out *how* I knew French."

"How terrifying that must have been for you," Professor Read murmurs. Dad shrugs awkwardly.

"In time I remembered that I'd been working with the SOE, but many of my memories of the war years remain blurry—especially the months leading up to that day."

"So you're looking for a man named Remy because…"

"The nurse told me that Remy dropped me off at the hospital clinic."

"But you're not sure if he was an agent."

"I do *think* he was," Dad says. "Am I certain of that? No. I was hoping you could tell me."

"Tell me this, Noah," Professor Read says quietly. "Does the village of Salon-La-Tour ring any bells?"

My father fumbles for the handkerchief and mops his brow again, but even as he does so, the color is draining from his face. This time, he keeps the handkerchief in his hand and he starts to twist it around his fingers.

"Dad?" I prompt uncertainly.

"My memories are so vague," Dad croaks.

"But you do have some memory of that village?" Read prompts.

"I think so." Dad's voice is little more than a whisper now.

"Were you injured at Salon-La-Tour, Noah?"

"Yes," Dad says. He clears his throat and lifts his chin. "Actually. Yes, I do believe I was."

"Your code name was Marcel, was it not?" Read asks. Dad nods again. *Marcel*. How strange to think of my father using someone else's name. "There was another agent with you at

Salon-La-Tour, wasn't there?" Dad squeezes his eyes closed for just a moment then nods silently. "Was there anyone else? Or just the three of you?"

"Just the three of us, I think," Dad says. "But she—Fleur—escaped somehow. I distinctly remember being alone with Remy."

"So you *do* remember Remy now?" I ask Dad, confused. He looks at me helplessly as he waves toward the professor.

"It's like I told you. I have random images that come into my mind...sometimes feelings that don't necessarily make sense. When the professor prompts me, I can see it just a little clearer. But it's all still very muddled."

"Let me tell you why I'm so fascinated, Noah, and why I had so hoped to speak with you one day," Professor Read says. "I believe the three of you left from a safe house outside of Limoges that morning. I've never been able to find out exactly what happened after that."

"Have you asked Remy...?" I interrupt. "Or... Fleur?"

"Unfortunately, Fleur did not survive the war," Professor Read says quietly.

Dad is an empathetic man, but as far as I can tell, he didn't remember this Fleur woman until a few minutes ago, so I'm confused by how stricken he seems to be at this news.

"Oh no. She was so young," he whispers, gaze dropping.

"As many agents were," Professor Read says.

"And Remy?" I press.

"Still alive, as far as I know," Read tells us. "I spoke with him on the telephone a few years ago."

"So you know him?" I exclaim, then I turn to Dad and beam. "This is marvelous news!"

"I'll just stop you there, Charlotte," Read says. "Yes, Remy is alive but his identity remains classified. The reason I spoke with him on the phone is because *he* called me and asked me to stop sending him letters."

"I did try to warn you," Theo says quietly, leaning forward past my dad as he offers me a sympathetic look.

"No," I protest, shaking my head. "Surely there must be some way around this. All my dad wants to do is thank Remy. There's no harm in that."

"We can discuss a few possible options in a moment," the professor says patiently as he turns his gaze back to Dad. "But first, Noah, perhaps you can tell me everything you remember from that day.".

"I barely remember that day at all. I already told you that."

"You also just explained to Charlotte that the memories become more distinct with a little prompting," Read reminds him softly. "I'd be keen to know if you can remember *how* you were traveling that day."

"No. That's all I remember." Dad runs his hand through his hair, then he blurts, almost defensively, "The pressure was on because of D-Day. We were just trying to get the mission back on track."

"On track how?" Read asks. Dad shrugs helplessly.

"Fleur was…" He breaks off, struggling for words. "It happened during the landing, I think."

Dad and Read stare at one another in silence. Dad looks away first, sucking in a sharp breath through his nose as he shakes his head. Dad doesn't just look uncomfortable now. He looks…ashamed?

"Noah," Theo says quietly. Dad turns toward him slowly. "Was Fleur injured somehow?"

"Her landing seemed perfect at first, that's what confused me," Dad blurts. "I'd seen bad landings before, I'd even seen one agent shatter the bones in her leg when she landed, but Fleur's looked to be perfect then she was on the ground. I wasn't sure what to do. I hadn't heard the sound of a gun, but a gunshot *was* the most obvious explanation for why someone would collapse like that. So many agents were captured or killed parachuting in—it was one of the most dangerous moments of a mission, and if the Germans were watching, I'd be putting myself at risk going to her aid." Dad is facing Theo so I can't see his face, but I can hear the strain in his voice. I reach up to rest my hand on his shoulder.

"Fleur wasn't shot though, was she?" Theo asks quietly. When Dad just stares at him silently, he prompts, "Was it her ankle?"

Read turns his attention to Theo, gaze narrowed, expression darkening by the second. It takes Theo a moment or two to notice this, but when he does, his eyes widen as if he's panicked. His skin flushes red and he suddenly looks out the window.

Dad doesn't seem to notice. He's staring at the floor now, his voice a hoarse whisper.

"I ran over to help her just as Remy landed. And yes, she'd sprained that ankle badly once…a training jump that went wrong. The doctors had long since cleared her for fieldwork, but the landing somehow aggravated the old injury."

Dad trails off again. Theo is also staring at the ground now. Read is once again staring at Theo.

The atmosphere in the office is thick with tension and I have *no* idea what's going on.

"Why does all of this matter?" I ask them, trying to get the conversation back on track. "What does any of this have to do with Remy?"

Read reaches into his drawer and withdraws a lined notepad and pen. I feel a brief burst of hope—is he about to give us Remy's details? But no. Instead, he scrawls today's date at the top of the page.

"How were you traveling that day at Salon-La-Tour, Noah?" he prompts, his tone firmer now. "You say that Fleur couldn't walk so I'm guessing you weren't on foot."

"No." Dad thinks carefully. "No, we were in a car."

"A car," Read repeats. He writes the word down and under-lines it three times. "And what was the date?"

"I told you, I'm not sure. Sometime just after D-Day."

"It was just after D-Day. You were traveling in *a car* and you attempted to drive *through* Salon-La-Tour. Were you driving?"

"I can't remember."

"Did someone *tell* you to take that route, Noah? Did someone tell you to take the car? Perhaps a contact at Baker Street—or maybe a contact in France?" Another grim shake of Dad's head. I can no longer tell if Dad is being evasive or if he genuinely doesn't remember. Beside him, Theo is now sitting with his elbows on his thighs, leaning forward. His expression is every bit as grim as my father's is pained.

The professor suddenly drops his pen onto the notepad and leans back in his chair. He looks at Dad, then seems to decide something, because he nods to himself and tents his fingers in front of his chest.

"I do understand your desire to thank Remy for saving your life. I can't tell you who he is, but I can ask him on your be-half if he would be willing to meet you. I have to warn you, when we last spoke he was resolute that he did not want to re-visit the war years. But I'll call him and explain, and we shall see how he responds."

"Thank you," Dad says, but he doesn't sound nearly as elated as I expected him to. His tone is heavy and his shoulders are slumped.

"All I ask in return is that you come back at some point in the future to undertake a comprehensive interview. We'll leave the students and your daughter out of this one—it will just be me and you, and if you don't want it recorded, I'll simply take some notes. I have a lot of questions about that day, Noah." He drops his voice and adds quietly, "I've long wondered about 'Marcel' and the things he got up to in France."

Dad, apparently, can't leave the room fast enough. He's on

his feet, walking past me toward the door, almost before the professor has finished talking. I scramble to follow him, but as I reach for the door, Professor Read calls.

"Theo." His tone is grim. I glance back just in time to see Theo wince. "Stay back please, son."

Dad charges out of Read's office, but I hesitate in the doorway, watching something unpleasant passing between Theo and Read. But I've been dismissed and I'm worried about Dad, so I jog lightly to catch up with him. Mrs. White is on the phone, but I wave to her and whisper my thanks as I pass, then I'm right onto the stairs, chasing Dad toward the building exit. He's still powering ahead, his footsteps heavy and his shoulders locked.

"Dad," I call. He turns back to look at me but his expression is twisted with frustration or pain or…guilt? "Dad, are you okay?"

"I just need a moment," he says abruptly, and he's already turning toward the carpark. I start to follow him, but I can't escape the feeling that we got Theo in trouble somehow, and I want to make sure he's okay too.

"I just need to speak with Theo," I blurt. "I'll catch up."

"Good." Dad raises his hand in acknowledgment without turning around. "I'll see you at the car." But after a few steps he turns back to me. His expression is carefully neutral as he adds, "Thank him for me, please, Charlotte."

"I will," I call.

I am completely, hopelessly confused. What on earth just happened?

I return to the park bench beneath the tree and watch the man with the lawn mower finish his job—but the minute the engine switches off, sounds of distant shouting echo down from upstairs in the history building. My gut twists uncomfortably as I look up and locate Professor Read's open window and those gauze curtains waving in the breeze. I can't make out any of the words, but Read sounds furious.

When Theo finally comes down the front steps a few minutes later, he looks even more frazzled than he did when we arrived. His footsteps slow as he approaches me.

"Well, that was odd," I offer uncertainly. He forces a smile.

"Indeed. I suppose it would all seem very odd."

"I hope we didn't get you into trouble."

Theo sighs and takes a seat beside me.

"Charlotte, the miserable truth is that I am more than capable of doing that all on my own. Is your father okay?"

"He seems so upset. I don't understand why the professor was laboring the point about how and where the agents were traveling that day. What difference does it even make in the scheme of things?"

"Ah. I suppose I can at least shed some light on that for you. Years ago, I sat in on an interview with an American POW who met Fleur on a prison transport a few months before she died. He told us that she was arrested after traveling in a car through Salon-La-Tour. At the time, Read assumed that the American had the details mixed up because car travel was banned in that part of France after D-day in an effort by the Germans to slow the resistance down, and it seemed so unlikely that three agents would ignore that. Read was probably trying make sense of that now that he finally has access to someone who was there."

"Oh," I said. I look at him curiously. "But...how did you know Fleur hurt her ankle?"

"Lucky guess." Theo shrugs, looking away, but he's not a great liar and he looks guilty as hell.

"Right..."

"It's clear your dad just wants to talk to Remy so maybe once he has some closure there, he'll be ready to talk to Harry some more."

"It's very difficult for me to imagine my father working as some kind of covert agent twenty-odd years ago," I confess. "Until a few weeks ago, I thought he was an army mechanic and I assumed he'd been based here in Britain the whole time. I found that hard enough to imagine, let alone him driving illicit vehicles through occupied France."

"It took me two years to complete my Master's with Professor Read," Theo says. "For much of that time it was my job to interview men like your father. You do a job like that for long enough and you come to realize that whoever someone is during war years, there is no guarantee that they will be the same in peacetime. Some of these men and women were completely broken by their experiences, but others came back from the war and drew a line under it…declared themselves entirely new people. Maybe at first they were trying to pretend they'd never seen and done the horrific things they had to do to survive, but sometimes they live the lie so long and so well they really do become someone different. You can't blame your dad for doing what he had to in moving on from the war, especially given his memory was disrupted in that accident too. And you *really* shouldn't blame yourself for struggling to picture him as whoever he was before."

"Thank you," I say softly. "And you? Are you okay?"

Theo smiles.

"I'm fine. The conversation I just had with Harry, as awful as it was, was several years overdue."

My father is silent as we drive home. I try to make small talk but he answers me in grunts and shrugs.

"That's strange about the letters never arriving…" I offer.

"It is," Dad says grimly.

"Do you know what might have happened there?" He shrugs noncommittally. "No theories at all?"

"I don't want to speak about this right now, Charlotte," he says. Dad isn't the kind to snap—but his tone is sharper than I'm used to, and I recoil in surprise. He looks at me, frustrated, then his expression suddenly softens. "I just need to think, okay? We can talk about it later."

"Okay, Dad," I say.

He retires to his room right after dinner, taking Wrigley with him. There is no light coming from under the door when the phone rings just after eight. It's my brother Archie, just as I suspected it would be. He's working for the World Bank in London, having been headhunted to some brilliant economics gig right after graduation. He often calls from the office when he's working late. Miser that he is, Archie doesn't like to pay for expensive long-distance calls on his own pence.

"How's Dad doing?" Archie asks me.

"Sometimes lately he's seemed a bit better but..." I break off, then ask, "Arch, did you know Dad was in the SOE during the war?"

"Huh? No, he was a mechanic."

"He was a flight engineer for the RAF and eventually joined the SOE."

Archie bursts out laughing.

"Lottie," he says, chuckling. "I don't know where you're getting this from, but there's no way that's true."

"It is, Arch," I protest. "Dad told me himself."

"You're trying to tell me Dad was a spy. *Our* dad."

"I know it seems unlikely. But yes, he says he went on secret missions to France."

"Bloody hell," my brother says. "Then why is this the first we're hearing of it?"

"He said Mum didn't like him to look back on those days."

"It'll be an ex-girlfriend," Archie says immediately.

"Archie."

"Seriously, Lottie. Mum was always so jealous. Was this before they were married?"

"Yes but I think they were already dating then."

We both ponder this in silence for a moment, then Archie says, "He cheated on her."

"He wouldn't!"

"Maybe he had an affair while he was off in France doing whatever secret things spies did in those days. No wonder Mum spent the rest of their marriage blowing her top if Dad even glanced at another woman."

"Don't say that," I hiss. "Dad is loyal to a fault. I bet Mum didn't want him thinking about the war because it was hard on the both of them. Dad said he was stuck in France for a year and she had no idea what had become of him for the whole time. That can't have been easy."

"Maybe," Archie says, but he sounds unconvinced. We were born only eleven months apart, which means we've been squabbling and fighting for pretty much our entire lives, so I recognize that burning emotion in my chest as defensiveness. If I don't change the subject now, we'll end up shouting at one another.

"How's Carys and Poppy, anyway?" I abruptly change the subject. Mum was livid when Archie came home during his first year at university with a pregnant girlfriend in tow. He was the golden child of the family until that day, the academic whiz who had scholarship offers to Cambridge *and* Imperial College. For a while, we all thought he'd have to drop out of his economics degree to support his surprise family, but Archie found a way to have his cake and eat it too. For two years, he worked nights to put a roof over their heads while he finished his degree during the day, and it's all paid off for him with this fancy new World Bank job.

"The terrible twos are no joke, Lottie," Archie says, but then he spends a few minutes regaling me with stories of his daughter's stubbornness and wit, and I feel myself relaxing again, the moment of tension gradually fading away. "I better go," he says, after a while. "I have to get home before Carys goes to bed or there'll be hell to pay. Tell Dad I said hi. I'll try to catch him next weekend."

"Okay, Archie. I love you."

We were not a family who said those words all that often, but since Mum died, I throw it in at the end of just about every conversation. Archie barely misses a beat before he replies, "You too, Lottie."

I hang up the phone, only for it to ring again before my hand is even off the receiver,

"Hello?" I say, startled.

"Charlotte." Theo's bright tone immediately tells me that he has some good news. "I don't suppose you and your father feel like taking a drive tomorrow morning? Remy has agreed to a meeting."

CHAPTER 9

JOSIE
Montbeliard, France
December, 1943

Even two weeks after the bombing, we were no closer to understanding how the village had been bombed instead of the factory. Noah was adamant he had the right coordinates, but it was becoming clearer that London wasn't convinced. Questions just kept coming with each wireless transmission and he was increasingly frustrated.

"We did everything right," he exclaimed one night. "Someone in London is responsible for this!"

"At least Turner has taken over the investigation," I said hesitantly. He had been one of my favorite instructors, tough but cheerful and positive, a dedicated and passionate Frenchman who, like me, had escaped occupied Paris during the early years of the war. I admired and trusted every member of the SOE's leadership, but I knew no one would hunt down a mistake that cost French lives like Turner would.

"That is a comfort," Noah said, scrubbing a hand down his face wearily. "Elwood is skilled and loyal to the SOE, but she's so busy training female agents now. And Maxwell works day and night but he has a full plate liaising with Churchill and the government. Booth is a genius when it comes to encryption, but unless the error related to messages between us and London, he'd be out of his depth. I fear if anyone but Turner took on the investigation, it might have fallen by the wayside, and this is too important to be forgotten."

In the meantime, we were stuck in limbo. A ground-based sabotage operation was still out of the question, but we knew a second air raid would never be planned until the error that led to the first catastrophe was identified. For several weeks, we trod water—me busy with the Travers family, Noah continuing a little work with the mechanic, but mostly focused on building the local Maquisards groups. But on a personal level, we were growing closer than we'd ever been. Lying side by side on that bed night after night, we had only two things to discuss—our mission, which had stalled, and our lives before the mission.

I told him more about my upbringing—about growing up there in the 18th Arrondissement, and what it was like to be an only child, homeschooled most of the time because I was usually too sick to go out. It was a comfort just to remember times when my relationship with Maman was simpler, maybe even easier.

"Sickness was my life," I told him. "Maman was always at work during the day, but if I was scared or upset when she came home, she would come and lay down with me. She used to play talking games to distract me. I think she just wanted to help me escape out of that bed…that room. And my body wasn't up to that, so she tried to use my imagination to free me. She would stretch out beside me and gently brush her fingers along the skin of my cheeks and forehead…"

Let's go somewhere lovely together, she would say if I was frustrated at remaining bed-bound, or if I was so sick that it felt exactly like life itself was slipping away from me, and I was terrified of what might come next. I would close my eyes and picture myself—in a library, at a candy store, walking along a beach with Maman holding my hand. *What does it smell like there, darling?* The familiar, reassuring scent of dust and aged paper, or the sweetness of candy, the salt of the sea. *What will we eat there, Jocelyn?* We would visit the café afterward for a treat, or gorge ourselves on that candy and never get a stomachache, or devour hot chips and fish. *How do you feel in your heart?*

Loved. Wanted. Known.

We played that game so often in my early years that by the time I was an adult, Maman no longer needed to say the words to me to relieve my anxiety. Just bringing the memory of that game to mind could ease my fears or distract me from my pain.

"I was her whole world, other than... I guess, Aunt Quinn," I told him, but I felt a pinch in my chest at the memory of my mother's friend.

"Her sister?" Noah asked.

"No, not her sister. They became friends at work," I said. "Westminster couldn't find enough men to train as doctors during the Great War, so for a brief window, they admitted women to study medicine. After the war, the administration decided that all of those women doctors should be nurses again, but Maman and Aunt Quinn refused to go back to their old jobs and ultimately won. I think they bonded over that and they've been best friends ever since. Every year they'd visit with one another, Quinn would come to us in the autumn, Maman and I usually went to London to visit Quinn late in the spring. They never missed a trip in all the years since Maman and I left London when I was a toddler."

"How did you end up in France?"

"My parents divorced," I said, throat tight. "It was very bitter. I had just been diagnosed with Coeliac Sprue. Maman found herself on her own with a sickly child and no child support. She said we had to move to France because the cost of living there was lower and the hospitals more supportive of women in medicine so she had some chance of promotion."

"And is that how you wound up in Paris on your own when the occupation began? Your mother had gone to Britain to see her friend?"

"Yes," I sighed heavily. "She wanted me to leave my classes at the Sorbonne to join her and I refused. I'd been doing so well with my English course and I didn't want to drop out just before my final exams. Besides, Parisian newspapers made it seem like an invasion was months away! We quarreled and Maman went without me. The next thing I knew, Germans were on the streets. Maman moved in with Quinn and still lives in her terrace to this day..."

He was silent as I paused, trying to figure out how to explain that last, terrible morning before I was deployed. Miss Elwood had just told me I'd be flying out to France that night, so I took a car from the barracks to Aunt Quinn's flat.

"I had been away at training for months but I wanted badly to see Maman, even though we just seem to bicker whenever we are together."

"Even before I joined the SOE and couldn't write anymore, it was clear from your letters that you and your mother weren't getting on all that well."

"I thought she'd be proud of me after I escaped France. I'd realized on my own what foods made me sick and I knew how to keep myself healthy. Instead, Maman just could not stop babying me. We were once so close, but after I joined her in London, all we did was fight. That last morning before I came here, I just wanted to share one *easy* conversation before I flew into the belly of the beast."

Aunt Quinn's house was quiet as I slipped inside that morning, but it was only half six, so I knew she and Maman might still be asleep. I pulled the door closed behind me just as there was movement in the hall, then turned around just in time to see my mother, half-asleep and wearing only a thin nightdress, coming out of Quinn's bedroom. Her face was puffy with sleep. Her hair was wild.

I was so startled and confused I couldn't quite join the dots at first. I knew Maman and Quinn sometimes stayed up late in the night on their visits—over the years I'd heard their footsteps on the hall, doors opening and closing. But to sleep in one another's beds? Dressed like *that*?

I must have made a sound, because my mother spun toward me and our eyes locked. I would never forget the shame in her eyes, or the way the color drained from her face.

"Darling?" Quinn called from the bedroom, alarm in her voice. "Dru? What's wrong?"

Maman and Quinn had always been so close, but it seemed I had failed to appreciate just how close.

"I didn't handle it well," I admitted to Noah now.

"Were you upset that they are…" He cleared his throat delicately. "…more than friends?"

"Not upset, but I was shocked. I was and am anxious for them—God only knows the hospital would not take kindly to two female doctors in a romantic relationship. But I know that Maman and Quinn love one another deeply and what form their love takes beyond closed doors is none of my business—I'm only glad they have each other. The problem isn't that they are lovers. The problem is the lies, Noah. Why not just be honest with me at least once I became an adult? Why let me think for my whole life that Maman had to move to Paris because of me?"

"There may still have been some truth in that," Noah offered gently.

I sighed impatiently.

"Perhaps a grain of truth. She *did* have to support me all on her own, but only because my father found out about her relationship with Quinn and blackmailed her. If Maman tried to insist that he give her money, he would tell the hospital what she and Quinn had been up to, and that would have ruined both of their careers."

"Oh."

Aunt Quinn had been a fixture in my life from my earliest memories, and the voice of reason when Maman and I were at war after my return to London, but I even managed to alienate her on that last, bitter morning before I boarded the plane for my mission. As we all sat together in a terse, awkward silence around the kitchen table, Quinn finally spoke.

"Your mother and I love one another, Josie. Try to understand. We never wanted to hurt you—"

"You've been lying to me for my entire life!" I choked. Maman made a sound of distress, and Quinn reached to squeeze her shoulder gently. "You both treat me like I'm still a child, even now! Don't tell me you didn't want to hurt me when you didn't even trust me with the truth."

"And this WAAF business you've been so busy with," Quinn countered, her face hardening. That was the lie the SOE had me tell people—that I'd enlisted in the Women's Auxiliary Air Force, and whenever I was away training or on mission, it was for them. "Have you told *us* the truth about that? Because I've never heard of any other WAAF recruit spending months away at training and returning tanned and covered in bruises and scrapes the way you do. And you're back unannounced this morning. You're here to say goodbye because you're being deployed?" I nodded silently, and Aunt Quinn pursed her lips. "Let me guess, Josie. The 'WAAF' is sending you somewhere top secret and you can't tell us a thing about your trip. Am I right?"

I was a hypocrite, and it seemed we all knew it. They had valid reasons for hiding their truth, just as I had valid reasons for hiding mine. But my emotions were running too high for me to be reasonable, and that's exactly why I had to leave that morning. I felt so fragile that if we kept trying to hash it out, we'd end up screaming at one another, and I couldn't leave for my first mission after a morning like that. I felt like a string pulled too taut already.

In time, we could all be honest—and maybe then, we'd finally understand one another. All we needed was some time.

"It must have been so different in your house?" I said, deflecting the conversation back to Noah because I knew I'd end up weeping if I kept talking.

"Oh, God yes," he chuckled. "Five boys? It was madness, just chaos all the time. But I miss that, even now." He paused for a long time before he added, "I want a family of my own, Josie. I want to settle down the minute the war ends. I want to move on and *forget* about all of this madness."

He told me more about Geraldine, his first love, and how important she had been in his life.

"We met at a dance just after I enlisted," he told me. "In lots of ways, she's my perfect opposite—I like to listen, she likes to talk. I like to stay in, she likes to go out. I wilt plants just by looking at them, she has a green thumb."

"Back when we were on the escape line, you seemed so certain you'd marry her," I remarked.

"I was," Noah said. "I might even have proposed by now except that my family was gone when I got back, and the grief seemed so heavy I wasn't sure how I'd get out from under it. *She* helped me to breathe again, but then the SOE invited me to try out. I couldn't tell Gerrie the details, obviously, but I did tell her I'd been invited to join the war effort in a way I couldn't explain, and she made it very clear that she wasn't willing to sit around waiting another year to find out if I was dead or alive. The thing is, the minute the SOE interviewed me, I knew I wouldn't even ask her to wait. We argued at first." He hesitated, then murmured. "I don't think I ever told you this, Josie, but she was always jealous of you."

"Of me?" I repeated, then I laughed softly. "That's madness."

"I was completely honest about you. I told her how much you helped me through that journey from Paris to London. I told her about our letters and even those visits we had back home," he said quietly. We met up only once or twice after our return. Geraldine was out of town the time I went to Liverpool, and Noah came to see me when I was stuck in a rehabilitation hospital after surgery in 1942, but they'd already broken up by then because he was about to start SOE training. "It didn't matter what I said. Gerrie was *always* convinced something more had happened between you and I."

"She must not have known you well, then," I whispered. "You'd never betray someone you loved like that."

"I'd like to think not," he said carefully, then he cleared his throat. "You just *never* know what people will do under pressure-cooker circumstances. And I do think it drove her a bit mad that she had no clue what was happening to me for the time I was missing. Before I was MIA for that year, she was just bright and bold and vivacious and lovely. But once I came back, she wanted to control just about every aspect of our lives. And besides…"

"…besides?" I repeated, startled. But the darkness of our apartment had been a shroud of privacy and secrecy, and as the silence stretched, it started to feel dangerous. Noah shifted suddenly, to prop himself up on his elbow.

"We never crossed a line," he whispered. "But she was right to be jealous anyway. You and I shared an experience that other people just could never understand and right from the early days, when we were traveling out of France and we barely knew one another, I've felt close to you in a way that seems…"

Now, I understood. I shifted too, propping myself up on my elbow so that we were face-to-face.

"Our bond is unique. It's just utterly unique."

"Exactly."

"That leaves us vulnerable here on our mission, you know."

"We won't let it get in the way of our work. It hasn't so far."

"I'm not a distraction to you?"

I heard him draw in a shuddering breath at that, and for a moment, I wondered if he was going to kiss me. But instead, he turned and collapsed down onto his back to stare at the ceiling, and his voice was tender as he answered, "Only in the very best kind of way."

The next transmission via Adrien's wireless set changed everything.

"Have you ever heard such nonsense?" Noah gasped as he read it. *"More than one hundred people are dead! Hundreds injured! And Baker Street is determined to attempt another air strike even though they still have no clue what went wrong the first time!"*

I was sitting on the bed while Noah paced back and forth, still shaking with anger. Another airstrike was coming within days. Even Adrien, our levelheaded "pianist," was shaken by the news.

The next time Noah passed me as he paced, I caught his forearm and turned him to face me. His eyes were shining with what I understood were tears of guilt and frustration.

"Every day that passes counts," I said, dropping my voice. "That's why Baker Street is talking about another air strike. If we don't move fast, the bombs that factory produces will take lives on the other side of the Channel. That's why this is *urgent*, Noah. We need to convince them there's a better way."

"How else can we destroy a factory of that size?" Noah asked, raw anguish in his voice. "We've been over this a million times. There is no other way."

I'd been stewing on an idea all week, trying to find the courage to suggest it. I still felt anxious to speak aloud something so outlandish—but it was clear we were out of time. I tugged

Noah's arm, and he sank onto the bed. I crossed my legs on the mattress as I turned to face him.

"While I was at work today, Jullien mentioned that Fernand Sauvage has been donating money and supplies to help rebuild the villages. Huge sums. He immediately understood that his factory was the target. And it's no surprise at all that he figured that out. A bombing raid of that size in a region like this could only mean one thing, yes?"

"I don't see how that helps us," Noah said, his gaze searching mine.

"What if we appealed to Sauvage directly." Noah blinked at me as his mouth dropped open in shock. In a rush, I tried to explain. "I just mean…what if we go see him and explain that his factory is going to be destroyed one way or another. The choice as to how that happens *can* be his. If he was willing to help us, to share with us the blueprints and maybe even to let us store explosives there on site somewhere, we really could destroy the whole factory safely. From the ground. In a single night."

"You don't seriously mean to suggest we expose ourselves to Sauvage to ask him permission to destroy his family's business?"

"I know it seems crazy," I said urgently, as I reached to take his hands in mine. "But if we cannot present an alternate plan to Baker Street, they *will* attempt another bombing raid and they seem to have already given up figuring out what went wrong with the first one. How many other innocent lives could be lost if they try a second time?"

"How do we know we can trust Sauvage?"

"We don't," I said simply. Noah flinched as if I'd slapped him. "But Jullien is a good man. I'm sure of it, and that's always been *your* instinct too, right? That's why you wanted to recruit him before we fully understood the situation with Mégane and the children."

Noah ran his hands through his hair, then gave me another incredulous look.

"This is madness."

"We present it to Sauvage as a choice—*his* choice. The factory will be destroyed either way but if he supports us, we can make sure it's done safely."

"I need to think about this," Noah mumbled, glancing at me in disbelief. "Either you've lost your mind altogether, or you're a genius."

"Both things could be true simultaneously," I joked weakly, and Noah barked a laugh.

When I arrived home from my work at the Travers house the next day, Noah was at the dining room table in our apartment, staring at a slip of paper. He had a pencil in his hand, and he tapped the end on the table anxiously.

"Still thinking about what we discussed last night?" I asked him softly as I sat beside him. Noah did not look up. I glanced down at the paper. In his now-familiar scrawl, he'd written the words *flowers blossom in the spring.*

"I needed to know if we had a chance of making your idea work before I took it to Baker Street," he said.

"Okay…"

Noah looked up at me, his gaze brimming with anxiety.

"I cycled to Jacou and called from a pay phone. I just called the factory and asked to speak to Sauvage. His secretary didn't want to put me through but I told her it was life or death. I told him that I am an agent of the British government and that his suspicions about the factory being the target of that last air raid were correct. I told him it's inevitable that the factory will be destroyed. I told him that there may be a way that we can ensure it is done safely."

I held my breath as I waited for him to continue. When he just stared at me, I prompted impatiently, "Noah! What did he say?"

"He didn't believe me at first. Not about the bombing—it's abundantly clear he understands his factory was the target. He didn't believe that I am who I said I am so I told him I'd arrange proof. He's going to listen to Radio Londres tomorrow at seven a.m." The Nazis prohibited the French from listening to the BBC station broadcast from London to France, but many French citizens kept a secret wireless receiver for the explicit purpose of tuning in. The broadcasts were mostly intended to counter Nazi propaganda and to motivate the French resistance, but from time to time they were also used to communicate messages to agents like us in the field—seemingly innocent phrases that communicated a deeper meaning. Noah dropped the pencil onto the paper and jabbed at the words with his forefinger. "If he hears this message on Radio Londres tomorrow, he'll give us everything we need." Noah looked up at me. "He doesn't want to see anyone else get hurt."

I snatched the paper up as I shot to my feet, intending to run to Adrien's apartment, to have him plan right away to send the message to London. But Noah stood and caught my hand. He tugged me gently forward, and to my shock, he pressed his lips to mine. Liquid fire shot through my veins—a delirious joy and pleasure that was both unexpected and somehow, inevitable.

"This operation will take every bit of our energy and focus for some time yet," he whispered, brushing my hair back from my face. "But the minute that factory is gone, you and I are going to figure *this* out."

CHAPTER 10

ELOISE
Rouen, France
February, 1944

"Papers, please, mademoiselle."

After several days in Rouen, I knew the drill and I handed over my paperwork to the young Milicien automatically. It was early afternoon, and I was returning to Madame Laurent's butcher shop, hopeful a third visit might yield me some progress. The young apprentice had so far made it clear he did not want to tell me more about his boss's arrest—he wanted nothing to do with the resistance and was determined to keep his head down and keep the business going. But I'd visited several other addresses from Basile's list and was yet to find a single contact still free in the community. The butcher's shop had been a hub of resistance activity only a few months earlier and I hoped that if I persisted, the apprentice would at least point me in the direction of what remained of the network.

"What is the purpose of your visit to Rouen, Miss Leroy?"

"Family, sir." I'd delivered the answer several times over those past few days. It rolled off my tongue without a second's hesitation. What would Giles think if he could see me there in Rouen? He'd have worried, but ultimately I knew he'd be proud of me.

"You don't have a *permis de sejour*," the Milicien said suddenly, frowning.

My stomach dropped. The other guards had not noticed my missing permit, but Basile had warned me that I needed one, just in case.

"Look, it's not the kind of thing every guard is going to pick up on," he had explained when he instructed me to secure one. "Some of the Germans don't know to look for it, some of the French militia think it's unnecessarily bureaucratic. But if you happen to get checked by the wrong guard, they might even arrest you for failing to secure it. Don't forget to register when you arrive, just to be safe."

Don't forget to register.

How had I made such a careless mistake? It was distraction… first by the Wehrmacht colonel's offer of a ride from the station the day I arrived, then because I was excited and anxious to see if Jérémie arrived to check the drop box.

I had missed an important step to my mission, and the worst thing was, Basile specifically *told me not to forget.*

I was so embarrassed and furious with myself there was nothing I could do to stop my face turning red.

"I…"

"Miss Leroy," the Milicien said sharply. "Even as a visitor from another town in the zone, you are required to have a *permis de sejour* for your time in Rouen. Can you offer any explanation for your failure to secure one?"

My pulse pounded through my head, leaving my thoughts cloudy with frustration.

"I just arrived this morning on the train," I blurted, but I regretted it immediately. It was a stupid lie and it might even be disproved if they tried to check. And what if they arrested me and took me to a prison or an office and I happened upon the Wehrmacht colonel I met when I did travel to Rouen? He would surely remember me. *Oh God.*

The Milicien frowned as he looked from me back to my papers, then he waved to a companion, standing by a nearby covered truck. This was the first time since my arrival that a second guard had become involved during a security check. The two men reviewed my papers together, and then the second guard looked up at me.

"Miss," he said. "Come with me."

They left me seated in a long hall at the Palais de Justice for eight long hours after my arrest. Strangers bustled through the hall, glancing at me, but never stopping to talk. There was a gallery to the right above my seat, and every now and then, I'd notice movement there. When I glanced up, I'd usually see an officer in uniform, staring down at me. Everyone was watching to see if I panicked.

But I wasn't panicked. I was still so frustrated with my carelessness that a self-directed rage was boiling away inside me and it was all I could think about. I could only hope it wasn't obvious that my thoughts were running wild and I was struggling to rein them back in.

Would they try to verify my arrival time—perhaps to ask the station attendants at Gare Saint-Sever if they'd seen me alight the train from Paris that morning? Or perhaps someone had been tailing me for some days, in which case, I was already exposed and the lie would only condemn me further. What if they searched my shoulder bag—what if they found the false panel in the bottom, which still contained my currencies, and forged rations cards and alternate identity papers? I carried it everywhere I went in case I had to flee in a hurry if my cover was blown.

If these men found that material, they'd take me to the Stand

aux Fusilles and shoot me then and there, and it would be all
my own fault.

Before I left for my mission, right at the airport as I was
boarding the plane, Miss Elwood had offered me the standard
SOE "L pill," a lethal cyanide pill. They offered every agent
the same on deployment—it was a comfort to some to know
they had on hand a quick, efficient way to end their life if a
situation became too intense.

I'd refused the pill, arrogantly convinced I'd be smart enough
to evade capture and even if I *was* captured, strong enough to
withstand any interrogation. I breezed through my mock interrogations during the SOE training. I was even lightly beaten
at one point, left with a black eye and some painfully bruised
ribs, and still, I held my tongue.

I never doubted for a second that I'd be able to do so in a real
interrogation, not until the minute I found myself in that hallway. A real-world test was potentially upon me and my courage was about to be tried—truly tried—by interrogators who
might opt to use no restraint at all, unlike my instructors. I
mean—hell—it was Mr. Turner who "beat" me that night, the
nicest of all of the instructors, even when he was attempting
to appear menacing. I'd have no such mercy from these men.
What if, the moment I felt physical pain, I started to babble
SOE secrets—names, addresses, code names, plans? It was *all*
there in my mind. Was that secure?

Stupid, stupid, stupid.

I had to calm myself down. An image of Chloe's face popped
into my mind and I remembered vividly a conversation I had
with her the day of our first real physical challenge during
the initial few days of SOE training, and the mental trick her
mother taught her to quieten her mind when life was hard.

Let's go somewhere lovely. What does it look like there? I let myself remember my husband's eyes, big and blue and sparkling,
framed in long eyelashes. I let myself imagine the unique, re-

markable safety that came with his arms around me, a circle of strength and restraint. *What does it smell like in the safe place?* I never did figure out the right way to describe Giles's scent. It wasn't just the soap or cologne he used. Beneath all of that, there was a deeper scent—masculinity and sensitivity and power and safety. Just Giles, and even years after his death, I could still bring it to mind. *How do you feel in your heart?* Loved. Wanted. Known.

He always said he loved how quick I was on my feet. He always told me he loved my fierceness and my resilience. If he was there with me in that hall, he'd be certain that I could handle whatever came next.

I was suddenly just like Chloe, standing at the start of the obstacle course, refusing to accept my failure before it had occurred. All was not lost just yet. I had to keep my cool so I could find a way out of the mess. My thoughts slowed, and my heart rate slowed too.

By the time the young Milicien returned to the hall to collect me, he had several more senior companions in tow, but I was undaunted. They took me into an opulent office, where a captain sat behind a wooden desk. His uniformed secretary perched on a chair beside him, taking notes.

"Miss Leroy," the captain said. He didn't seem aggressive, only bored. Maybe a little impatient. "Please explain yourself. What are you doing in Rouen?"

"My uncle is missing." I said. *Think about Giles. Think about Hughie.* "My aunt asked me to look for him. She is worried he might have been injured in the recent bombings."

"And you arrived today, you say?"

"Yes, sir." It had been a foolish lie, but I was locked in to it now.

"You took the train from Paris."

"Yes, sir."

I tried to imagine myself as the captain saw me as I stood there before him. Chestnut hair, set in waves around my face.

Bright blue eyes—my whole life, people had been telling me they were striking, my best feature. An hourglass figure, accentuated by my pretty woolen dress and coat.

The captain had no idea who I was. The things I'd been through. The lengths a woman like me would go to for revenge. What was it Madame Laurent had said? *Men are all too quick to believe a beautiful woman runs entirely on sentiment and knows nothing of substance or value.*

That was it—my way forward. I was going to convince them I was just a terrified girl, too stupid to even follow the basic procedure of moving around in the forbidden zone along the Atlantic Wall.

"I'm so sorry, sir," I mumbled, as I reached up and began to twirl a lock of my hair around my finger. I dropped my gaze back down nervously and kept my voice soft. "I didn't know what I was supposed to do."

"Have you registered your uncle with the lost and missing persons office at the Town Hall?" the captain asked. I looked up at him, feigning confusion.

"No, sir. The Town Hall, you say? Is that…"

"That *is* the procedure, Miss Leroy. You should have registered as a visitor immediately upon arrival and you should have registered your uncle's details with Town Hall so that the local authorities would know that someone is looking for him."

"That seems so much easier than just asking around after him as I planned to," I said, keeping my voice small and uncertain. "Is it too late for me to do that now, sir?"

The captain looked up at me, sighed impatiently, and waved toward the woman taking notes.

"Give her the name of your hotel. Your uncle's name too. If we hear from him, we'll let you know. Now get out of here but don't go to the Town Hall until morning. You'll need to hurry to be back to your room before curfew."

"Thank you, sir," I said, and I walked all the way to the door before he stopped me with an abrupt, "Miss Leroy?"

I turned back to him hesitantly.

"Yes, sir?"

"Next time you're outside of Le Havre for any reason, be sure to familiarize yourself with the procedures of the township you're visiting."

"Yes, sir."

Even as the door closed behind me, I heard the captain berating the young Milicien.

"You are not required to bring every silly girl you come across to my office! There was nothing at all about that timid mouse to suggest even average intelligence, let alone an indication she was deserving of suspicion."

I had lost a precious day sitting in that hallway in the Palais de Justice and all because I had allowed myself to become distracted for just a few moments, right at the start of my mission. Never again, I promised myself. There was too much at stake for me to make such a careless mistake again.

CHAPTER 11

Noah and I sat together at the little table the next morning. We kept a small wireless receiver hidden in the top of the laundry closet most of the time, but that day, we drew the curtains for privacy and sat with the wireless between us.

"This is London! This is the French speaking to the French…" My eyes locked with Noah's and we held our breath as we waited. "Before we begin, please listen to some personal messages…"

This was the typical Radio Londres format for each broadcast. The "personal messages" were always obscure, sometimes amusing. The broadcasters knew the Germans listened every bit as much as the French did but they did not try to hide that these messages were actually coded messages for agents and specific French citizens. I had the sense that sometimes they liked to toy with the Germans, to give them the impression operations were underway on a grander scale than we had actually managed.

"Tea is best served steaming hot. Flowers blossom in the spring. Olivier is very tall."

Noah closed his eyes, exhaling with relief.

"What next?" I whispered. He opened his eyes.

"I call Sauvage back today to arrange a meeting."

"That's a risky move."

"This will work. I know it will."

"I think it will too…but…"

"I trust my gut," he said simply, and then he reached to cover my hand with his. "And even more than that, I trust yours."

The first rendezvous with Sauvage would be in a busy park, late in the afternoon, a few days after the radio broadcast. Noah was to sit at a particular bench, reading a newspaper. Adrien sat some distance away, pretending to read a book, but in truth, keeping watch.

Noah's instructions to Adrien were that if the meeting was a trap, say if Gestapo arrived instead of—or with—Sauvage, Adrien should not attempt to rescue him. There would be little he could do to help him in that moment. Adrien was there only to observe. If the meeting went badly, the best we could hope was to use our local contacts to mount a rescue later.

I was sick with nerves that afternoon as I worked at the Travers house, supervising the twins and preparing dinner. Noah promised to come to the kitchen to let me know he was okay once the meeting was over. When his face appeared in the window, I was so relieved I could have wept.

"Monsieur Martel!" Aimé said, surprised but overjoyed to see him. The girls had only met Noah a handful of times, but both had quickly come to adore him.

"Hello, Aimé," he said, smiling softly, and I knew in an instant that the meeting had gone well. Noah looked at me then and his smile deepened. "How is your day, my love? Mine has been excellent."

"I'll see you at home a little later?"

He nodded and tipped his hat as he left. When Jullien came

home a few hours later, I flew along the street and burst into our apartment. Noah was standing by the kitchen sink, but he turned to me and said, "Tomorrow. We start tomorrow."

"Tomorrow?" I repeated, dumbfounded.

"Nine a.m. We disguise ourselves—I'll dress in my suit as if I'm a businessman. You'll need to wear office clothes and pretend you're my secretary. We'll meet Sauvage at the factory and he's going to show us around the entire facility. He's also going to arrange for a set of plans for us."

"Noah! I can't just *not* go to work."

"That's the other thing," he said carefully. "He wants Jullien to help us. We have to tell him the truth."

"Oh, no," I protested, shaking my head. "No! It would be too risky for them to know what we—"

"As Sauvage reminded me, your presence in their lives is risky enough already for them. Can you imagine if the Germans discovered what you and I have been up to? They would interrogate Mégane and Jullien half to death just because you have worked in their house!"

My breath caught in my throat at the very thought.

"But..."

"I know we wanted to protect them, but we inadvertently put them at risk the minute we made contact with them," Noah said gently. "Sauvage assures me that Jullien will want to help. We should give him the opportunity to make the decision for himself."

"So...you are not a child minder?" Mégane said in shock later that night, after Noah and I arrived unannounced and asked to sit with her and Jullien for a chat. The four of us were seated around a coffee table in their expansive lounge, the girls long asleep upstairs. I felt a pang of sadness that I'd no longer spend my days with the family. I'd quickly become so fond of them all. "But the girls love you, Béatrice—*Chloe...*"

"And I them," I rushed to assure her.

"The minute we understood your situation, we agreed we would do nothing at all to put you at risk. We were never going to attempt to recruit you to help us," Noah said, glancing between Mégane and Jullien. "But Fernand was adamant that you would want to be a part of this."

"I suspected," Jullien sighed, and even Mégane turned to stare at him in surprise. "Oh, not the specifics. I sleep poorly since the war began and the back gate off your courtyard squeaks just a little. I'd heard you coming and going at all hours, so I knew one or both of you were up to something." He scrubbed a hand through his thinning hair then nodded. "I hate every aspect of the occupation. I loathe that they have co-opted the factory for these evil purposes. It kills me to think it will be destroyed, but to refuse to help you would mean blood on our hands."

"You will still help me, won't you?" Mégane asked me hopefully.

"She is needed elsewhere, my love," Jullien told her gently. "We will find a new nanny immediately." He rose suddenly and waved toward us. "Marcel. Chloe. I have blueprints in my study from the retooling project. We can begin planning right away."

Six weeks after that disastrous bombing raid, Noah and I led two small teams of local resistance operatives to the Sauvage factory at 11:00 p.m. on an overcast night.

Sauvage and Jullien were safely at home, but they had given every imaginable support to the operation. Jullien liaised with key staff to make necessary arrangements—manipulating a rostering "mishap" that meant there were no security guards stationed on the night of the operation, and returning himself earlier that evening to unlock the necessary gates and doors. And as airdrops from London built up our supply of explosives over those preceding weeks, Sauvage arranged for workmen to pick up the crates of explosives and stockpile them right on the factory floor, disguised as components for the coming munitions project. I got a particular thrill imagining German soldiers supervising work in the plant, unknowingly walking past the largest explosive supply the region had ever seen.

Noah led one group of local operatives into the facility and I was responsible for the other. We both knew the layout by heart by then, and we'd planned the demolition to ensure all critical infrastructure was destroyed. Sometimes, I felt the handful of weeks of sabotage training we received preparing for the field was laughably inadequate, but as Noah and I planned that operation, I discovered we knew just enough to be very effective indeed.

We had placement of explosives to ensure maximum destruction with minimum manpower. And in the end, even working silently in the dark, it took us less than an hour to rig everything we needed to, and to secure the doors and fasten the padlocks on the gates. The latter was my idea. If any of that external infrastructure survived the blast, say if a gate was discovered intact somewhere, it needed to appear that it had never been unlocked for Sauvage and Jullien's sakes.

Just before midnight, Noah and I dismissed the workers and they scattered into the night. We continued to work in silence, just the two of us now, rolling ignition wire behind us as we slipped back through the last unlocked gate. I hooked the padlock back on and clicked it closed, then ran to catch up to Noah, who was already in a deep ditch, a few hundred feet away. There was a heavy cloud cover that night. It was dark, but not so dark that I could miss the anticipation in his eyes.

"Ready?" he whispered.

"Do it," I said flatly.

The explosion was everything we had hoped—maybe a little more. The force of it was phenomenal, like a physical wave had crashed through our chests, even as we crouched there in that ditch. Noah and I were thrown hard against the back wall of the trench, and my ears rang painfully even though I had covered them with my hands. Immense steel factory doors flew dozens of feet into the air, traveling on the force of a massive fireball that triggered secondary explosions in fuel tanks elsewhere in the plant.

"Are you okay?" Noah asked me. It looked like he was shouting but I could barely hear a word. I nodded, and scanned my gaze down his body, searching for injuries.

"You?"

"Better than good," he said, but then he took my hand and led me toward our bicycles. It was difficult to ride at first—I was still so dizzy. I kept overbalancing, and I'd shoot my foot out to try to steady myself, only to find the ground was not where I expected it to be. But we could not stop—we couldn't even afford the luxury of riding slowly. We went swiftly over dirt paths and back roads, zigzagging back toward our apartment. The lights were on in the Travers household and the girls were crying, likely roused from their sleep by the sound of the blast. I felt terrible for startling them, and likely other children across the town, but reassured myself: if we had not blown that factory up, we risked a second air strike hitting other innocent children. Disrupted sleep tonight might have saved those children's lives. As we dumped our bicycles and slipped inside the apartment, I noticed that one of our back windows had shattered from the impact of the explosion, even from more than a mile away.

"Let's change into our nightclothes then go out into the street," Noah said, taking my hand and leading me to the laundry room. He wiped a smudge of dirt from my face with a washcloth then I did the same for him, blotting the sweat that had run across his brow. "Everyone else will be outside to see what the fuss is about. We should make sure we're seen doing the same."

We left the yard again, this time by the front gate, and found that he was right—bleary-eyed locals were standing along the street. The fire raged so hot and so bright that an orange glow was cast over the entire town, almost as if the sun were rising.

"Fire at the factory," one of the neighbors, an older gentleman, told us knowingly. "I bet the power plant exploded."

"I didn't hear planes," his wife said uncertainly. "But this surely must have been the British."

"No way to be sure," Noah said easily, then he stifled a yawn and tugged me back toward our apartment. "Back to bed for you, Mrs. Martel. I don't want you out in the cold."

I stifled a laugh as he drew me back into the apartment, but the laughter faded the minute the door closed behind us. Noah was staring at me with an intensity in his gaze that set my stomach abuzz with butterflies.

"We did it," I whispered. "Can you believe it?"

He took two steps toward me, slipped his hand behind my neck and pulled me to him for a kiss so fierce and joyous it took my breath away.

Later, when the town was asleep again and the night was still, and the scent of smoke and burning fuel hung in the air, Noah and I lay entwined in our bed, a blanket covering our naked bodies.

"We make a fantastic team, Josie Miller," he whispered, and I shivered with pleasure as he wrapped his arm around my waist, pulling me even closer.

"We really do," I whispered back.

Noah and I knew that suspicion would fall on Jullien and Sauvage long before it fell on us. Before the operation had even taken place, we tried to prepare them for their inevitable arrests. I felt preemptively guilty for what they were about to endure.

"Perhaps they pretend they know exactly what involvement you've had—but even if their version of events is close to the truth, they'll probably just be guessing. They might threaten you. Your family. It's all designed to wear you down, so as it escalates, take that as a good sign, not a bad one. The harder they try and fail to break you, the closer you are to release."

"If you're kept in a cell with someone who appears to be an ally, don't fall for it," Noah added urgently. "And when they do release you—be careful! They might let you out just to watch your movements so assume you're being watched."

"Speak slowly, clearly and firmly," I added. "Don't attempt heroics or argue. Deny everything that you cannot easily explain, but don't lie unless you absolutely cannot avoid it. Keep your answers as close to the truth as you can without giving yourselves away."

"Marcel. Chloe," Sauvage said gently. "Thank you for your advice, but whatever happens, we did what's right and we can only do our best from there."

Sauvage was arrested the morning after the explosion, and most of his senior staff, including Jullien, were arrested in the days that followed. Jullien and the other staff were released within days, but they held Sauvage for a full week.

In the meantime, the town had become a hotbed of suspicion. German officers of all stripes swarmed upon the place and I couldn't move much beyond the apartment without having my papers checked. Noah had temporarily abandoned all other operations within the circuit—no more training for the local network, no more late-night meetings. Adrien and I communicated only via dead drop, exchanging notes at a series of hidden locations.

"This will all blow over," Noah kept assuring me, and I believed him, but I was starting to worry about Adrien. The notes he left with each transmission from Baker Street seemed ever more alarming.

One of my contacts was arrested today—just after I broadcast from her apartment.

*Suspect there is a D/F vehicle in town. Several close calls this week.
It's becoming more and more difficult to find somewhere to broadcast.
I was almost picked up today.*

Mégane told me a rumor she'd heard via their new nanny.

"Germans were waiting when the service at the church ended
this morning. They detained anyone who was carrying a bag,
then they checked all around the place—they even searched
the attics of the buildings nearby."

Adrien had established a series of places to broadcast from, all
around the town and even on farms outside of it. That church
was one of his most convenient spots. He had an arrangement
with the priest and could access the spire.

"Adrien might need to go silent for a while," I suggested
to Noah.

"He's our only channel to London, Josie," he said uneasily.
"He can't go silent."

We had done so much good, but now everything had been
put on pause, and every day it seemed like more innocent locals
were being dragged in for questioning. I was most distressed to
hear the local shoemaker had been violently interrogated after
the Gestapo became inexplicably convinced he knew something about the destruction of the factory. I walked past the
shoe repair shop days later. The shoemaker was back at work,
sporting two black eyes and what looked to be a broken arm.

"*We* did that to him," I said, throat tight. "Indirectly, of
course, but it was still a consequence of our work."

"I feel guilty every single time I recruit someone into the
circuit—what if they're found out? What if they're beaten or
killed?" Noah told me. "We have to accept that sometimes innocent people will suffer as we reach for a greater good. I hate
it too—but we *have* done good work here. Every day we work
toward the end of the war means these innocent locals are a
day closer to freedom too."

The following day, I left the house early, intending to collect some meat for dinner. On the sidewalk outside of the first store, two SS officers were stopping people as they passed. As I neared, one asked me for my papers. This was a regular occurrence, and I wasn't fazed in the least—not even as the first officer skimmed my identity card, or the second asked me where I was going and stared intently at me as I explained the morning's chores.

"We're looking for a British man," the first one told me as he returned my papers to my hand. It was all I could do to maintain eye contact with him. My stomach had dropped and there was a buzzing in my ears. "Possibly going by the name Adrien. Brown hair, straight and thick, possibly with green or brown eyes."

"I'm sorry, sir," I said. "I don't know anyone like that."

I went about town just as I'd planned after they dismissed me, intentionally taking my time just in case someone was watching me, even though my stomach was in knots. Noah was sitting at the table studying a map when I got home. I set down my bags of produce and rushed to his side.

"Noah," I whispered frantically. "This is not going to blow over."

We didn't have much time—and even fewer options—to deal with Adrien's situation. His cover was blown, and one way or another, he would need to move on from Montbeliard. Baker Street decided they would evacuate him to London, but with the full moon only days away, this would happen right away.

Two nights later, Noah, Adrien and I stood in the tree line around a short field, waiting to hear the drone of the engine so we could guide the Lysander to the ground with the battery-powered torches in our hands. The air was still, the moon a perfect, silver circle above us. I felt a heaviness in my chest that went beyond the gravity and danger of the moment.

The months I shared with Noah in that little studio in the

Travers' backyard had been the most intense period of my life. There had been no time to stop and reflect on the emotional roller coaster—the lows of the bombing mishap, the highs of the destruction operation, the bliss of falling so deeply in love with Noah. There had been no time to question what the future looked like, to wonder what would come for us in the short term, and the longer term. Adrien's departure seemed the beginning of a new chapter. The uncertainty of what came next was something I could no longer ignore.

"We did some good work here," Noah said solemnly, glancing between us.

"I will never understand how that village was bombed," Adrien said. "It still keeps me up at night."

We all stood in silence at that, until Noah said hesitantly, "They'll debrief you thoroughly, Adrien. You'll have days of questioning."

"I know. And I'm ready."

I could see there was more Noah wanted to say, and yet he stood frozen, as if the words were stuck at the end of his tongue. Just then, we heard the plane approaching, and the next moments passed in a blur as we guided it to land.

Adrien clambered into the body of the plane and our new w/t operator, François, scrambled out to the field to replace him. And soon we were helping François to Clément's farmhouse where he would stay for several days, until Noah could secure a bicycle for him, at which point he would cycle the six miles to the nearby village of Donzenac and secure himself a room there.

As the circuit courier, I would soon spend much of my time cycling back and forth to ferry messages, but this was the safest option given the likelihood that Germans were wandering the streets with D/F units, scanning for signals.

It was only much later, when Noah and I finally fell into bed beside one another, that I had the chance to ask, "When

Adrien was leaving, I could see you wanted to say something more to him."

"Yes," he said seriously, but then he gave a chuckle. "Josie. You read me so well."

I knew how his shoulders would slump when he was tired. I knew how his footsteps grew heavy when he was frustrated. I knew Noah Ainsworth's every expression—his every mood. He knew me just as well. It was part of the wonder of our relationship—how perfectly in sync we had fallen.

"What did you want to say to him?"

Noah tensed even as he pulled me into the circle of his arms. "He knows about us. I'm certain of it."

"What? But how?" We were so rarely all together. I was the go-between as the circuit courier, and we had stuck to that arrangement faithfully, even when we were planning the factory sabotage.

"You probably didn't even notice, but I brushed my hand against yours as I passed you at the field," Noah said, frustration in his voice. He was right—I hadn't noticed. Noah was so affectionate that he was constantly touching me when we were alone, and we were well out of the habit of remembering we were *not* actually married when in the company of other people. "I forgot myself for a moment. I looked up and realized he was staring at us and I just... I don't know how to explain it. His expression was so dismayed. So serious. I *know* that he knows."

"Okay," I said, but adrenaline was surging in my body, my heart pounding against the wall of my chest. "That doesn't mean he'll tell Baker Street."

"My love," Noah said helplessly. "Adrien is a faithful agent. He has risked his life for this work, and he will no doubt do so again in the future. I couldn't even bring myself to ask him to lie for us because I knew that he would never agree."

"So he tells them he suspects a romantic entanglement," I said, throat going dry. "That doesn't mean they'll separate us.

We've done incredible work here, you said so yourself. Surely they'll see—"

"Josie," he interrupted me, his arms contracting around me. But he didn't need to contradict me because I knew why our relationship was an issue, and it had nothing to do with our effectiveness.

The intimacy Noah and I shared was a strength when it came to our bond. It was a weakness when it came to our work. An agent needed to keep a cool head if he or she was interrogated. Romantic love, or even close friendship, was a vulnerability the Germans could easily exploit, and this was exactly why Miss Elwood had warned me about my friendship with Noah in the first place.

"What do we do if they recall one of us? Or if they send us elsewhere?" I asked miserably.

"We need a plan," Noah agreed, brushing his lips against my hair.

"How can we plan for this? We don't know when the war will end. We don't know where we'll be when that happens. How will we find one another?"

"Twice now, life has brought us together. I have to believe we will find one another again. We have to do our jobs now, and even if that means we work apart for some months or even years, it will all be worth it when we can be together in a better world later."

"I don't have a key to my old apartment in Paris but the upstairs window frames are all a little worn. If you climb up onto the balcony, you could jiggle one open...climb inside and stay there until I arrive," I said suddenly. "If the war ends and I'm in France, I'll find a way to get myself there."

"Good. And if we have made our way back to England by then, Baker Street will connect us."

"If the war ends," I whispered sadly.

"We have to believe the war will end, my love," he told

me softly. "If we entertain any other possibility, we'll find ourselves too depressed to be of any use."

It came as no surprise a few days later when François received a message that our circuit was being disbanded. Noah would be sent to initiate a new circuit in the Corrèze commune and was to sit tight and await instructions as to when, but I was being immediately deployed to join the *Success* circuit in Paris.

There was no time to grieve, no time to sulk. After a sleepless, tearful night in Noah's arms, I found myself on the train station platform the very next morning.

All around us, other people were saying their goodbyes, but those people faded into oblivion for me. I only had eyes for Noah—and because we were supposedly husband and wife, we didn't hesitate to show the pain of the moment or our affection for one another. Tears ran down my face and there was a sheen in his eye. The platform attendant blew the whistle and Noah pulled me into his arms for one last embrace.

"Don't go," he blurted against my hair. "Stay. I'll tell them I can't be without you. We'll tell them we—that you—" But there was nothing more to say—no way to avoid our separation, and we both knew it. With palpable frustration, he finally whispered, "Josie, this is all my fault. I'm so sorry."

"It's like you said," I whispered unevenly. "Life has brought us together twice. We will find each other again."

"Josie, I love you."

A sob built in my chest, and I barely suppressed it as I whispered back, "I love you too, Noah. I always will."

I had always wanted to find someone of my own. Even in my younger years, when a fulfilling, healthy life was just a dream, I'd imagined my own prince like Noah—someone sensitive and kind, courageous and in his own way, brilliant. Our love had been born under pressure but it all stretched before us— the coming of peace, and years and years to learn who we each were in ordinary times, to build the family and the home we both dreamed of.

But first, we had to face this separation. It was time to focus individually on the work that was so much bigger even than the love we shared. The woman Noah saw when he looked at me was brave enough to follow the order to Paris. The man I *knew* Noah to be was brilliant enough to survive whatever came next for him too.

A kind older gentleman reached down to help me climb up into the carriage, and I stowed my suitcase at my feet and stared out the window at the platform. My eyes locked with Noah's as the train began to pull away.

"I love you," I mouthed, and the last time I saw him, he was mouthing it right back.

CHAPTER 12

ELOISE
Rouen, France
February, 1944

Several days had passed and the butcher's apprentice was still refusing to speak to me about the arrest of his boss or the work of the circuit.

"My boss has been arrested and his family *and mine* are relying on me to keep this business going," he hissed, when I offered him money in exchange for information. "I cannot risk speaking to you!"

I went instead to each of the addresses Basile had asked me to memorize. Some had once been safe houses. All were empty now. There were homes that had been secret training venues for Maquis groups, but as far as I could tell, these had also been abandoned. I made my way to the garages where Basile and his operatives had stored the tons of weapons and explosives Baker Street once dropped to fields near Rouen.

"A garage is the perfect place for such storage because no one bats an eye when cars or even lorries transport the shipments there. Our caches are behind false walls that were installed with the blessing of the business owners," Basile had explained. "Go in and ask to hire a bicycle but drop the phrase *blue basket* into the conversation. If the owner is there, he'll take you to his office and you can verify that the weapons caches are intact."

But at both garages, even though I batted my eyelashes and asked to hire a "bicycle, maybe something with a basket—oh, even a stylish little blue basket!", I saw not so much as a flicker of recognition from the men I spoke to.

"Miss," a worker at the second garage told me, scratching his head. He'd been to ask the other workers if they knew anything about hire bicycles. "Most of us are new but as far as we know, we've never had bicycles for hire. Sorry."

"Could I perhaps speak to the manager?" I asked in desperation. He shrugged.

"He's away on business. No one knows when he'll be back."

Basile had described his key operatives at each garage in detail and told me they should be easy enough to find, but I didn't locate a familiar face at either business. At a loose end, I lingered in the street after the first garage closed and followed two of the young workers from there to a nearby café bar. I sat near them, but almost as soon as I took my seat, another man approached me.

"Perhaps I could buy you a drink, mademoiselle?"

I offered him a polite smile, and he suggested I might enjoy a cup of coffee. I bit back a sigh as I nodded.

We spent a lot of time in SOE training drinking absurd amounts of alcohol to practice maintaining our cover story while drunk, so it was a real surprise to me to step into a bar on my second afternoon in Rouen to discover that, as a woman, the rations rules prohibited me from buying so much as a sip of wine. I'd now been in Rouen for almost a week and I was starting to wonder if any one of the senior SOE trainers had spared a single thought as to what a *woman* in the field might need to know.

As for the coffee, I knew the bar would likely prepare me a cup of roasted corn coffee and the thought of it turned my stomach, but a woman sitting alone in a bar was always going to attract the attention of male patrons and to blend in, I had to work with that reality.

"I'm Régis," the man said once he'd placed our orders. "And you are…"

"Fleur," I said politely. "Thank you for the coffee."

"It is my pleasure."

Fortunately for me, Régis was a poor conversationalist, more interested in talking at me than engaging me to talk, so as he drank his wine and I forced down the corn coffee, I let him chat aimlessly about himself while I focused instead on the conversation taking place between the two young men from the garage. I could see their reflection in a mirror behind the bar, so I knew they were leaning close toward one another, talking quietly as they smoked and sipped wine.

"…so many arrested. Did you even know what they were up to right in front of us…?"

"…can you believe we were working right next to a weapons cache like that? My God! When the Gestapo pulled down that wall…"

"I only found this job because of Blaise, you know. We've been neighbors for years and I had no idea…never suspected he was involved in the resistance! But last night, they came for him too. They woke half the neighborhood up when they smashed in his door…"

My companion was midsentence when I watched in the reflection as the men behind me rose. I slid off my stool and at his scowl, offered an apologetic look.

"I'm sorry, Régis," I pleaded, pressing a hand to my stomach. "I'm feeling terribly unwell." His irritation was palpable, and that in turn irritated me. God save me from men who thought they were entitled to so much as a minute of a woman's time just because they bought her a drink! I needed to leave quickly and I wanted to make this man squirm a little. I bent forward and winced as I dropped my voice and added, "I have *terrible* women's problems, you see."

At that, Régis recoiled as if I'd slapped him and nodded hastily to indicate I should go.

I followed the garage workers into the street and tailed them from a distance over the next half-dozen blocks. They stopped to exchange farewells, at which point I hung back, leaning against a lamppost and pretending to search through my handbag. One of the men walked to the entrance to a small block of apartments, and the second continued walking.

I couldn't easily check inside the apartment building to see if any doors were damaged like the one they were discussing in the bar, so I made a mental note of where the building was, and continued following the second man. After another four blocks he turned into the yard of a small house. Next door was a house that was the mirror image of his own except that the front door was boarded up.

And best of all, behind the faded curtains on the windows at the front of the house, I could see that lights were on inside. Someone may have been arrested last night, but someone else had definitely been left behind.

It was close to curfew now—I would have to move fast. I jogged to the laneway behind the houses and located the small courtyard attached to the home with the damaged front door. I pulled open the wooden gate slowly then crept inside. Here the curtains had not been drawn, so I could see right into the house, where a young woman was feeding a little boy as he sat in a wooden high chair. The child was just a toddler, with light brown hair and big brown eyes, rosy cheeks and a little graze on his forehead, as if he'd stumbled trying to walk. The young woman's nose was red and raw and her eyes swollen as if she'd been crying. Still, she looked at the child with such love in her gaze. As if he were her most precious treasure. As if he was all she had left in the world.

My vision blurred, and for just a moment, I was in her shoes, staring into the eyes of a child who trusted me completely. A child I would die to protect.

Just then, the woman looked up, and saw me through the window, and opened her mouth as if to scream. I pressed a finger over my lips and with the other, fumbled into my brassiere. I withdrew a small wad of cash and pressed it against the glass.

Her mouth remained fixed in a shocked circle, but the scream I'd feared did not come. Money was a powerful motivator, especially to a woman who had just lost her breadwinner. Instead, she lowered the spoon, allowing the toddler to take it. He immediately began to bang it on the nearby table, happily singing to himself in baby talk as the woman cautiously rose to her feet.

The back door swung open, just a crack.

"I don't want to make trouble for you," I said, voice low, staying back just far enough from the light seeping through the door that my face remained in shadow. "But I heard your husband was arrested last night." She nodded, still staring at me suspiciously. I extended the notes toward her then asked carefully, "Was he working with the resistance?"

Her eyebrows knit. She glanced between the money in my hand and her son, behind her.

"I can't—"

"If I were loyal to the Germans I'd have nothing to gain in asking," I rushed to assure her. She hesitated, so I pressed, "Right? They already know the answer to the question. So the very fact that I am asking it should tell you I'm an ally."

"I don't know much at all. He had been sneaking out after curfew," she said, her eyes welling with tears. "He told me he was just visiting his brother, but he was also arrested last night. My sister-in-law said that many of their friends have now been taken too."

"This sister-in-law—"

"Her name is Nathalie."

"And Nathalie is still free, will you give me her address?" The woman nodded. I passed her the cash then stepped back into the shadows.

Nathalie lived in an apartment above a restaurant. I sat in a café across the road for hours the next morning, trying to figure out the best way to make an approach. The Gestapo may have been watching her apartment building, so arriving unannounced to her front door was out of the question. I couldn't even chance a phone call—switchboard operators listened in on calls for the Germans all the time.

In the end, there were no easy, safe ways to make contact. I watched until I'd seen the same woman come and go from the building several times, until I was reasonably certain this must be Nathalie. When I saw her leaving again, I followed her down the street and into a grocer. While she stood in front of the tinned beans, I pretended to bump into her.

"Oh, I'm sorry!" I exclaimed, as I slipped a note into her pocket. Her gaze followed my hand, confused, but I pressed my finger to my lips quickly. She reached into her pocket and nodded subtly.

"It's no trouble," she replied quietly. I turned and walked away, and waited for her in a nearby park, where I found a retaining wall behind a park bench. I perched on the low wall and removed a novel from my bag, resting it on my lap so I could pretend to read it.

The minutes passed and I began to wonder if she'd join me as I'd requested in the note. I wouldn't blame her if she didn't—her whole life had likely been upended by her husband's arrest, and the secretive nature of my approach indicated that I represented still more trouble. But then, after a few minutes, I saw her coming up the path, the newspaper I'd instructed her to buy tucked into a woven grocery bag. We exchanged a polite smile, and then she sat on the park bench behind me, facing away from me to read the newspaper.

"You are Nathalie?"

"Yes," she said, surprised. I heard movement and realized she'd turned to stare at me.

"Don't look at me," I said sharply, still staring at my novel. "Lift the newspaper so if anyone see us together, they won't realize we are talking."

"Who are you?"

"A friend. Your husband was arrested?"

She hesitated for a long time, until I realized that if I wanted her to take the risk of opening up to me, I would have to reveal a little more of myself first.

"Do you know Basile?"

"Yes!" She seemed relieved by the mention of his name.

"Basile and I have much in common," I said carefully. "I'm here at the request of our mutual friends. We knew one another when we worked as janitors…"

She turned the page of the newspaper and then said softly, "You're with the SOE?"

"I'm here at Basile's request," I said, deciding quickly it was best not to confirm her suspicion. "What can you tell me about the circuit?"

"Basile had maybe a hundred or more men and women organized in Rouen alone. We were meeting in small groups. Mine was undertaking training for sabotage. My group had about a dozen members and our leader was…" Her voice grew rough. She paused, cleared it, then finished in a whisper, "He was my friend. His name was Thierry. About a week after Basile left, the Gestapo came to arrest Thierry and the stubborn fool pulled a handgun, and…" She broke off, overcome with emotion.

"I'm sorry," I said.

"For a long time the rest of my group seemed to have escaped German attention but a few weeks ago the arrests began and this time, they snowballed. Every night, more arrests. When they came for Claude a few nights ago, I was only surprised they didn't take me too. But listen to me, if you're here for London, you need to tell them what's been happening."

"The arrests?"

"They've started constructing concrete runways all along the coast, perhaps ten meters long, beginning underground in a cavity, and sloping up from there. I know for certain that there are some just north of here, but I've heard rumors they extend every ten kilometers from here all the way to Cherbourg!"

I pictured a map in my mind and felt an icy chill run down my spine. Elwood warned me there were rumors of German rockets that would reach Britain from the continent. That curve from Rouen to Cherbourg ran roughly parallel to the English coastline.

"Claude spoke to a lorry driver who was bringing deliveries of sand for the construction," Nathalie continued. "He had been throwing iron filings into the sand, hoping that whatever these weapons are, they use some kind of magnetic orientation and the metal will throw them off. I know Thierry was planning to launch sabotage attacks against the bases and the runways, but with him gone and the circuit in disarray—everything has stalled."

"Who else do you know who has escaped arrest?"

"There are just a few of us…"

"Nathalie, you all must go into hiding immediately," I whispered urgently. "If they've detained most of your group, it's only a matter of time before someone exposes the rest of you."

"I have nowhere to go," she said miserably. "I have no family to hide me and no money. Most of our friends were involved with the circuit. I'm a sitting duck."

With just a handful of operatives and only two weeks left in Rouen, sabotaging those platforms was out of the question… but with the help of Nathalie and her friends, perhaps I could at least confirm their existence, and take details of the infrastructure back to London with me.

"I can help you hide, Nathalie," I said, thinking of the money hidden in the bottom of my bag. "But I'm going to need your help in return."

CHAPTER 13

CHARLOTTE
Collingham, England
1970

"You don't have to come with us, you know," I tell Theo the next morning when I find him waiting for us on the footpath outside of his flat in Manchester. It's a busy street and we couldn't find a place to park out front of Theo's flats so Dad's waiting in the car half a block away. I volunteered to fetch Theo to bring him to the car, in part because I wanted to talk to him privately.

"I've come this far," he says wryly. "I figured I should see this through to the final act. How's Noah?"

"Not good," I admit. Theo motions for me to turn around to return to the car, but I shake my head. "He's barely said a word since we left the professor's office yesterday. I told him about this meeting this morning as soon as he woke up and he agreed to come but he's so anxious, Theo. It's awful."

"It is perfectly understandable though," Theo says gently. I'm suddenly struck by two things—his ease with this awkward, uncomfortable situation, and the kindness in his eyes. I'm so grateful to have met him right when we need this kind of support the most. "The war is a period in his life he's rarely

revisited over the years and now he's trying to face it head-on.
That can't be easy."

"I know," I say. "But you should know that in the last ten
minutes he's decided he doesn't want us to come in when he
speaks to Jean."

Remy's name, it turns out, is Jean Allaire. He lives a few
hours' drive away in Collingham, Leeds. We were almost at
Theo's flat before Dad changed his mind about us joining him
for the meeting and he's far too stressed for me to argue the
point. He agreed that Theo could join us for the drive if he
wants to, and I'm really hoping that's what he decides to do.

"Oh no," Theo says, wincing. He glances back toward his
flat. "Well, that's his prerogative, of course."

"But you're welcome to come for a drive if you didn't have
plans…" I add hastily. Dad's behavior this morning is not at
all what I expected when Remy agreed to meet with him.
Theo has obviously had some experience dealing with men and
women who served and the difficulties of speaking about their
experiences. I'd be relieved to have skilled backup to support
Dad if the meeting doesn't go well.

"No plans to speak of," Theo says, then, "I'll still come along.
Moral support and all that. If you don't mind…?"

"I'd appreciate that," I say, relieved. "He really doesn't seem
himself today."

"He may well feel better after he sees Jean."

I insist Theo take the front seat beside Dad. He protests at
first but soon acquiesces—he's much taller than me, and Dad's
car is small enough that the back seat is cramped. The trip to
Remy's will take us a few hours and as we set off, Dad locks
both hands on the wheel, his gaze fixed on the road as if the
very act of driving requires every ounce of his concentration.
We've only made it a few blocks when Theo twists around to
speak at me.

"Where do you work? What grade level?"

And at that, we're chatting away—at first, the conversation a little forced as we try to fill the space around Dad's stony silence, but soon we're engaging in an easy back-and-forth. Theo works at a boys' independent school and teaches both modern and ancient history. "For fun," he manages the school's chess competition and astronomy club.

"It's not what I imagined for my life," he admits. "I thought I'd be an academic. Probably a military historian like Harry. But my mother always says 'man makes plans, God laughs,' and…" He shrugs. "Here we are."

He tells me about the dedicated characters of family history group and some of the remarkable discoveries they've made about their ancestors since he started it eighteen months ago. I'd thought of him as awkward, but it turns out Theo is easy company once he warms up.

After Theo and I have been swapping teaching stories for an hour or so, Dad finally clears his throat and asks, "Your…er… your wife doesn't mind you giving up your Saturday to drive with us, Theo?"

When Theo explains there's no wife to speak of, my father's eyes meet mine in the rear-vision mirror and he gives a wink. I glare at him because this car is way too small for such an awkward matchmaking attempt, but inwardly, I'm relieved to see a spark of my dad's usual, cheeky self.

Remy's extensive cottage is on a leafy street in Collingham. Once Dad's parked the car on the cobblestone drive, he closes his eyes and draws in a shuddering breath.

"You don't have to do this, Noah," Theo assures him. "If you've changed your mind, I can just go to the door and tell him so."

Dad opens his eyes. He still looks anxious, but he puts his hand on the car door handle.

"I set out to thank him, and I'm grateful for the opportunity to do so," he says unsteadily. "But I also have a lot of questions and I'd be lying if I said I wasn't nervous about hearing the answers."

With that, he leaves Theo and me behind. We watch as Dad approaches the house, but before he can even ring the doorbell, the door swings open to reveal a man about my father's age. Jean Allaire's shoulders are slightly stooped, and he wears what's left of his black hair in a long, sparse comb-over.

But from my vantage point here in the car, I observe a moment of pure, awkward nothingness where they just look at each other, as if neither is sure how to begin. Jean seems wary and Dad is shuffling his weight from foot to foot like a child on his first day of school. After an excruciating moment, the men disappear inside the house.

"God, I wish he'd let us join him," I say.

"He'll tell you about it when he's ready," Theo replies.

The door opens again and a woman emerges. She's wearing pearls and a fitted floral dress, and her golden hair is set in curls that frame her face. She approaches the car and Theo winds down his window.

"I'm Marion, Jean's wife," she introduces herself. "I assume you two are here with Noah?"

"Yes, Mrs. Allaire," Theo confirms. "Charlotte here is his daughter, and my name's Theo. I'm a friend."

"You really don't need to wait out here. They'll go into Jean's study if they need privacy," she says firmly, then she grimaces. "I've been anxious all morning so I did some baking to keep myself busy. We'll need some help to eat it all."

We follow her into the house and to a large formal dining room. The long oval table is set with a beautiful woven runner, and atop of this sits a steaming teapot and all manner of delicious treats. But Dad and Jean are already seated there, and when we enter the room, Dad looks up at us, slightly alarmed.

"I saw them waiting in the car and told them to come in," Marion announces. "You two can retreat to the study if need be."

I sit between Theo and Dad, and Marion and Jean sit opposite us. Theo takes a sandwich and nibbles at it. Jean rubs his hands together as if he's warming them, even though it's a beautiful summer's day. Dad takes a scone, spreads it carefully with jam then cream, but then he sets the cutlery down and stares at his plate. The seconds tick by but no one speaks.

Theo and I share a wince. We should have stayed in the car.

"Darling, to start with why don't you catch Noah up on what you've been doing since the war," Marion prompts. Jean clears his throat.

"I trained as an architect when I came home and after that, I joined my father's practice. He retired in 1963 and I manage the firm now." He falls silent. Marion elbows him gently. He clears his throat again then asks, "So…what do you do these days, Noah?"

"I was a flight mechanic at the start of the war. I retrained as a car mechanic after. In the early '50s I started my own business, then expanded it into a chain. I married after the war, to Geraldine. She passed last year."

Jean and Marion both murmur polite sympathies. Then the room falls into an excruciating silence that's broken by what's possibly the least subtle change of topic in the history of the world as Jean blurts, "We bought this house in 1960. It's hundreds of years old but was close to being condemned at the time so we bought it for a steal."

"Jean primarily does heritage architecture these days," Marion tells us. "He's prevented dozens of older structures from being destroyed, haven't you, darling? Some of the most important historic buildings in Britain have been saved because of you."

"You might say heritage architecture is my passion. In the case of this home, I designed the remodel myself, then managed the tradesmen over the next eighteen months."

Jean proceeds to spend more than ten minutes describing the

remodel project, right down to the way he and Marion ago-
nized over the style of the faucets—should they use a traditional
style, perhaps restored from the original period, or should they
modernize? We are not exactly waiting with bated breath by
the time Jean informs us they restored original fixtures and
have felt satisfied with this decision in the ensuing years. Dad
nods as if he's fascinated, but his eyes glaze over, and I know
he's not listening to a word. I'm about to suggest Theo and I
return to the car when Marion interrupts.

"This is all so interesting, darling, but perhaps we need to
move on now."

Jean breaks off, then nods. He turns his gaze back to Dad,
takes a deep breath.

"I love history, Noah," he begins, "but I don't like to think
back on my own. I do understand that has been intensely frustrating to Professor Read, but he stressed upon me that you
wanted to see me today so I agreed. Having said that, I couldn't
sleep last night wondering what it was that you needed to say."

"I appreciate you making time for me," Dad says gruffly. He's
back to staring at the still-untouched scone on his plate. "I did
want to speak to you about—" He breaks off, then turns to look
out the window into the garden, blinking rapidly. I reach across
and squeeze his hand, noting the sheen of tears in his eyes.

"Dad," I say. "Do you want me and Theo to go back to the
car?"

Dad reaches down and squeezes my hand, then shakes his
head.

"Not just yet, love. I just need a moment..." When he's com-
posed himself, he draws in a breath and turns his attention back
to Jean, who is now looking back at him warily. "I was obviously badly injured. At Salon-La-Tour, it would seem."

"Yes," Jean says stiffly. "That was a very difficult day."

"I don't recall much about it, to be honest. Just flashes of
images and some vague, troubling feelings," Dad says. For the

first time, I notice how often Dad says things like this when he talks about his memory problems around the time of the war— *troubling feelings. Feelings that don't make sense.* A shiver of confusion and concern runs through me, especially when I consider that Dad clearly did not want us to hear whatever it is he has to say to Jean today. Beside me, Dad is finally on a roll but he's talking almost to himself, his eyes downcast and his voice low.

"I suppose the last time you saw me was when you were dropping me at the hospital."

"That's right."

"Most of my memories returned eventually, but what I recall of those last few weeks is patchy to this day."

"I'm sorry to hear that."

"By the time I'd recalled even that I was an agent, the liberation was well underway. I waited at the hospital until Paris had been set free, then I went there because I couldn't remember why but I just had this feeling—" He breaks off abruptly, swallows, then clears his throat. "But…in the end, I was at a loss in Paris too. It wasn't just my memory that was damaged in those early days, my whole mind seemed scrambled. I couldn't concentrate or plan properly. I was alone in Paris looking for something that I felt certain was important although I could not remember why. I had no money or documentation and no idea how to get home. I lived on the streets for a few weeks because I didn't know what else to do."

On the streets? I blink away hot tears of surprise at this revelation, then reach to rub Dad's back.

"I'm sorry, Noah," Jean says. "But if you've come looking to confront me about that, I really had no choice about leaving you there. Our team had been given a mission and two of the three of us were out of action. I had to carry on alone."

"No, no. I'm not telling you that because…" Dad breaks off, flustered. "I just want you to understand. Why I didn't track you down to thank you right away."

"To *thank* me?" Jean repeats blankly, but Dad continues as if he hasn't heard him.

"It was just fortunate that I saw a poster about the SOE apartment. I don't know what would have become of me otherwise."

"SOE leadership had a devil of a time locating us all," Jean says slowly. "I was rather lost too until a wireless operator told me about that apartment."

"What was this apartment?" I ask.

"With hundreds of agents spread all across France, some of the key SOE leaders came across to Paris," Jean explains, "They set themselves up a base and spread word far and wide that agents should come in. Most of us made our way home via that apartment." His gaze grows cloudy. "Those who survived, anyway."

He and Dad both fall silent, probably lost for a moment in thoughts of their fallen comrades.

"The SOE brought me back to the UK and that's when I really started to recover. I reunited with Geraldine shortly after that and life just sped on by, you know? There was never any time to stop and look back."

"It was much the same for me." Jean nods, then he and Marion share a quiet glance. "There was a wave of jubilation when the war ended, but what comes next? You have to move on and then you're focused on career and family and life just rushes on by you."

"Exactly. But since my wife died, I can't help but think back. I'd have missed so much if you hadn't saved me that day. All of those wonderful years with my wife. We'd never have had Charlotte here, her brother Archie, my beautiful granddaughter Poppy—but for you, I'd have missed all of it." Dad delivers each word carefully and his voice is thick with tears. "I just needed to say thank you." Dad turns his gaze to Marion and says, "I wanted to make sure that Jean's family knows that he is a hero."

I finally flick a glance at Jean, only to find him staring at the ceiling now, visibly uncomfortable. He sucks in a breath then exchanges a slightly panicked glance with Marion who winces and shrugs.

"I'm sorry to tell you this, but you've got it all wrong, Noah," Jean says. "We weren't alone that day. Do you remember that?"

"Fleur was with us at first but then she was gone," Dad frowns, then pauses. "Wasn't she?"

"Well, yes, but—" Jean scratches his neck awkwardly then tries again. "Do you remember the roadblock?" Dad gives a helpless shrug. Jean inhales sharply then to my surprise, he narrows his eyes. "We drove right into a trap and we were virtually defenseless. Do you remember that?"

"I…"

"Do you remember you wanted to surrender? To *surrender!*" Jean repeats himself as if he can't believe this even now, his voice rising as he does so. Dad's mouth falls open in shock. Jean's fist thumps against the table now and he leans forward as he hisses, "Months of training where they drilled into us to *never allow ourselves to be captured* and you were telling me to pull the car over and surrender right when the Germans were finally on the back foot! I wouldn't—Fleur wouldn't…!"

"Love," Marion says, her voice low and urgent. Jean breaks off to stare at her. "Stop and take a breath," she says gently. He nods, swallows, and turns back to Dad.

"I kept driving and tried to turn around, but the Germans shot out the back tire and we went off the road for a moment, colliding rather violently with the wall of a ditch. That's when you struck your head. That's probably when you were shot, because the car took a lot of bullets about then too. But it all happened very quickly so I don't know for sure. What matters most here is that it wasn't me who saved your life. It was Fleur."

"*You* took me to the hospital. You even thought to take me some distance away for help in case the Germans were looking for me, isn't that right? Why else would you take me all the way to Brive-La-Galliarde—that's...what...forty-five ki-lometers? Fifty?"

"Noah, God. *No*," Jean mutters, his face flushing. "I was twenty-two years old. It was my first deployment and I'd been in France for less than a day. I was impatient to get to work and I thought I knew everything, but the minute I saw that road-block, I panicked. Fleur told me to hide with you in a farmer's barn while she drew the Germans away from us. I waited there with you until things were quiet again, but she didn't come back and you wouldn't wake up and the God's honest truth is I had no idea what to do."

"But..."

"Luckily for you—an old farmer had watched the whole thing unfold. He saw us go into his barn, but he couldn't come to help at first, because Fleur was in a gunfight with the Ger-mans not far from his house. She held them off for at least half an hour, but they eventually captured her and left. Only once the farmer was sure they were all gone did he come back to check on us. He loaded us into his cart, hid us under some hay, and drove us to Brive-La-Galliarde. *He* thought to take you some distance away in case the Germans knew Fleur had been traveling with others and checked the hospitals. None of that was my doing. If anything, I was a liability that day and to be completely frank, if the farmer hadn't insisted otherwise, I might have just left you there in that barn."

"But Fleur didn't make it," Dad croaks. "Professor Read said she didn't survive the war."

Jean shrugs. "All I know is the farmer saw her captured."

"But..."

"I did try to help her before I left," Jean says, almost to him-self. "I found the local Maquis group. The last I heard they were going to try to find out if she was in a local prison to see if a rescue attempt was feasible. But I couldn't stop to help. You and Fleur were out of commission, so it was up to me to continue alone."

"This is just awful," Dad whispers hoarsely. "My God. To think that brave young woman traded her life for mine...it's just..."

"Noah," Jean says sharply. "Is this really why you tracked me down?"

"I just wanted to express my gratitude."

Jean sighs impatiently. He looks from Dad to me and Theo, then stands abruptly.

"We should continue this in my study."

Dad rises and follows Jean from the dining room, leaving me, Theo and Marion. She forces a smile.

"Talk of war is never easy," she says. "Jean really was very troubled last night," she murmurs, then she glances hesitantly toward me. "He was hoping your father might be coming to apologize." At my blank look, she drops her voice and adds in a whisper, "To make peace."

"Apologize?" I say, alarmed. "What on earth..."

"I shouldn't say," Marion says, flushing. She stands and starts to clear the food from the table. "Honestly, it's between them. I really... I just..."

"Please, Mrs. Allaire," I say urgently, and I stand too. She's frazzled—stacking plates full of food on top of one another and avoiding my eyes. Theo stands too and he takes a plate gently from her hand.

"The female agent. Fleur. She *was* hurt so I do understand why your father insisted they take the car that day," she says. Beneath the powder on her face, Marion Allaire is flushing. She gives me a desperate look. "But your father was the circuit leader. Don't you think it's terribly bad luck that the route he insisted they take happened to be guarded by four trucks full of Germans? That your father tried to insist they surrender the minute they saw them?"

"What are you suggesting?" I gasp.

"This is why Jean never wanted to speak to Professor Read," Marion says to Theo, frustrated. "There had been rumors of a double agent among their ranks for some time. Jean didn't want to speak out of turn and potentially ruin your father's reputation but he always suspected—"

"Charlotte," Dad says stiffly. Theo and I look up at the doorway. My father is white as a sheet. "It's time for us to leave."

It is a long, uncomfortable drive home with Dad. He grips the steering wheel so tightly his knuckles stay white, and every now and again I see him shake his head as though in frustration or disbelief. Theo and I make a few gallant attempts at chitchat, but the tension radiating from my father in the tiny space is oppressive and distracting now and we can't seem to find a rhythm.

This time, Dad doesn't bother looking for a parking spot on Theo's street. He just stops in the middle of the road outside the building, blocking traffic. The car behind him honks impatiently but Dad doesn't seem to notice.

"Thank you for letting me come along," Theo says as he's scrambling from the car. He gives me a helpless, apologetic look. "If I can help at all with anything else, please don't hesitate to call me. You both have my number—"

"Thanks for joining us," I reply, as Dad gives a distracted wave and starts to drive away. I can only hope Theo isn't insulted by the way Dad is behaving. I lean out the window to call back to Theo, "You've been very generous to try to help us—!"

Dad continues on toward Liverpool after that. I settle in the back seat and try to figure out how to talk to him. Finally I decide that nothing I say is going to make things any better, but I can at least express my support.

"I know that was intense, Dad. And maybe not at all what you expected. I hope you're okay."

"I'll be fine."

I'm not convinced by this at all because his shoulders are up around his ears.

"The agent... Fleur?" I say hesitantly. "Was she your friend?"

"I barely knew her. We had a mutual friend."

"It wasn't your fault, Dad."

"You weren't there," Dad snaps, and I look at him in surprise. I expect him to immediately apologize, but he's still staring at the road. "You have no idea what was or wasn't my fault."

I leave it after that. We drive in silence for some time until Dad says quietly, "Your mother was so wise, wasn't she? She was always so sure I should never look back at my SOE days. Perhaps I should have thought some more about that before I started all of this."

Chapter 14

ELOISE
Paris, France
March, 1944

Three weeks after I left Paris, I returned to Madame Célestine's apartment. I dropped my bags to the ground and tapped the cast-iron knocker against front door, aching with exhaustion from head to toe.

It had been the longest weeks of my entire life. I was arrested twice—that first time for my missing permit, the second time a random detainment, but I once again played the part of innocent fool and was released within hours. They were difficult days, but every day in Rouen was difficult. In the end, with Nathalie's help, I did find the tattered remains of Basile's circuit—a handful of citizens still free in the community, some still bearing the bruising from their arrests. Through them, I connected with what was left of the wider resistance community in the region—other independent resistance organizations, and a few *Marquis* groups that existed outside of Basile's orbit.

It was clear that every group had been ravaged in that spate of recent arrests, and not nearly enough operatives remained at Rouen to rebuild any meaningful resistance efforts, especially if the D–Day landings were, as expected, to take place over the coming summer, just a few short months away.

I knew that Basile would be shocked by my findings, and I fully expected him to argue that things couldn't nearly be so bad. That's why, in the hidden compartment of my shoulder bag, I had folded two Wanted posters—one that bore his likeness, and another that noted he might be using the names Basile or even Henri Edgar Pueyrredón. Was that his real name, or one of his cover names? In any case, it was clear that the Germans knew exactly who he was. I was dreading delivering the news to Basile that his once-proud network had been reduced to rubble, even though the handful of operatives remaining had done him proud in their efforts over that past two weeks.

We didn't waste a moment of my time there and my mind was bursting with new information to report to Baker Street. I'd identified a series of bridges, munitions factories and warehouses that might be vulnerable to air attack. I could report in detail on the rapid increase in German security efforts in the region over the past few months. Those who'd been arrested and released all told me the same story—their interrogation was almost entirely about preparations the resistance was making in readiness for a coming landing.

In addition to all of that, I managed to get close to several of the mysterious rocket sites. Nathalie kept watch for patrols while I crept through the fields around each site, to peer through perimeter fences or scale trees for a better view through the binoculars she had secured for me. I could not make sense of what the sites were intended to do exactly, but it seemed clear enough that this new technology was close to ready: all of the locals who worked on the initial construction had been laid off and were prohibited from returning.

I managed to get to within just a few dozen feet of one of each type of site, both the long runway style platforms, possibly designed to launch some kind of "air torpedo," and the square "launch pad" infrastructure, which was believed to be for a larger, more powerful explosive device. I had managed to record enough detail to memory that I felt certain I could sketch out the layout of each once I was back in London.

In the end, I left Rouen in a rush, two days earlier than planned, and I would not be returning. I had moved around during my stay as Basile had instructed me to, but at the last boarding house I stopped at, the host was known to be an ally. When I emerged from my room that very morning for break-fast, she pulled me into the kitchen and let me know she'd had a visit from the Gestapo.

"They are going door-to-door along the street, asking if we've seen a woman from out of town, possibly named Fleur," she told me, dropping her voice. "They described you to a tee, mademoiselle. They said there may even be a reward for any information about your whereabouts."

She helped me cut my hair right there in her kitchen, until the lengths that once reached my shoulders now sat roughly below my ears. She gave me some of her clothing—a hideous felt hat, several layers of undershirts to hide my shape, covered by a cotton dress that smelt strongly of mothballs. I wore deeply unstylish, handmade leather shoes that she'd worn for so long the stitching on the sides was coming undone. She secured some sponges, which I fashioned into inserts to rest against my bot-tom teeth to make my cheeks look fuller. I'd washed my mouth with iodine to temporarily stain my teeth yellow.

The sum of all of these efforts was that the woman who stared back at me in the mirror seemed decades older, espe-cially once I adjusted my posture to stand with a hunch and made an effort to walk with a stiff limp. We learned such dis-guise techniques at "finishing school," and in this case, they were a temporary measure, designed to last just long enough for me to leave Rouen.

Within an hour of that shocking conversation in the kitchen,

I was limping my way to the train station, and just three hours later, back in Paris. I walked around the city for hours after my arrival, checking and double-checking that I wasn't being followed. My contingency plan loomed large in my thoughts—if I saw even a hint that anyone was tailing me, I'd have to find somewhere else to sleep for the night, then to begin the mammoth task of trying to figure out how to reach help in Spain.

By the time dusk was falling, my feet were aching from the dreadful shoes and my back was aching from the artificial stoop, but I'd seen no sign at all that anyone was following me, and so I had finally been reassured enough to go to Célestine's house.

The door opened, but the woman who greeted me was not, as I'd expected, Madame Célestine. Instead it was my old training partner and roommate Chloe. For a moment, we just stared at one another, then she squinted at me.

"Fleur?"

"Yes!" I said, laughing as I recovered from the shock. "What on earth are you doing here? Are you staying here?"

"I am!" she said, stunned, and once the door had closed behind us, Chloe threw her arms around me. I'd never been much of a hugger, but Chloe was, and over the months of our training I'd grown to love our embraces. Embarrassing tears filled my eyes at the sheer relief I felt at seeing a friendly face, and when she released me, I tightened my arms around her for just a few extra seconds.

"Are you okay?" she asked. She sounded tired too, weary and heavy in a way I'd not seen in her even during our training.

"Of course," I said, blinking the tears quickly away. "Just tired. How long have you been here?"

"I only arrived yesterday. And you? Madame Célestine didn't mention you were coming…"

"I'm a few days early," I said. A vital doctrine of our field operations was that agents should avoid prolonged contact unless it was strictly necessary to the mission, so I suspected that the overlap of our stays at Célestine's house would not be tolerated for long.

I removed the awful modifiers from my cheeks then took the hat off, too, and shook out my hair. All day I'd been thinking only about bathing and changing my clothes, lying flat to stretch out my spine, but now that Chloe was here, the urgency of all of that seemed to ease.

"Sit! Rest!" she insisted, as she took the hat from my hands and set it gingerly on a nearby sofa. I left Rouen in such a rush I only packed the most essential items of my clothing, and had just one suitcase and the leather shoulder bag with me. Chloe took these from my hands and rested them on the chair beside the hat. "I'm guessing you'll want some tea."

"No, I definitely need something stronger today," I laughed weakly, but I let her guide me to an armchair, and I sighed with pleasure as I sank into it.

"I'm going to go tell Célestine you're here and to fetch us some drinks. And then... I guess we can swap notes about our first real-world missions?"

"Mine is still very much active," I said reluctantly. "I'm not sure how much I should say."

"Understood. I'll be back soon."

We swapped as much information as we dared divulge that night. I told her I'd been in the Normandy region on reconnaissance.

"I had some hairy moments," I admitted, flicking her a glance. "I owe you a favor, actually."

"You do?" she said, bemused.

"*Let's go somewhere lovely together,*" I said softly, and her eyes widened in surprise. "I used that trick you taught me for staying calm more than once. Thank you for sharing it with me."

"I'm so pleased you found it useful," she said. "My Maman would be proud if she knew."

She told me, in much greater detail, about months at Montbeliard, the destruction of the factory there, the exposure of their w/t operator. We tumbled into bed late and I thought I'd sleep like a log, but as the grandfather clock in the hall outside counted down the hours to midnight, I was still wide awake, repeating key facts from the mission to myself over and over again, a memory trick I'd learned to keep track of so much information I could not afford to write down.

In the early hours, I started to think about Giles. I remembered the very moment we met—that charming smile he offered me on his first day of his pilot's course at the Hatfield flight school. I'd been in England for eighteen months by then and had just won a civilian position with the Elementary and Reserve Flying Training School.

We talked every day over the two months of his course— sometimes he'd sit at my desk and distract me for hours after he finished his training. I didn't mistake the way his eyes would linger on mine or the faint flush on his cheeks when I smiled at him. He was shy—but not so shy that he wouldn't talk to me. And even after all of those weeks, he'd never asked me out. I couldn't make sense of it and as his course was ending, I'd run out of patience and time.

"Well?" I said impatiently, when he walked past me on his final day at Hatfield flight school, giving only a polite nod.

"Well, what?" he asked, turning back to me in alarm.

"Are you going to ask me out, or not?"

"Do you...do you *want* me to?" he said. He seemed shocked by this.

"Only if you want to!" I exclaimed. He paused, staring at me quizzically, and I deflated. "Giles, I don't understand. You seem to like me, but you've made no move to ask me out."

"I wasn't sure if my feelings were reciprocated," he said, raising his chin proudly. "I thought it better to be left wondering than to inadvertently cause offense."

It was a whirlwind courtship and we were married within six months. Pushing Giles to ask me out was the single best decision I had ever made. The depth of grief I felt at his loss was a testament only to the depth of love I felt for him in life.

And then there was Hughie—the piece of our family we didn't even know was missing.

During my mission, I had blocked most thoughts of my homecoming from my mind. I could not afford to lose focus when I was in Rouen, and the idea of reuniting with my son and even my mother tended to leave me impatient and anxious. But now that I was relatively safe in Paris, I let myself imagine that moment for the first time—how it would feel to open the door to my apartment and to see them both there, safe and well and no doubt overjoyed to have me home.

Counting the weeks of preparation with Basile at Baker Street, I had been away from Hughie for the better part of six weeks this time. We'd endured long separations during my training so I knew to expect a little hesitation from him at first, but within an hour or so he'd be smothering me with hugs and messy kisses.

It was that thought that tripped me up.

The tears came unbidden and I was too exhausted to resist so I let them run down my face and into my pillow. I *loved* my son. I loved every little thing about him—from his desperate curiosity about the world to those beautiful blue eyes. I had tried, in the beginning, to speak to him in both English and French so that he might be bilingual but he had taken to French so much more quickly than English. I loved the way he would babble at me in my mother tongue. I could not wait to hear his little voice call *"Maman!"* again.

"Are you okay?" Chloe asked, her voice thick with sleep from the other side of the room. My face flushed with embarrassment, and I sniffed and rolled toward the wall.

"Sorry. I'm fine."

"If you need anything—"

"I don't."

I spoke more sharply than I intended to, but Chloe's breathing deepened again within minutes, and she was back to sleep.

"Can I ask you something?" Chloe said. It was midmorning the next day and we were sitting at Madame Célestine's table sharing yet another cup of tea. Her home was lovely, but both Chloe and I were at loose ends waiting for the next phase of our deployment, and neither one of us was accustomed to having free time. "You have a family at home, don't you? You don't have to tell me the details," she added quickly at my surprised look. "It's just that when we first went for training, I noticed you had a tan line on your ring finger. And you've never mentioned any names but..." She cleared her throat. "Sometimes you toss and turn in your sleep. I think you might cry in your sleep sometimes too."

"My husband is gone," I said. It was against the rules to tell her anything at all about my personal life—but I could see no harm in telling her this much. As the words left my mouth, a memory flashed before my eyes. He was home on leave the last time I saw him. I had finally adjusted to the shock of finding myself pregnant after his previous visit home. Giles could not stop touching my belly. He kept telling me how beautiful I was—how excited he was that we were going to be parents.

We went for dinner with one of his squadron pals who happened to bring his camera along. After the meal, the friend insisted on taking a photograph of us. Giles was leaning against the wall of the restaurant, standing right behind me. He was beaming at the camera, his arms around me, hands resting proudly on my belly. I looked as carefree and happy as I'd ever remembered feeling.

Giles was a man of deep faith, raised Catholic by his mother. When he left for North Africa two weeks later, I gave him a copy of that photograph and a set of rosary beads attached to a little medal.

"St. Michael," he had murmured, running his finger over the medal. "Patron saint of the military. He'll watch over me to keep me safe."

If only.

My eyes filled with tears at the memory and I blinked them away, embarrassed.

"I'm sorry," she said, her voice sympathetic, and I felt myself bristle. I didn't want pity—not even from Chloe who I genuinely liked and trusted, and who seemed a little distracted herself that day. In stretches of silence that morning I'd caught her staring off into the distance, her expression heavy with grief.

"That's not why I— You don't have to—" I broke off, then stopped and took a breath and all of a sudden words were pouring from my mouth and I could not stop the torrent. "That *is* partly why I'm here. My husband was killed in action and it's so cruel how abrupt it was. One minute you're a wife and the next you're a widow, and the only thing that separates those two moments in your life is a damned *telegram*. There's not even someone from the government there to shake your hand or to thank you for his service. Not even someone around to offer you an explanation, or even a bloody hug. It's brutal and it's cold and it's cruel, and there's no justice on offer at all for the spouse left behind." My thoughts went to a parcel I had been given, still wrapped and unopened, in the drawer beside my bed. It was from Giles's CO, and I knew it would contain his most personal effects—maybe even a letter for me. Two years after his death I had yet to open it. I was curious, but once I opened that parcel, there would be no more from Giles, and I could not bring myself to face that. "When Baker Street approached me for the SOE, it seemed like an answer to my prayers. I was going to lose my mind sitting at home grieving him. I had to *do* something."

"That makes sense," she said.

"But when I…couldn't sleep last night, I wasn't just think-ing about him," I said stiffly. I cleared my throat again. In for a penny, in for a pound, I supposed. "I have a son. It's never been easy to be away from him, even if it is necessary."

"Where is he now?"

"My mother…" I sighed and reached for one of Madame Cé-lestine's cookies. They were made with saccharine and bread-crumbs, and had a coarse, dry texture that meant they could only really be enjoyed with a hot beverage. "My mother and I have never been particularly close, but her marriage ended just after my son was born and she came to stay with me. It turns out she's a much better grandmother than she was a mother."

That was an understatement, but I was sharing more with Chloe than I knew I should, and it was the easiest summation of a difficult situation. Maman was already pregnant when she married my father at just seventeen, and by the time she was nineteen, she was divorced with a toddler in tow. It seemed to me that she had always been searching for something and she'd gone looking in all the wrong places—trying to find peace within herself in boyfriends and her multitude of husbands. She left France a few years after I did, settling down with a Welsh farmer she met on the ferry, but by the time Hughie was born and I wrote her to let her know I was not just a mother, but a widow too, her marriage was on the rocks and she showed up on my doorstep.

I almost turned her away. At that stage, I felt only resentment toward her and I already felt overwhelmed by the circumstances of my own life. But I was also out of my depth, struggling to care for Hughie adequately in my grief, so I agreed to let her stay for just a few weeks.

Two years later, she was still there, and our relationship was better than it had ever been. My mother adored Hughie and but for her presence in our lives, I'd never have been able to train

with the SOE. Sitting there with Chloe, I was shocked to realize I was almost as keen to see Maman as I was to see Hughie.
That was a miraculous shift, especially given the reason I left
France in the first place was that she and I could barely stand
to be in the same room.

The joy of watching my son grow up together had brought
healing to our relationship in a way I had never anticipated.

"Well, since you broke the rules and told me something about
yourself, I'll return the favor. I fell in love on my mission."

"You…" I was almost speechless, until I burst out a shocked
laugh. "Chloe! *What?*"

"I have you to thank for it, too," she said, laughing in spite
of herself. "They were going to send you to Montbeliard except
that you hurt yourself on that test parachute jump."

"I don't need to tell you that you're not supposed to have
romantic dalliances on mission," I scolded, still shaking my
head even as I laughed. "You're the last agent I expected to
break a rule like that! You seem such a stickler for the straight
and narrow."

"I am," she said, her smile fading a little. "But my circuit
leader was actually an old friend and our cover story was that
we were married. Now that I think about it, it was probably
inevitable that something more would develop between us."

"What happens from here?"

"We both survive the war," she told me firmly. "And then
we reunite and get married and live happily ever after."

"I hope that's what happens for you."

"And you?"

"I finish out this mission. Get back for my debrief. I go
home to my son and my mother. I can't think ahead any further than that."

It was my idea to wander the stores. We were going a little
stir-crazy with nothing to do at the apartment and unlikely to

get ourselves into much trouble shopping as any ordinary young Frenchwomen might on a spare morning in the city. I even helped myself to some of the money I had left over from the supplies Basile gave me for my trip. This was a little cheeky of me, but I couldn't imagine Baker Street minding much, given it was forged currency anyway.

"What exactly are we shopping for?" Chloe asked me, and I shrugged.

"A gift for my son if I can find something suitable. Then my mother. Finally, Miss Elwood."

"Ah, Miss Elwood. What an idea! I do like her a lot."

"Me too," I said. "Although in the beginning..."

"She seemed terrifying. I mean—she *is* terrifying," Chloe chuckled. "But beneath that, she has a heart of gold."

Miss Elwood had been heavily involved in our training and in my case at least, across just about every detail of the preparation for my mission. I knew that she, Turner, Booth and Maxwell were thick as thieves, but she seemed to be most deeply invested in the female agents. Elwood could be brash, almost abrasive, but in a strange way, that was what had endeared her most to me. I suspected people thought the same about me sometimes.

Chloe and I walked from store to store, considering various options for gifts. They had to be small enough to fit within my leather shoulder bag as I'd be leaving my cases behind. The gifts also couldn't be terribly expensive. I decided on a small flacon of *Soir de Paris* for Maman, a perfume I hoped she'd love that would remind her of home. For Miss Elwood, we found a beautiful brooch—a large cluster of green and red beads with two tiny pearls hanging below.

And then, on our way out of the jewelry store, I paused at a chaotic display of dusty, used goods. Inside the cabinet was a beautifully carved wooden box with the Eiffel Tower etched onto the top, not much larger than the palm of my hand.

"I'll take that too," I said quietly. One day, I would open that parcel from Giles's commanding officer. Inside, I knew I'd likely find the St. Michael pendant I bought for Giles the day before his deployment, along with his wedding ring and the photo of us at the restaurant.

Through these little trinkets, Hughie could have tangible reminders of the milestones of our family life—the photograph, representing the brief moment we were all together, and all of our hopes and dreams that would never come to pass. The pendant, representing Giles, and his deep faith and hope. And the box itself—a little piece of Paris that would represent the city of my birth. The city that made me.

The following day, I had a difficult, uncomfortable meeting with Basile, who was unfazed by the wanted posters and was still adamant he was going to find a way to return to Rouen.

"And if Baker Street tell me I'm not to return, I'll work the *Success* circuit here in Paris," he told me stubbornly. "It seems to have more than enough challenges. I'm not going to let them evacuate me. France is where I need to be!"

It wasn't my job to convince him—I would leave that up to Baker Street. We said our farewells, and I went back to Célestine's apartment to say goodbye to Chloe. Before I made my way to the field outside of the city to meet my Lysander, she pressed a small scrap of paper into my hands.

"I won't ask you to do anything that breaks the rules," she said softly. "Give it to Miss Elwood or Mr. Turner. They can read it to check I'm giving nothing away. There's just a lot left unsaid between my mother and me and…"

I took the letter and slid it into my pocket.

"I'll pass it on," I promised.

"I doubt they'll send it. The rules are strict about contact with home when we're in the field. But perhaps they can put it into my file," she said. "I just need to know that I've cleared the air with her in case…"

"Don't make contingency plans, Chloe. You don't need them—you're skilled, courageous and strong. When all of this is over, you and your boyfriend will come for dinner with me and my mother and son and it will feel like this was a strange dream we once had."

"I hope you're right."

"Of course I'm right. You're going to do brilliantly."

After five full days of debriefing sessions, I had all but lost my voice. I'd been quizzed by familiar faces—Booth, Turner, Elwood, even Colonel Maxwell, the head of the agency and a man who had a direct line to Churchill.

"Basile should come home," I told Maxwell.

"He is still adamant he should stay," Maxwell said.

I jabbed a finger against the Wanted poster.

"Look at this likeness! Paris is only eighty miles from Rouen. He will be so much use to you here, but it's only a matter of time before he's arrested if he stays."

I drew maps and diagrams, made lists of observations and names and dates. The minute I mentioned those rocket sites, high-ranking officials from the Ministry of Defense were called in, and that kicked off another round of questioning and more maps and more sketches and Elwood started bringing in cups of tea with honey and strong coffee loaded with sugar to keep me going.

I had a sore throat from talking and a headache from the thinking and an aching neck from sleeping on the lumpy mattress in the little apartment at Baker Street I'd been given for the duration. I'd left my SOE-issued clothing in Paris with Chloe, and I was sick of wearing the starchy, dated clothes Ms. Elwood had supplied me.

I wanted to hold my son, take a hot bath, don my own

clothes, and eat several servings of whatever my mother would cook me.

"That's about it," Elwood finally said just after lunch on the sixth day, and I was so exhausted and relieved I could have wept with the force of those words. We were alone in an office at that stage and had just finished a very long session checking the transcription of my recollections of infrastructure along the Seine.

"Wait," I croaked, and I fished around in the pocket of the dress she'd loaned me. First, I withdrew the letter from Chloe, still folded neatly in half. "She knows it's against the rules, but Chloe wrote a letter for her mother. I haven't read it, but she assures me it's completely benign, and—"

"I'm sure it would be, knowing Chloe," Elwood said, taking it from me. "But regardless, I can't send it on. As you well understand, even simple words can be used to express covert meanings. What if it was a coded message that simply looked like a letter? What if it's an encryption key? I'll hold onto it though. If anything happens to her, I'll make sure her mother gets it."

"Thank you. And there's something else." I reached back into my pocket and withdrew the brooch. "A gift for you."

"A gift?" she repeated, thin eyebrows arching high. "How on earth did you pay…"

"Best not to know," I said, winking at her, and she opened the box and gasped.

"My goodness, Fleur. This is so thoughtful of you."

"Just a little something to say thank you. I did a fantastic job, and no wonder, because that's exactly what you all prepared me to do."

"Well," she said, blinking down at the brooch, then at me. She hesitated, then reached back down onto a leather folio on the table and swung it open. "I was going to give this to you later, but this seems a better time now. I met your son, you see."

"You met Hughie?"

"Your mother was called away on business for a few days and asked us to arrange alternate care of him. I have no children myself, but the men here seemed to think that I was the only one of us qualified for such a job. My mother lives with me and was thrilled at the prospect so I found it hard to say no." She rifled through the papers in the folio, then withdrew a tiny black-and-white photograph. "On the first day he seemed a bit sullen and there was a fair at the park near my flat so Mother and I took him for a walk. A man was taking photographs for a few pence. Hughie was having so much fun by then, I knew you'd enjoy sharing the moment."

I was utterly bewildered as I took the photograph, but there was my son, looking off beyond the lens, laughing at the camera as bubbles floated on the air around him. Hughie was wearing clothes a size or two too big, and he had that little rash he sometimes got around his mouth when a new tooth was coming in. But he was holding a strawberry in one hand and he was grinning—his eyes shining, his entire face alight with joy. In the background I could see carnival rides.

"But…what business would Maman…?" I trailed off, completely baffled.

"I'm not exactly sure. Turner spoke with her and arranged it all. She's back now and everything is fine. I know they'll be thrilled to see you, so I won't keep you a minute longer. Thank you again for the brooch."

"And thanks for the photo," I said but I could not help a pang of alarm. Maman was all but penniless—I had been supporting her since she came to live with me and she had no business to attend to, as far as I knew. God, had one of her scoundrel ex-husbands returned? Or had she followed some new man—leaving Hughie behind, just as she'd so often left me behind as a child?

The thought made me feel ill. Had I been wrong to trust that she'd turned over a new leaf?

"Ready, Fleur?" Turner was in the doorway. His usual smile was strangely absent, and he didn't attempt to make small talk with me as we walked to his car. Once he had pulled his Vauxhall out into the street, I sighed with pleasure and relief that it was finally over.

"You probably know this, sir, but my flat is at Bexley."

Turner was silent for a moment. He cleared his throat, then said, "I'm sorry, but we can't go to your flat just yet."

"But—"

"I know you're tired but this is quite important, Eloise," he said, startling me with the use of my real name. Of course he *knew* it, officials at his level knew just about everything. But this was the first time I'd heard my name in the context of SOE business ever since I was called into a room at the Northumberland Hotel for a meeting on what I thought was a matter of confusion around Giles's war pension, but what turned out to be the wildest imaginable job interview.

"Is everything okay?" I asked, but I waited in silence as Turner stared at the road. My pulse started to race. "You're making me uneasy, sir. What's going on?"

Just a few blocks from the SOE office, he pulled the car into a parking space then flicked the ignition off. Still staring out the windscreen, he said, "Almost everyone in the SOE is brilliant. Almost everyone is loyal. There are exceptions to the rule."

"Every agent I've worked or trained with has represented the agency with skill and pride." I frowned. "During our training, you and the other officials were very quick to weed out those who lacked the necessary character."

"The system is not perfect, I'm afraid. The miserable reality is that there are double agents within our ranks."

A burst of defensiveness immediately surged through me.

"Mr. Turner, I do hope you are not suggesting—" I said hotly, but he quickly interrupted me, his tone calm but firm.

"I'm not accusing you of anything and this conversation will be much easier for us both if you just let me speak."

I wanted to go home. I had completed my mission carefully and faithfully. Until just that very minute, I'd assumed the SOE officials were all thrilled with my work, but I was suddenly questioning everything. Had I made a mistake? Had I missed something?

"I know of at least one double agent. There are possibly more," Turner said grimly. "I cannot tell you how I know, or who I suspect...rather, who I know them to be. But I will tell you this much because you need to know—Eloise, by the time you left Rouen, the Germans knew you were there. They know your real name. More than that, they know your mother and son's names."

"No," I gasped. "No, sir. That's impossible."

The SOE was an agency that prioritized secrecy above all else—that's why we used code names, why we went to such lengths to maintain distance from one another. I'd never before heard of an active agent's family being exposed.

"I can't tell you how I know this," Turner repeated. "But I assure you, the threat is very real."

"Are they in danger?" I demanded. On their own, they were vulnerable. I needed to get home to keep them safe! "Is this why my mother was called away on business while I was in the field?"

Turner turned to face me.

"About a week after you left, my secretary called me at home," he said. "She was working late when a call came in on Elwood's line. It was one of your neighbors. She heard your son crying inside your flat but your mother wasn't answering the door. The neighbor and her husband broke a window to get inside. They found your mother. She had collapsed." The conversation was starting to feel like a bad dream. I shook my head numbly. "They tried to revive her," he continued. "I'm sorry. It was just too late."

"No," I said, ridiculously. "She can't be gone. She just can't—"

"I know this is distressing but we have a lot to get through, Eloise," he said calmly, and he reached into his jacket, passing me a freshly pressed handkerchief. "Please try to focus."

My eyes were dry, but I took the handkerchief anyway. I wrung it through my fingers as I nodded for him to continue.

"They found Ms. Elwood's number on a card in your kitchen."

"Yes. Just before I left, she gave it to me to give to Maman in case anything went wrong while I was away," I whispered absently.

"Your neighbors weren't sure what to do with the boy. They said they barely know you." I closed my eyes at that. It was true—Giles and I inherited the flat from his mother, who was a vibrant, active part of the community in that block of flats. But the neighbors were all so much older than me and I was convinced we had little in common. I never got to know them beyond the occasional nod in the hallway. And then Maman came to live with me and we formed a little bubble around ourselves. "I arranged for Elwood to take your son for a few nights. To be honest, I learned of your mother's death around the same time I…" He paused, cleared his throat, then finished carefully, "Well, I understood the Germans had your real name by then. I assumed her death was suspicious."

"You think they killed my mother—"

"The timing was concerning," he interrupted me. "I've since spoken with a doctor at the morgue and he said it was most likely natural causes. But at first, my only concern was keeping your son safe and I knew Elwood wouldn't let a thing happen to him even if they did manage to track him down at her place. She lives with her mother, and her mother is a fierce sort, but maternal, you know? It was the best I could come up with on short notice."

"But where is Hughie now?" I blurted. "Elwood said she had him for four nights. It's been weeks!"

"I found an excellent child-minder. She has no idea who he really is—she doesn't even know his real name. She knows only that his security is potentially at risk."

I felt crushed by the conversation—the news about my mother, sheer terror for my son. How long had he been left alone with Maman after her collapse? Was he traumatized? How could he adjust to so many strangers? His whole life until then, he'd only had me and Maman.

He was probably beside himself, even now. He was probably crying for me, wondering where I went.

"Please, take me to him," I said. Mr. Turner cleared his throat.

"Elwood and Maxwell are already planning to ask you to return to France."

"I'll refuse," I gasped incredulously. "Everything has changed now! Surely you understand that."

"Did Elwood give you the photograph she purchased?"

"She did, but…"

"Then you saw how settled he was. That was just two days after your mother's passing. He is well settled where he is, and more importantly, he is safe there. Even if you retrieve him tonight, all you do is to make him identifiable again. And if you do choose to return—"

"I won't!" I interrupted him rudely. "My priority must be my son now, Mr. Turner. I can keep him safe better than anyone can."

"The work is not finished, Eloise."

"But it is finished for me now that my mother is dead!" I exclaimed roughly. "I did everything the SOE asked of me. I went to Normandy. I've—"

"That's precisely my point," he interrupted me. "You have knowledge of the Normandy region that could be vital in the future. You will need to take time to process the news today and to make sense of it, but I know the fierceness of your spirit—I saw it every day when you were training. D-Day is surely approaching, Eloise, and France is the key to ending the war so that Europe can be free—" He broke off, then his voice dropped as he whispered, "So we can *all* be free."

"There is no precedent for the Germans injuring the families of agents on British soil, sir. Is there?" I said, throat tight.

"There are few precedents for any of this, Eloise," Turner said, and suddenly he seemed almost as tired as I was. He dropped his head back against the headrest and closed his eyes. "It's not uncommon for the Germans to figure out who our agents really are if they are arrested and now, we have someone on the inside sharing personal details so…who knows what comes next."

"But you can't seriously suspect a double agent at the very *top* of the organization," I said. He looked right at me, stricken as he nodded.

"That's exactly what I'm saying. Who else knows your real name? The details of your family? Those files are secure—only the highest echelons of the SOE can access them."

"But Mr. Booth would never," I said fiercely. "And Miss Elwood? Not a chance! And my God, if it's Colonel Maxwell, we're all doomed. It makes no sense, sir."

"You're just going to have to trust me when I say that I know for certain someone has divulged your identity and I am certain that there is a double agent. You must not breathe a *word* of this to any of them—not Elwood, not Booth, not Maxwell."

"But Elwood had Hughie for days after my mother died," I whispered. "If you don't trust her, why leave him with her?"

"It is an exceedingly difficult situation to understand, let alone to explain to you without putting you in still more danger. Maybe this person found themselves in an impossible situation," he said wearily. "And Eloise, you are just unlucky enough to have been sent to Normandy—the most contentious commune in France. Some bastard German was utterly determined to know who you were and our double agent possibly had no choice but to give you away, perhaps not even realizing your family would be exposed too. Every agent who goes into occupied territory gambles with their life, but *this* mission always put you at an extra level of risk."

"You make it sound like the double agent is powerless but there is always the choice to do the right thing. The betrayal is unforgivable," I said furiously. "Unimaginable! They should hang! Tell me you're close to exposing them."

"It *is* unforgivable. But it's also no surprise to any of us that these Germans are utterly ruthless. And please trust me when I tell you that I am handling this the best way I can," he said firmly, then softer, "Please believe me when I tell you I am doing my absolute best."

"I do, sir," I whispered. My eyes were burning with unshed tears, but I hated anyone to see me cry. I turned away from him to stare out the window. "I need to see my son, Mr. Turner. Please take me to him."

"I don't think you'll retire from the SOE—not until the war is finished. And if there is any possibility that I'm right about that, I strongly suggest you leave your boy where he is."

I closed my eyes. I imagined a future where I collected Hughie and took him back to our flat. We grieved my mother together. We established a normal life again—visits to the library, the park, the grocery store. Perhaps, if the Allies won the war, I would eventually come to terms with my decision to step back from the SOE. I'd unwrap that parcel of Giles's belongings. I'd learn to live with the reality that my husband's death was unfair and unjust and that was just the way it was.

But if the Allies lost? Britain would fall one day. My son

would grow up in a world where Nazi hatred reigned supreme. And I would have to live with the knowledge that I didn't do everything in my power to make the world a better place for him.

My heart sank. As exhausted as I was, as unthinkable as it was, I realized that I would return to France if the SOE did indeed ask me to. Maybe this time not for Giles, but for Hughie himself.

"I will need to meet this woman," I said. "I need to see where he's living. If you want me to entrust my son to her, I'll need to know who she is."

"It should be very apparent to you now that in the field, anything can happen. If you return to France and you're captured, you will take with you the details of every surviving shred of the Normandy networks with you in your mind. You can only be sure that your interrogation would be especially fierce—you cannot predict how you'll cope with that. If you genuinely have no idea where Hugh is, that is one less vulnerability they can use again you." To my frustration, a tear slipped from my eye, onto my cheek. I brushed it away impatiently. Turner sighed gently and dropped his voice. "I'll arrange for you to see him from a distance. Without his carer seeing your face, without *him* seeing you because that would be unsettling, you'll see that I'm right—he's perfectly safe and content."

"So only you will know where he is."

"That's right."

"And if something happens to me in France?"

"He'll be well cared for with this woman and her family."

"How can I go back to France, knowing there is a traitor in Baker Street?"

"You have to trust me when I tell you that there is one bad apple but the rest of our team are exemplary," he said heavily.

"And if something happens to you while I'm gone? What happens to my son?"

"The moment I resolve the situation with the double agent," he said, "I'll be sure to update your file with the precise detail of where he is."

"How did you find this woman?" I asked Turner the next day. We were sitting in his car on one side of a stretch of parklands opposite an historic convent. I was holding binoculars. Turner was tapping the steering wheel.

"Through a trusted friend," he said.

I didn't sleep a wink the previous night after he dropped me to my flat, in such a state of shock that at first, I collapsed in a heap on the sofa. After a while, I became cognizant of the smell in the flat. Food was rotting, laundry needed attention. I cleaned for hours, busying my hands while my mind adjusted to my new reality. Later, I lay for a while in Hughie's little bed, curled up in a ball. Then I moved to my mother's bed, still unmade, and I rested my head on a spare pillow, so I could lay and stare at the imprint from her head on her own pillow. I wept for the years when I resented her, and for those beautiful, unexpected years when we were close.

Turner told me he'd arranged a quiet, respectful graveside service at Sidcup Cemetery. My neighbors attended and so did he. He prepaid her headstone but said it didn't feel right for him to decide upon the inscription. Instead, he left it to me to contact the stonemason upon my return.

Mixed in with all of that grief and concern and shock was a thread of disbelief: a double agent in our ranks? Somewhere near the top of the agency? I was grateful that Turner, at least, could be trusted. Otherwise, I wasn't sure how I could even consider a return to the field. Agents were beyond vulnerable in occupied territory—entirely dependent on Baker Street to guide our decisions to keep us safe. I asked him to promise me that if I went back, he would keep a hand in my mission. He told me that he was already doing everything he could for all

agents in the field. "They're as safe as they can be," he assured
me. "And you will be too."

"Here they come," Turner said now, pointing.

For some reason I'd pictured Hughie's carer to be about
my age but she was older—maybe in her forties. They walked
slowly across the path because Hughie was holding her hand
but also because he stopped periodically to crouch low to the
ground, his other hand reaching toward various treasures. My
hands shook as I lifted the binoculars to my eyes. He was smiling, chattering away as he pointed to a flower.

There was something so reassuring about his smile in the
morning sunshine that day. I had feared that his cheeks would
be tearstained or that he'd be pale or lethargic from grief and
fear. That simply wasn't the case. He was well dressed, his hair
combed and his cheeks rosy, his smile and his speech both easy
and free.

"Does she speak French?" I asked, turning the binoculars
to the face of the woman standing in my place to care for my
son. She had a soft smile as she chatted with him, her expression fond and gentle even as Hughie dawdled. In that moment,
jealousy and gratitude were at war in my gut. I wanted to hug
her to thank her with every ounce of strength I possessed. At
the same time, I wanted to tear my son away from her and to
take him into my arms.

"Of course," Turner confirmed. "She speaks French so they
can communicate, but she is also teaching him English."

I stared through the binoculars at my son's face until it hurt
to keep looking. If I was going to do this, I would have to do
it quickly before my heart overruled my head. I dropped the
binoculars to my lap as if they had suddenly become too hot
to hold.

"One more mission," I said flatly, turning to Turner. "And
then I never want to hear from anyone at Baker Street ever again."

"If the next few months go as we hope they will," he said

soberly, "everyone at Baker Street will soon be busy trying to forget these years entirely."

"And if something happens to me in the field this time?" I asked, throat tight. "What will happen to him?"

"Had you not returned last time, the carer would have adopted him. That plan has not changed."

"And you'll update my file with his location the minute you resolve the security issue in our ranks."

"The moment I'm sure it's safe to do so."

"What do I tell Elwood about this? What do I tell Booth?"

"Nothing at all, Eloise," Turner said heavily. "They won't know to ask, and you can't breathe a word of this until I tell you otherwise."

We drove home from Beaulieu to Bexley in silence, each of us lost in our thoughts.

"Did you happen to see Chloe while you were in Paris?" Turner asked suddenly as we neared my flat.

"Yes," I said, but then I added quickly, "There was a crossover of only a few days. I didn't divulge any details of my mission to her."

"Did she talk to you about hers?" I hesitated, and he cleared his throat. "It's quite fine if she did. Her mission was complete by then, you're a trusted colleague. I know you trained together."

"We did talk about it a little," I admitted. "It sounds as though her circuit did some extraordinary work."

"Oh my, they truly did," Turner agreed. We fell silent again as he continued driving, and I thought the conversation was over until he said, "Did she mention her circuit leader?"

"Ah—" I was caught off guard by the question. "Why do you ask, sir?"

Turner cleared his throat.

"There was an indication at one point that she and her circuit leader may have become close. The consensus from Baker

Street was that she's a fine agent—a rule follower too—and that there was likely to be little substance to that rumor. It's obviously not ideal for agents to be in one place for too long so we shifted her to Paris anyway, but I wondered what your thoughts were."

"Well, you probably know even better than I do," I said carefully. "She and her circuit leader have been friends for years, and who knows what becomes of a relationship like that when two people are under pressure in the field."

"Who knows indeed…"

"But you can be sure that she's an agent with true integrity and she would never compromise the work of the SOE," I added hastily. "She's just not like that. Chloe is one of the good ones."

Turner nodded slowly.

"Yes," he said. "Yes, that's exactly as I thought."

Later that night after Turner returned me to Bexley, I sat cross-legged on my bed, the parcel from Giles's CO on the duvet in front of me. I stared at it for a long time, then finally, picked it up and opened it. Just as I'd expected, it contained a short note from his CO, offering sympathy for my loss, explaining that Giles had instructed that if he should perish, I should be forwarded the contents of the parcel.

Giles was a great man. You and your son can be very proud that he died a hero, Eloise.

Died a hero. What did those words even mean? Did it somehow make his death more meaningful that he had worked with courage until it happened? It certainly did nothing to ease the sting of the loss. I stared at the letter with frustration and scorn, but I quickly felt grief taking the place of my anger. I had to believe Giles's dedication to freedom, his belief in justice, his passion for peace—that all of this did make both his life and his death somehow worthwhile.

I had to believe that he and his sacrifice mattered.

Deeper in the parcel, I found an envelope addressed to me.

I opened it with shaking hands, and out first fell the photo of Giles with me during his last visit home. I looked so young in that photo, a different woman altogether than the one who stared back at me in the mirror now, even though only three years had passed.

And Giles? Staring into his eyes in that photograph made my chest ache and my eyes sting. He looked so *content*, so thrilled with the surprise twist in our story that Hughie represented. I missed my husband with every waking moment, but as I looked at that photo again, I felt my grief would overwhelm me for the rest of my life.

I couldn't do it. I could not read his letter. It would be the last words he ever spoke to me and that would mean he was really gone. I pushed it away as if it represented a physical danger to me, but then a thought sounded—if not now, *when*? I'd been tempted to open the parcel before my first mission, but I had the luxury then of knowing that if anything happened to me, my mother would know to share its contents with my son.

Just as Giles had left instructions to his CO to send me this parcel, I was the only person left who could do the same for Hughie, and I could be called up for my next mission at any time. Just like Chloe in the field, lamenting whatever the disagreement with her mother was, I had to ensure there was some kind of closure for my loved one left behind.

Weeping now, I unfolded the letter slowly, savoring the touch of the paper against my skin, knowing that it had last touched Giles's hands. A sob burst from my lips at the sight of his handwriting—that pretty, careful scrawl, almost too flowery to come from the pen of such a strong man.

Eloise, my love,
You have been the greatest blessing of my life. Whatever happens, know that I have loved and adored you with every breath since the moment I saw you behind that desk at Hatfield.

If this war takes my life, but one day you and our baby live in a world at peace, it will have been worth it. Make sure that they know that their father loved them even from afar. Make sure they know that I was certain that they would be good and brave and brilliant.

And as for you, Eloise, do not let rage consume you if I am lost. Be safe and be well, and be happy. You deserve all of those things, my love, with or without me.

I love you. I love you. I love you.
Giles

With shaking hands, I folded the paper up, and rested it gently in the little box I had picked up in Paris for Hughie. On top, I rested the photograph, and atop of that, the final item from the parcel: the rosary beads I gave to Giles the very last time I saw him.

The metal links were a little rusted now, the medal of St. Michael slightly bent. I tried not to think about whether Giles had those beads with him when he died. I tried not to picture another airman gently taking them from his pocket and washing them so I might have them back.

When I was called back into Baker Street just two days later for a meeting with Turner, I took that little box with me, stuffed with precious items for my son, including a note from me. It was so difficult to write and I could manage only a few lines before my emotions overtook me and I wound up weeping over the paper, but it was something. Giles's last words meant the world to me, and I wanted to do the same for my son.

Hughie,
It is so impossibly hard to leave you but I step back into this war driven only by the need to know that I did everything I could to build a better world for you. Be safe, and know that you were

loved and adored by both of your parents from the very first min-ute of your existence.

　　Be a great man, my son, just as your father was a great man. He lived his entire life in compassion, love and humility, and it is my hope and prayer that you will do the same.

Love always,
Your maman

"Make sure Hughie gets this if anything happens to me," I told Turner. "It's not much, but it will tell him who we were."

After seeing Hughie in the park that day, the only way I could convince myself to leave him again was to promise my-self that I was finishing my work for him, and only him.

CHAPTER 15

JOSIE
Paris, France
March, 1944

The Paris operation was nothing like the tight triad Noah, Adrien and I had formed. The *Success* circuit had several w/t operators, a dozen couriers, and when I first joined, one somewhat battered circuit leader, César. At our very first meeting he warned me that the circuit had suffered a recent spate of arrests.

"A few of my agents were here too long and maybe they got complacent…" he said, pinching the bridge of his nose. "One agent was arrested after he made a habit of eating lunch at the same place every day. Some agents probably pushed too hard in their recruiting. But we've had some baffling arrests. One of my w/t operators just disappeared into thin air. Local contacts I thought were completely secure have been captured. I'm starting to think the only explanation is that the Germans have someone in London. Maybe someone right near the top."

This prospect was fanciful—close to paranoid! The top ranks of the SOE were comprised of the most dedicated personalities I had ever encountered—Elwood, who was stern and could be cold, but who lived and breathed her work. Booth, who had been known to fall asleep midsentence, nap for a few moments, then wake up and get right back to working on some cryptography challenge. Turner, who loved to drink and would always offer a few pounds if the opportunity arose to gamble, but who was quick with a smile or to offer support, and who loved France with every fiber of his being. And Maxwell, who had a wife and children at home but made it very clear that so long as the war raged, his home family would be secondary to his work family.

"Not a chance," I told César. He seemed dejected to the point of depression, and at my dismissal of this idea, he sighed wearily.

"Perhaps it's someone here in France, then, but someone is exposing our methods and operations to the Germans. As you join us, you should know to watch your back."

I got to work right away. The *Success* circuit was a hotbed of resistance activity—stretching across the city and into the regions around it. I was constantly on the move, cycling or walking or catching trains, delivering messages directly or via dead drop. Sometimes I helped move supplies from one place to another, smuggling cash or small weapons or medicine.

I constantly wished that Noah had been transferred with me, or even in my place. The challenges the *Success* circuit faced were so immense and he was such a skilled agent—I was doing my best, but felt certain he'd have been better able to rise to the challenge than I was.

At times, the loneliness of my new role seemed more than I could bear. The very nature of my work in that large circuit was that I was moving between other agents and contacts constantly, never forming close bonds with any of them. As I sat alone in my room night after night, I had so much time to worry and to ruminate. I worried about Noah. Was he safe, was he well? Would we both survive to reunite after the war? I worried about Maman, and even Aunt Quinn, and everything we said to one another on that final, awful meeting.

German eyes were on me everywhere I went, the danger

every bit as intense in Paris as it had been in Montbeliard right after the bombing. In the first few weeks after my arrival, I heard of seven new arrests. I even had a close call myself during what I thought was a meeting with another courier. I arrived at the apartment to find the door unlocked, just as I had been told to expect, but when I pushed it open, two Gestapo officers were waiting.

"Name and papers," the first one said. After a split second of panic, I retrieved my falsified papers from my handbag.

"I'm Margot Barre," I said, giving them the new cover name I'd adopted with the move to Paris. I was trying to sound innocent, but my voice came out rough and uncertain. Their gazes sharpened as they looked back down at my papers. I forced a cough and peered around. "Is this the home of Dr. Le Lievre?"

"There is no doctor in this building."

"I have been very unwell," I said, dropping my eyes to the ground as I forced another miserable cough. "It is the scarlet fever, my mother thinks." I didn't miss the way both Germans took an automatic step back away from me. I raised my eyes to them now, trying to channel my genuine fear into artificial tears. "None of the doctors in Bougival could determine a cure. I'm staying with an aunt who tells me she was treated by Dr. Le Lievre at this address when she caught the fever herself in her childhood..." I let my voice trail off. "She did say it was many years ago and he might have retired..."

The men conversed quietly, but I caught enough of the conversation to know they were immediately in agreement that they should get me out of the apartment as quickly as possible. I tried to imagine myself through their eyes. A small, rail-thin woman with bags under her eyes—a woman who was genuinely shaking now, although in fear, not because of sickness. I was starting to look ill again—something I loathed but had so far been powerless to change. Fresh food in Paris was so difficult to come by. My faked ration card entitled me to purchase a small allotment of bread and cheese each day and a small portion of pasta and margarine once a week. I didn't dare eat a bite of any of that so had been swapping this food on the black market as much as I could. The trouble was there wasn't much worth swapping it for.

"Do you know Raimund Leandres?" one of the Germans asked. Raimund Leandres was the cover name of the courier I was due to meet, and my heart broke for him, knowing he was likely somewhere in a cell, facing unimaginable torture. "I don't know anyone in Paris except my aunt, officer," I said hesitantly. I'd be done for if they insisted on verifying my story with this "aunt." To my relief, they gingerly passed me back my papers and dismissed me.

Just a few days later, a message came from Veronique, one of César's w/t operators. Baker Street was alarmed at the way the circuit was crumbling and was recalling him to London immediately. Our new circuit leader would arrive within days.

I was waiting at the entrance to the Gare Saint-Lazare, pretending to read a newspaper. This was my third day waiting and I'd continue returning each day to meet the 2:00 p.m. train until the new circuit leader arrived. I knew only that he would be wearing a green tie, and he would be looking for me by my beige blouse.

I was eager to meet our new circuit leader to hear his plan to stabilize the situation. Even in the days since César was recalled, there had been more arrests of local resistance contacts. The network felt like an unstable floor beneath me, planks giving way just as I reached for them.

A fresh wave of travelers emerged from the station as the 2:00 p.m. train departed and I straightened, scanning the crowd until it thinned to a trickle. I was almost ready to go back to my room and try again the following afternoon, but then a familiar face appeared. I struggled to contain my surprise as my gaze dropped to the green tie against his chest. He nodded subtly, to indicate he'd seen me, and I began to walk in the opposite direction, knowing he would follow.

Once I was safely in the laneway, I tried to make sense of it. Mr. Turner? Here in Paris? It seemed a desperate and risky move for the organization to send one of its most senior officials. Things must have been even more tenuous for the circuit than I'd realized.

"Sir," I breathed when he finally joined me. "Is it true? Are you the new circuit leader?"

"Difficult times call for extraordinary measures and I convinced the others that I could manage things best from here." His eyes were kind as he smiled. "So here I am, back on home soil—as you are, Miss *Barre*."

"I have adopted an alternate cover story," I told him. "I had a close call last week. I'm now *Honorine Deschamps*."

"A close call?" he repeated, frowning. His gaze scanned me from head to toe and he asked, "Are you quite alright?"

"I went to a meeting and…" There was something strange about the way Mr. Turner was reacting to this news—as if it was especially shocking, or of unique concern. The miserable reality was that for someone in my position close calls were inevitable and Mr. Turner knew that as well as anyone. He had been part of the training regime that had taught me to expect it. "Sir, it doesn't really matter. I talked my way out of it and I'm fine. But we never quite know what to expect when we go to meetings in Paris now. You must know agents are dropping like flies."

"It is a concern," he said, still staring at me intently. "Listen to me, Chloe. We are going to work very closely together now. You are vital to my plans to restore stability here, do you understand? Take no unnecessary risks."

I gave him the address of a safe house where he could shelter for the night, and we agreed we'd meet the next afternoon once he'd secured a longer term apartment.

It was such a surprise to see Turner in Paris, but it was also a relief. He'd always taken a special interest in my training—offering an extra level of support and advice along the way. Mr. Turner was almost a father figure to me, and it was reassuring to know that once again, I'd be working with someone who knew me. Someone who genuinely cared about my welfare. After the loneliness I'd felt in those early weeks in Paris, that was an immense comfort.

Turner had been in Paris for a month and it had quickly become apparent that he was going to have to operate under his real name. His family was renowned in the city, famous for the expansive furniture business he managed until the occupation began. Everywhere he went, people knew who he was.

In training, they had warned us that if we found ourselves in a place we once called home, we were to refrain from meetings or accommodation in any areas we had previously frequented. That was easy for me—I'd lived most of my life on two blocks of the 18th Arrondissement, with forays to the Sorbonne while I was studying. It wasn't nearly so simple for Turner. The more I thought about it, the more shocked I was that he'd decided to return at all.

"It's a complication, but I do think it may be a blessing to be so well connected," he told me, the first time he showed me around the apartment he had rented. It was unusually plush for an agent, on the fifth floor of a large apartment block, featuring several living spaces and multiple bedrooms. It seemed excessive to me that one agent would opt to rent such a place, but Mr. Turner was an expert in SOE procedure. If he was able to rent the apartment cheaply through an old friend, and he was confident there was no risk in that, who was I to question the decision?

We established a system where, if he needed to see me, he would put a particular vase between the drapes in his living room—a window I could easily see from the street below.

"Walk past thrice daily," he instructed me.

"And how will I know where to meet you?" I asked.

"To start with, we'll meet here."

"Here?" I said, eyebrows high. "But…"

"This building is secure," he assured me. "It will be perfectly safe."

"Sir, my cover story is that I'm a nurse who works night shifts," I said uncertainly. "I need to maintain that so I can be on the street after curfew when you need me to work late. If I'm picked up or questioned, what will I say if they ask why I've been coming here repeatedly?"

"Good point. We'll need to change your cover story," he said, nodding. "Look, given I'm now operating under my own name, your new cover story will be that you're my commercial secretary, assisting me to rebuild my family business. Use one of your spare identity cards and adopt a new name."

"Is that your cover story too? That you're rebuilding your business?"

"Yes. Our furniture was once the finest in Paris, you see— that's why I'm so recognizable. We employed hundreds of people and had several factories and outlets across the city. It broke my heart to shut down operations but once the occupation began, the city was in such flux it became impossible to procure the raw materials we needed to operate."

"Will people really believe the business could function again? Wouldn't you have the same problems now?"

"I don't actually intend to rebuild it, of course," he said. "But yes, I believe it's plausible that I might be able to access the necessary materials now that the occupation has been in force for several years. People still need furniture, and supply chains exist if you know where to look."

"It must have been very difficult to walk away from your family legacy, sir," I remarked. Turner's expression dimmed.

"You have no idea. I used the last of my savings to escape to Sweden and from there, to London. As chance would have it, I went to boarding school with Freddie Booth so once he heard I was back in the UK, he begged me to help set up the SOE. They had no one in the agency with recent experience in France so I was happy to be of service."

As instructed, I walked past Turner's building morning, noon and just before curfew, but although I'd anticipated meeting directly with Turner only a few times a week, from the outset that vase was in the window at least once a day. It was well against our procedure for me to be coming and going from his apartment so often, but I told myself this was no different to the scenario in Montbeliard when Noah and I pretended to be spouses.

"Good day, Mlle. Fournier," the doorman greeted me one morning.

"Good morning," I said, trying to cover my surprise. How did he know my new cover name? I asked Turner, and he shrugged easily.

"I had to tell the staff something. They all seemed to assume you're my lover."

"People have already noticed me coming here?" I repeated, alarmed. He'd only been in the city for a few weeks!

Turner straightened and looked away as he murmured, "People always notice a woman like you."

But before I could even process such a comment, he was on to the next thing, passing me a notepad so I could scrawl down some instructions. It was only later, when I was alone at my new room, that I had the time to pause and reflect on the dynamic between us.

I wasn't sure how to interpret Mr. Turner's close attention to me. He'd never once been inappropriate, but he did ever-so-casually breach my personal space at times. He'd touch my lower back just gently as we went to move into a new room, or our fingers would brush as he passed me a notepad or took a cup of tea.

Maybe I'd have missed those moments if I saw him only occasionally, but I was with Mr. Turner every single day, and I was more perplexed with every passing hour. Sometimes, he'd put the vase in the window to call me upstairs, only to have me sit and wait *in case* courier work arose. I mentioned in passing the difficulties I was having finding fresh produce, and twice in that week I arrived to his apartment to find a basket of black market goods waiting for me. And the drinking! Turner had always enjoyed a hearty libation and during training this had presented no problems at all. Maybe he arrived a little ragged for early morning training now and then, but he'd always done his job brilliantly anyway. But now, not a day passed without him suggesting we share a bottle of wine. I always declined, preferring to keep a clear head, and sometimes he would drink the whole thing himself, right in front of me.

He was busy—rushing out to meetings, lamenting late nights recruiting. Sometimes he'd take on a strange, manic mood that I didn't know how to interpret. I'd see the vase in the window and rush up expecting orders, and instead, Mr. Turner would be drunk and rambling about his recent successes, seemingly unable to stop chatting or sit still. On one of those afternoons, he was lamenting the loss of the family business, talking about his frustration as his father's legacy slipped through his fingers in 1940.

"...and then of course, the Germans commandeered the factory," he told me, shaking his head. "That was the beginning of the end."

I frowned. "I... I seem to recall you said you were unable to get raw materials. That's why you had to cease operations."

"It was a combination of both," he said dismissively, and

then he went back to rambling about the "glory days" when his family's product was in every high-society home in Paris.

Which version was correct—the story where the business ran out of raw materials, or the story where the Nazis took it over? In the scheme of things, the confusion of facts did not matter much, except what possible reason did Mr. Turner have to lie?

Soon, he had been in Paris for six weeks. The arrests had all but stopped and he was making excellent progress, expanding our network of local contacts quickly and efficiently, preparing the city for what was hopefully an inevitable wave of Allied troops. But he'd also reshuffled the entire circuit, breaking it into two branches which would no longer interact. Given his unusual visibility operating under his real name, he had decided to keep some distance between himself and most of the network.

"Should I stay away from the apartment now, sir?" I asked him, more than a little relieved at the thought.

"I've got particular work in mind for you in the future so you'll maintain distance from the rest of the network just as I will. I'll still have you liaise directly with Veronique for updates to Baker Street, but any other messaging you're involved in will be completed by dead drop only."

I assured Mr. Turner I was at his disposal and prepared to start the new arrangement but felt a pang at the thought of being cut off from the other agents. Life in the field was lonely and it seemed the circle of allies around me was to shrink even further.

I shifted a few small sacks of flour, exposing the wooden shelving below, then stuffed a note into a large crack in the shelf, and put the sacks back in place. This grocer was a supportive local contact, and his flour shelf was my most frequent dead-drop location to reach an agent known as Campion. On my way out, I stopped to purchase some Jerusalem artichokes to mash for my dinner.

As I slipped back into the street to walk away, I saw Campion standing on the balcony across the street. He was leaning on the railing but the minute he caught my eye, he turned to walk back into the apartment, gesturing with his hand as he left, as if to draw me closer.

I wasn't sure what to do at first. Turner had made it quite clear that I would not liaise in-person with agents like Campion, but Campion was visibly distressed. In the end, I decided I had to investigate.

A few minutes later, I climbed the stairs to the apartment, my heartbeat thudding in my ears. Campion met me at the door and ushered me inside.

"I can't find Mahaut," he told me anxiously. Mahaut was a w/t operator, one I'd liaised with previously myself. "He missed a meeting with me a few days ago so I went to the safe house where he had been staying. His belongings are still there but the host told me he hasn't been in since last week. A local source said she'd heard a rumor that one of our agents went to a scheduled meeting and found the Gestapo waiting for him. Have you heard of any arrests in the last few days?"

"No," I assured him. "The arrests stopped shortly after César left."

"What are you talking about?" he said. "There have been countless arrests of local resistance operatives and I'm certain some of our agents have been arrested too. Hell, I've seen no one except you all week. No couriers, none of the w/ts. Something doesn't seem right."

"I'll talk to Turner," I said, bewildered. "Just sit tight."

I rushed back to the apartment, only to have Turner dismiss Campion's concern.

"I suspect Campion is simply hearing old rumors. We haven't lost a pianist—or an agent of any kind—since I arrived."

"Have you seen Mahaut yourself lately?"

"I have," Turner assured me. "He is free, active and doing good work."

"I need to go back to let Campion know," I said.

"Certainly. But remember—dead drop only."

"He's somewhat distressed, sir," I admitted. "I think he needs reassurance."

Turner nodded and reached for a notepad. He scribbled down a brief note, then handed it to me.

"Use your drop box. I'll meet him myself tonight—the details are all in the note. It won't take me long to clear this up."

Turner seemed every bit as comfortable in Paris as he had in England—still quick to offer a smile, at ease and relaxed. Not a single thing about his body language suggested to me that he was lying about Mahaut's fate. Still, I still tossed and turned that night, mulling it all over in my mind. I told myself that while a certain degree of paranoia was helpful and useful in the field, Turner—of all people!—knew what he was doing. I was in a position where I *had* to trust him, and second-guessing his every decision was not helpful. I had to let it go.

A few days later, I rode my bicycle to meet Veronique to deliver another update.

"Turner requests some munitions and more cash—both francs and marks," I told her. "Another week of no arrests."

She frowned.

"But that's..." she blurted, but quickly broke off, shook her head and looked away, pursing her lips. "Never mind. Copy that."

"What's wrong?"

"It doesn't matter."

"Veronique. Please, tell me."

"Campion was arrested this week," she said flatly, her tone almost accusing. I stared at her in shock.

"What? When!"

"A few nights ago. He went to a meeting and the Gestapo were waiting for him."

"That's..." I glanced at her uncertainly. "Are you sure? When was this meeting?"

"I don't know. I heard about it secondhand. All I know is that he was anxious about his situation the last time I spoke with him and now he's probably at Avenue Foch." The mention of that address was enough to send chills down any agent's spine. It was the headquarters of the counter-intelligence branch of the SS, the *Sicherheitsdienst*.

I had little rapport with Veronique. We'd only met in person a few times, and at every encounter, I'd found her cold almost to the point of hostility. W/t operators had the hardest job of all—their encryption methods were incredibly complex and they were constantly on the run, stalked endlessly by the Germans with their radio direction finding equipment. Veronique had already outlasted the rumored six-week average time frame a w/t operator in Paris evaded arrest. At times, when she'd been abrupt with me, I'd wondered if she was buckling under the strain.

Now, I wondered if she, like me, just had no idea who she could trust.

Something was definitely off. I just did not know how to figure out where the rot was coming from.

I was treading very carefully with Mr. Turner now. I wanted badly to trust my circuit leader, but the timing of Campion's arrest left me uneasy. A few days after I spoke with Veronique, he called me to his apartment and asked me to deliver some cash to an address in the 4th Arrondissement. As I was leaving, I noticed a slip of paper, curled up beside the hallway runner.

I didn't break stride as I bent to scoop it up, stuffing it into my brassiere as I walked down the stairs to the street. And only once I'd completed my drop and returned to my own room did I fish it out to read it.

It was a notice of debt—1000 francs, due within a week. There was no name on the notice—not even an address. But beside the total due, someone had scrawled the word *blackjack*.

I told myself it didn't matter one bit if Mr. Turner was gambling after hours at some sketchy underground club. Even during SOE training schools, when the instructors would walk us to pubs, to ply us with drinks to see if alcohol loosened our tongues, Mr. Turner was known to always seek out the local bookmaker. Like his drinking, gambling had never hampered his work. And perhaps *this* gambling club was where he was recruiting new contacts.

If I hadn't already been feeling uneasy, I'd have convinced myself to ignore that little slip of paper, but my senses were on high alert. I buried it under a loose floorboard in my room, the place where I kept my spare counterfeit currency and identity cards—my other "insurance policies."

CHAPTER 16

CHARLOTTE
Liverpool, England
1970

"I just wanted to check in on Noah," Theo tells me quietly when he calls a few days later. "I've been thinking about him. I hope he's alright. I'm just so sorry the meeting with Jean was…"

"…a disaster?" I finish miserably.

Theo sighs.

"Is your dad ready to talk about it yet?"

"No," I mutter. I've tried—*God*, how I've tried. Every time I strike up a conversation with Dad, he snaps at me or makes an excuse to leave the room. Each night, he retires early, locking himself in his bedroom with the dog. He wasn't this irritable even in the depths of acute grief and I am beside myself with worry. "I know he's a good man. He would never, *ever* have done anything to put those other agents in danger. And if Marion or Jean were trying to suggest my dad was a double agent, then—" I break off, indignant. "Of course he wasn't! I mean, right? Just because Dad's memories of the time aren't the best and he says he feels a little guilty about something does *not* mean he betrayed his country. It sounds like it made good sense for them to pull over that day. Maybe if they *had* surrendered, Fleur would still be alive and my dad wouldn't have wound up in hospital. Right?" Theo doesn't say anything, so I try again. "Right, Theo?"

"It was very hard to get a read on their conversation at Jean's house, especially because your dad isn't ready to discuss it yet. This isn't the first time I've heard a rumor of a double agent in the SOE ranks. But to lead a group of agents directly into an ambush would make little sense even if your dad was conspiring with the Germans. I mean—why risk his own life when he could have just called them and given them the location of a safe house?" Theo breaks off, then adds quickly, "Not that I'm suggesting he *was*..."

I know my dad wouldn't betray his country, but I've been too outraged by the very suggestion of it to think it through as logically as Theo has.

"Thank you," I say, exhaling with relief. "Yes. That's right."

"What's your plan now? Will you just wait and see if your dad decides he wants to talk about it some more?"

"Actually, no," I say. "Dad set out to thank the agent who saved his life, remember? He was content to just lay flowers on Remy's grave if he'd died."

"You want to keep going."

"I know Fleur died in the war, but I figure there's probably a grave or memorial somewhere and I want to try to find it. Maybe even a living relative. Remember Dad said he'd be content just to make sure Remy's family knew what he had done? Perhaps the same will apply to Fleur. I know we're back to square one, but I just don't know what else to do. This obviously means so much to Dad and I feel like I've let him down somehow."

"Charlotte," Theo says thoughtfully. "I don't suppose you're free to meet for lunch?"

Theo and I meet at a small pub just a few blocks from the house I share with Dad. Today, he has a smudged thumbprint on the lens of his glasses, and I can't stop wondering if it's obstructing his vision. One errant wave in his hair has formed a curl that sits at a wild angle away from his forehead. But his eyes are always so soft and kind, and I'll be eternally grateful to Theo for his support over the past week.

"I love being a teacher," I tell him. We've ordered our meals and we're sitting at the bar as we wait. "But summer break is great, isn't it?"

"I don't disagree with you there," Theo says, knocking his glass of beer gently against mine before he asks, "Why did you go into teaching?"

"Mum was a teacher and I always felt drawn to it," I say, my gaze dropping momentarily, before I clear my throat and ask, "And you? Why did you choose this career?"

"I loved the idea of becoming knowledgeable about history so that I could help people piece together their own family stories, just as I do with the family history group at the church. But I also have to earn a living, and trying to get the next generation excited about history is a great thing too."

"That's noble," I say. Theo shrugs awkwardly.

"What we read about in reference texts is the equivalent of viewing the events of the past from a thousand-foot view. When you narrow your focus down to individuals you realize that what makes these lofty events world-changing is that they change a whole lot of individual lives, and through that, they change the future. Just look at your father. If this agent hadn't saved your father's life at Salon-La-Tour in 1945, *you* wouldn't exist. Professors speak of history at university in generalist, abstract terms, but when you break it down, it really couldn't be more personal."

"So history has been a lifelong passion for you?" I ask him. He hesitates for just a moment.

"My degree says I studied 'modern history,' but my passion is narrower than that. My birth parents died in the war and

I never had the chance to know them. My fascination stems from there."

"I'm sorry."

"I've made peace with the fact that I'll never understand who I might have been if things had worked out differently, but it took me a very long time to reach that place. I remember what it felt like to know that there were questions about my past I could never resolve. I love the idea of helping others to avoid the torment of working through that. That's probably why I want so badly to help your father."

The waitress places our food on the bar and Theo flashes me a smile.

"Bon appétit," he says.

I get halfway through my bacon sandwich before I pause to ask, "Do you think I'm right? Do you think Dad might feel better if we find a way for him to honor Fleur somehow?"

"I'm not sure you should ask me for advice on this, Charlotte, given my efforts so far have only made everything worse," Noah says wryly. "Perhaps we can make some inquiries and if we find out something of her *then* we could let your father know?"

"That's not a bad idea. But we really are back to the drawing board."

"Looking for a female agent might be easier than looking for a male agent," Theo muses. "There weren't nearly as many, for a start."

"How many were there?"

"There were hundreds of men but maybe only a few dozen women. There were media reports about some of the women of the SOE in the first few years after the war ended. There were even some biographical films, you might recall."

"Yes, I watched a few of those films at school," I murmur. "That's probably why I assumed this would be easy. It's such a contradiction that those films were made and readily available to the public, yet decades later, there's still such strict secrecy around other facets of the SOE."

"It was a hugely controversial program and I can see why. When it all boils down, women with no combat experience to speak of were dropped behind enemy lines. At best, they had a few months of intensive training. Many had even less than that. They were treated very harshly if they were captured, and I suspect that many died in terrible circumstances. It makes sense to me that the families of the wives and mothers and daughters who never came home would want their heroism to be known...that some might contact newspapers or work with filmmakers whether the government wanted them to or not. If you like, I can search through the microfiche at the university library to see if I could find some of those newspaper articles. Perhaps we'll get lucky, and this 'Fleur' might belong to one of those families who spoke to the press early on."

"Genius!" I exclaim. "Thank you. And do you think perhaps we should try Professor Read again?" Theo's face falls, and I hastily explain, "I just meant because he did manage to help us find Remy. And quickly, too."

"Yes, he did rather," Theo murmurs. He looks down at his plate, sighs, then looks back to me. "Charlotte, Harry is quite upset with me so I suggest you contact him yourself this time. Mrs. White will probably let you through now that she knows you, but you should leave me out of it—for your own benefit."

"Oh, yes," I mumble, wincing. "Sorry. I didn't mean to suggest... I can call the office on my own."

"Don't apologize." Theo smiles sadly. "I made an error of judgment, and Professor Read caught me out in it. Don't hold that against him, please. He has every right to be angry with me."

I want desperately to ask him for the details, but that feels like invading his privacy, and so I leave it there. But as we part that day, he reminds me that he'll go searching for those news articles, and we agree to meet again for coffee the following afternoon.

* * *

"Tell me you have good news," I greet Theo when I open the front door the next day. "I called the university six times today. Six! The phone is just ringing out. The same thing happened last week when I called, but at least then, Mrs. White finally answered after lunch. No such luck today."

"Ah. Harry barely answers the phone even when Mrs. White tells him he has to and he never touches it when she's not there. Mrs. White does work some interesting hours over the summer, so you might have to keep trying for a while," Theo says, just as Wrigley hops down the hallway toward us. Theo's face lights up. "Cute dog! I always wanted a golden retriever when I was a kid but my dad is allergic to dogs." Wrigley, clearly recognizing a new ally when he sees one, makes his way toward Theo. His tail wags vigorously as Theo crouches to scratch his head. "Hello, boy. Who's a good boy, then?"

"He is indeed a very good boy," I confirm, watching as Wrigley looks up at me, deliriously happy to have the attention from this new friend, and without pausing to brace myself or consciously deciding to say it, I add, "He lost his leg trying to get help to my mum last year. He's a hero."

Theo frowns as he rises to his full height again, his gaze gentle as he looks into my eyes again.

"I'm sorry about your mum, Charlotte. I'm not sure if I've said that before now."

"Thanks," I say. I look away and blink to try to clear the tears that rise.

"That sounds like quite a story," Theo says gently. "I'd like to hear it one day if you want to talk about it."

"Let's make some tea and we'll see how we go," I sigh, welcoming him inside. Theo follows me to the kitchen. I take two cups from the drawer and flick the kettle on.

"This house is beautiful," he remarks.

"My parents' dream house," I say, but when I turn back to

face Theo, all I can see are my mother's favorite features of the house—the pine paneled cathedral ceiling, the dark exposed beams, the cork floor. Behind him, through the double glass doors that lead to the backyard, I see the garden where Mum and Dad spent so many weekends side by side.

"There were times when I was younger when I felt every-thing that happened in my life—big or small, happy or sad—led my mind right back to the question of who my biological parents were and what became of them," Theo says. I wince inwardly, cursing myself and the rawness of my emotion. Here I am complaining about losing Mum after sharing more than twenty years with her to someone who never knew his parents at all. Theo smiles kindly as if he's read my mind. "Grief isn't a competition. It can't ever be compared, actually. I'm just tell-ing you that because I want you to know that as I got older, I learned how to live with the reality I faced even though I'd never have chosen it."

"Mum was a teacher. She was teaching grade six last year. She was always a morning person and she always loved to walk, so she'd get up before dawn and take Wrigley for a nice long stroll before school," I blurt. "Dad woke up that day to the sound of Wrigley crying, scratching at the window to their bedroom." I wave vaguely toward their room—the largest bedroom, right at the front of the house. "There was blood everywhere—all over the window and at the front door. His front leg was badly broken and he was alone. Dad woke me up so I could try to help Wrigley. I had no idea what was going on but I knew it was bad. I carried the poor thing inside and he was howling in pain and distress. Dad knew Mum's walking route, so he ran to check on her."

I turn toward the kettle as it starts to whistle. I flick it off at the switch then reach for two tea bags, frustrated with myself. Why am I telling Theo all of this? I barely know him, and this is going to make me cry. I can't seem to stop myself though.

The words are tumbling out even as I'm making cups of tea, my voice rough with tears and anger and frustration at the injustice of it.

"Dad found Mum a few blocks away. Someone had run off the road—pinning Mum and probably Wrigley between a fence and their car. But the bastard reversed out and drove off and left them both to die, and the police never found out who did it. That dog ran three blocks on a shattered front leg to try to get help, and because of his bravery, Dad got to be with Mum as she took her last breath. He got to…" I pause to clear my throat and collect myself. "To tell her he loved her one last time and he got to hear her say it back. When I say Wrigley is a hero, I really mean it."

I exhale when I finish, and I'm startled to find the breath comes easier than the ones before it. I haven't talked much about Mum's death since Billy and I broke up. He told me that I had to let it go. It had been months since her death but I just kept going on and on about it and I "wasn't fun anymore." I told myself I'd stop burdening him and tried hard to stop talking about Mum and my shock and my grief, but within a week of that conversation I realized I resented Billy McDougal so much I could barely stand the sight of him.

Not *fun* anymore? Of course I wasn't fun. I missed my mother so much it hurt to breathe.

I told Billy I needed some time and he called me a miserable bitch. I handed back my engagement ring then and there, and that was the end of it.

I crawled inside of myself after all that. I stopped talking about Mum altogether, even to my friends. You're not supposed to be depressed and grieving for a parent in your early twenties—you're supposed to be out enjoying life and building a career and making good things happen. I tried to pretend that's exactly what I was doing, even if I felt miserable the whole time. I couldn't talk to Dad because he was grieving too.

I couldn't talk to Aunt Kathleen because every time I saw her, my throat seemed to close over. Almost every moment I spent with her for most of my life, Mum was there too. Aunt Kathleen never wants to spend time with me *and* Dad, but it hurts to be alone with her.

It's been hard to carry my grief all alone but I told myself it was easier to do that than it was to try to share it with someone else only to have them push me away.

I turn back to Theo, expecting to find him staring awkwardly at the ground. But no—Wrigley is at his side, tail wagging vigorously as he leans against Theo's leg, but even as he pets the dog Theo is looking right at me, his eyes brimming with compassion.

What a relief it is to find myself in the company of a man who is not terrified of difficult emotions.

"No one should have to lose a loved one like that," he says softly. "Life is so unfair sometimes."

"It really is," I say, then look down at the cups in my hand and offer him one with a feeble laugh. "After all of that, do you actually want a cup of tea or did I just make you one to give myself something to do while I was spilling my darkest trauma at you?"

He laughs gently too as he accepts the cup, but quickly sobers.

"I couldn't find anything in the microfiche about 'Fleur.' I'm sorry, Charlotte."

"Ah," I say. "That would be too easy, wouldn't it? Thanks for trying anyway." A sudden thought strikes me. "Oh no! I've also gotten nowhere with Mrs. White so you drove all the way up here for nothing."

For a minute, Theo looks dumbstruck, but then he says unconvincingly, "Oh, I had a friend to check in on up here anyway."

I don't believe him, but I am starting to suspect Theo might be enjoying my company as much as I'm enjoying his, and that sends a warm flush through me.

"Want to come and sit out in my dad's beautiful garden?" I suggest. His glasses are askew. There's a faded stain on the white T-shirt he wears. But he smiles all the way up to those big, kind eyes and I never want him to leave.

"I'd be delighted."

The afternoon has flown by, and Theo and I are still in the garden chatting when I remember I've been meaning to try Harry's office again. He refreshes our cups of tea while I'm inside sitting at the hall table, listening to the number ring out. I sigh impatiently as I hang up, then we automatically wander back out to the garden and take our seats again.

"No luck?" he surmises as he passes me my tea. I shake my head. "She'll answer eventually. Keep trying."

"I will," I say. He hesitates, then he clears his throat.

"I suppose that must have seemed strange last week with me and Harry."

"It did."

"You might have noticed a rather imposing locked door behind his desk."

"I wondered about that."

"Harry has access to all manner of classified files. With supervision, his students can assist with recording or transcribing oral histories, but from there, every little record is kept under lock and key—usually at the national archives, although from time to time he brings specific objects to the university for concentrated work. He treats every single object as sacred. I'm certain that's why he has Mrs. White sat way down the other end of that hallway—it makes no sense given how closely they work together, but she smokes like a chimney and he won't allow cigarette smoke near historic documents. Every object that he signs out from the archive is taken under lock and key into that secure room."

"What does that have to do with you?" I ask. Theo stretches out his legs and crosses them at the ankles, then looks up to the blue sky above us.

"Do you remember I asked your father if they took the car that day at Salon-La-Tour because Fleur had injured her ankle?"

"Yes. How *did* you know to ask that?"

He turns toward me. Our eyes meet and lock, and we're fully clothed and sitting outside, but there's something almost intimate about this moment.

"Remember yesterday when I told you that history is personal?" When I nod, he goes on. "It is true that I am most likely an orphan, but I know virtually nothing about my birth parents. I lived in an orphanage until I was seven, and then went to live with the Sinclairs. I adore them, truly. They're a brilliant couple and they did everything they could to build a family around me. As I grew older, my curiosity about my birth parents started to really burn within me, and that always felt like a betrayal of the Sinclairs. It didn't help that when I tried to ask them about my other family, they would only tell me that my biological parents both died in the war. That I should be proud of them for fighting for their country, but that I had to leave it at that."

"They were afraid of losing you."

"Yes, I think so. And perhaps they were worried I'd be disappointed if I went looking for answers and couldn't find them. I wanted to respect their wishes, but around the time of my eighteenth birthday, I thought I'd go mad if I didn't try. I waited until they were out one day and went through the drawer in their bedroom where they kept special paperwork. I found my official adoption documents and the name of the orphanage, along with a transcript detailing some very curious remarks from the judge who officiated over court proceedings about me."

"Curious how?"

"The words 'unknown identity' and 'undocumented surrender' featured heavily," he says, smiling weakly as I gasp. "I couldn't leave it alone after that, regardless of how much Mum and Dad wanted me to. A few weeks after my birthday, I told Dad I had to drive to the university to clarify course options and he let me borrow his car. Instead, I drove to the orphanage. It was hours away from our house in London, way down in Hampshire in the middle of nowhere."

"Were your parents angry?"

"They still don't know," he admits. "I don't suppose they would be angry now. At the time, it was probably the worst thing I'd ever done. I was a child who liked to please, you see."

"I'm sure," I say wryly. "I'll have you know, I was an angelic child, too."

"Yes, even from this angle I can see the faintest trace of your halo," he says wryly, and I smile in spite of myself. "My memories of the time before the Sinclairs took me in had been foggy but as soon as I arrived, I remembered the place. St. Brigid's, it's called—it's a convent, but they also run a school and an orphanage. Once I introduced myself, the Mother Superior remembered my surrender because it was such an odd situation. Out of the blue, a man arrived with me in tow and begged her to help. He said my mother had been posted overseas and there was no one else to care for me. He assured them she would be back to collect me within a few months."

"Wasn't there paperwork? A birth certificate, or some kind of admissions form?"

"No," Theo says, sighing. "Mother Superior had been told that my situation was fraught and it was best if she knew little about me—for my own protection, supposedly. It seems madness by today's standards but you have to remember, the world was in chaos. She really thought she was doing the right thing. It was an immense shock to learn that I was surrendered without so much as a surname or a date of birth."

"Of course it was," I murmur. "You poor thing. What birthday do you celebrate?"

"What my parents call my birthday is the day I was surrendered. They rounded down by a few years—so it roughly matches my biological age, I suppose."

"And that was just...it? Your parents never returned for you?"

"Mother Superior said they came back just the once a few weeks after my surrender. The man—my father?—called and asked them to take me to a park some distance away. He specifically insisted that someone not wearing a habit or identifiable clothing be the one to accompany me. Mother Superior agreed because she assumed I was still in grave danger. That was the last time anyone heard from either one of them. The orphanage cared for me for a few years after the end of the war, hoping my parents would return, but they never did. They just disappeared without a trace."

"How awful," I say. I can't even imagine what it would be like to be as disconnected from my own history as Theo is from his. I feel my mother's absence every minute of every day—but at least I know the shape of the space she used to fill. "I'm really sorry about all of this, I really am, but what does this have to do with Professor Read?"

"Ah, this is where it gets complicated," Theo says. "At eighteen, I was upset by what I'd learned but too anxious about having disobeyed my parents in digging into it, so I kept it all to myself. Time marched forward. I went to university and majored in history and gradually narrowed my study focus to the war. That's when I discovered that I had been wrong in my estimation about that little convent orphanage in the middle of nowhere. I mean, it is little, and it is a convent orphanage... but it happens to be in Beaulieu. That's the tiny village right in the epicenter of the cluster of properties used for the SOE's finishing school."

"Oh!" I say, comprehension dawning. "You think your father was in the SOE?"

"I suspect both parents may have been, actually," he says. "It's the only explanation I can think of for the secrecy. I suppose the other thing you need to know is that when I arrived at that orphanage, I didn't speak a word of English."

"Were you mute?"

"Oh, no. Mother Superior told me I was quite the chatterbox and I learned English quickly enough, but when I first arrived there I spoke only French."

"My goodness," I say, shaking my head. "You are an interesting man, Theo Sinclair."

"Only in this aspect," he laughs. "The rest of the time I'm a dreadfully uncool history teacher. My dad is an Oxford man so I'd been studying there, and he just about disowned me when I transferred to Manchester, but when I joined all of the pieces of my own past together, it was clear to me that Professor Read was probably the only person on earth who could figure out who I really was."

"And did he?"

"Much like you and Noah, I assumed that I would be able to tell him what I knew and that he would fill in the rest of the picture. As you now know, it doesn't work that way, but Harry is a very kind man. He told me he was very sorry for my situation but that he couldn't reveal anything that remained classified. I was disappointed at first, but also genuinely fascinated by his work, so I did spend a lot of time lurking in his office in my final year of undergrad studies. After a while, he told me there was one agent who had a child around my age, but that child does not share my name and was never surrendered to an orphanage. So, I had to let it go, and for a long time, I did. I had just about completed my Master's, and Harry was help-

ing with my PhD application—he was to be my supervisor."
His eyes grow distant for a moment and I know he's thinking
about what might have been, but then Theo shakes himself and
continues. "One day, I left his offices. I got all the way to my
car before I remembered I left something on my desk I needed
that night. My office was in one of those little rooms in the
rabbit warren hallway between Mrs. White's desk and Harry's
office, and he obviously didn't hear me come back. He's a mild-
mannered sort and it's rare for him to raise his voice, but he
was so excited he was just about shouting into the phone. It
was something about a medical record accidentally placed in
another agent's file. All I remember is Harry laughing and saying, 'You have to admit it was starting to look as though she
disappeared into thin air—this is all we've ever found.' Well,
obviously *that* caught my attention—especially when I heard
him explaining that this file mentioned a woman's abdominal
surgery in 1942 and speculating about whether this was a eu-
phemism for an 'illegitimate' pregnancy."

"No!" I gasp.

"I couldn't just barge in and let him know I overheard a call
he'd obviously timed for after I left, but I barely slept a wink
that night wondering. I hoped he'd fill me in the next day, but
he didn't say a word. We were working together in his office
that afternoon, reviewing a transcription I'd made from a recorded interview, when Harry got up to go to the bathroom
and I realized he'd left his keys on the desk..." Theo sucks in
a breath, then covers his eyes. "Charlotte, you can't tell anyone this. Promise me. Both Harry and I could get in all kinds
of legal trouble."

"Of course I won't," I promise.

"I pulled the fire alarm."

"Oh! Wow," I say, jaw dropping. "That's brave."

"It was absolutely not brave. It was impulsive and quite stupid."

"What happened?"

"I assumed Harry evacuated when the alarm rang, but I also knew the campus staff would quickly realize it was a false alarm and I probably had no more than ten minutes before he'd return. I took his keys and opened the secure room. Inside, there was a long, high bench lit by a line of very bright study lamps. And right there on the bench sat a file for an agent code-named Fleur. Hundreds of pages were sorted into neat piles."

"The woman who saved my dad's life!" I gasp. "You've seen her file?"

"Very briefly, yes," Theo says. "It was immensely thick, so I knew she wasn't the agent Harry was excited about. I mean, he just mentioned only ever finding a single page, right? And *that* was the page I wanted to find so I started searching around the desk. Right on the top of one of the piles of paperwork, I found an incident report about a parachuting accident—Fleur landed badly in training and injured her left ankle. But I was running out of time and as interesting as all of that was, it wasn't worth risking my career for, so I turned to leave. That's when I realized that in a darker corner of the room, a corner I'd assumed was just more filing cabinets, was an area Harry has set up specifically for close photography. He has fixed flash light stands and a tripod and the like there, and in the center of all of that was a single page from a medical report for an agent with the operational name 'Chloe.'"

"Oh my God."

"The report was very short, so even in ten seconds I just about memorized the whole thing. Chloe was much slimmer than her examiner would have liked, so he was recommending she be provided with extra lard and bread at breakfast and dinner. Her medical history was unremarkable except for 'abdominal surgery' in early 1942."

"That's it?"

"That's it," Theo sighs. "That's all I learned."

"When were you taken to the orphanage? And how old were you?"

"I wasn't surrendered until 1944—about six months after that medical examination. And given my size and development at the time, the director thinks I was probably two."

"It's a fit!"

"Yes. I wonder if my father was caring for me while she trained, perhaps even when she was deployed, and then he surrendered me when his own work called him away. Without more of her record...without knowing who *he* was...there's no way to know for sure. So...imperfect as it is, I still believe this random page is the closest I've ever come to identifying an agent who *might* have been my mother."

"Did you find out Chloe's real name?"

He sighs sadly. "If only. That page only listed her operational name. I'm guessing that Chloe's own file was lost or destroyed, perhaps in that dreadful fire in 1946."

"That's such a shame. But I still don't understand why Read was so angry with you that day we met him."

"Ah, that's the simplest part of all of this. Your father mentioned they had to drive because Fleur couldn't walk. He seemed to be struggling to explain himself, so I tried to prompt him and asked if she'd hurt her ankle. Remember?"

"I do."

"I completely forgot that I only knew Fleur had a history of ankle issues because I read the incident report in her classified file."

"Of course." I wince. "So Harry didn't catch you that day?"

"He suspected right away, actually," Theo says, groaning as he covers his face with his hands. "Harry went to the evacuation point after I pulled the fire alarm and there were only a handful of people there so it was obvious I was missing. He confronted me as soon as he came back upstairs. Maybe we could have gotten past it if I'd been honest, but like the bloody idiot I am, I flat-out denied I'd been in the file room and we argued. Eventually he gave me the benefit of the doubt and allowed me to stay on to finish up my Master's but our relationship was never the same. I changed paths after that. To be honest, I was so ashamed of lying to Harry, I realized I had to make peace with the uncertainty of my origin, and to do that I had to move on from that area of study. I suppose I probably set up the family history group as some kind of penance. I can't change what I did that day in Harry's office, but I can help others to find their own stories. I do get a lot of joy out of it. You should have seen Mrs. Underwood a few weeks ago when she managed to find her grandfather's birth certificate all on her own! It's so fulfilling seeing those men and women finding their own pasts, even if I can't find mine. And I do enjoy teaching, even if it's not what I thought I'd wind up doing."

"Thanks for telling me," I say. Theo gives a self-conscious shrug.

"So now you know. Mrs. White dumped you and your dad into the hands of a criminal mastermind so ineffective he accidentally confessed to his accuser right at the scene of the crime."

"Have you considered the possibility that this Chloe might still be alive?" I ask Theo suddenly.

"I have to believe that if she survived the war, she would have come back for me."

A sudden thought strikes me.

"I could ask Dad…"

"If he knew Chloe?" Theo pauses, then shrugs. "I suppose you could. It's certainly true that the male agents outnumbered the women ten to one. The odds aren't astronomical that he might have met her. But even if he did happen to come across her, it doesn't help me much. He wouldn't know her real name or any details about her life."

"Even if he has a memory of her, that would be something

that you could *know*," I say, thinking of the way I *knew* my mother, and how every aspect of that knowledge is precious to me now. Theo smiles sadly.

"I suppose there's no harm in asking."

CHAPTER 17

ELOISE
Paris, France
June, 1944

"I don't care if the weather is bad," I exclaimed, as I stood beside a bomber at RAF Harrington Airfield, mirroring the pilot's posture as he stared up at a stormy sky. Beside me stood Remy, an agent I'd met two nights earlier on our first attempt at the flight. "Bad weather in England does not mean bad weather in Corrèze. Let's *go*."

"What do you think?" the pilot asked Remy, who shrugged.

"We can always turn back again if it's too rough."

I'd never been a patient woman, but now, every night we delayed meant another night away from my son. I just wanted my mission to begin so I could come home.

The bad weather that week did at least help the cause in a roundabout way. While Hitler's men were listening to fake radio chatter from Dover and preparing for a fair-weather invasion at Pas de Calais, the Allies launched a surprise invasion during a break between two thunderstorms the previous night, successfully landing via the sloping, inhospitable beaches of Cotentin Peninsula near Caen. The mood across the UK was euphoric. We had a long way to go, but the tide of war was turning. And now, as soon as I could convince this pilot to take me there, I'd be parachuting to a field outside of Limoges to meet with my new circuit leader.

"Okay." The pilot turned back to nod toward Elwood, who was standing a few feet away, reading from a clipboard. "I heard this weather might last another week, so this might be as good as it gets."

An hour later, I was walking through the usual procedure—Elwood double-checking each item of clothing and my pockets, issuing me my new identity documents.

I'd called Turner's secretary a few times since I received my orders, but she was noncommittal about his availability. My last attempt had been that very morning, when I called into her office and told her in-person that I was being deployed.

"I really need to speak with him before I go," I said flatly.

"I'm sorry," she said, giving me a bewildered shrug. "I can't tell you where he is because I don't know where he is. It's top secret."

I had not spoken to Mr. Turner in two months—not since a week after my return from Normandy, when he called me at home, sounding harried and rushed, to ask me to take over his role training new recruits until my mission details were finalized. Higher priority work was taking him away, he told me, but I wasn't to worry—he had everything under control.

I'd been grateful for a distraction and had stepped into his shoes happily—but now that I was about to head back to France, I wanted reassurance. Had the security issues at the top of the organization been resolved? Was I in safe hands? Was my *son* still safe?

Turner specifically told me *not* to mention our conversations about a double agent to Elwood, but this was my last chance to inquire about him, and so I drew in a breath and asked, "Is Mr. Turner coming to see us off?"

She seemed confused by the question.

"Didn't he explain this to you when he asked you to step in with the recruit training? He's been called away."

"He didn't say when he'd be back," I said.

"Is something wrong, Fleur?" she asked, eyebrows knitting. "Anything you would speak to Gerard about you can also speak about with me."

But that wasn't true at all. I still could not imagine that Elwood was the SOE's bad apple but I also couldn't take the risk of being wrong about that and perhaps ruining Turner's operation to expose her.

"Everything is fine, Miss Elwood," I said quietly.

She assessed me carefully, then nodded and signed the final line on her paperwork.

"Colonel Maxwell sends his very best wishes," she murmured. "We all know you'll represent us—and Britain—well."

"I won't let you down," I said.

"That's the last thing in the world I'm worried about," Elwood said, as I spun on my heel and walked to the plane.

The pilot was right to worry about that trip—it was one hell of a flight. Even flying low to avoid radar, we did not escape that turbulent weather. The first few hours were so rough that Remy spent much of them curled up in a ball clutching a bucket. By the time we were at the drop zone, I was so happy to be leaving the stench in the body of that plane, I insisted on going first.

The jump went perfectly—my first contact with the earth smooth and steady, until all of a sudden, my ankle just gave way. In a miserable re-enactment of the jump that went so badly wrong during my training, I was dragged along behind the chute, clutching desperately at the grass trying to slow myself. When I finally came to a stop, I lay limp against the earth, trying to catch my bearings. I released myself from the parachute as I twisted to sit up, only to find that just touching the bottom of my shoe to the ground was enough to spark a pain so intense, I barely noticed heavy footsteps on the ground as a man approached me.

"I'm Marcel," he said uncertainly. "That was quite a landing. Are you hurt?"

"My ankle," I whimpered, reaching to gingerly touch it through my flight suit.

"The safe house isn't far from here but we will have to walk," he said hesitantly.

I didn't feel up to walking anywhere, but I realized the alternative was probably lying on the field until the Germans found me. There was a flurry of movement to my right, and then Remy landed gracefully nearby.

"If you two can bury the parachutes," I muttered, "I'll try to figure out how to walk."

The safe house was a little over a mile from the drop zone, but I knew from my first step that it was going to be the longest hike of my life. My ankle couldn't support my weight, so I had to drag myself across the French countryside, hopping on one foot and leaning on a stick Remy found for me. He and Marcel were walking behind me, carrying our cases.

"Can I help you?" Marcel asked uncertainly, after a while.

"No thank you," I said stiffly. I hated to ask for help even at the best of times, but I did *not* want to appear weak in front of these men I was now to serve so closely with. I was busy trying not to panic. It took weeks for my ankle to feel strong again last time. What would I do if this injury was just as slow to heal?

"You have to cycle a long way tomorrow," he said, after a while.

"Almost sixty miles from here," Remy reminded us.

"I'm aware," I said, but even though I couldn't see his face in the dark, I sensed Marcel flinch at my flat tone. It would do me no good to offend my new circuit leader before we even started working together. "I'm sorry. This is an old injury and I don't know what I'll do if I've aggravated it badly again."

"We will figure it out," he assured me gently, then he offered again, a little more insistently this time, "Try leaning on me. We have to keep moving but you don't have to do this on your own."

Reluctantly, I wound my arm around his waist and he mirrored the posture, then we began to shuffle forward together along the track through a thatch of trees.

At the safe house, Marcel prepared some food for us while Remy washed up. I gritted my teeth as I eased my boot off my ankle, heart sinking as I saw the extensive swelling beginning to bloom around the joint, the skin already mottled purple and red.

"There's no way you'll be walking on that tomorrow, let alone cycling such a long way," Marcel remarked, setting down a plate of bread and cheese beside me on the sofa.

"Perhaps," I said. He walked back to the kitchen and returned with a glass of wine, which he handed me.

"For pain relief," he offered. I took it greedily, hoping the alcohol might silence the voices of doom and gloom in my mind. "Don't worry. Worst-case scenario, we signal London and ask for an evacuation—"

"No," I said, sitting up immediately. Marcel leaned forward in his chair opposite me.

"I don't want to do it," he said firmly. "But we have to be realistic."

"Even if you send me home, you won't get another agent right away. I have a lot to get home to, but I have a job to do first. I don't intend to let this ridiculous injury stop me."

"Sometimes things don't happen as we expect in the field and we have to adapt. A few months ago, my circuit tried to coordinate the destruction of a large factory and the air raid went terribly wrong, but my previous courier had a real knack for lateral thinking. She came up with a much better way to achieve the same result, and safely too. That's the kind of thinking we need for this situation."

"That wasn't Chloe, was it?" I asked hesitantly. Marcel's eyes widened.

"It was!"

"I trained with her. I'm not surprised to hear she saved the day with a little creativity."

"She told me she trained with another woman. She said you were the best agent she knew."

"Well, I'm not much good to you now, am I?" I muttered.

"What would Chloe do right now?"

"Honestly? She'd pretend to cry and convince some burly man to carry her the whole way," I said wryly. Marcel threw back his head and laughed.

"Good grief," Remy said, wincing as he joined us in the living room and saw my ankle. "Well. What's the plan?"

"We pray that we wake up and my ankle is miraculously healed," I deadpanned.

"There is no plan," Marcel said, sighing. "Not yet, anyway. Fleur will rest it tonight and we will see how she is in the morning."

I knew as soon as I woke up that my prayers had not been answered. My first thought was that my ankle felt monstrously swollen, just as it did the first time I sprained it. When I tentatively moved my foot, pain shot up my leg. Leaning on the stick Remy had found for me, I hobbled all the way outside to use the outhouse, and by the time I made my way back, Marcel was seated at the dining room table. He winced when he saw my ankle.

"I'm okay," I said even though I knew I was not. Marcel tapped his fingers against his cheek thoughtfully as I made my way to the table. "Can't I just stay here for a few weeks, until it heals? I know it's not ideal for the mission but..."

Marcel shook his head.

"One of the Maquisards owns this house. We need to be gone before his family returns from a trip tomorrow. We simply have to get you to the next safe house."

"I can try to cycle," I said uneasily, peering down at my swollen ankle. "Walking is painful, but cycling might not be so bad."

I pushed my chair back. I thought I'd limp to the bicycles to try to ride, but as soon as I took a first step, my weakened ankle gave way and I only kept myself from falling by awkwardly catching the chair to hold myself up. Marcel pinched the bridge of his nose.

"I find it so frustrating that they ask so much of you women," he said, scowling in frustration. "You get injured falling out of a plane but I'm still supposed to ask you to cycle halfway across France. They send Chloe halfway across the country, all on her own to a city where she knows no one, and I had to let her go. Whatever happened to men protecting women? It's just not right!"

I knew for sure then that this was the man Chloe had fallen in love with during her mission. The concern and affection in his eyes as he spoke about her was unmistakable.

"Marcel," I said flatly. "Chloe may be slight, but she is far from fragile. She doesn't need you to protect her. Nor do I. My gender has nothing at all to do with this ankle and I am every bit as capable as a man."

Marcel rubbed his eyes wearily.

"Sorry. Of course. I don't mean to insult you, Fleur. Nor do I mean to suggest that Chloe is anything but fiercely capable. Sometimes I feel this war goes against every piece of common sense and social convention I've ever understood. And I don't just mean about women—I mean, my God. These bastards have no respect at all for human life, and I always thought that was one thing we'd evolved to agree upon. It's like the rules are topsy-turvy and sometimes I just can't make sense of it."

"I understand that," I said heavily. "Boy, do I ever."

"I can't figure out how to make an evacuation work, either," he said suddenly, groaning softly. "The full moon was days ago and there was barely enough light for the landing last night. Perhaps they could try tonight—but it's sixty miles ride even to reach my w/t, so I'd have to cycle all the way there and back in one day, *and* we'd still have the problem of where to put you today."

"Can't you get a car?"

"The Germans have prohibited car travel. They're trying to slow the resistance down after the landings."

"But we needn't drive the whole way," I suggested. "And perhaps we can take the back roads…"

"I really don't know," Marcel muttered. "A dead agent is no good to anyone."

"Can you think of an alternative?" I asked him. "It sounds very much like even if you're to send me home, you still need to get me to the next safe house to wait for the next moon."

"Okay," he said, pushing himself to his feet. "I know of a Citroen we can borrow. We'll leave in an hour."

The trip was uneventful at first. It was a beautiful day—a light breeze had blown in overnight and pushed every hint of cloud away. But despite the beauty of my surroundings and the calm start to our journey, I couldn't shake a sense of foreboding that morning. My injured ankle left me unusually helpless. Baker Street sent some munitions with Remy and I to be distributed to the Maquisards around Brive-La-Galliarde. Marcel wanted to hide the Sten gun and ammunition in the boot of the car, but I insisted they remain in the back seat with me. If things went awry and I couldn't run, I could at least try to shoot my way out of trouble.

"It will only take a few hours even traveling the back roads," Remy said. He had made it very clear that he agreed that the car was the smartest way for us to travel. It seemed that Marcel was the only one with any reservations, but even he could see there was little alternative.

They took the front seats automatically—Remy driving, Marcel beside him in the passenger seat with the map. On an ordinary day in the field, I might have argued for a more active role, but I was distracted, staring down at my misshapen ankle and wondering how long it was going to take me to be useful again. As we neared the village of Salon-La-Tour, I was startled out of my reverie when Marcel suddenly cursed.

"What's this…" Remy asked uncertainly. A few hundred feet ahead, at the bottom of a hill with a long, gradual slope, a cluster of German vehicles stretched across the road.

"It's a roadblock," Marcel muttered.

"Turn around," I said, leaning forward to rest my hands against the back of the front seat. Remy did not react, so I said it again, more urgently this time. "Remy, turn the car around."

Marcel glanced back at me, and his gaze dropped towards my foot.

"Our options are limited…" he said, then he swallowed. "There's nowhere to turn off unless we try to drive through a field, and that will only draw attention to us. And if we turn around now, they'll surely follow us."

A sudden vision of Elwood and Booth at the airfield flashed through my mind. Turner assured me it was safe for me to return to the field, but what if he was wrong, what if the Germans had already been alerted to our mission, and by someone right there in Baker Street?

"There's every chance that roadblock might have been setup to *look* for us. We have to turn around!"

Marcel looked at me, stricken.

"Fleur, we can't out-run them. We'd have to ditch the car at some point, and you can't even walk!"

"What's the alternative?" I said fiercely. "Surrender? *Never!*"

Remy cursed and spun the car around in a U-turn so violent I rolled from one side of the back seat to the other. Just as the car shifted direction, a shot sounded, and the car veered wildly off the road. Marcel was caught off guard by the sudden shifts, and as he was thrown around, his head hit the window beside him with such force that the glass shattered and he slumped in his seat.

"Remy!" I exclaimed. "For God's sake, keep your head!"

"The car is pulling!" he shouted, his voice shaking. "The tire is gone. What do I do?"

Just then, the back window shattered behind me and the scent of gunpowder tore through the car as I fumbled for the Sten gun. We spent weeks at training learning how to assemble them quickly—how to move our hands without pinching the skin between the components, how to put the pieces together without conscious thought, eventually how to assemble the whole thing blindfolded, working by muscle memory only. I was grateful for that now as the gun came together in seconds, and I swung up on my knees to peek out the back window of the car. The Germans were scrambling into armored cars to give chase, and it wouldn't take them long to catch up to us.

"Fleur," Remy cried, and when I glanced back, he was flicking his panicked gaze between the road and Marcel, who was limp and unconscious. There was a wound in his left shoulder and blood was already seeping through his shirt. Behind us, the Germans again fired at the car but the shots flicked up dust on the road behind us.

They were trying to shoot out the rest of our tires. If they caught up to us, Remy could run, but Marcel and I would be defenseless.

"There!" I shouted, pointing to a barn off the main road.

"But they'll follow us—" Remy protested, voice thick with tears. He was panicked beyond reason now, and I knew I had to take charge.

"I have a plan. Pull into the damned barn!"

Remy pulled the car off the road and brought it to a stop in the barn so abrupt that Marcel was thrown forward. I grabbed his bloodied shirt and caught the fabric just in time to stop his head from slamming into the dashboard.

The path forward was crystal clear. There was no way to save all three of us—but there was also no reason we all had to be captured.

"Get him out of the car," I ordered, dragging the canvas bag with me as I limped from the back seat. Remy was moving slowly and visibly in shock. "Remy, *now*. Do it now!"

He shook himself, then raced around to the passenger side to hoist Marcel over his shoulder.

"What do I do?" he asked me. He looked like a child in that moment—a frightened little boy who needed reassurance and guidance. Just the thought brought my Hughie to mind, and my frustration with the young man softened.

"Climb into the loft and pull the ladder up behind you," I instructed him quickly. "Hide yourselves and the ladder behind the hay—and don't come out, no matter what you hear or what happens. If the Germans come in and Marcel makes a noise, hold your hand over his mouth."

"But—"

I couldn't spare any more time to reassure him. I drove away then, spinning the wheels violently as I went. I glanced up into the rearview mirror in time to see Remy struggling up the ladder with Marcel over his shoulder. It wasn't a great plan, but it gave them at least a chance, especially if I could draw the Nazis away to buy them some time.

Could the Germans have seen how many people were in our car from that roadblock, even at such a distance? If it all happened so fast, perhaps they didn't even realize there were three of us in the car. If I got lucky, maybe they wouldn't even go back to look for Remy and Marcel.

It was easy to drive haphazardly running on only three tires. I swerved from one side of the road to the other, driving as fast as the car would allow me to travel, moving toward the armored vehicles even as they drove toward me.

The gap between their vehicles and mine seem to be shrinking by the second. When a shot rang out and another one of the Citroen's tires blew, I jammed on the brake. As the car came to a stop I threw myself from the driver's seat, pulling the canvas bag behind me. There was a tree ahead—just an apple tree, but it would give me something like cover. I scrambled across the ground on all fours to reach it, then lined up the boxes of ammunition on the ground in front of my legs.

Behind me, the German cars came to a stop right near the Citroen. I glanced back and did a quick count of vehicles.

My ploy had worked. All four German cars had followed the Citroen. There was shouting—in German, and then in clumsy English and French, ordering me to give myself up. But I had been praying for a moment like this one for years. The revenge I craved was right in front of me now—all I had to do was take it.

I leaned around the tree and fired off rounds in warning toward the Germans. It would not deter them, but it seemed only fair to give them a chance to flee before I started shooting *at* them.

Shots came back toward me in return, and the time for warning fire was over. I had eight boxes of ammunition but the Sten shot so quickly that if I wasn't careful, I would burn through it in minutes. I had to draw this out to make sure that Remy had a chance to hide properly.

For the next thirty minutes, I toyed with the Germans. I rationed those bullets as if they were made of pure gold—firing rounds, pausing and allowing them to come closer, firing more. I felt no guilt when I saw some of those men go down hard, but I was somewhat surprised to find I also felt no joy. Collectively, the Germans had taken so much from Europe and they had taken so much from me, but when the moment for revenge came, I fired that gun for an altogether different reason.

The first time I went to France for the SOE, I was seeking revenge for Giles. That second time, I was there seeking peace for Hughie.

Sometimes in war, impossible calculations needed to be made. The death of those German soldiers would never bring my husband back to life but might just save Marcel and Remy… and who knew what good those two might bring to the world.

A sense of acceptance came over me as I fired the last bullet. I looked down at my ankle, now purple and yellow and black, so swollen the skin had stretched. There was no way I could run. All I could do was accept that I would be captured, and to do my best to honor my country through whatever my imprisonment brought.

"Well, what are you waiting for?" I shouted, glancing cautiously around the tree. The Germans, sheltering behind their cars, peered out at me. I threw my useless Sten gun away from the tree and slumped back against the trunk. "I can't walk. If you want me, you're going to have to come and get me."

CHAPTER 18

JOSIE
Paris, France
May, 1944

I excelled in the art of evasion during my training. During practice sessions, I was commended by Mr. Turner himself for my high level of skill identifying when someone was covertly following me.

Since my arrival in France, I'd discovered that the real world was very different to the calm environs of Beaulieu, the location of the SOE "finishing school." The streets of Paris were often busy, sometimes even crowded with pedestrians, and most of the time it was impossible to be certain I was not being followed.

A skilled operative might have followed me for days without me realizing. Fortunately for me, Veronique did not appear to be particularly skilled.

I spotted her within a block of leaving my hotel one morning. She was hanging back a few dozen feet and at first, I assumed she was trying to contact me—perhaps to slip a note into my hand as she passed, perhaps requiring urgent help. I stopped to look in a shop window to give her an opportunity to catch up but when I looked back to see where she was, caught sight of her ducking into a laneway to hide.

I kept walking but slower now, turning the situation over in my mind. Obviously a confrontation was in order, but where, and when? After another few blocks, I stopped to rummage around in my purse, and looked up to find her bending over unconvincingly to adjust her shoe. She didn't even think to turn away from me, so I got an excellent view of her face.

Enough. The time was now. At least in part because the girl needed to realize she was terrible at this.

I turned and walked directly toward her, and she spun on her heel, as if she was going to try to outrun me, but there was little chance she'd lose me without breaking into a sprint, and to do so would be to draw too much attention. I caught up to her just as we neared the laneway she hid in just a few minutes earlier. I hooked her by the back of the arm to tug her into the lane with me.

"You're following me," I said, when we were deep in the laneway, sheltered from prying eyes. She scowled at me.

"I was just—"

"There's no point lying. I *know* you were." She stared at me defiantly, but there was also a glimmer of fear in her eyes. I released her arm and stepped back, bewildered. "Veronique. My God, relax, we're on the same side. Why on earth are you tailing me?"

"What possible reason could you have to be going to Malgier Labelle's building every day?" she demanded, raising her chin.

"What are you talking about?"

"Malgier Labelle. He works with the *Abwehr*." The *Abwehr*— the German military intelligence organization.

"I've never even heard of him, Veronique! The only place I regularly go is Turner's apartment."

"You meet Turner at his apartment?" she repeated, raising an eyebrow. I felt myself flushing as I nodded. "But you aren't going *to* his apartment for your meetings. Not regularly. That's…"

"It is in keeping with our cover story!" I said defensively.

"I've seen you go to Labelle's building," she said, crossing her arms over her chest.

"When?"

"Yesterday. The day before. The day before that!" If her effort that morning was any indication, my failure to notice her following me was an indictment that I'd become too complacent there in Paris, lulled by the regularity of my routine with Turner. "Yesterday you walked past the building at ten, but you only walked a few blocks away, stopped in at a café, and then returned. The second time you passed, you went inside."

"You're talking about Turner's building." I walked past at ten and the vase was not in Turner's windowsill. I walked past again an hour later because it was almost *always* there by lunchtime, and it was. "Is this building on Rue Lapointe?"

Veronique suddenly deflated, the air leaving her lungs in a rush. She closed her eyes as she nodded.

"Before he disappeared, Mahaut told me he'd heard a rumor that Labelle lives in that building."

"Mahaut is still operating. Turner has seen him!"

Veronique scowled at me.

"*You* are the only agent I've seen in weeks," she said abruptly. "The whole reason I was tailing you was that everyone else seems to be missing. When César was here, I was working with three other couriers. In the last two months, I haven't had a message from any of them. I knew of Mahaut, plus another w/t operator. Of course, we hide and we move and we shift, but we were all periodically in touch until Turner arrived."

Suddenly I realized that her cool manner toward me had not been stress, or as I'd suspected, just her way. Now that we were face-to-face, airing all of this, I realized she was deeply suspicious of me. It was right there in her eyes as she weighed up how much more to say.

"You can trust me," I said. "Some things have troubled me

lately too. We can work together. I want to help you untangle all of this."

"I went to the safe house of one of the other couriers," she blurted. "It's been ransacked. He's gone. I have to assume he was arrested. And Mahaut. And Campion. I've sent the messages you've given me to send, but every message that reports a stable situation here in Paris is a lie."

I was in the dark about so much and Turner himself was the common thread to all of it. I looked at Veronique, unsure if I should say as much, but just then she crossed her arms over her chest and demanded, "I've only seen Turner *once* since he arrived—just at the initial meeting. Is he really still here? Is he really still free?"

"You thought *Turner* had been arrested." I sighed, sinking back against the wall. "You thought I was working with the *Abwehr* to feed you false information so you'd transmit it to London."

"I had to wonder," she whispered, casting her gaze down. "But if Turner lives in the same apartment block…"

"I've trusted him…"

"Just because he's *nice* does not mean he is *innocent*."

We both fell silent for a moment, pondering that.

"What makes you so sure Labelle lives in that apartment block?" I asked.

"It is only a rumor, but Mahaut shared it with me long before Turner arrived."

If Turner was a traitor, my situation was beyond dire. Veronique and I were pawns in a game that we could not even begin to understand.

"Turner loves France," I said. "This is his home. He wants, more than anything, to see it freed."

"You obviously know him much better than I do," Veronique said. There was still a hint of accusation in her tone, but she and I needed one another now. The very first thing we had to do was to establish some level of trust between us.

"Follow me to Turner's apartment," I told her. "I'm going to try to confirm if Labelle lives in the building, and I want you to go to the café opposite. Sit by the window. Stay there all morning if you have to. Sooner or later, Turner will leave. You'll see with your own eyes that he is still here and he is still free."

"I can tail him," Veronique said. That was the logical way forward, but having seen her in action, I was concerned.

"If you do, please be more careful," I told her. "I spotted you right away this morning."

"You didn't see me the last few days," she pointed out.

"I wasn't looking closely enough," I admitted. "But if Turner really is working with the Germans, he'll be paranoid. He won't miss you if you're as obvious as you were today."

"I know Turner is very close with Booth."

"They went to boarding school together."

"It was clear while I was training that he and Elwood and Maxwell are plenty chummy too. What if he is here on a mission so secret that even you and I are not privy to it?"

"You think he is a triple agent?" Hope blossomed in my chest. It was an answer which meant Mr. Turner was not a traitor, and I wanted desperately for it to be true.

"It's a real possibility, isn't it?"

But as quickly as the hope had surged, it deflated.

"But if that were true," I asked, "where are the other agents?"

Veronique slumped.

"Turner could be passing Labelle the names of our agents without even leaving his apartment block," she said miserably. "Perhaps there have been dozens of arrests while he uses you and I to keep up the façade so Baker Street has no idea how dire things are."

"Or perhaps Labelle has just been spying on him. Perhaps

this is all a symptom of Turner's inadequacies, not malicious intent," I said.

Veronique's gaze suddenly softened as she stared at me.

"You want to believe he's innocent, don't you?"

"Of course I do," I muttered. "If he's guilty, our days are probably numbered."

I rushed from the laneway once Veronique and I had finalized our plan and made it to the apartment just in time to see the postman leaving the lobby. I expected to find him there. He almost always arrived at Turner's building by about 9:00 a.m., the same time I went to check for the vase in the window for the first time.

I waited until the postman was out of sight, then I rushed to the concierge.

"Sir," I said, feigning distress. "Is there any mail for my boss, Mr. Turner? We are waiting on an important letter."

"Allow me to check," the concierge said. There was a stack of letters on his desk, and he began to rifle through them. "I'm sorry, mademoiselle. No mail today."

"Please, can I double-check? It's important and really should be in that pile," I said. The concierge hesitated only for a moment before he handed me the pile. I flicked through it quickly, and there was—the third letter in the stack. An envelope addressed to M. Labelle, Apartment 15. Turner's apartment, the apartment I had been spending most of my days in, was right next door—Apartment 16. If they were collaborating, Turner could be slipping the Abwehr information without so much as walking down the stairs.

"Never mind," I said, handing the concierge back the pile of letters. "We'll try again tomorrow."

I met Veronique just before curfew that night. For the first time ever, we met at her room. We needed somewhere private for a longer conversation.

"I followed Turner all day," she told me. "He had lunch with a man at the Café Dupree then he walked to an apartment nearby. He was there for about two hours then he walked home. There was nothing suspicious at all in his movements, although I'd love to know who that apartment belongs to. Men were coming and going all afternoon."

"He likes to gamble," I said, thinking of the debt I'd discovered. "It's possible it was some kind of underground gaming club."

"And Labelle?"

"You were right, he lives in the building. But there's more."

After I confirmed that Labelle lived in the apartment building with Turner, I had to confirm that he was involved with the *Abwehr*, as Veronique suspected him to be. I was stumped by this at first. I knew and trusted so few people in Paris.

In the end, I found myself right back where I started—at Madame Célestine's apartment. When she opened the front door and found me on the stoop, she looked left and right frantically before she pulled me inside.

"Child," she said. "What you doing here?"

"I'm sorry. I need help and didn't know where else to go."

"I'm not sure I can help you at all," she said wearily. "Surely you know that everything has changed."

We did not so much as take a seat—it was clear she wanted me out of there as quickly as possible. In uneven, anxious bursts of speech, she told me about dozens of arrests across the city.

"Every day there are more," she said. "If the rumors are true, some of your own agents are at 84 Avenue Foch even as we speak." Célestine's eyes began to swim, and she swallowed hard before she whispered, "Even Basile was arrested three weeks ago."

I had not worked directly with Basile but knew of him by reputation, and I knew that Célestine was his aunt. Part of the reason why I went to her apartment that day was that I had hoped she could connect me with him so that he might help me figure out a plan of action.

My very presence was a risk, and Madame Célestine was not in any position to help me. I had to leave the apartment quickly, but before I did, I asked, "I just need to know, Madame, have you heard of Malgier Labelle?"

"Labelle is a senior official with the *Abwehr*," she said, as the color drained from her face. "By all accounts, a vicious monster of a man." I put my handle on her doorknob, and she gently touched my arm. "I'm sorry to say this, Chloe, but when you leave here today, please don't come back. I want to help, but the resistance within Paris right now is on fire, and I cannot afford to get burned."

"It is bad, Veronique," I said quietly. "I spoke with a local contact who confirmed your suspicions of many arrests, including some of our own agents."

"What are we going to do?" Veronique asked me. There was a tremor in her voice. I reached across the table to squeeze her hand.

"You have a transmission window tonight." One of the strangest parts of my day had been returning to Turner's apartment to find the vase in the window. I didn't want him to know that I suspected him, and so I went back upstairs, and spent a full hour talking to him. How bizarre it was to sit in the living room and know that a senior *Abwehr* official was potentially right next door. How uncomfortable, to sit opposite Turner on those luxurious leather sofas, to sip tea with him while he dictated a message for me to ferry to Veronique for transmission that night, knowing that his report of extending the resistance circuit and protecting his agents was entirely lies. He seemed unusually quiet that day, but in his typical way, was still quick with a smile and oh-so-*likeable*. It broke my heart to think that this man I had thought so highly of was betraying the Allies with every word.

"There is no going back if we report him to London," Veronique whispered. "Are you sure?"

"I am."

"And then what do we do?" she choked, and she pressed her fists to her hair. "I just want to go home. God help me, I just want to go home. Three months training? They really thought we could handle this kind of situation with three months training? I'm a child-minder, for God's sake! I don't belong here!"

"Listen to me," I said firmly, leaning toward her. "I have a little cash—just enough for us to catch a train. My old circuit leader will help us, I'm sure of it." My heart leaped at the thought of reuniting with Noah. I would not feel safe again until his arms were around me. "We signal London tonight to alert them to our concerns and then we will leave right away."

I would go with her to broadcast the message but we wouldn't wait for a reply. We each had a spare set of identity papers. We would adopt new names, hide our hair under hats, spend the night hiding behind a warehouse a few blocks from her safe house. Then in the morning, we would buy tickets and board a train to Corrèze.

I wasn't sure exactly where I'd find Noah there, but I knew that if he heard about the situation I was in, he would trust me to find a way forward. I had to trust myself to do so too.

Veronique fetched some paper and I picked up the pen to write. Together, we crafted a simple message expressing our concerns about Turner's loyalty—the arrests he had not reported, his proximity to Labelle. I structured the message in five-word phrases, a system designed to ensure the wireless operator was transmitting for the shortest period of time possible. Once I'd finished, Veronique drew up a long table and began the complicated, arduous process of double encoding the message using her encryption key.

"Where will you transmit from?" I asked her.

"I have access to a room in an apartment on La rue de la Faisanderie," she murmured.

I felt useless watching her work, so I made a cup of hot water for myself and some ersatz coffee for her. I had just placed both mugs on her little table beside her notepad when there came a fierce knock at the door.

"Open up!"

Veronique froze, the pen hovering over the paper. Her face went pale, her eyes were wide.

"Don't panic," I said, dropping my voice. I motioned to the paper on the table and indicated that she should hide it. She scooped it all into her arms but before she was even on her feet the door flew open—kicked open by the mountain of a man on the other side.

Veronique screamed in fright and the papers fluttered from her arms. I scrambled frantically—thinking I could tear up that top page, the most incriminating page, and maybe even swallow some of the pieces before the huge man at the door reached me. The Gestapo would realize that we had been about to tell London of our concerns about Turner and that was bad enough, but that top page contained Veronique's encryption key. If the Germans had that entire page and her wireless set, all they would need to message London was her security check—something Gerard Turner could tell them in seconds. I simply couldn't let that happen.

"Stop," a man said, but even though I assumed he was speaking to me, I ignored him, throwing myself at the paper. I scrambled for the top page and reached it, but just then, I realized Veronique was putting something in her mouth.

"Veronique! *No!*" I cried, but she stared at me with terrified eyes.

I'd refused Elwood's offer of an L-pill during my preflight checks. I knew some agents preferred the option for a quick death should their mission spiral badly off course, but I had always told myself I'd try to cling to hope instead. Now, looking into Veronique's tear-filled eyes as she swallowed the cyanide pill, I was not sure which of us were smarter.

The room was suddenly full of men, some in the plain clothes of the Gestapo, a few in SD uniforms. The men swarmed around Veronique aimlessly until one shouted, "Take her outside and make her vomit."

It was a distraction and that meant an opportunity for me. As they dragged her from the room, sobbing and crying, I ripped the top sheet of our notes in half, intending to stuff it into my mouth.

A brutal hand closed around my wrist. The sudden shock of the pain made my knees give out, then another man rushed at me, snatching the paper from my hands.

CHAPTER 19

CHARLOTTE
Liverpool, 1970

Later that night, I'm sitting in the living room watching TV. Dad has just come home from work and is at the dining room table behind me, eating the steak and eggs I prepared for him. Dad is too polite to mention it, but I've managed to overcook the steak and undercook the eggs.

My stomach is aflutter with butterflies. I have a million questions about the SOE I want to ask Dad, but I know he's not ready to answer them so I haven't asked. It's different when it comes to Theo. He's helping us out of the goodness of his heart, and I know my dad would want to help him in return if he can.

"Hey, Dad?" I say gently, twisting in my seat to face him.

"Hmm?" Dad stares down at his plate as he saws at the tough steak. He scoops the slice up and drops it to Wrigley, who's lying beneath the chair. Dad would never have allowed Wrigley to sit so close to the dinner table before Mum died, let alone feed the dog from his own plate.

Dad looks exhausted. There are bags beneath his eyes and his shoulders are slumped. My heart sinks as I realize I can't ask him. Not tonight.

"Never mind," I say, and I turn back to the TV, but I'm trying to watch the news and all I can think about is teenage Theo borrowing his father's car and driving across the country only to discover he didn't even know his own birth date. I suck in a breath and force myself to turn back to Dad. "When you were training with the SOE, did you ever come across an agent known as Chloe?"

Dad's cutlery clatters as he drops it against his plate.

"Why on earth did you ask me that?" he asks me sharply. I open my mouth to tell him about Theo but at the very last second, think better of it.

I can't betray Theo's confidence. This is his story to tell, if he chooses to tell it at all. It's hard to explain any of this without explaining that Theo broke the law and snuck into Professor Read's secure room.

I gnaw my lip and decide to lie.

"Theo mentioned he'd come across that name in his studies with Professor Read."

"I knew her," Dad says abruptly. He pushes back his chair and stands, then, giving up any pretense of eating my rubbish meal, bends to scrape his entire dinner into Wrigley's bowl.

"Did you work with her?" I ask hesitantly. Dad is silent for a long moment, staring down at the dog as he licks his bowl clean. My father's expression is so tense, a shiver of concern runs through me. "Dad?"

"I knew her well," he says. "We were good friends." He looks across at me and his gaze is completely hollow. "What did Theo want to know about her?"

"Did you train with her?"

Dad scrubs a hand over his face, then walks slowly across the room to take a seat in Mum's armchair. He leans forward toward me and his expression eases to something closer to weariness.

"We did serve together late in the war, but I also knew her well before the SOE."

"You did…?" I gasp, then, so excited I can barely bring my-self to breathe, I whisper, "Dad, does that mean you know what her real name was?"

"Of course. Her real name was Josie Miller," he says softly, but then he pauses. "Actually, her name was Jocelyn Nina Miller. She much preferred people use her nickname—Josie."

"Was she French?"

"She was born in London. Her father was some well-to-do lawyer and her mother a doctor. There was an especially acri-monious divorce when she was an infant and her mother moved her to France. She grew up in Paris and lived there until the occupation." A sad, distant look comes onto Dad's face. "Do you remember I told you I traveled with a woman on the escape line? That was Josie. She was a tiny scrap of a thing but God, Lottie, her spirit was immense. We walked dozens of miles in a single night and every one of my footsteps meant two or three for her. She was exhausted, but there was no stopping her—she just kept going." He pauses, then laughs suddenly. "I was absolutely terrified and wanted nothing more than to crawl into a little ball to hide beneath a tree, but I had to keep going because I was too proud to admit any of that in front of her."

"She sounds remarkable."

Dad sighs sadly.

"She really was, love."

"Do you remember anything about her personal life?" I ask uncertainly. "Did she have children, for example?"

My father looks so pained by this question I instantly regret asking it.

"She wanted children and she was marvelous with them," he whispers, then he swallows heavily. "But no, she never had the chance to have her own."

"And you saw her often through the war?"

"We wrote letters for a long time after we made it out of France. I was serving at first, training flight mechanics you recall, and about the same time, she was here in England, quite unwell." That's interesting. Perhaps, if Theo is correct and Josie Miller's "surgery" was a covert pregnancy, Dad might not even have known. "Later in the war we were posted together." A warm fondness crosses my father's face and it strikes me that this is the very first time I've seen him reminisce about the war without becoming visibly pained by the memories. But his expression sobers, and he tilts his head at me. "Why is Theo so interested in Josie?"

"Oh, you know these history types," I say, laughing uneasily. "Curious just for the sake of curiosity all the time."

"She was…" Dad trails off, his gaze distant again as he stares past me to the TV. "She was extraordinary. One of the most incredible women I've ever known."

"Did she die serving?" I ask.

The wistfulness evaporates in my father's expression. His jaw sets hard and his lips thin. The shadows return to his gaze, and right along with them, that vague, sickly sense of guilt.

"Yes," he says, and he pushes himself to his feet as if he's going to return to his room. I'm struck by the realization that it cost my father something to delve into his memory to retrieve that information about Chloe. He wanted to look back when we started this process, but maybe the reason he's become disengaged since our visit to Jean Allaire's house is that he just can't bear to let his thoughts remain with the past.

"I'm sorry for asking, Dad," I blurt desperately. He pauses and gives me a miserable look.

"I've had questions for all of these years and your mother always encouraged me to forget them. In the beginning, I wasn't so sure of that, but she always did have a way of changing my mind."

"She did." Mine too, I think, and I'm surprised by a surge of bitterness that runs through me at the thought. I immediately feel disloyal, as if I've tainted her memory somehow just by acknowledging that. Mum was loving and kind and clever and supportive. But if I really stop and think about it, she did tend to go out of her way to make sure the rest of the family complied with her thoughts on particular subjects.

She never liked Billy, for example, and when we first started dating she launched a concerted campaign to convince me not to see him. Now I see that she just wanted the best for me and most of the time, she was right. Billy is the perfect example of that! I'd have saved myself a lot of heartache if I just listened to her in the first place.

But was it really so helpful for her to constantly point out his flaws to me? Was it healthy for her to suggest other boys in our circle I should date, sometimes even in front of Billy? Was it fair of her to refuse my requests to invite him to family dinners, even a year after we were dating?

"I think I convinced myself I could shortcut my grief for your mother by distracting myself but all I've really managed to do is to drag my memory back to the last time I tried to shortcut my own emotions," Dad laughs weakly. "Your father, I am sorry to say, is the kind of man who needs very little encouragement to run away from his feelings rather than to confront them full-on."

"These feelings you keep talking about," I say, cautiously meeting his gaze. "You said you have 'troubling feelings' when you think about the war."

"I made a lot of mistakes in those days," Dad says. "I have all of this…" He waves his hands around his chest vaguely. "…*guilt* that surfaces when I force my mind to go back and I can't always make complete sense of it. I find myself surrounded, with aged, overdue feelings coming at me from all sides."

Dad takes a step toward the bedrooms, but I stand and catch his hand. He turns to look at me, his eyes swimming in tears. I'd never seen him cry before my mother died. Now, I can't help but wonder if this tender side of him was buried beneath a facade for decades. I throw my arms around him, and he returns the hug automatically.

"Dad," I choke. "I'm sorry for all of it. I'm just sorry this is all so hard."

"Life goes by so fast, doesn't it?" he whispers roughly against my hair. "Most of the time my SOE days feel like something that happened to someone else, but when I really let myself think about it, it feels like it all happened no more than five minutes ago."

Just then, Wrigley joins us, pushing his way between us to join in the hug. Dad and I both laugh half-heartedly, and as we separate, Dad brushes away a tear and bends to scratch Wrigley's neck.

"Why don't you watch some TV with me tonight?" I ask him, pointing to Mum's armchair. "We can watch Monty Python and forget about our problems for a while."

Dad pauses, and I think he's going to refuse the offer, but then he shrugs and forces a smile.

"You're just jealous because Wrigley always wants to go to bed early when I do."

He sinks into his own recliner, right next to the one my mother always sat in, and I chuckle triumphantly when Wrigley struggles his way up onto the larger sofa, next to me. The dog falls asleep with his head in my lap after a few minutes, my hand resting in his soft fur.

I'm not sure we manage to forget about our problems, but we do laugh as we distract ourselves with a few hours of TV, and that's enough for now.

If Dad had retired early, I'd have called Theo with the new information about Chloe right away, but it's too late to call once Dad is in bed, so it will have to wait for morning. Still, I toss and turn in bed, unable to sleep because I'm haunted by visions of a young Theo sneaking into his parents' room to investigate his own adoption.

A sudden thought strikes me.

My mother also had a drawer full of special paperwork. Even in all of the months since her death, it has never occurred to me to see what's inside.

I haven't been into my parents' room since Mum died, but I slip through the door the next morning as soon as Dad leaves for work and am immediately startled by how confronting it is. Her clothes are still in the wardrobe, lined up on the hangers by color, items in the drawers folded to the perfectly sharp edge she preferred. Her shoes are lined up too, although my gaze sticks for a long moment on the empty space where her running shoes should be. I run my hand along the dresses and jackets on the hangers and let my vision blur.

I miss you, Mum.

Her marriage to my father seemed a happy one, except for one bewildering period when I was seven or eight. She and Dad were fighting all the time, and me and Archie convinced one another that a divorce was imminent. In a way that only children can, we decided that we had done something to cause all of the fuss, and as the big sister, I decided it was my responsibility to figure out what we'd done wrong so I could fix it. The next time I heard them shouting, I left Archie to hide under the bed as we'd taken to doing, but I crept across to press my ear against their door.

"I know you're in love with her!" my mother cried. "Why else would you be spending so much time at the workshop?"

"Because I'm trying to build a business, Geraldine!" Dad shouted back. "For God's sake, you knew these years were going to be hard until we got the second shop up and running. I'm no more having an affair with that woman than I am a potato!"

"What's an affair, Daddy?" I asked him the next day, and his eyes bulged.

"Where did you hear that word?" he asked me, voice strained.

"I heard you and Mummy shouting last night."

"Mummy has the wrong idea about something," he said, and he seemed very tired in that moment. I didn't understand it at the time. I adored Mum. It just didn't seem a prospect worth considering that she might have been in the wrong.

That was the last time I'd hear them shouting, but it was far from the last time I'd see a vicious jealousy in her. They loved to entertain and had a large group of loving, warm friends— but it was not at all uncommon for their dinner parties to end in Mum sulking because Dad spent too much time speaking to one of the other women.

I go to my mother's chest of drawers and pull the bottom one open. It's the deepest drawer and there's an organized stack of paperwork in there—Mum's old folio organizers, bills marked paid before their due dates, birth certificates, pay slips—each fastened to like documents with colored paper clips. I flick through all of it but find nothing at all unexpected, until I leaf through one of Mum's old organizers and note the little cross marks in the corner of certain dates. This was how she tracked her period, which I know she did religiously until she entered menopause. I pack the drawer back up and walk to their en suite.

Dad hasn't packed away her toiletries or makeup, and the sight of those bottles and tubes scattered across the counter-top makes my heart ache so desperately, I have to sit down on the closed toilet lid for a moment to compose myself. Her perfume is there on the bench—some cheap brand she discovered a few years back and fell instantly in love with. I spray it into the room and breathe it in, and I miss her so badly I would give anything—*anything*—to be embraced in her arms again.

I didn't come into that bathroom to torture myself. I just know that there is only *one* area of the house my father would never venture near, and that's the box under the sink where my mother always kept her sanitary items. He's always been

deeply squeamish about the finer details of the female repro-
ductive system.

I slide the box out and open the lid to find it fully stocked
to the top with sanitary pads, even though my mother hadn't
had need of them for a few years. I dig through the box, and
my hands begin to shake when my fingers close around a stack
of envelopes buried at the bottom.

"It's me. It's Charlotte. Mum had hidden the letters from
Professor Read," I tell Theo in a rush when he answers the
phone. "The first one they ever sent Dad was open, so I know
she read it. The others were unopened, but just like Read said,
his office sent letters to Dad at semi-regular intervals for more
than twenty years. Mum must have been intercepting them
when they arrived."

"Probably trying to protect him from having to relive troubling memories," Theo suggests gently. I twist the cord of the
phone around my finger as I ponder this.

"I suppose so," I say. But why keep them for all of that time?
She could have destroyed them or even thrown them away.
My gut twists as I consider the possibility that my mother did
not want Dad to see those letters but felt bad enough about
her behavior that she couldn't bring herself to close the door
completely.

But that reminds me—those letters aren't the only reason
for this phone call.

"Oh! And I asked Dad about Chloe," I say in a rush. "He
knew her. Quite well, actually."

"He did?" Theo gasps, but his tone is guarded as he asks
slowly, "So…what could he tell you?"

"She worked on an escape line. They escaped France together in 1941 and wound up friends."

"He knew her before the SOE…" Theo whispers, stunned.

"Her real name was Jocelyn Nina Miller. She used the name

Josie. She was born in London but grew up in Paris. Dad did say she didn't have children, but he also said she was particularly unwell around 1942 and there was a long period where they corresponded via letter so—"

"So maybe my theory about a hidden pregnancy bears out," Theo blurts.

"What do we do now?"

"Now that we know her full name and place of birth, I can try to order a copy of her birth certificate." I hear a rush of air as he exhales against the receiver. "Maybe I'll even get lucky and it will list a parent or sibling we can try to find."

CHAPTER 20

JOSIE
Paris, France
May, 1944

In training, they taught us that if we were tortured, the first fifteen minutes would be the worst. If we could survive that without our tongues loosening, we could survive anything.

They did give us some terrible advice in that training, but this was among the worst.

I lay on the floor of my cell at 84 Avenue Foch, dazed and confused after another day of torture and interrogation. Was this day two or three? No, it had been longer. Maybe this was day four or five.

Two of my toenails had been removed. One of my molars was cracked, and I suspect that several of my toes were broken too—one of the interrogating offices kept stomping on my feet in his jackboots. I suspected I had some broken ribs. My lungs were angry and inflamed after hours of water torture.

The worst of it was that they already knew so much about the SOE. They knew where I had trained, they knew about Maxwell and Booth and Elwood, they even knew that initial interviews were being conducted in the Northumberland Hotel. I wasn't tortured and interrogated because I knew anything that those men did not know—after all, it was certain now that my circuit leader was working *with* them, and likely had been for some time. This was never an exercise in information gathering, as much as they made a show of demanding I answer particular questions. I knew, from the very first blow, that this was an exercise in revenge.

The hours of misery since my arrest had collapsed into one confusing medley of memories that ran together, but one stood out from the blur: Gerard Turner, sitting opposite me as I slumped on a chair, my hands cuffed behind the backrest, bleeding and beaten down and exhausted.

"I'm trying to get you out of here," he whispered hoarsely. "You weren't supposed to be at her house that night. You told me you were meeting her before curfew to hand over the transmission. She was tailing me! I had no choice about her. But you?" I stared at him, seething with hatred, but I did not answer. It was a bizarre thing to see grief and shame and remorse in the eyes of the man who had, ultimately, condemned me to such suffering. His voice broke as he finished miserably, "I was trying to protect you. You were *never* meant to get caught up in this!"

"I thought you were a good man," I blurted then, as tears of disappointment and pain filled my eyes. My lips were swollen, a heavy lisp in the sounds because of my injured teeth.

"I made one bad decision in 1941. My father's business was going under."

"You took money from them," I croaked, stunned.

"I was desperate, and at first, they only asked me to pass them low-level intelligence—details that didn't even seem important. But as soon as I took that money I was trapped, and they've demanded more and more from me over the years..." His eyes swam as he stared at the table. "Every time I think I've found a way out, there's something more, but it's not my fault. I had no idea what I was signing up for. You have to believe me, Josie."

"Mr. Turn—" I broke off, then squeezed my swollen eyes closed, the disappointment almost overwhelming me. But then I felt a sudden surge of fury and I opened my eyes and I stared at him as I said fiercely, "*Gerard*. There is no circumstance on earth that could justify the things you've done. If you have a shred of moral courage, you'll contact London. Turn yourself in."

"It's too late for that," he said dully, but then the door opened, and an SS officer was there—Schulte, the one who liked to stomp on my toes. I cowered in spite of myself, but Schulte only told Turner that his time was up and he had to leave.

"I'll try to come back," Turner said. I wanted to tell him not to bother, but my entire body had frozen at the sight of Schulte, my throat so tight I could not force the words out.

I didn't see Turner again after that, but I saw plenty of Schulte and his kind.

"Do you know what a *Nacht und Nebel* prisoner is?" he spat at me during one interrogation. "We will disappear you. There will be no trace of you left behind when all of this is over—no paperwork or body for anyone to find, no sympathetic witnesses to your fate. Did you think you were suffering *for* something? You aren't. The war is all but over, and the Reich will be the victor."

In that moment, all I could think about was the last time I spoke to Maman, and everything left unresolved from that day that might now forever remain unspoken. I had to believe Fleur had managed to convince Baker Street to break the rules and send my note to her. The thought of my mother and Aunt Quinn forever wondering what became of me hurt more than anything the Germans could ever do to my body.

I lay there on the floor that night, collapsed as much in despair as pain, and my bleary eyes fell upon a remarkable inscription on the wall, low and almost out of sight. It was a list of names—other people who'd passed through that cell, visible only to someone too weak and broken to hold themselves up.

A tiny nail rested where the wall met the floor. With my bloodied, swollen hands, I picked up that nail and marked my name at the bottom of the list, so that one day someone might remember that I had been there too.

I had done my best to make a difference. I had done my best to survive. If there was any justice in the world, that had to count for something.

I tried not to count the days. Time meant something different now, and I knew I would be more afraid if I understood how long my imprisonment had been. The physical torture stopped once I was moved to Pforzheim Prison, but the mental torture had only just begun. I was in my cell alone all of the time— each day punctuated only by the morning and nightly visits from unfriendly guards. I had no bed—just a simple wooden plank affixed to the wall, with a thin, dirty blanket to cover myself with. I had no toilet, only a metal bucket. I was still wearing the clothes I was arrested in. I was shackled at my hands and my feet.

They brought me two meals a day, sometimes a miserable, watery soup with a few chunks of potato or carrot floating in it, sometimes a boiled potato or even two, almost always with a chunk of stale bread. In the first week I refused the bread, but by the second week my hunger was so intense I could not resist it, even knowing that it would make me ill, and it did. But still, I ate that bread because the bloating and the cramping were worth even a short break from the constant, gnawing hunger.

I dreamed of mattresses and cushions and the soft embrace of my mother's arms. I dreamed of Noah—simple dreams of watching him smile or sleep or reach toward me, love shining in his eyes. I dreamed of softness, because my entire world had been reduced to hardness, and even more than the pain of stone walls or a wooden bed against my bony body was the monotony and coldness and *aloneness* of it all.

There was a window in my cell. It was small and high, covered with metal bars to prevent escape, and the glass was filthy and smeared. But through that window, I had a glimpse of sunlight and the spectrum of gray and white in the clouds and the smudgy blue of the sky.

I loved that window because through it, I saw change—night and day, sunshine and rain, even while everything else in that cell remained constant.

I had never learned how to pray—never thought I'd be someone who would want to. But in that prison cell, every single day, I prayed to thank God for that window.

I knew right away that I was no ordinary prisoner. The Germans around me in the prison assumed I did not speak their language, but I did. They used one phrase repeatedly—almost every time they spoke my name.

"Nacht und Nebel." Night and fog, a special designation of prisoner. Schulte told me they would "disappear me" and I had no doubt that's what was happening. The sounds of the prison through the day led me to believe it was full and busy, and I knew instinctively that solitary confinement was not a punishment meted out to all prisoners. The endless aloneness was punishment for my role with the SOE.

And endless it seemed. My ribs showed through my skin and I developed pressure sores that would not heal. There was never enough water so I lived in a perpetual thirst. My broken tooth ached and the taste in my mouth left no doubt that it was festering.

How best to make the days of monotony and pain mean something? I asked myself this question day and night. If every human life had value, and I believed that to my core, how could I make those days matter? I couldn't connect, or help, or create.

All I could do was wait. All I could do was to tell myself that there was dignity in surviving and power in holding onto hope, especially because the enemy wanted nothing more than to leave me hopeless.

Chapter 21

CHARLOTTE
Liverpool, 1970

"I can't tell if you've been avoiding spending time with me or if I've been avoiding spending time with you," Aunt Kathleen says as she hands me a cup of coffee the next morning. She glances across her dining room, to the chair where Mum always sat—the one near the big bay windows. "But either way, we need to get better at catching up. She would want us to do better."

"I know, Aunt Kathleen," I say. We've spoken on the phone, but this spontaneous visit I've made to her home today is the first time we've been in the same room for months.

It's hard for me to sit here with her now, to sip coffee alone, just the two of us, when almost every other time in my life Mum would have been seated at this table too. They'd talk in that unique way they shared, talking so fast they almost spoke over the top of one another. And I'd sit here, the third wheel to their duo, nursing my coffee while I waited for one of them to ask me a question so I had my chance to join into the conversation.

"It's not the same, is it?" Kathleen asks, still looking at that empty chair. "Nothing is the same since she died. I've been divorced twice and both times were very bloody hard, but neither hit me like your mother's death has." She offers a wan smile. "Husbands come and go, but sisters are for life. I really thought she'd outlive your dad and we'd end up in side-by-side beds in a nursing home." I smile sadly at that. I can easily picture the future Aunt Kathleen had imagined for them, though knowing the way those two could talk all night and day, some long-suffering nurse would probably have had them separated before long. "This isn't just a catch-up, is it? I can see something in your face."

"You knew my dad before the war."

Aunt Kathleen picks up her coffee and straightens her spine. She flicks me an irritated glance, then sighs.

"We're talking about this then, are we?"

"Please. I really need to understand."

"I'm guessing you didn't manage to convince your father to forget about his trip down memory lane."

"He needs to do this, Aunt Kathleen," I say emphatically. "And to help him, I need to understand what it all means."

"Gerrie had been besotted with him from the first moment they met. She didn't want him to enlist in the first place, not even as a flight mechanic. She thought it was too dangerous, but he just would not listen. Do you know he was missing in action in France for over a year?" I nod, as Aunt Kathleen's gaze hardens a little. "We all told her he was probably dead, but she waited for him. He returned and then his whole family was gone and of course that was terribly sad, but you know how hard she loved him, Charlotte? Day and night, she was there for him when he felt like he had lost *everything*. And how does he repay her? They'd been talking about marriage. He sat her down and she was convinced he was going to propose then and there and do you know what he does instead?" Her nostrils flare. "He *broke up* with her. He didn't really explain at the time. Just said he wasn't ready to settle down and she should move on with her life."

"Ouch," I say, wincing.

"Of course, we later learned about the SOE secrecy rules, but you'll never convince me he couldn't give her some clue about what was really going on. He disappeared for years after that. Your mother and I graduated and we started our first jobs and she mourned that relationship for such a long time. In early 1944 she finally started seeing a lovely young man and *bam*, your dad reappears to throw it all into chaos. Again."

"You've never liked Dad much, have you?" I say.

Aunt Kathleen sniffs before she says, "I grew to love him in time especially after he blessed your mother with you beautiful children. But no. For too many years, I was too angry with him to *like* him."

"I found letters from a university professor who wanted to interview my dad about his wartime service. Dad had never seen them. Mum hid them in her sanitary napkin basket."

"Ah," Kathleen says and I know immediately that this is not news to her.

"She told you?"

"I knew some archivist had been trying to reach your father regarding his service, and Geraldine thought an interview was a horrible idea," Kathleen says. She pauses, carefully sips her coffee, then admits, "I didn't know she'd gone as far as to hide letters from him, but it doesn't surprise me much. She was ruthless in her love for your father right from the minute he resurfaced in 1944, even though he was an absolute mess when he came back."

"Because of his head injury?" I ask hesitantly. She raises one slim shoulder.

"Partly that. Partly the trauma of the war, I suppose you'd say. And of course, at the time, he was grieving another woman."

"Another woman?" I repeat, eyes wide.

"Oh yes, darling," Kathleen says, pursing her lips. "Your lovely father broke my sister's heart to go off to fight that noble battle for freedom, and while he was in France, found the time somehow to fall in love with someone else."

"Mum wasn't put off by this when he returned?" I say, stunned.

"My God, she was so hurt. But he was in desperate need of help and she still loved him. She rearranged her whole life for him—broke up with the new beau, convinced Mum and Dad to let him move into the spare room. I'm not sure how he'd have managed if she hadn't, to be honest. The SOE just dumped him back in London and left him to his own devices."

"That's so unfair!" I exclaim.

"You don't know the half of it, love. His memory was shot, he couldn't concentrate to so much as read a newspaper headline, and all he ever talked about was the war." Kathleen murmurs, "In those first few weeks, he was like a broken parrot—just weeping all the time about his 'guilt.'" There's that word again. My heart sinks. "Oh, yes, darling. Whenever we asked him what he'd done, he'd just weep—he couldn't tell us. Well, he *wouldn't*. Perhaps part of the memory loss was the head injury, but I'm convinced a big part of it was that he did not want to remember. Your mum always discouraged him from looking back at the war years not just because she was worried it would set him back, but because we were all terrified of what he'd find if he did."

"And despite all of this, he and Mum still somehow ended up married?" I say, rubbing my forehead. "At the start of 1946, no less?"

"In late 1945 Gerrie told me they were dating again. The war had just ended and the whole world was celebrating, so I figured they'd just gotten a little carried away and I begged her to take some time to reconsider. I wasn't just concerned for her, believe it or not. I was still angry with Noah for everything he'd put her through over the war years, but he was obviously vulnerable. You probably don't want to hear this about your own parents, but they rushed into that second courtship, racing toward the altar like marriage was a competitive sport. It was not a good combination of desires. Noah just wanted to settle down, to have a family quick smart because he was all alone in the world. And Gerrie just wanted to tie him down, probably before he could fall in love with someone else and leave her heartbroken. Again."

"Aunt Kathleen," I say defensively. "Don't say those things. They were madly in love."

She peers at me thoughtfully, then lowers her cup to the table so she can reach across and squeeze my hand.

"Darling," she says. "I loved Gerrie with every bit of my heart and I will miss her every waking hour. But surely you know—your dad is not perfect. Hell, your *mum* was not perfect." I open my mouth to protest this, but Aunt Kathleen gives me a pointed look. "She was a jealous woman. Controlling. She could be downright *mean*. She was arrogant—God, I never heard that woman admit she was wrong, not once in fifty-three years! And you know what?" I stare at her, eyes narrowed, but her face softens as she finishes, "I adored her anyway. I don't need to pretend she was someone she was not in order to honor her, Lottie. Frankly, if I pretend now that my sister was an angel I'd be doing myself a disservice." She gives me a sad look, and reaches to brush my hair back from my face. "Sweetheart, we have to grieve who she really was, not who we wanted her to be. And she and your dad ultimately built a great life together, but that does not mean it was a healthy relationship, especially right at the beginning."

"So this is why you never liked Dad? Because you're convinced he did terrible things during the war?" I blurt. Aunt Kathleen sits back in her chair and sighs softly.

"All I know for sure is that he came back from France twice, and both times he'd been with that same woman. The first time he tried to convince your mother that their relationship was platonic, but Gerrie never really believed it. There was something about the way he described that other girl—even I could see the magic in his eyes. And then he went back to France for the SOE and this time he *did* admit he'd been madly in love with the other woman. And—"

"It wasn't the same woman though," I interrupt, frowning. "Was it?"

"Oh yes, my darling. It absolutely *was* the same woman. He walked the escape line with her and then by some mysterious coincidence she ended up with him on whatever mission he was sent into France to complete. *That's* the woman he was heartbroken over in 1944. Now tell me that's not suspicious as all hell."

Dad was *in love* with Josie Miller? That's shocking enough, but another thought hits even harder: Could Theo be my half brother? Oh God. My stomach churns violently at the thought and I decide I had better examine that reaction more closely later.

Aunt Kathleen squeezes my hand again. "Over the years, as I said, he endeared himself to me, and believe it or not, I do love your father now. I just never wanted my little sister to wind up with a man who would not choose her first and always."

CHAPTER 22

ELOISE
Karlsruhe Region, Germany
September, 1944

"Where do you think they're taking us?"

I was shackled at the ankle to Romilly, a young French woman who was arrested for carrying resistance newsletters. We had been stuck for hours in a crowded boxcar as it crawled across Europe at a snail's pace. At first, Romilly didn't seem to want to speak to me, but as time passed and our dignity faded away, she was opening up. She was about my age but was not coping particularly well. I found myself trying to console her.

"I imagine we'll end up in camp," I told her gently. "Whatever happens though, we will hold our heads high. The end of the war can't be too far away."

Was I really so optimistic? I had been forcing myself to appear so for long enough that I was no longer sure how I really felt. In the months since my capture at Salon-La-Tour, I had been volleyed between Fresnes Prison near Paris and 84 Avenue Foch for interrogations. I'd been beaten so badly that my nose now sat at an angle. They had almost drowned me more times than I could count. I was threatened with rape and paraded around naked before the eyes of leering German soldiers.

Sometimes, they would offer me special treatment in exchange for the simplest of facts about the SOE—day trips, fresh clothes, better accommodations. Other times, they would point out to me that they already knew almost everything anyway.

"Milton Maxwell has two cubes of sugar in his tea," a smug interrogator told me one day. "And he prefers scones to cake. That's the level of detail we hold about your organization. Why would you put yourself through this suffering for nothing? If you work with us, you'll only be telling us what we already know and your life will be so much easier."

They were toying with me but I knew it, and that made it easier to keep my mouth shut. They might have known what Colonel Maxwell had for morning tea, but that didn't mean they knew anything of consequence. The Germans sometimes seemed panicked, and many of the questions they pushed me on were things I had no idea about anyway. Things like the advance of the Allies across France, and their terror at that prospect was music to my ears. I just had to hold on, and liberation might still come.

And then all of a sudden, a group of us prisoners from Fresnes were crammed into boxcars. I suspected we were presently en route to Germany and I took that as another good sign. If the Germans were moving political prisoners back into secure territory, the Allies were likely in or at least nearing Paris.

"At least we are far away from Avenue Foch now," I said to Romilly, who mumbled something in agreement, but still sat drooping and despondent. At least I'd been prepared for the torture during my training. Perhaps part of Romilly's problem was that she was just a civilian who had been trying to do her part to help and was unlucky enough to be caught.

A distant explosion rang out, and the train suddenly braked, throwing Romilly and me into the prisoners beside us. The sound of buzzing overhead brought another explosion—much closer this time—and then boots on the ground as guards ran past our carriage, fleeing the train to hide. The rapid thumping of bullets hitting the ground rang out as the planes buzzed again.

"They're just going to leave us here to die, aren't they?" Romilly said miserably.

"It must be the Allies," I reminded her. "They might destroy the railway tracks but they won't hit the train intentionally. If the guards had any sense at all, they'd stay onboard."

But she seemed unconvinced as we heard still more boots on the ground, and panicked cries from the Germans as they fled the train. Romilly cowered beside me, crying softly, but I stiffened, my ears tuning in to another sound.

"Help! Is anyone there? Can someone help us?"

An American man was shouting out for help in the next carriage. No one said anything in reply at first but when he called again, his voice breaking with desperation, I called back, "Sir! Are you on the train?"

"Yes! Do you have water? We haven't had water for many days," he shouted, and I detected now in his voice a level of utter desperation.

"I'm so sorry. We don't have any water either."

The man fell silent for a moment, and I collapsed back against the wall of the carriage, deeply regretful that I could not help him. I was thirsty too—but I'd only been on the train for a few hours, and I'd had ready access to water at the prison. This man was suffering in a whole other way.

"There's nothing we can do," I said, more to myself than to anyone else. "We are trapped, just as he is."

Near me, an older woman cleared her throat.

"Well, maybe not," she said hesitantly. "Our door is unlocked."

"It is?" I said, startled. "But…"

"I've been on this train for three days," she told me. "Didn't you notice how they were rushing when they brought you in? The Germans are in a panic and often forget to lock the doors."

"Sir!" I called out, sitting up. "Some of the guards have run away from the bombing. Perhaps all of them! If your door is unlocked, you could try to jump off the train. Perhaps there's water nearby?"

"Miss, we're all shackled to the floor in here." I looked around my carriage. The women around me were all shackled in pairs, but none of us were secured to the floor. The man continued wearily, "A few men in here are loose but they are in no state to escape."

"Romilly," I whispered. "Let's try to help them."

"But we will be shot!" she exclaimed. "No!"

"We can at least go to the door and see if it really is unlocked. And if it is, I can try to get an idea of where we are." She didn't move, so I leaned my head close to hers and whispered, "Listen—there are still planes around, the guards won't return until they go." She avoided my gaze, and I nudged her. "I can't do this without you."

She sighed impatiently and carefully, awkwardly, we scrambled to our feet and made our way through the throng of women to the sliding door of our carriage. I pushed it open a crack, and although the older woman had warned me, I was shocked to find it was indeed unlocked. This was the boost to my morale I sorely needed. After all, if the Germans were so lax with carriage security as we traveled, perhaps I really did have a chance of escape once we reached our destination.

Outside, the morning sun was rising, casting a romantic glow over the fields that extended as far as I could see to the east and the tiny village in the distance on the north. I couldn't see any guards—I assumed they'd run to hide among the civilian houses. Behind us, all of the women were shifting to get closer to the open door.

"There," Romilly whispered, pointing with her free hand. She'd spotted a cattle trough just a few dozen feet from the train line.

"But how do we bring it back for them?"

"Take this," one of the women in the carriage muttered reluctantly, and the women worked together to pass her empty canteen to Romilly and me at the door. "Take some water to the men then refill it and bring it back. I will share it with you as we travel."

"If we get shot doing this…" Romilly muttered uneasily, as we began the exceedingly awkward process of climbing down from the carriage, still shacked at the ankles and wrists.

"Then we will die knowing we were doing our best," I said flatly. I heard the sigh she tried to swallow, but soon we were scrambling toward the trough, our footsteps in sync so the shackle didn't slow us down any more than it had to. We quickly drank a few handfuls of water ourselves, then filled the canteen and made our way back up the slope to the other carriage. The women from our carriage were pouring out now, making their way down to the water.

"Please go as quickly as you can," I called to them anxiously. They ignored me, continuing down to the trough, and I was relieved by the sound of more planes overhead. The Allies were unlikely to shoot at innocent civilians, and the soldiers were unlikely to return while the air raid was still active. Would this be my chance to escape? Perhaps. But first, I had to help those men.

"Sir?" I called, as we approached the other carriage. "I have water—"

The door slid open, and I couldn't hide my shock at what was inside. There were only eight of them, but these were airmen—American and British by the looks of their tattered, bloodstained uniforms. The men were filthy. Their faces were marked with dirt, their eyes sunken and hollow…their lips cracked and bleeding. Two men were unconscious or worse, and the other six were shackled to the ground. They leaned toward us anyway, as if so desperately thirsty that they just wanted to be as close to the water as they could get.

"Here," I said urgently, passing the canteen to the man at the front. "Just a few sips, then pass it on. When it runs out, we'll refill it and bring it back. As long as we have the time, you'll get a second turn."

But by the time the canteen was empty, other women from the carriage had their fill of water. Romilly and I stood beside the open door of the men's carriage to talk to Captain Jock Mendleson, the man who'd called for help, while other women went down to refill the canteen for the men a second time.

"We're done for," he said heavily, staring at the floor of the carriage. "This isn't how you treat a prisoner of war. This is how you treat someone you're going to execute."

"You can't know that, Captain," I scolded him. "If they were going to execute you, you'd most likely be dead already. Hasn't the war brought twists and turns to your life already? Perhaps the next twist will bring the end of it. Perhaps you'll be home with your loved ones before you know it."

Now that the men had been able to have a few sips from the canteen, the urgency was gone when the woman from my carriage returned with it a second time. The men savored the water now, sipping it slowly, sighing with contentment as the moisture drained over their parched throats. Jock took his second pass at the canteen, then handed it to one of his companions as he looked to me again.

"What did you do to get yourselves captured?"

"Resistance work," Romilly said.

"I'm a spy," I told him, and his eyes widened in surprise. "France is riddled with British spies—men, women—all ages, all backgrounds. The war is far from over, and you are far from doomed." And then I told him about the success at D-day, and the circumstances of my own capture at Salon-La-Tour…my regret at the decision to travel by car.

"But it is what it is," I said, shrugging, as I tried to keep the conversation positive. "And now we just have to get through each day until we can escape or the Allies liberate us."

"The guards are coming back!" one of the women shouted. I looked around—wondering if it was too late for Romilly and me to make a run for it, but she was standing beside me staring at the ground. If I were on my own, perhaps I could have run. My ankle still ached sometimes but was healing.

But I could never escape shackled to another woman if she weren't in the right frame of mind to accept the risk, and I didn't need to ask Romilly to know that she wasn't.

I gave the American men one last determined look and a whisper of good luck, before they slid the door closed. Slow as we were, Romilly and I were still the fastest on our feet, so we rushed back to refill the canteen one last time. When I handed the full canteen back to its rightful owner, an older woman who seemed far too frail to have run down the hill herself, she caught my hand.

"My mother used to say that even in the worst of times, we must look for ways to do good," she said quietly. "I think I had forgotten until just now. So thank you."

I felt Giles with me in that moment. This was the spirit with which he'd lived his entire life, and it was how I too could find meaning, whatever came next, even with all of my fear for my son and my uncertainty about my own future.

CHAPTER 23

JOSIE
Pforzheim Prison, Germany
September, 1944

I tried not to mark the passing of time, but that window meant that I had no way to ignore it. I had seen the end of spring from that cell and had watched summer pass.

One day, a guard came to my door. They usually changed over my waste bucket in the morning so I pushed myself off the bed and picked it up to hand it to him, following the same routine I'd had for months. This time, the guard shook his head in and motioned for me to follow him. Stunned, I took a wobbly step out the door.

"What is the date?" I blurted.

"13 September," he said curtly.

I had been in that cell for close to five months. Had the war ended in that time? If so, and the Allies lost, it was entirely possible that nothing in the German prison would have changed. I was already struggling to walk on wasted muscles, but my knees gave out at the thought that I was leaving that cell to enter a world where Hitler had won. The guard grabbed me by the arm to drag me into an office after I collapsed. He dropped me unceremoniously into a chair, then sat opposite me to complete paperwork. I sat bewildered as he flicked from page to page, every single slip of paper marked with the words *Nacht und Nebel.*

Was this sudden change in my circumstances a good thing, or a bad thing? I had no idea, and I was so worn down—so overwhelmed—that I could not even bring myself to ask. Eventually, the guard slipped the paperwork into a folder, propped it beneath his arm, and motioned for me to follow him back out into the hallway. I pushed myself to my feet and collapsed again. He huffed impatiently and once again was dragging me by the arm as I stumbled after him—but then—we walked through a door and I was outside. I looked up at that vibrant blue sky and I sucked in a sharp breath, greedy for fresh air.

All too soon, he pushed me into the back of a van and zipped the canvas door closed behind me. Was this an opportunity to escape? But no. I was still handcuffed, still weak. I had no way to cut the canvas open anyway. I sat alone in that van for an hour or more as it drove, thrown mercilessly from one side to the other with every corner. When it finally stopped, I was once again manhandled from the back and found myself standing outside of another prison.

"Karlsruhe," the guard said abruptly. "You've been transferred."

There was an all-female wing at Karlsruhe—even the guards were women. A brusque guard named Hertha oversaw my paperwork, and the pitying glances she kept flicking at me as I waited told me I looked every bit as rough as I felt. When she handed me my prison uniform, I thanked her in German, and she was visibly relieved.

"Where am I?" I asked her.

"Karlsruhe is a civilian prison."

"But…why am I at a civilian prison?"

"You aren't the only prisoner of war they've sent us in the past few days but we have no idea why you're being sent here. And your N&N designation means we are not supposed to let you associate with the rest of the prisoners. We're supposed to keep you in solitary confinement permanently..." She paused, glanced at the door, as if checking that we were alone, then dropped her voice. "But we don't have enough cells for that, so you'll be bunking in with another N&N prisoner."

"*Nacht und Nebel,*" I whispered. "I know it's 'night and fog.' What does that mean?" It was well and truly obvious to me by that point that being an "N&N" prisoner was no positive thing, but I was still curious about the term.

"It's just a designation of political prisoner," she said. "Come."

She led me patiently through the long corridors of the prison, stopping automatically when I slumped against a wall because my muscles were too weak to hold me up. I was exhausted from the effort of carrying myself upright for the first time in months even though I was grateful that Hertha did not man-handle me like the male guard did.

Most of the cells we passed were empty, but I saw hundreds of female prisoners outside in the yard through the windows. When Hertha pushed open a door and I saw long rows of showers inside, I could not help but to weep. I was still wearing the same outfit I'd been in when I was arrested five months earlier and had not bathed since that day. My clothes were so stained with blood and dirt and sweat that most of the fabric was stiff.

Hertha went back to the door and peered through the small window, looking back into the hallway, then she reached into her pocket and handed me a slip of soap.

"Thank—" I started to say, but she cut me off with a low hiss and shook her head. I nodded in understanding—she was obviously concerned she'd get in trouble for helping me—but I was certain my gratitude showed in my eyes.

The water in the showers was icy cold, but I didn't care one bit. I washed every inch of my body with that soap. To pull on even that stiff prison uniform, after months in the same filthy clothes, was one of the most pleasant sensations I had ever experienced.

Once I was dressed, Hertha took me back through the prison block, all the way to the front office, then down another corridor. Here the doors were much closer together, but unlike the main dormitory, each cell was enclosed. She stopped, unlocked a door and swung it open. I gasped in surprise. This space was much larger than my previous cell, with two chairs and a low table, and a cupboard, and even a bed with a straw mattress on it. A woman lay on the mattress, facing the wall so I could not see her face.

Perhaps other prisoners would not smile at a shared cell with a single bed, topped by a thin, filthy mattress that was already occupied. But there was so much for me to be excited about in that room. Human company! Soft furnishings! A toilet and even a sink!

Oh, even if I could just drink as much water as I wanted, I would be in heaven.

Hertha motioned for me to step into the cell, and the prisoner rolled over on the bed and sat up with a start. As the door slammed closed behind me, I wondered if I'd finally lost my mind.

"Chloe? Is it really you?"

"Fleur?" I croaked. She rose from the bed and rushed to my side as my knees gave way, catching me just in time to help me to the bed. My whole body shook with sobs, but she held me close, and rubbed my back.

"Eloise," she said firmly. *"They* know my real name, so it only seems fair that you do too."

"I'm Jocelyn," I wept. How had I survived for so long without so much as an embrace? Now that I was hugging a friend again, it seemed as vital to my survival as air or water and food. "My friends call me Josie."

"…so, Veronique and I decided that was enough, we'd alert Baker Street. But as we were preparing the transmission, the Gestapo arrived…" I swallowed roughly. "She took an L pill.

The last time I saw her, they were dragging her outside to try to force her to vomit. I have no idea if she survived."

Eloise listened silently as I explained about the circumstances that led to my arrest. I could not bring myself to explain the torture I had endured at Avenue Foch. Even bringing it to mind was enough to make me weep.

I was distracted pushing those memories away for a moment but when I looked at Eloise, I saw that she had wrapped her arms around her chest and was trembling, staring at me with sheer terror in her eyes.

"Turner is the double agent," she choked.

"Yes," I said gently. "It's shocking, I know."

"You don't understand," she whispered. "I trusted him to arrange care for my son. He's the only person who knows where Hughie is."

There was nothing we could do from the prison cell. No way to raise the alarm, no way for her to check on her little boy's welfare. All I could do for her was to hold her while she rode the wave of panic and frustration. And later, when I tried to talk about the five months I'd spent in solitary confinement but the words just kept sticking in my throat, she held me too.

All we had was that we were together. Regardless of how dire our situation was, I knew we were blessed to have that.

CHAPTER 24

CHARLOTTE
Liverpool
July, 1970

A few strange days have passed since my conversation with Aunt Kathleen. I'm trying to find the courage to ask Dad about Josie Miller again. This time, I plan on asking him straight—were you really in love with her? *Could you have fathered a child with her?* But before the opportunity arises, Theo calls, and he does not sound like his normal self.

"I'm sorry to ask this," he says, his voice high and a little strained. "Perhaps you could come to my flat? There's something I need to show you."

"There's something I should talk to you about, too," I say, although I'm still not sure if I should tell him about Aunt Kathleen's suspicions about Dad's relationship with Josie. I don't want to get his hopes up that we might have stumbled upon his mother *and* his father in one fell swoop. I make the trip over to Manchester right away and find Theo a ball of chaotic energy. He tells me to take a seat at his little dining room table, and he bustles about the kitchen, making cups of coffee and chatting nervously about the cricket game he watched with his friends the previous night.

"Theo," I interrupt him after a while. "What's going on?"

"The birth certificate came," he says, suddenly incredulous. "We *found* her."

Jocelyn Nina Miller was born in London in 1920, and at that point at least, was the only child of Tobias Andrew Miller and Drusilla Rose Miller, *née* Sallow. Drusilla and Andrew had married two years before.

"So...these people might be your grandparents?"

Theo chews his thumbnail anxiously.

"I went to the library and looked in the phone books. I can't find Tobias or Drusilla Miller anywhere."

"I'm sorry..."

"Wait—it's just...." He gnaws at his lip then cracks his knuckles. "Your dad told you Jocelyn's parents had an especially unhappy divorce, right?"

"Right."

"Well, I can't find a Drusilla Miller anywhere. But Drusilla is such an unusual name and Sallow is *incredibly* rare and I did find a Dr. Drusilla Sallow."

"Dad said Jocelyn's mother was a doctor!" I gasp. "She must be using her maiden name again?"

"It makes sense, doesn't it?"

"Where is this Drusilla Sallow?"

"That's the thing, Charlotte," Theo says urgently, then he jabs his forefinger against the table. "She's right *here*."

"Here?" I look around blankly.

"In Manchester! Her listed address is only a few miles from here." I gasp again, and he runs his hands through his hair then says bleakly, "But it's probably not her. Right? I mean, it could be. But it's probably not. What are the chances that my grandmother would be living just a few miles away from me?"

"I really don't know."

"I just keep thinking if I drive past, I might catch a glimpse of her."

"What good would that do you? Are you hoping she looks like you?"

"No, I'm more thinking that if *this* Dr. Drusilla Sallow is much younger than Jocelyn's mother would be, I can rule her out." He looks at me pleadingly, then, as if he's asking for my permission, he asks, "Would it be so bad to just drive past her house?"

"It wouldn't be *bad*," I say carefully. "I'm just not sure it would do you any good."

He sighs as he nods, but after that, the silence is tender.

I've grown to like and admire Theo. I see him as a man who has spent his whole life searching for a family he knew he would likely never find—and he's used that unresolved desire to do good in other people's lives. Over the past few weeks he's told me about that family history group, and all of the joy his members find in digging deep into their own pasts.

I think about that in the context of my grief for my mother. If there was some tenuous link that might make me feel reconnected to her...some tenuous link that might help me understand her, I'd chase it down hard. A burst of pure empathy washes over me.

"Let's drive over," I say, reaching for my handbag. "Together. Now."

Theo looks at me in surprise.

"Why did you change your mind?" he asks.

A vivid image of my mother flashes to mind and I'm not sure I can explain myself without crying, so I just shrug and push myself into a standing position.

"It's summer holidays and we're both teachers. What else do we have to do with our spare time?"

The jittery, uneven tone of Theo's breathing betrays his anxiety as he drives toward the house, but we don't speak. We turn into Drusilla Sallow's street and Theo starts tapping his thigh with his fingertips to a manic, frantic rhythm.

Not quite eight minutes after we left Theo's apartment, we are parked right opposite the cottage.

"When I was younger I used to daydream about inadvertently walking past a blood relative, but it's always been a kind of fantasy. It feels strange to acknowledge to myself that perhaps it was a real possibility at least for the last few years since I moved here."

The cottage is quiet and still, the curtains drawn and the front door closed despite the oppressive heat. The expansive garden is lovingly tended, hedges trimmed into careful shapes to frame beds of colorful petunias.

We sit staring at the cottage for a long time. Every now and again I draw a breath, intending to ask Theo what he's thinking, but when I look at the expression on his face I fall silent again. He is staring at that house, a lifetime of hope and longing in his blue eyes, and I feel like an intruder on the moment even though he invited me to be there.

But every attempt I have made to help my father seems to have gone awry. He's abandoned his project and he seems to be plodding along as he was before, focusing on work and spoiling Wrigley at every available moment. I don't think I helped Dad at all in the end, and I'm starting to worry that I've just led Theo to disappointment too.

"Josie might—I'm just saying Josie might not even be your mother," I blurt. Still staring at the cottage, Theo nods.

"I know that."

It's so hot in the car that I have sweated through my nylon blouse, and every now and again, a rivulet of moisture runs down my forehead or down the gap between my shoulder blades. The windows are open but that's not enough, and just when I think I can bear it no more and I'm about to suggest that we leave, a taxicab pulls into the driveway. Theo sucks in a harsh breath.

The driver steps out of the car and rushes around to the front passenger side, where he helps a diminutive woman from her seat. She appears to be in her seventies or eighties. She stands awkwardly, leaning on a cane and pressing a hand to her back as if she's in pain, but even from a distance it is clear that her conversation with the driver is not a happy one. The woman is pointing fiercely toward the back of the cab, and the man is pointing at his watch, and for a minute or two they just squabble like this. But then the man throws his hands into the air and walks to the back of the car. He opens the trunk and pulls out a collection of paper bags of groceries. One by one, he sets the bags down hard on the lawn in front of the house, until he reaches for the final bag, this time spilling some of the items onto the ground as he drops it.

The woman shouts and waves her cane at him as he drives away, then she looks down at the groceries on her lawn and her shoulders droop.

Theo is out of the car before I can even stop him. I leap from my own side and follow him as he rushes toward the mess of groceries on the ground. The woman looks at us warily as we approach, her chin high and her gaze haughty. We've not exchanged a single word, but I already know this is not a woman who is comfortable asking for help.

But if we don't help her, she's going to have to make a dozen separate trips from the drive to her house, leaning on that cane. I tell myself that we're not actually meddling, but rather helping a woman in need.

"Sorry. S-sorry," Theo stammers, as he exposes his palms to the woman and slows his steps as he nears her. "I didn't mean to startle you, but we were sitting in our car chatting over there and I saw what just happened and wanted to come and offer you some help."

"I appreciate that, young man, but I'll be quite fine on my own," the woman says stiffly. But then she looks down at her cane, and the groceries, and her shoulders slump again. "Actually…"

She unlocks her door and then holds the screen open while we take the bags into her kitchen. There are framed photographs all along her hall table. There's a black-and-white photo of a young girl, frail and sickly looking, smiling bravely into the camera. Around it, there are photos of two women together through various stages of life. At the back of the table, there's a photo that is unmistakably the woman we've been helping. She's younger, dressed in a lab coat and standing out front of what I suspect is a hospital. I catch Theo's eye and nod as subtly as I can manage toward the photos. I watch his shoulders rise and lock somewhere near his ears as he surveys them.

"Thank you," the woman says. "I recently injured my hip and I'm not yet able to drive. I got into a disagreement with that dreadful taxi driver about the fare."

"Are you a doctor?" I ask her, pointing to the photo in the frame.

"Yes, I was a doctor. I retired only a few years ago." She sighs wistfully. "That was a terrible mistake. The human spirit is not designed to stop."

"Are you Drusilla Miller?" Theo asks. I gasp, and he gives me a panicked look, as if he'd suck the words back in if he could. So much for taking this slow and just "driving past." The woman's eyes widen then narrow. Her grip on the cane tightens. I have no doubt she'll use that thing to drive us from her house if we make one wrong move, so I step toward Theo and slip my hand into his elbow, intending to tug him back toward the door.

"Who are you? Who are you really?" the woman asks sharply.

"My name is Theo Sinclair," Theo says, but then he pauses and repeats, "Theo. My name is *Theo*." Clearly he was hoping that Drusilla Sallow was somehow aware of a lost grandchild and would react with joy at the sound of his name, but her face remains perfectly blank. He clears his throat and pushes his glasses up his nose. "I...the thing is, I..."

"Theo is a postgraduate history student." I blurt out the lie before I even have a chance to think it through. "He specializes in the SOE."

Drusilla sighs and gives us a disappointed look.

"I see."

"We wondered if perhaps you are Jocelyn Miller's mother," I say weakly.

"If you are here, young lady, you know the answer to that question," she says tightly. "What is it you want?"

"Truthfully, I don't know much about Jocelyn at all, but I was hoping you could tell us a little bit about her," Theo asks softly. "Who was she? What was she like?"

Drusilla eases herself into an armchair.

"If you're going to scam your way in here and start dredging up the past—" she points to me with her cane "—you, make me a cup of tea." She turns the cane toward Theo. "And you. Unpack these groceries. I'll rest until you're done, then we'll talk."

"You might not have thought of her as strong-willed if you met her—she was sick all of the time as a child and I know she seemed very timid to most, but she had a real knack for getting her own way. I mean, just take her name, for example. I named her Jocelyn after my grandmother and I loved that name, but some terrible child down the street from us in Paris once told her it sounded like his grandfather's name. She was so stubborn about it, and by the time Jocelyn was eight or nine, everyone else in her life called her Josie," Drusilla says, chuckling, but then she sighs. "I was the only holdout for most of the rest of her life."

"She was an unwell child?" I ask. We're all seated in the armchairs now, nursing cups of tea, the groceries packed away. I'm getting the sense that once she got used to the shock of our visit, Drusilla might just relish the opportunity for a trip down memory lane.

"For most of her childhood, I was convinced I'd lose her young," Drusilla says, her eyes misting. She clears her throat. "She had Coeliac Sprue. At that time, no one really understood what it was or how to treat it, and somewhere around thirty percent of children who suffered from it didn't make it to adulthood. Of course, since the '50s we've known that it's an autoimmune disease—in some small percentage of the population, ingesting gluten triggers the body to damage its own small bowel. Well, long before medical science figured that out, Jocelyn modified her diet to relieve her symptoms. She and I used to bicker about it because there seemed to be no scientific basis for such a cure! But you see what I mean about her strong will?"

"So she was frail and unwell," Theo says hesitantly. "And yet she somehow ended up enlisting in the SOE?"

Doctor Sallow sips her tea delicately, then sits the cup down on a saucer on a little lamp table beside her chair. She takes a long, slow breath in, as if fortifying herself, then she folds her hands in her lap and says, "Every year, I liked to come to London to visit my friend Quinn..."

"So that was it? She finished her training and you never heard from her again?" Theo asks, an hour later. We have listened, riveted, as Drusilla Miller explained the story of her daughter's involvement with what appeared to be the WAAF, but she now understands was the SOE. She's been into her room to retrieve a small photo album, which I'm flicking through as she talks. There are a handful of photos of Josie, mostly as a girl, some of which reveal a child looking so ill it almost breaks my heart.

"She did come back briefly one morning—just to tell us she wouldn't be in touch for a while," Drusilla says, suddenly avoiding our gazes. "Suffice to say we quarreled. I was half-asleep when she arrived and completely unprepared for the difficult conversation we had that day. I had no idea it was the last time I'd ever see her."

"And did the SOE keep you abreast of whatever she was doing?"

"Not at all," Drusilla says, her tone fierce. "She'd told us she had enlisted in the WAAF, although by the time she left, I knew that wasn't the whole truth. Still, in lieu of any useful contacts, I kept calling various WAAF offices, hoping if I made a nuisance of myself someone would figure out where she really was and put me through to the right agency. One day, I found myself on the phone with a man named Gerard Turner. He wouldn't tell me which agency he represented, but he was at least a helpful fellow, at least initially. He confirmed my suspicion that she'd been posted somewhere overseas but assured me that she would be well cared for. I called him every few weeks for a while, but then one day I called and *he* was unavailable too. And this time, his secretary suggested I stop calling—that I'd hear from them as soon as they had news. Well, France was liberated, and still *nothing*! Jocelyn could have walked through the door without warning one day, just as she had done in 1942. Or she could have been long dead. I had no way of knowing and for the longest time it was as though both realities were true."

"The authorities eventually did update you, didn't they?" Theo asks uneasily. Drusilla's eyes are hollow as she nods.

"In late 1944, I opened the door one day and a stranger was standing there. I could tell the minute I made eye contact with him that something was wrong, but for a long time, he just stared at me…it was quite unnerving. Then finally, he asked me if I was Jocelyn's mother. It was dreadfully awkward. He looked as if he was going to cry. I didn't know what to do, but by then, I was starting to wonder if this chap was her friend. She made so few friends in her life—my Jocelyn was quite self-sufficient—but she returned from France with a young man—"

My heart leaps. Theo glances at me, then croaks to confirm, "Was it Noah Ainsworth?"

Drusilla nods.

"Yes! After her return to the UK they were constantly exchanging letters and I think they even managed to meet up a few times, although I never met him personally. So when I saw how upset the man on my doorstep was... I just assumed he was a friend and, well, Noah was the only male friend she had once she arrived here so..."

"Was it him?" I manage.

"No," Drusilla murmurs. "No, but as soon as I asked if he was, the man's entire demeanor changed. He introduced himself as Gerard Turner and told me that Jocelyn was gone. I didn't believe him at first, but he was adamant and I had no choice but to accept it eventually. It seems she made a crucial mistake on a mission in France. According to Mr. Turner, that error led to her capture *and* the capture of another agent." Theo and I both gasp in surprise. Drusilla's gaze drops again. "I was very concerned that my daughter's mistakes would become public knowledge and that this would be how people remembered her. He assured me I need not worry—everything was highly classified, so as long as I kept her story to myself, no one else would ever know she'd been involved with the SOE at all." She flicked a glance at us. "But now you've tracked me down, so I'm guessing that wasn't an accurate take on the situation."

"Her records are still classified," Theo said quickly. "No one outside of this room will know what you just told us."

"Even if she made some mistakes, Doctor Sallow, she still did an incredibly noble thing," I say.

"I know. And I knew my daughter so I'm certain she went into that crazy role with the very best of intentions." Drusilla reaches into her pocket and withdraws a handkerchief. She taps delicately at the corners of her eyes as we all sit in a horrified silence, pondering everything she had shared with us.

"Dr. Miller," Theo asks suddenly. "Did your daughter have a child?"

Drusilla lowers her handkerchief. She reaches for the photo album and starts to flick through the pages. I entertain a fantasy of Drusilla turning to a page featuring a beautiful baby with a striking likeness to Theo. I'd get to bear witness to an emotional reunion between mourning grandmother and lonely grandchild.

But instead, she turns to a page in the middle of the book and I am suddenly staring into the eyes of an adult woman who is clearly very ill. Her cheekbones jut out from her face, and her hair hangs limply around her shoulders. She's wearing a hospital gown and sitting slumped in a wheelchair.

"You don't have to be a doctor or even a woman to understand how taxing pregnancy can be on a woman's body. Does that look like a body capable of the demands of pregnancy and childbirth?" Drusilla says, pointing toward the photo.

"But... I believe she was hospitalized in early 1942," Theo says urgently. "Perhaps she had a child and you didn't know—"

"That photo was *taken* in early 1942," Drusilla interrupts him. "Yes, she was hospitalized—she had surgery to remove a significant ovarian cyst and her body just would not heal. That's it. She wasn't physically strong enough at that point to bear a child. Why *are* you asking me this?" Her gaze narrows. "And how did you come to hear about my daughter, anyway?"

"Part of Theo's work is looking for the children of the SOE agents who served," I say, surprised at how easily the lies are rolling off my tongue. Drusilla nods and closes the album, giving us a thoughtful look.

"It must have been very difficult for those women to leave their children behind to go to war," she murmurs. "Just as it was very difficult for those of us left behind to learn our children were gone too. I only wish Jocelyn's sacrifice meant something. To know that she is gone, all for nothing, haunts me to this day."

I understand senseless loss better than I might have, once upon a time. We thank Drusilla for her time and walk slowly back to the car.

"Not her, then," Theo says lightly.

"No, it doesn't seem so," I say. "Are you okay?"

He assures me he's disappointed but otherwise fine, but when I offer to come in to his flat for a while to keep him company, he tells me he needs some time alone to think.

"This is a nice surprise," Dad says. I can't remember a thing about the drive back to Liverpool but I find myself in his office at the main branch of his workshops. I'm sitting opposite his desk, my foot tapping impatiently against the floor. Dad peers at me, frowning. "Unless this isn't a social visit."

"When I asked you about Josie Miller a few weeks ago," I blurt, "you said she was one of the best women you ever knew."

"She was."

"I hate to ask you about her again, but I have to know." I suck in a breath. "Dad. Was she competent?"

"What a strange question," Dad says, startled. "Why are you still thinking about this?"

"Theo and I found Josie Miller's mother," I say, and then it all trickles out—how easy it was once we knew Josie's real name, how Drusilla lives so very close to Theo's flat and how it felt like the universe was smiling upon us because before we knew it we were in a room with her. I tell my father just about everything except for Theo's real motivation for trying to find Josie's family. That still does not seem like my story to tell.

The words tumble out of me in a rush, and when I finally trail off, my father pinches the bridge of his nose as if he is developing a headache. He sits back in his chair, and then he slides down it, until he is resting the back of his head in the middle of the backrest. For a long moment he sits in silence, staring up at the ceiling of his office.

I am an adult, fully grown and independent, but I feel like a child waiting for a scolding after confessing a schoolyard sin. When my father finally speaks, his voice is so faint I have to strain to hear it.

"I remember barreling into my parents' house without knocking when I was about your age. I caught my parents kissing rather passionately in the lounge. They were fully clothed and it was all appropriate, but I remember feeling so confused at the affection they had for one another, and the fact that even after all of those years of marriage they still seemed to want to express it like teenagers. To me, they were just my mother and father, and I knew them only through that lens. I sometimes forgot that they were also human."

"I know you're human, Dad," I protest. He sits up, and rubs his eyes.

"It was such a shock to me when my parents died, Lottie. You have a taste of this now that your mother is gone. While your parents are alive a part of you remains a child. But once they are gone…"

"Everything feels different," I finish for him, throat suddenly tight. "Like your safety net has disappeared."

Dad nods sadly. Since my mother died I feel I have been thrust into adulthood in a whole new way, and I am unprepared and floundering. Perhaps the bitterness I have struggled with for these months is rooted in a childish sense of injustice— I needed more time with her. I *deserved* more time with her.

"I've been in love three times in my life," Dad says suddenly. His gaze meets mine. "I loved your mother first. But you remember I told you I walked the escape line with a friend? Well, that was Josie—"

"So you and Josie Miller did have an affair while you were dating Mum?" I gasp.

"No. God no," Dad says hastily. "At first, we just shared a special friendship, forged through an incredibly difficult moment in our lives."

"Good." I exhale.

Dad pauses, then says reluctantly, "I don't think your mother ever really believed that though. It didn't matter how many times I assured her otherwise—she wanted me to cut off contact with Josie from the minute I came back to the UK the first time. I loved your mum, but I needed my friends more than ever at that point in my life, and I just couldn't push Josie away."

"You broke up with Mum when you joined the SOE, didn't you?"

"I did. She was furious with me, but I figured by the time I came back from France, I'd run into her at a pub or the post office and she'd be holding hands with some other bloke and it would break my heart, but I'd be happy knowing she was happy. I knew I had to join the SOE, but I couldn't put her through another period of waiting, so I let her go."

"And *then* you fell in love with Josie," I whisper. He nods.

"I'm not ashamed of that. We had a unique relationship and we were both single at the time," Dad says. "But you asked me was she capable? The truth is, there was no one better. She was brilliant. Dedicated and creative. Cautious and persistent. Even in the face of unimaginable danger, her resolve never wavered once, and all of the best things I did through the war, I could only do because she was my partner at the time. I brought out the best in her—and I felt she did exactly the same for me. But..." Dad trails off, his voice breaking, and a strange tension crosses his face. "It all gets a bit blurry after our main mission was complete. I do remember saying goodbye to her at a train station and feeling as if my heart had been torn from my chest. And then of course, my accident happened a few months later—and when I started to get my wits about me again I felt a very strong pull to find her in Paris, but for the life of me, I could not remember the details. I was utterly lost until I saw that poster inviting SOE agents to meet at the apartment the officials had set up. That's when one of our officials told me she was dead."

"I'm sorry, Dad," I say. He sighs, looking out the window wistfully.

"Grief has a way of hitting a person like a ton of bricks sometimes, as you now understand all too well. When I finally came home, I went to your mother because I really didn't have anywhere else to go. I told myself I'd just ask for her help until I was on my feet again, maybe just a few months, but my recovery took so much longer than that. And your mum always was the kind of woman who found it easier to love wholeheartedly than she did to accept love herself. She was there for me at the worst moment of my life. Of course I grew to love her a second time."

"I found the letters," I say slowly. "The ones from Professor Read. Mom had hidden them."

Dad looks briefly surprised, but his expression quickly shifts, until he's just resigned. He walks around the desk to sit in the visitor's chair beside me.

"I wanted to track Remy down right after you were born," he admits.

"You did?" I say, startled.

"I was so happy and the future felt so bright. I wanted to find him...maybe to show him the beautiful baby girl I would never have known if he hadn't saved my life that day. But when I told your mum, she just about blew a gasket. Reminded me of what a mess I was when she took me in after the war. I felt so guilty for that, I never brought it up again."

"How did Josie die, Dad?" I whisper. My dad is very still as he thinks about this question.

"I don't know the specifics," he admits heavily. "They just told me the Gestapo executed her."

"Could Doctor Sallow have been given incorrect information about her daughter's death?"

"I'm really not sure, love. I doubt it."

"It's just she was told that Josie made a mistake. Something that led to her capture, and the capture of another agent."

Dad hesitates, then rubs his eyes.

"She *was* dropped into a war zone with just a few months training. I suppose anything is possible, but the Josie I knew was careful and diligent."

We sit in silence, until I ask hesitantly, "Is there any chance that Josie might have had a child?"

At this, my father looks at me blankly.

"When on earth could she have had a child?"

"Early 1942?" I suggest. His gaze grows skeptical.

"She was definitely not pregnant when we parted in 1941, and after that, she was so unwell. There's no chance she managed to have a baby at that point in her life."

It is exactly as Drusilla says, but I am disappointed for Theo anyway.

"Does Josie's mother understand that even if her daughter did make a mistake or two, she was still an incredible agent? The only thing I know for sure is that the war ended because women like Josie stepped up," Dad says.

"I really don't think Drusilla does understand that, Dad," I whisper, thinking about the sadness in Drusilla's eyes as she talked about her daughter.

"Maybe one day I could meet her."

"Maybe one day, that would be good for both of you," I agree. I might even facilitate such a meeting myself. There's just someone else I have to speak to first.

Chapter 25

"What do you think will happen?" Josie asked me on that first night together. It was late, and we were lying side by side on the bed, staring up at the ceiling. I was still shaken by the events of the day—by the reunion with my friend, or what was left of her, as tortured and starved as she had been, and by the news that my son was not safe from the risk of the war, as I'd long believed. "I am months behind what is happening with the war, of course. Has there been any good news?"

I told her everything I knew about the D-Day landings, and about the joyous, relieved mood that swept Britain at the news.

"So…do you really think we will win?"

"It was looking very promising for us when I was captured," I told her. "I suspect and hope that's why they moved us all further into Germany—the Allies must surely be advancing. Europe will soon be free and the world will be at peace. I'm just not sure…"

"If it will happen in time for us?" she said, finishing my sentence. I nodded sadly.

"I don't think the Germans will give up without a fight.

I'm imagining the advance of the front will be slow." My chest ached at the thought of never seeing Hughie again. I intended to keep a lookout for chances to escape and to keep my spirits up, but I had to be realistic about it too. Josie and I were in a terrible predicament, and now even further from home.

"If we survive, I'm going to meet Noah in Paris," she said, smiling softly. "We're going to have a family. Build a life together."

"If we survive," I whispered, "I'm going to go find my son and he will be enough for me for the rest of my life. I will make my life's work raising him into a good man, the kind of man who cares about other people. A man who cares about what's right, just as his father did."

"Do you think it has been worth it? Even if we don't survive?"

I thought about missing my mother's funeral, about my son being in the care of strangers, perhaps disconnected from the very record of our family. I thought about everything I'd seen and the hours of fear and anxiety and pain I'd experienced.

But then I pictured Hughie growing up without the anxiety of the looming shadow of the Nazis just on the other side of the Channel. I saw him growing up in a world where hate had been conquered, and freedom had won. Surely, if the Allies won the war, humanity would reject bigotry and cruelty and the world would be a better place forever. Surely, if the Allies won, the world would learn to reject hate, and embrace love.

Even if he never knew the role I'd played, it would all be worth it if he could be free.

"Absolutely," I said, my voice cracking with emotion. "My role in all of this has been so small, but at least I did something."

"Even if it costs me my life," Josie whispered, "I will be proud to have sacrificed it for France and for freedom. It means something that we fought for what we believed in, doesn't it?"

"We might still make it," I reminded her, wiping my eyes.

"You've survived all of those months in solitary confinement already. Perhaps we'll just stay here in this cell together until we are liberated."

"That wouldn't be so bad," she said, smiling. "I can certainly think of worse fates."

The first time there was an air raid, we heard the rest of the prison being evacuated down into a basement, but Josie and I were left behind. I could hear others, not far from us, shouting for help in English and French.

I went to the door and thumped on it furiously to add to the protest.

"You can't just leave us here! Help!"

For a few minutes, there was nothing, but then Hertha came to the door. We saw her most days and had become familiar with her, if not friendly. Perhaps she was privy to what Josie had already endured, because Hertha had been allowing us a few special privileges. We were supposed to shower once every three weeks, but she'd been taking us to the shower block every Sunday, and occasionally she would slip us extra food. One day, she even allowed us a whole hour outside, instead of our regulation thirty minutes. As the air raid continued Hertha spoke, frustration in her voice. Josie translated for me from the bed, where she was sitting with her knees drawn up.

"She tells me that the warden says we must stay here."

And then Hertha was gone, her footsteps thumping along the hallway.

It was dark in the cell, but I could see Josie's big eyes and her pale face through the moonlight filtering through the window. I sat beside her on the bed, trying to think of how we might keep ourselves safe if a bomb happened to land on the building, and quickly came to the conclusion that there was nothing we could do to protect ourselves. Even if we lay beneath the bed, that simple wooden plank would offer no protection at all.

"This N&N business…" I asked hesitantly.

"I don't understand the particulars but I know it is not a good thing."

We rode out the air raid sitting on the bed, holding one another's hands. There wasn't much to say when we were both aware that we could die at any second, but I drew comfort from knowing I was with a friend, even as I was frustrated almost to tears at my own powerlessness. Within an hour, the all clear sounded, the prison guards led the other prisoners back to their cells. I stood at the door and thumped until Hertha came back.

"Is it really the intention to leave us here to die if the prison is hit by a bomb?" I asked her. Josie came to stand beside me and translated the words into German through the door, and Hertha replied, her tone low and rushed.

"We are supposed to be isolated. The only reason we are allowed to share a cell is that they do not have the capacity to house us individually. She says they don't really have the capacity to house us at all and the warden is furious that we are here." Josie paused, listening as Hertha spoke, then looked at me anxiously. "Oh no—she says the warden is doing her best to move us on."

"Where to?"

"She just said to a prison equipped to handle political prisoners, not a civilian prison like this," Josie sighed. "God, I hope that doesn't happen."

Life at Karlsruhe was surprisingly tolerable. We had three meals a day delivered to our cell through a hatch, and even "coffee" at 4:00 p.m. each day, which was generally acorn coffee or sometimes bitter, watery tea. The food was woeful by the standards of a free citizen but Josie assured me it could be much worse. There was bread with a small portion of margarine and soup, often with a serving of vegetables at lunch and dinner, and on the weekends, sparse chunks of meat in a thin stew with noodles. Periodically we'd be surprised by a few slices of sausage or milk with our coffee, and Hertha was forever slipping us extra plates if she was on shift.

Josie and I quickly came to an arrangement where I'd eat the bread, and she'd eat her fill of everything else. She had been thin even when we were training, but since her time in the prison, she was all but skin and bones. I was happy for her to have more than her share.

The thought of being moved on, and maybe even being separated from Josie again, filled me with dread. She was so worn down, I already feared I would wake up one morning and find her dead.

CHAPTER 26

JOSIE
Karlsruhe Prison, Germany
October, 1944

Eloise and I were woken by the sound of thumping on our door before dawn one morning. We'd been at Karlsruhe for a few weeks and the routine had been much the same day to day, until that early-morning wakeup call.

"Come," Hertha called. "You need to take a shower." There was a strange tone in her voice I couldn't quite identify.

"Why?" I called back. It wasn't Sunday.

"You're being transferred," she said. This time, her tone had a strange lilt to it—like a note of forced positivity. I was confused, but translated for a sleepy Eloise, just as Hertha opened the door. She was carrying a pile of folded clothes in her arms, two fresh pairs of prison espadrilles on top. The rest of the prison was still quiet and still as we followed her to the shower block.

"Here." She handed us the clothes, then reached into her pocket for a full block of soap and a comb. "Make yourself as neat and tidy as you can."

More soap, and this time, a comb! I stammered my thanks as I took it into my shaking hands.

The skirt she'd given me was far too big and kept slipping

down over my hips, so Eloise helped me tie a knot in the waist so it would stay on. The blouse hung on my frame, but I had a lovely knitted cardigan to wear over it. Eloise gently pulled the comb through my wet hair until it was smoother than it had been in months, and when I looked down at myself, I felt beautiful and feminine, a far cry from the ragged mess I'd been in solitary confinement.

Soon, we were led to the prison's administrative block. Hertha sat with us, tapping her foot against the floor as she stared at the door.

"Is everything okay?" I asked her. Her gaze slid to my face but she didn't say anything. "Hertha?" I prompted. She cleared her throat.

"It's all fine," she said, then more firmly, "Everything is just fine."

"Do you know where we're being transferred?"

"The warden has been very concerned that this situation is so unorthodox," she explained. "We do not have enough staff or the space to care for political prisoners like yourselves and she fears that while you are here, we are vulnerable to Allied air attack. It has been distressing her more and more and she insisted some of you be moved."

"So where are we going?" I repeated.

"It's a farm," she said suddenly, then she forced a smile. "Just a work farm. Lots of fresh air and hopefully much better food! This is a good thing." But her voice was laced with guilt. She was lying, but why? My heart sank as Eloise leaned toward me.

"What is she saying?"

It was my turn to force a smile. There was no point worrying Eloise given we were entirely powerless to change our situation anyway.

"She said we are being moved to a work farm."

"Oh!" Eloise said, brightening. "That doesn't sound so bad."

Two other female prisoners joined us then, their hair also wet and freshly combed. Hertha and another guard led us through the front door where a transport was waiting in the soft pre-dawn light.

I caught Hertha's eye just as she pulled the zipper down to close the canvas at the back of the truck. The other guard was back further, out of sight, so I mouthed *thank you*. As Hertha looked away, I saw the unmistakable sheen of tears in her eyes.

Eloise began chatting with the other women in the back of the truck right away. Wendy Jones and Mary Williams were also SOE agents. They had trained together but had been arrested separately and only reunited when they arrived at Karlsruhe, just like me and Eloise. Wendy's reception party was ambushed by the Germans so she'd been taken straight in the minute she landed. Mary was a wireless operator, and she was arrested a few weeks after arrival when a D/F van tracked her down. Both had been imprisoned for just a few weeks.

"We're going to a work farm," Eloise told them.

"Oh, good," Wendy said, exhaling with relief. "It was all a bit strange there, wasn't it? I had the sense the jail didn't know what to do with us. Maybe it will be better at this new place."

As we boarded the train for Strasbourg that day, I could not stop thinking about the distress in Hertha's face as that truck pulled away, but I let Mary and Wendy and Eloise enjoy their optimism. There would be no harm in a moment of peace and positivity, even if it turned out to be unmerited.

CHAPTER 27

CHARLOTTE
Liverpool
July, 1970

I've been sitting on the park bench under the tree outside of Professor Read's office for three hours when he finally walks along the path past me. When I call his name, he startles, as if he hadn't noticed me there.

"Oh, hello there," he says, brows knitting. It's clear from the puzzled look on his face that he recognizes me but can't quite place me, so I leap to my feet and rush to fall into step beside him as he walks toward his building.

"Charlotte Ainsworth," I remind him. "Noah Ainsworth's daughter?"

"Of course," he says, momentarily relieved before wariness crosses his features. "Did I have a meeting booked with you and your father today?"

"No, sir," I say politely.

"Ah, well, Mrs. White is on vacation at the moment but she's back next Monday." That explains why no one answered the phone during my dozens of attempts to get through yesterday. He looks at me hopefully. "Perhaps you could call then and make an appointment...?"

"This won't take long, Professor," I say firmly. It's a hopeful lie—the truth is I have no idea how long it'll take. Read sighs and rests his briefcase on the ground as he pulls a large ring of keys from his pocket and unlocks the door to his building, then motions for me to step inside first. We walk in silence up the stairs toward his offices, and I hold his briefcase while he unlocks the next door. The smell of Mrs. White's cigarettes lingers heavily.

"Come right through," he sighs again, and I follow him down the long corridor to the next locked door. Inside his office, I take the seat opposite his desk and wait while he stows his briefcase beneath the desk. He looks at me expectantly.

"I'm not sure if you're familiar with the SOE agent Jocelyn Miller," I say, and he frowns, but not before a split-second expression of surprise crosses his face.

"It should be abundantly clear to you by now that I'm constrained by the law when it comes to discussing the details in classified records," he says, pursing his lips.

"I know," I say hastily. "It's just that... I came across her mother, and—"

"Her *mother*?"

"That's right, and—"

"How on earth did you *come across* Josie Miller's mother?" he demands, folding his arms over his chest.

"My father..." I can't tell him about Theo's role in all of this. I clear my throat and say, "Dad and Josie were posted together on a mission in France and he knew her real name. I...ah...came across her birth certificate, and it had her mother's name on it."

"Miss Ainsworth, I can't tell if you're being disingenuous or if you really do fail to appreciate how unlikely this is."

"Unlikely?"

"There was a concerted effort to locate Josie Miller's mother in the late '40s," he says stiffly. "I believe another attempt was made in the '50s. No one has ever been able to track her down."

"Her name is Dr. Drusilla Sallow," I say. "She lives here in Manchester."

"Here in *Manchester!*" he repeats incredulously. He reaches for a notepad and pen, scribbles something down, then looks up at me. "Sallow, you say? Not Miller?"

"Her maiden name," I croak uncertainly. "He—I mean, *I* couldn't find Drusilla Miller and Dad told me Jocelyn's parents had a particularly acrimonious divorce, so…er…so I wondered if Drusilla would have gone back to her maiden name. It was right there on her birth certificate."

"*You* found her, did you?" Read's gaze is piercing. "Alone?"

"Theo helped," I mutter. I don't want to get him in any more trouble, but the professor has clearly seen right through me anyway. I try to wrestle the conversation back on track. "None of that matters anyway, Professor Read. I'm only here because Dr. Sallow says that her daughter was executed in Paris in 1944 after making a mistake of some kind in the field. It's just my dad thinks so highly of her, you know? And maybe Josie did make an innocent mistake—but her poor mother to this day thinks she was incompetent or something and… I just wondered…if there's been a mix-up, perhaps you could help Dr. Sallow find out the truth." I trail off helplessly. Professor Read has leaned back in his chair now and is staring at me in slack-jawed disbelief. After a moment, he reaches for the phone and dials a number from heart.

"Helen," he says. "You need to come to my office. *Now.*"

CHAPTER 28

ELOISE
Strasbourg, Germany
October, 1944

The train stopped at Strasbourg, and we were led up into the back of another covered truck. Once we were seated, a guard climbed up to lock our handcuffs to a chain attached to the floor. He climbed back down and this time, left the back open.

The truck began to move, making its way through Strasbourg then along a country road. Wendy and Mary and I chatted about what might come next as we watched the scenery through the back of the truck becoming more and more open. I was feeling hopeful, and it was evident they were too, as we imagined working in green fields with crops just like the ones we could now see, fantasizing about the possibility of more fresh food, but beside me, Josie was silent.

"You're awfully quiet," I murmured to her.

"Just tired," she said, but her smile was wan.

"Did the breakfast not sit well with you…" I said carefully, nodding toward her stomach. She shook her head and forced another thin smile.

"It was utterly delicious. And I'm fine."

It was a long, winding journey, and the truck began to climb along the mountain roads. The scent of pine filled the air as it grew cooler, the expanse of the mountains stretching out beyond and around us. Every now and again, I could see the stonework of an old castle, occasionally the boundary walls of an old monastery or the steeple of a church.

"It's so beautiful up here," I whispered.

Beside me, Josie nodded and said softly, "Imagine how beautiful it would be if it were free."

Something was weighing on her, but it was clear she wasn't ready to discuss it. I wondered if she was feeling uncertain about speaking freely in front of Wendy and Mary, and hoped we'd be lucky enough to find ourselves housed together again so we could talk alone later that night. The truck continued through dense forests, then through beautiful villages scattered with well-loved houses, their window boxes in full bloom with flowers, the curtains open. Every now and again I'd see people walking down the street in their wooden clogs, carrying baskets to market or walking hand-in-hand with their children.

Hughie. I had no way to know who the woman I saw in the park that day really was now that I knew I could not trust Turner. All I could do was to trust the kindness in her eyes as she looked at my son, and to hope and pray that wherever he really was, he was loved, and that I would one day have the chance to straighten it all out and to explain to him how our great big mess came to pass.

When the truck finally came to a stop, a guard came around and unlocked us, releasing both the chain and the handcuffs that locked me to Josie the whole trip. We'd been so well treated on the journey that I was hopeful the worst of it was over, that wherever we'd be staying would be somewhere more pleasant. But as I climbed down from the truck and looked around, my breath caught in my throat.

"We take to Kommandant," the guard said in stilted English, and he motioned with the rifle slung from his shoulder for us to move forward. Josie reached for my hand and squeezed it. I looked at her in shock.

"This isn't a work farm," I whispered.

"Perhaps a stop along the way," Wendy offered uneasily.

There was little color in the scene before me—just endlessly eerie shades of gray and white and black. Masses of men stood watching us in their striped uniforms. Their faces were gaunt and their eyes were hollow, their heads invariably shaved close. They were standing around an expansive yard that was entirely devoid of grass, just exposed pale dirt as far as the eye could see. I could not spot a single female prisoner. Beyond the men, in the near distance, were rows of wooden huts built on tiers, surrounded by guard towers. Beyond that, high fences topped with rows of razor wire.

"Quickly to inside," the guard snapped, pointing his rifle at us as he hurried us toward the entrance to an office. "No looking!" he shouted at the prisoners, swinging the rifle wildly around. The men quickly turned away from us, but as soon as the guard's attention was elsewhere, some turned back again.

Why had Hertha made us dress so well if they were only going to imprison us with these men? I thought about the food on the train and even the small mercy of leaving the back of the truck open so we could have fresh air and watch the scenery as we traveled from Strasbourg. My heart rate slowed as I considered the kindness we'd been shown along the way. Surely, all of that meant something.

We waited in an office for some time, two SS guards seated beside us, barking at us to keep quiet whenever we talked. A woman, possibly a secretary, brought us water at one point, and later the guards took us to use a bathroom. Then officials arrived, in all manner of German uniforms, high-ranking officials from the Wehrmacht and the SD and the SS. These men were led past us, down a hallway until they were out of sight.

Finally, the secretary returned, and motioned for us to follow.

We walked single file down the hallway, the SS guards falling into line closely behind us. The nameplate on the door to the room told us this was the office of the Kommandant.

The light fixture hanging from the ceiling of the large office gave off a gentle yellow glow, making it almost seem homey, with wide leather couches, soft drapes on the windows, even a vase of flowers on top of a filing cabinet. But the air was thick with tension. Six officers seated around the room wore expressions of open hostility while the Kommandant stared at us impassively from behind the heavy desk. His hands rested on a stack of paperwork, his fingers linked together. The secretary stood in a corner, her arms crossed.

We were made to stand in a row in front of the desk, then the Kommandant motioned toward the secretary and handed her some of the papers. She read our names in heavily accented English, handing us each a stack of pages as she went.

I looked down at the page I'd been given but it was in German, and even as I skimmed the words, few made sense to me. The letterhead said *Reichssicherheitshauptamt*, which I knew to be the RSHA—the Head Office of Reich Security. But the paper was titled *Vollzugsettel*. What did that mean? I would have to ask Josie later.

The Kommandant spoke in German, several other men spoke too, and then the secretary collected the paperwork back from us and the guards motioned for us to follow them from the room. Whatever the meeting had been, it was over and I turned to leave—but then Josie cleared her throat and blurted something in German. Her voice was breathless and desperate, almost pleading.

The Kommandant was clearly unimpressed—he barked a harsh phrase at her and waved his hand to dismiss us from the room.

"What did you say?" I asked her, as I filed into the hallway behind her.

"No speaking," the SS guard snapped.

We were led from the room, and I was no more enlightened than when we went in.

"Follow please," the main guard said. We waited in the hallway again for a moment as an announcement played over the speakers. The noise from the prisoners outside faded to quiet, then we were taken through the grounds to an orderly room—the barracks' meeting space. The guard pointed to two trellis tables at the back, where an urn, a box of tea and some cups sat waiting.

"Please to refresh." At our blank looks, he spoke in frustrated, irritated German, pointing to the table and another door. Josie cleared her throat and translated stiffly, "he said we should help ourselves to the tea and take a moment to freshen up. There is a toilet through that door."

We'd been walking in single file since we left the office, so this was the first time I had the chance to see her face and when I did, a shock ran through my body. Josie was white as a ghost, a look of sheer terror in her eyes.

The guard closed the door and Mary and Wendy made a beeline for the tea, chatting easily as they went. Josie went to follow, but I caught her arm.

"What on earth is going on?" I whispered. Her eyes were wild as she looked from me to the others.

"Nothing," she said, her voice high. "I just want a cup of tea."

She tried to take a step, but I tightened my grip on her arm.

"What was the paperwork? What did you say to them?"

"Eloise," she whispered, squeezing her eyes closed. "Please don't make me tell you."

"The paperwork," I said, heart sinking. "It was bad, wasn't it?"

She hesitated, then all of a sudden deflated.

"A *Vollzugsettel* is an execution order." I gasped in shock. Josie took my hand and squeezed it hard. "I'm sorry," she whispered tearfully. "I'm sorry."

"Why allow us to change? Shower? Why feed us so well today?"

"All Hertha's doing, I suspect," she said. "One last act of kindness. I could tell something was wrong this morning. She seemed distressed."

"When is it happening? What else did they tell you?"

"Tonight, by lethal injection. I asked the Kommandant how they can execute us when we haven't so much as had a trial or a court-martial." Her nostrils flared and her eyes filled with tears. "He seemed shocked I spoke German—I don't think they intended for us to know. But then he said I should be grateful to them for being so humane. They could hang us or shoot us."

"How generous of them," I said numbly. On the other side of the room, Wendy was smoothing her hair down and Mary was making cups of tea, as the two women relaxed, completely unaware of their fate. I looked back to Josie. "You weren't going to tell me, were you?"

"No," she said sadly. "If I thought we could do anything at all to change things I'd have found a way to tell you right away. But..."

I took a quick inventory of our situation, trying to think of a way to escape. I quickly reached the same conclusion Josie had. We were surrounded by SS officers and barbed wire and guns. Death was the only outcome here—the only question was whether we went peacefully or painfully. Across the room, Wendy and Mary looked tired but were still calm. The camp was distressing, the incident in the office probably unnerving, but they had no idea of the gravity of it all.

"Do I tell *them*?" Josie asked, her voice thick with tears.

"No," I said quietly, exhaling. My heart was beating faster, a dull thud that seemed to echo through my body, as if my very spirit were clinging to those last few precious beats. "I'm glad you told me, but your instincts were right. Sometimes courage simply means letting someone else feel peace for as long as they can."

"Hey. Hey you!" A man was at the window to the orderly room, a prisoner with sunken eyes over a gray face beneath his shaved head. He was whispering through the gap where the window had been pushed up to let fresh air in.

We had been waiting in the room for hours, long enough that a light fog blew in over the sunny day then thickened, until the whole camp had become shrouded in cloud. Mary and Wendy had long finished their tea and decided to lie down on the floor to nap, claiming exhaustion after the early start. Josie was in the toilet and had been for some time.

When I noticed the man, I rushed to the window.

"Hello," I said, in English. The man gave me a sad look.

"I'm RAF. Are you all French?"

"French and British," I told him. "SOE."

"Bill!" someone hissed from the yard. "They're coming."

He reached up and put his hand over mine on the windowsill and squeezed once.

"They'll shoot me if they see me talking to you so I have to go but…go well, and thank you for your service," he said seriously, then squeezed my hand again. "They tried to hide you from us, locking us in our barracks when they moved you through the camp. But a group of us saw you arrive and we all know what…" He broke off, wincing. "I mean, it's just we all know how this works."

"I know," I whispered miserably. "I know what's coming."

"I wish there was something I could do but…"

"Thank you," I whispered back, but as he moved to leave, I caught his hand one more time. "There's no way out of here, is there? No chance we could escape?"

"I'm sorry, miss," he said heavily. "The place is crawling with guards. If there was a way out, I'd be long gone."

There was an announcement over the loudspeakers, and the man gave me one last look then ran away. When Josie returned, she took the seat beside me and rubbed her red-rimmed eyes.

"Did you hear the announcement?" she asked.

"What did they say?"

"The prisoners are being sent back to their barracks and they've been told to close the shutters and doors," Josie said. "I doubt that's just because of the fog. It won't be long now, I imagine."

Outside, the general chatter and movement quickly faded until the whole place seemed to have fallen into an eerie silence.

"Are you scared?" I whispered.

"Not scared. Just sad. I doubt my mother knows I've been captured and we parted on difficult terms. I wish I could talk to her one last time—to tell her how sorry I am for everything and to tell her that I love her. I just wish she would be proud of me. I just wish I could make her understand why I chose to take these risks even though I ended up here."

"She'll be proud!" I protested. "Of course she'll be proud of you."

"But everything is so secretive," Josie whispered tearfully. "What will she be told about my death? Will they tell her gently? Will she hear of my successes, or just that I was arrested? And Noah? No one even knows that we were in love. Who will think to tell him what became of me?"

"We can't change any of it now," I whispered, my throat tight. "I don't even know where Hughie is. I just have to trust that the truth will find its way to him one day."

"I wasn't even crying in there because of what's about to happen," she whispered unevenly. "I was crying because I know now I won't get to hold my Maman or Noah again. I wish I could embrace them one last time."

"Hold them in your heart at the end," I said to her softly. "Even when the world around us goes to hell, we can find peace in our minds. You taught me that, Josie."

"That's what you'll do?"

"Giles will be waiting for me on the other side. But—" I broke off, emotion overwhelming me. When I spoke again, I could barely get the words out. "It will be Hughie I think of in the last moments. Like you, I suppose, I'm not so much scared as sad."

The door opened, and the SS guard was back. He spoke directly to Josie now, giving up altogether on his attempts at English. She replied in German then stood, holding her chin high.

"It's time to go to the infirmary," she said, eyes filling with tears again. I rose too and hugged her. The guard barked something at us, and we separated. Wendy and Mary roused and pushed themselves up.

"The infirmary?" Wendy queried, frowning.

"Typhus inoculation," Josie said lightly.

As we walked along the path toward the "infirmary," I could smell smoke in the air. The sun was starting to set, but when I looked toward the building ahead of us, I could just make out smoke rising from a chimney at the back of the building, rising up to reach the heavy fog.

They sat us at a low bench in a corridor. All of the doors leading off the hall were closed until two men in lab coats entered the room. One was younger, maybe only in his twenties. He looked uncertain. The other man was short, with a thick mustache and a shiny bald head.

"One at a time. You'll come with me," the bald man told us in clear English. He pointed to Wendy. "You are first."

"No," Josie said, raising her chin as she reached to take my hand. Her palm was sweaty and although her voice was strong, she was trembling. "Keep us all together."

"But you must undress for the exam," he said impatiently.

"No," I said. He scowled at me. "We won't undress unless a female doctor is present. We don't need to undress for an injection, anyway."

Wendy and Mary gave us bewildered looks, no doubt surprised to hear our defiance to the German doctors. But the doctor sighed impatiently, then muttered something under his breath. The young man walked out of the hallway to a door at the end and returned quickly carrying a tray. I stared at the tourniquets and the small brown vial, a single syringe and needle beside them.

Hughie, I love you.

The first doctor swept an impatient glance over the four of us. "Expose your arm then, please."

I released Josie's hand and undid the buttons of my blouse. The doctor quickly measured the liquid, drawing it into the syringe, while the younger man moved along the line and applied tourniquets to Wendy and Mary's arms. After the older had injected Wendy and Mary, the young man moved the tourniquets forward to apply them to me and to Josie.

When the bald man bent toward me with the syringe, I looked him right in the eye.

"I have a son," I whispered to him. There was a flicker in his eyes. "He's a baby—not even three years old. My husband is dead. I am all that child has in the whole world."

"Very sad for your son," the doctor said stiffly.

I felt the slight pinch as he punctured my skin. My heart began to race as he injected the liquid. Josie reached to take my hand again. Beside us, Wendy and Mary were watching quietly, both calm and both, so far, still well.

The doctor lifted the syringe to prepare it for Josie, then paused. He reached to the tray and picked up the little vial. He shook it, as if checking to see how full it was, then sighed and sat it back down.

"Is the dose not sufficient?" Josie asked him, her voice strained. He pursed his lips.

"You are small. It will be enough."

"I feel dizzy," Wendy said quietly.

"It's just a side effect from the inoculation," the doctor said dismissively. "Please wait here, we will just be a few minutes."

He didn't look back at us as they left the corridor. Josie and I stared at one another.

"Gosh, that's making me sleepy..." Wendy said, but she trailed off.

"I feel very strange too," Mary said, but her voice was coming from a long way away.

"Let's go somewhere lovely together," Josie whispered. I closed my eyes, and brought to mind an image of my son. I saw him pink and angry when I held him in my arms the first time. I remembered the milky, sweet smell of his cheeks as I nuzzled him close when I'd fed him in the night. I remembered the feel of his soft body collapsing into my arms after his first triumphant steps toward me, the sound of his laughter when I played with him during the months when my ankle was healing.

I'm sorry, Hughie. I love you. I hope you'll be free. I hope you'll be happy. I hope one day you'll find the truth.

As the room began to grow dim, the images faded too, and I used my very last breath just to love my son.

CHAPTER 29

I was still conscious, but my mind was foggy. I could not keep my eyes open.

I was walking down a beach, Maman on one side, Noah on the other. He was holding my hand now. Maman had looped her arm through my elbow. Aunt Quinn was ahead of us, smiling and waving us closer. *What does it smell like there, darling?* The air—so fresh and crisp, and salty too. *What will we eat there, Josie?* Ah, we will stop at a kiosk for chips and fish wrapped in newspaper, drizzled with sharp vinegar, and I'll eat as much as I want but I won't get sick at all. *How do you feel in your heart?*

Loved. Wanted. Known.

The fantasy was abruptly interrupted when the doctors came back into the room, talking quietly among themselves. They were speaking German and it was so hard to focus. Two voices, one deep, one higher and breaking with emotion.

"They told me these women were all English or French and had no idea what the injection was. They specifically said we did not need the Gestapo here to do this because there would be no resistance!" The deeper voice dropped to a furious whisper. "I was not expecting to have to argue with them about undressing. I admit—Gustaf, I was thrown by that, and I wasn't concentrating as I should have been. I think I have given one of them too much—there was not enough left by the time I got to…"

"She is skin and bone," the higher voice said uncertainly. "Will it be enough to keep her unconscious at least until…?"

The grating sound of metal on metal as the wheel on a trolley squealed, then silence. I was awake enough to wonder what the sounds were, too drowsy to open my eyes at first. Long minutes passed, then the trolley and the footsteps returned. My eyelids were fluttering and the darkness in my mind was receding. The trolley went again. I was barely even dozing now, lethargic but awake. I was still holding Eloise's hand until they disentangled our fingers. I remembered all over again what was really happening and grief for her might have overwhelmed me.

I hoped she went peacefully. I hoped she was with her husband already, looking down on their baby boy.

I was in an in-between place—my mind wanted to go, but my body kept pulling it back. And was that smoke in the air? No, something so much worse. Something that made my stomach lurch and my heart race.

I opened my eyes abruptly. I was alone in the hallway on the chair, wide awake and panicking. The door opened, and the two men were there, staring at me. The youngest was standing aside from the older again. This time, he looked as if he might cry.

"What do we do?" he said, sounding panicked. He turned to the older man. "There is no more phenol. Doctor, what do we do?"

There was a moment of horrifying silence. They stared at me, I stared at them, and not one of us in that room knew what to do. I flicked my glance toward the other door, the one we'd entered the building through. It was a long hallway—a few dozen feet back to the outside. And even if I made it, where would I go? Escape *into* the camp?

"Just hurry," the older doctor said.

"Hurry?" the youngest was alarmed. "But—"

"Just get this over with so we can go!"

Get this over with. My life meant nothing to these men. My murder was one last task they had to tick off before they could leave for the day.

All my life I had been written off, underestimated, forgotten. Wendy and Mary were gone. Eloise, gone. But me? I was still there, and I had no more left to lose. I was in the last moments of my life and nothing I could do now would change the outcome. In some roundabout way, that made me the most powerful person in the room.

A burst of furious adrenaline shook the last of the grogginess from my mind and I shot to my feet and took off toward the door. But the older man bolted toward me, quickly catching up. He scooped me up from behind, tightening his arms around my waist and hoisting me into the air in front of him. I fought with everything I had—throwing arms and legs wildly, screaming for help as he dragged me down toward the younger man, who looked at me, stricken, but did nothing to help.

"Gustaf, for God's sakes," the bald doctor hissed. "Open the door!"

The younger man slumped in defeat, and pushed the door open, revealing a steaming hot, cavernous room. At the center of the room was a large brick structure, set beneath a massive chimney that disappeared up into the roof. The structure had four arched doors. Three were locked closed. One was open, and a long metal bed on rails hung out of it.

Behind the bed was a raging fire.

"No!" I cried, and I turned toward the younger man. "Please. Don't let him do this."

He was already scrambling toward a cupboard. He threw

the door open and started searching, knocking vials all over the place as he went.

"There has to be something—" he stammered. "Anything! Something to just—"

"I told you, it's all gone," the older man grunted as he struggled to drag me closer to the furnace.

"We cannot put her in there alive! *Awake!*"

With every step, I felt the blasting heat grow stronger and I struggled harder, screaming until my throat ached. "Help! *Help me!*"

"The Kommandant said there must be no witnesses! Get over here! Someone will hear if she keeps shouting."

The younger man hesitated again, but then he straightened his spine and ran toward me. He caught my upper arm in his fist but held me too loosely, and I tugged my arm out straight away, setting my hand into a claw and swinging wildly toward him. I connected with his face, gouging a deep, angry scratch across his eye and cheek. He cried out, taking a hasty step back, and just then I kicked behind me, managing to inflict enough pain that the bald doctor's viselike grip around my waist relaxed.

I landed awkwardly… heavily, winding up sprawled on the hot concrete floor, looking up at them, just five or six feet from the furnace.

"I'll be gone soon," I said, my voice shaking not with fear, but with fury. "…but I will only be set free into peace. You'll never know how that feels, not either one of you, because your role in this war will haunt you for eternity." I was a shy girl, then a quiet woman, but now I was a lioness and my roar became louder, echoing from the walls around me. If I shook, it was only with the injustice of it all. I had moved to a place past fear—even past regret. "One day you will stand before your God and try to justify even this moment and *you will fail* because there is no justifying what you've done. You'll never even convince yourselves this wasn't an execution tonight—it was cold-blooded *murder*."

I fought with every precious breath left in my body, even though I knew they would overpower me. And as they pushed me down onto the tray, the flames from the furnace burning so hot the pain was already blinding white, I used my very last breath to shout one final war cry.

"Vive la liberty! Vive la France!"

What lay beyond what I could see—the universe, and all of the sparkling stars and planets and galaxies? In the vastness of the one life I had lived, I had given my all to what I knew to be *right*. I had used my days for good, in every way that I could manage, even when it was hard and even when it didn't seem enough.

Pain left my mind cloudy but I knew it would be over quickly—I could already feel myself slipping away. I reserved my precious last thoughts for those I had loved the most. For Aunt Quinn, who I so wished I'd had more time with. For my mother, who had given me everything and who had shaped me into a woman who would try to make a better world, even against the odds.

I'm sorry, Maman. I'm so sorry. I love you. Forgive me, please. I hope you're proud and find happiness.

And for Noah, who had been my hope for the future. With my very last breath, I set out a prayer that he would find a different path without me—a happy path, in freedom and in love, in the world that we had hoped so much to build together.

CHAPTER 30

CHARLOTTE
Liverpool
July, 1970

I'm sitting at a long boardroom table surrounded by confused people. Theo is beside me, scribbling absentmindedly on a notepad. Dad sits to my right. He's slurping the coffee I made in Professor Read's kitchenette. Opposite us, Drusilla Sallow is sitting with the woman from the photos in her hall table.

We haven't so much as introduced ourselves yet. As soon as we walked into the meeting room, Helen Elwood handed us each a piece of paper and asked us to sign it before we said a word.

"Harry and I have permission to talk to you all about some incredibly sensitive matters today but what you are about to learn should never leave this room. If you'd all be so kind as to sign this agreement to that effect, we can speak a little more freely." She's a tall woman, maybe in her sixties, with short silver hair and an imposingly stiff posture. She collects the agreements, checks each signature carefully, then takes a seat at one end of the long table, opposite Professor Read, who is already scribbling notes at the other end. "Now, if you could just introduce yourselves." We progress around the table, each of us just saying our names. The woman beside Drusilla Sallow introduces herself as "Dru's roommate, Dr. Quinn Madison."

"Dr. Sallow," Helen says suddenly, a depth of emotion in her voice. "Let me say from the outset that I am so sorry for everything you have been put through."

The whole tone of the room shifts in an instant. To see this brusque, proud woman so close to tears only as the meeting is just beginning makes me nervous. I glance at Dad, and see he's staring at the table, jaw locked tight. I reach across and put my hand over his.

I threw a cat among the pigeons when I ambushed Professor Read four hours ago. In the time since, I first met with Harry and Helen on my own and the two of them all but interrogated me about how I found Drusilla Sallow. I've asked them a million questions about *why* this is all so shocking but they keep telling me they'll answer when we're all together.

I then sat in Harry's office while Helen made the difficult call to Drusilla to ask her to come in, before Harry handed me the phone and said grimly, "Call your father. And…since it's clear he's had a hand in this too, call Theo too."

And now, I hope, we're all about to understand exactly what happened to Jocelyn Miller in the last days of her life.

"You said on the telephone that you need to clarify the circumstances around my daughter's death," Drusilla says.

"I do. I will," Helen says firmly. "But first, please let me explain that we *have* made an effort to contact you over the years. Starting in late 1945, then again as late as the 1950s, I tried very hard indeed to track you down."

"I moved to Paris to help rebuild in 1946 and I lived there for about fifteen years, until I moved back here to take the teaching position I held until I retired," Drusilla says. "I was still in London in '45. I was living at Quinn's terrace where Josie also lived for a time. It would have been quite simple to find me if you'd bothered to look."

"As we'll explain soon, much of Josie's record was destroyed," Helen says softly. "That made things exceedingly difficult. I didn't have her full name or her birth date, let alone any of your details, Dr. Sallow—not a name, not an address, not even an occupation. I spent months looking for a birth certificate for a 'Josie Miller.' I even searched birth registrations in Paris, because I distinctly remembered her telling me about growing up there."

"How on earth could this happen?" Dad asks stiffly. "I *know* the SOE had extensive files for each of us."

"We certainly did during the war years. In 1946, there was a fire in our records department at Baker Street—an immense collection of records was lost. At the same time, our secretarial staff was sorting through the mountain of documentation we'd collected during the war. I was in Germany then and unfortunately, the person we left in charge of that process was not as trustworthy as we'd hoped. It's a tragic aspect to this mess that all of Jocelyn's records went missing, either through the fire or the records purge or some other human intervention around the same time."

"We found a single page from her personnel file about four years ago," Harry interjects, shooting Theo a pointed look. Theo clears his throat and shuffles awkwardly on his chair. "That page detailed scant notes a medical examiner recorded when Jocelyn first attended the student assessment board at Winterfold House. It had been incorrectly filed in behind the equivalent notes for another female candidate, and was a truly unremarkable page of documentation, except that it belonged to an agent who for all intents and purposes disappeared from our records entirely after the war ended."

"Noah, do you recall the wireless operator who served with you at Montbeliard?" Helen asks Dad, who squints, then grimaces.

"Nice chap. An excellent w/t operator. I don't recall his cover name."

"He was known as Adrien. His cover was blown, and we evacuated him."

"That's right—" Dad trails off. "Yes. I think that's right."

"In his debrief interview, Adrien told us that he suspected your relationship with Jocelyn was closer than it should have been. Romantic in nature."

"We knew it was against the rules, but it never influenced our work. We achieved incredible things together."

"I know, Noah," Helen says reassuringly. "In fact, given the two of you had single-handedly arranged for the safe destruction of an entire munitions complex, something even the entire RAF couldn't do, I was of half a mind that you should continue to work together."

"Jocelyn did that?" Drusilla asks.

"Yes, ma'am," Dad says. "The RAF tried and failed, at a tremendous cost to those in the villages around the factory. Your brilliant daughter found a way to get the job done without it costing a single human life."

Quinn rests her hand over Drusilla's on the table.

"One of our senior officers was deeply concerned about your relationship," Helen tells Dad quietly. "He argued that we should move Josie. The *Success* circuit in Paris was in a state and we all knew she was an excellent agent, so eventually, we agreed to shift her there."

"Who was that?" Dad asks.

"That was Gerard, Noah. Gerard Turner."

Dad nods silently. Helen takes a sip from a glass of water on the table.

"We know that the arrests were continuing around her in Paris, but we didn't know much more than that. There was a degree of panic from those of us at Baker Street, watching that circuit flounder just as the D-Day invasion seemed to be looming. We had high hopes our troops would eventually reach and reclaim Paris and *that* milestone would bring an important morale boost to the entire continent. Our circuit there needed to be robust and extensive to support the Allied advance. Gerard convinced us the only way forward was for him to go to Paris to sort the circuit out himself."

"I trained under him," Dad tells me. "He was a tough instructor, but a good man."

"Yes, unfortunately that was my assessment of the man too," Helen mutters. Dad's eyebrows lift in surprise. "It seemed an excellent arrangement at first. Gerard was sending through regular updates via his wireless operators and the circuit seemed to have stabilized and even expanded since his arrival. Obviously, the D-Day landings were a success and our men began to advance across France, but just as fighting began on the outskirts of Paris, a message came through from Turner. There had been a sudden spate of arrests and dozens of additional agents, including Jocelyn, had been executed. It seemed like tragic timing given the city was liberated days later."

"Gerard Turner came to my house in 1944 to tell me this." Drusilla sounds exasperated. "I don't understand why you've dragged me in here today to tell me again."

"One of our agents found Jocelyn's name carved into a cell at the SD headquarters in Paris which seemed to corroborate the story Gerard told us about her death. He only stayed in Paris for a few weeks after it was liberated—"

"That's when I saw him," Dad interjects. "At the apartment there. He's the one who told me Josie had died."

"After that, he came back to London to hold up the fort here and to notify various family members of deaths in the field. He also supervised the administrative staff at Baker Street as they began the cleanup of our offices and files."

"And through all of this," Read says quietly, "it's important to note that Helen was still in France. All of the senior SOE officials were, except Turner."

"Yes, that's right. As the occupation collapsed, we had hundreds of agents still missing, scattered all over. Even once we'd spread word far and wide that those agents could safely reveal themselves and find help via an apartment we established in Paris, we still had almost 120 agents unaccounted for. They were mostly men, but there was also a group of women."

"How could you just lose track of that many people?" I ask.

"I call it 'the fog of war,'" Harry explains. "Europe was in a state of utter chaos. The SOE had scattered, traumatized agents all over the place, and dreadfully disjointed communications to boot."

"In late 1944, I began a project to search for these agents," Helen says. "A handful of missing agents resurfaced from the Paris circuit in the months after liberation and I was shocked to find most of those who'd survived had been in hiding. Some were highly suspicious of Gerard, citing lax security procedures once he arrived back in France, but Freddie Booth and I were both certain that the problem was prolonged and intense stress, not disloyalty. It's no excuse, but my focus was still elsewhere. Most of our agents, especially the women, were designated 'Night and Fog' prisoners, which meant the Germans tried very hard to make them altogether disappear. There were no paper trails to follow, so I had to rely on in-person interviews to track people down. I asked a guard at Pforzheim Prison if they'd imprisoned any of our women there, and to my shock, he distinctly recalled Josie. He said she was at Pforzheim for months after D-Day."

"That's not right," Dad says, after a stunned moment of silence. "Gerard said she was executed in Paris *before* the landings."

"I know that's what he said," Helen says gently. "But it seems that was never the truth."

"But why on earth would he lie about something like that?"

"It took me a very long time to figure that out, Noah," Helen admits. "I kept traveling, interviewing people all across France and Germany, searching for all of those missing agents—

and now I'd added Josie to the list of women I needed to find. Every one of them mattered, but I especially wanted to figure out what became of her given the situation was so baffling. For a while, I feared I'd never find her trail again, until a guard told me that a handful of political prisoners were sent to civilian prisons in the rush to keep ahead of the advance of the Allied troops."

"Jocelyn was accommodated at a civilian prison named Karlsruhe for the last few weeks of her life," Read says quietly. "She was housed in a cell with an agent named Fleur. Noah, you will remember her from Salon-La-Tour."

Dad nods. His hand is shaking slightly beneath mine. He and Drusilla both seem to be in shock.

"A guard from Karlsruhe told me that Fleur and Josie were as close as sisters," Helen says. Although she's a stern woman, her tone has eased and softened, and now she speaks very gently, her eyes brimming with sympathy. "When the transfer order came through and that guard realized these women were to be executed, she did her very best to ensure their last day on earth was dignified. She arranged fresh clothing for them and even bribed a colleague to take them by passenger train instead of a boxcar to Strasbourg. She packed them a special meal for the journey and did her best to hide what was coming so they wouldn't be scared."

Beside me, my father makes a sound that could almost be a sob. He withdraws his hand from mine on the table and presses it over his mouth, looking away. My own eyes fill with tears as I gently rub his shoulders.

"Jocelyn was executed just a few hours after she arrived at Natzweiler-Struthof in August 1944," Helen finally says.

A hush falls over the room, until Drusilla straightens her spine and says flatly, "Did this guard personally witness her death?"

"No, the guard remained at Karlsruhe."

"You said there was no paper trail." For the first time, Helen looks uneasy. She shifts awkwardly in her chair. "For twenty-four years I have imagined the entirely wrong scenario for my daughter's last hours. You need to be completely transparent with me now." I see the low-key panic in Helen's eyes as she looks to Read and my stomach drops. There's more here, and I'm not sure any of us are ready to hear it. Drusilla's voice breaks as she adds desperately, *"Please."*

"I…" Helen is apparently at a loss for words. She clears her throat, then sips again at her water.

"Was anyone arrested for her murder?" Drusilla demands hoarsely. "Was she alone when she died? Did she suffer? I don't care if the answers are distressing, I just need to know!"

"Jocelyn was executed with three other agents," Harry says suddenly. "They died by lethal injection."

"Then what is it you aren't you telling me?" Drusilla says flatly, staring at Helen, who swallows anxiously.

"Miss Elwood?" Dad prompts uneasily.

Helen looks resigned. "I interviewed an orderly who was there with this group of women until their last moments. He believed that Jocelyn was the only one in the group of women who spoke enough German to understand what was going on—the others believed they were being given an inocula-tion. He remembered her being incredibly courageous in keep-ing calm so that the others would not die afraid. But after—" Her eyes have filled with tears. "Jocelyn fought until her last breath. The orderly said her last words were *'Long live freedom, long live France.'* She made quite a ruckus—many of the pris-oners I interviewed from that camp recalled hearing her shout those final words."

I cover my mouth with my hand. I'm trying to stifle my own emotions, but the pain in the room is palpable. Quinn has her arms around Drusilla, who is drawing in big, shuddering breaths. Dad sits in silent misery, tears running down his face.

Theo and I exchange a glance that's part *can you believe this* and part *what on earth have we uncovered.*

"Did she make a mistake?" Drusilla whispers hoarsely. "Is that why she was arrested?"

"I don't believe so, no," Helen says. "I interviewed one of the Gestapo officers involved in her arrest. He told me that Turner sent them to arrest a w/t operator, and when they arrived at her rooms, they discovered that she and Josie had drafted a transmission to alert Baker Street that Turner was a conspirator. They managed to get the w/t's encryption key too, despite Josie's best efforts to destroy it. The Germans were able to impersonate that w/t successfully for months, right up until just before Paris was liberated, which is why we at Baker Street had no idea how dire things were on the ground in the city."

"So this Turner fellow sent Josie to prison and then…*lied* to me about her death for revenge?" Drusilla says, stunned.

"Actually, there's some evidence that he tried to have her released from the prison," Helen admits. "I spoke to several German guards and officers who recalled Gerard making desperate attempts to speak with her, even trying to supply new information from our agency in exchange for her release."

"Well, that just makes no damned sense," Dad says, pinching the bridge of his nose. "The bastard was a traitor who conspired with the Germans and allowed Josie to be arrested, then he tried to *help* her?"

"He did always have a soft spot for her," Helen tells us with a sigh. "I interpreted it as an almost fatherly admiration when we were training her and she showed such promise, but who knows? It's no consolation at all now, but for whatever reason, he did try to help her. People are complex sometimes."

"I just can't believe he'd betray his country like this. Both countries," Dad says, his voice cracking with emotion. "He seemed like such a good man."

"It's no excuse at all, of course, but Gerard was already in dire financial straits when the occupation began, having gambled away his family's fortune," Helen explains. "Every decision he made from there was likely influenced by the Germans. He sought Freddie out the minute he arrived in Britain and at the time, we were so relieved to have help from someone who had recent experience in France, no one suspected a thing, but we know now that he was already working with the Germans, even then. There is some evidence he tried to extract himself from their clutches a few times—but it always came back to money. Even here in the UK, what appeared to be a casual gambling habit was a catastrophic weakness the Germans exploited time and time again. Every shred of the man's integrity was traded for the cash. Perhaps earlier in the war, he'd have been able to buy Josie's release—but by the time she was arrested, the Germans knew the war was just about over and nothing he could offer was valuable to them."

"But why lie to us about her death?" Dad asks brokenly.

"The same reason he made such a mess of the SOE files, Noah. He was covering his tracks," Helen says. She glances across to Drusilla. "Why do you think he told you that dreadful lie about her carelessness in the field, Dr. Sallow? He wanted you to be ashamed. He wanted to keep her story secret, and he really didn't want you asking questions because they would have led you straight to us. Later, he destroyed her file so that there was no chance *we* would find you either."

"So where is he now?" Dad demands, thumping his fist onto the desk. "Tell me the bastard is in prison for what he did."

"It took us far too long to realize that he was still creating chaos even once the war was over," Helen admits. "I didn't make it back to London until 1946. I was shocked to learn then that Booth and Maxwell were growing suspicious of Gerard in the wake of the mess he made in the records department. They had looked back at the chaos of the war and could finally see the connections between Turner and so many incidents that made little sense at the time. MI6 arrested him to conduct an interview, but I'm sorry to say he took a cyanide pill in the car on the way to questioning."

Dad's face falls.

"So he never even faced trial?"

"Not in this life, Noah. I'm sorry."

"My daughter and I...we parted on very difficult terms and for twenty-four years..." Drusilla whispers numbly.

"She regretted that, Doctor Sallow," Dad says urgently, as his gaze flicks between Drusilla and Quinn.

"She actually tried to write you," Helen adds, and from her file, she withdraws a sheet of yellow notepaper. "She passed this letter back to me via another agent who was briefly posted in Paris with her. I wasn't allowed to send it to you at the time. The rules were very strict about agent contact with home during their field missions, but it's clear she was desperate to make amends."

She passes the note across the table. There's a long, strained moment where Drusilla just stares at the note, frozen.

"Read it to me," she whispers to her friend. Quinn reaches out and takes it gingerly, then in a low, unsteady voice, reads,

"'Maman, I am so sorry for the way we said goodbye that morning. I love you, so very much, and I only want you to be happy. You have always fought so hard for me. You have always fought so hard in everything you do, and that is the example I follow now as I go to fight. I am stronger than I ever knew and I want only for you to be proud of me. Please don't worry too much. I am exactly where I am meant to be. With love, always...'" Quinn pauses. "It's not signed."

"She couldn't sign it," Helen explains. "She wrote it in the field and she knew better than to leave evidence like that. But I assure you, it came from Josie."

"I recognize her handwriting." Drusilla weeps, picking up that little letter and cradling it against her chest. "Oh, my baby."

"I'm a highly organized woman," Helen tells us. "I'd have

filed that letter in Jocelyn's personnel file and it would have
been lost in the fire, except that the D-Day planning began in
earnest right about the same time and I was run off my feet. I
forgot all about the letter for years—I only found it in my desk
when I returned to pack up once I'd finished searching for the
missing agents. By then, of course, we had no idea how to find
you, Dr. Sallow, but I've held onto it for all of these years…just
in case…" Drusilla and her friend are holding one another close
and sobbing now, and I feel like an intruder in this room. I look
away, as Helen murmurs almost to herself, "I kept all kinds of
random things I discovered when we cleaned out Baker Street.
Gerard's office was such a mess! The man was a real pack rat.
During the investigation, MI6 went into his flat and his office
to search for classified materials and as they went, they boxed
up everything else for disposal. I convinced them to keep it all
in storage. Maxwell told me I was mad to think there'd be anything of worth in Gerard's old trinkets and clothing and crock-
ery, and maybe he was right. We just had no way of knowing
what damage Gerard had done along the way, so I wanted to
keep every scrap of evidence from his life, just in case we ever
found we needed it."

"He told me he'd ensure Jocelyn's name was suppressed if the
records were ever unsealed. He told me it was for the best if no
one knew of her mistakes," Drusilla says now, her voice shaking with anger. "For twenty-four years I thought my daughter
died in shame. I thought her death meant *nothing*."

"Your daughter was a bloody hero," my dad insists, tears
streaming down his face. "It's a travesty that you were ever
allowed to think otherwise. But this is my fault. It's *all* my
fault." He covers his face with his hands, shoulders shaking as
he weeps.

"Dad," I say, bewildered. "What on earth are you talking
about?"

"I knew she'd make a good agent. And I wanted to see her

again, so…" He breaks off, stricken. "I nominated her. Tell them, Miss Elwood. Tell them what I did."

"During his training, Noah told us about Josie." Helen nods. "He had correctly identified in her the qualities of a brilliant agent after what he'd seen on their journey on the escape line. That's why we invited her to try out for the SOE."

"It wasn't just that. I touched her hand in front of Adrien—that's the only reason Baker Street found out we were in love—the only reason she was sent to Paris! I failed her, time and time again," Dad chokes. He turns his hollow gaze to Drusilla. "Your daughter is dead because of me, Dr. Sallow. You have every reason to hate me. I'm so sorry."

"Did my daughter love you, Mr. Ainsworth?" Drusilla asks stiffly. Dad draws a surprised breath, then nods, almost to himself.

"Yes. Yes, I believe she did."

"Then we'll leave the blame for her death where it belongs. Not on your shoulders, Noah, but on the shoulders of the men who killed her." She reaches across the table, stretching out her hand toward him. Dad's fingers are shaking as he reaches to meet her halfway. "Let it go, son," Drusilla whispers. "Forgive yourself. If Josie loved you, that's what she would have wanted."

Hours have passed. Dad and Dr. Sallow are still sitting at one end of the table swapping stories about Jocelyn, while Quinn watches on and Professor Read frantically scribbles down notes.

Theo, Helen and I have made ourselves fresh cups of tea and we mingle away from the other group. Their conversation is starting to feel like a long overdue wake I wasn't invited to. It's been an exhausting day for everyone, but there's a peace in my father's face that I wasn't anticipating. If he set out looking for closure when we first decided to track down Remy a few weeks ago, he's finally found it. It just wasn't where we first thought to look.

"I feel such a relief," Helen says on a sigh. "Honestly, it's like a weight has been lifted from my shoulders."

"My dad set out just to thank the agent he thought had saved his life, but I can't help but feel like he wound up getting exactly what he needed, in a roundabout way."

"Yes, Harry told me about your father and Fleur," Helen says. "She actually brought this brooch for me, smuggled it back from Paris in 1944." She taps a brooch on her cardigan, a brightly colored cluster of green and red beads with small pearls dangling below. "Fleur was entirely on her own for her first mission, and as we now know, managing somehow to stay one step ahead of the Germans as Gerard fed them information about her. And then of course, to save your father's life that day at Salon-La-Tour. She was a truly remarkable woman." Helen stifles a yawn, then looks out the window again. Her voice is distant as she murmurs, "I still wonder sometimes how Gerard could fool us all for so long, but then again, when I look back at what seemed to be an intense dedication to the work we were doing, I can still scarcely believe he was disloyal at all. He worked day and night for years right beside me. He pushed our agents in training, helped us to plan the missions, even went above and beyond to clear away any obstacle to their service, just as I tried to do." Her eyes crinkle suddenly. "God—at one point, he even got involved in finding child care for Fleur's own child! Her mother was called away unexpectedly and he all but browbeat *me* into looking after the boy. Luckily for the child, my mother was there to help, because God knows I had no idea what to do with a toddler."

"What became of the child when she died?" I ask hesitantly. Theo is staring at the ground, his jaw set. I have an inkling he's listening intently, but I know, especially after what happened when we met Drusilla, he would be trying very hard not to get his hopes up again.

"Fleur's mother took him back as soon as she returned from

her business trip. The boy was the cutest little thing. Didn't speak a word of English and my mother's French wasn't the best, but we managed."

My eyes lock with Theo's.

"He didn't speak English, you say?" I repeat.

"Not a word."

"And...Fleur's mother. You're *sure* she cared for him after her death?"

"I never had reason to doubt it..."

"Did you speak to her? At any point?"

"Well, no." For the first time, Helen appears uncertain. Her brows knit as she says, "Gerard had spoken to her on the phone so he was the one to return the boy when it was time."

"But who told Fleur's mother that she was dead?" Theo asks cautiously. Helen's gaze shifts between us.

"It would have been Gerard," she admits. At our shocked gasps, she says, "Please remember that was months before anyone had cause to doubt the man! Why are you even asking me about this?"

"Theo," I whisper. He looks at me. His glasses are askew, his eyes are wide and shiny with tears of hope. "*Tell* her."

It unravels quickly from there. After a quarter of a century of silence and lies, Theo Sinclair discovers the truth about his family of origin in the very place he spent years searching for it.

"What do you think Mum would make of all of this?" Dad asks me. It is almost 3:00 a.m., and we've only just returned home from Manchester. Poor Wrigley was beside himself when he saw us, and he's now stretched across the lounge, his head on Dad's lap. Dad's voice is raw and his eyes are puffy from crying. He seems exhausted, but I think this is the good kind of tired. I'm slumped in Mum's armchair, too wired to sleep, too tired to hold myself up.

I think about Dad's question for a few minutes before I try

to answer it. He is sitting to my left, and that silvery scar is just above his ear on the side of his head nearest to me. I know that beneath his pajama shirt there's other scars, puckered and round, mirrored on both sides of his shoulder. Even if there was some surgery that could hide the mark left behind by the trauma life inflicted upon my dad, the mark would still be there in some invisible way. Those scars are part of the man who raised me. Those imperfections part of the man I have known and loved for my entire life. The version of him who did not have a brain injury and had never been shot ceased to exist long before I was even born.

In Dad's case, the scars he wears are marks upon his body I can see and hear in his voice, and maybe for Mum, the scars were in places that were harder to spot, but in the end it's all the same: our scars become part of who we are. Every mark life makes upon us creates a new version of our identity because there is simply no going back to who we were before those experiences.

To truly love someone, we must accept the real version of them, scars and all.

"Mum wasn't perfect, was she, Dad?" I croak, and my eyes are suddenly stinging again, even as Dad gives me a slightly startled laugh.

"Lottie," he says. "She wasn't ever meant to be. None of us are."

I think about my mother and the love I had and have for her. I think about the happy upbringing she gave me and Archie, and her years of important work as a teacher. I think about her relationship with Dad, and how, despite everything, I know she would want him to be happy.

And for the first time since her death, I let myself acknowledge that maybe it's not disloyal to admit Mum made mistakes too sometimes. Like Aunt Kathleen said to me, I have to mourn who she really was, not who I wanted her to be.

"If Mum knew how much time and energy we've put into

this, the jealousy would have driven her mad," I finally admit. "But she *kept* those letters, Dad, and that's how I know, deep down, she understood that one day you'd need to look back at those years and face them head-on. She'd be proud of you for doing that."

"War is hell, love. History nominates a winner, but every single person touched by war loses something—even those one step removed from the oppression and the shooting and the bombing. People like Dr. Sallow and her friend. People like your mum," he whispers. "But Gerrie and I got to be together and to raise you and Archie in a world at peace *because* of the sacrifices of women like Josie and Eloise."

"That's an awfully big shadow to live in, isn't it?" I say, and Dad nods slowly.

"I'm happy for Theo," he says, but he sounds stricken again. I know he's thinking about Fleur, and this new knowledge that she saved his life at the cost of her own. I squeeze his forearm gently.

"Do you remember what you said to me when I asked you if Josie might have made a mistake?" I say. Dad doesn't respond, so I remind him. "You said that war is messy but that Josie was just a kid dropped into a war zone with just a few months training. I think you need to keep some of that grace for yourself. Because of *you* and your courage in looking back to find Remy, Theo has found his family." He's asked me to come along when he and Helen Elwood meet tomorrow. They're going to start a thorough search through the boxes of Turner's belongings together, hoping they might find something to confirm their suspicions about Theo's identity.

"The truth has a way of finding its way to the surface," Dad concedes. "Maybe in knowing the truth about his parents, Theo can find meaning in their loss."

"I don't know about that," I say. "I think meaning is something we make, not something we find. And you know—in a lot of ways, Theo has been doing that already. His whole life's work has been making meaning out of the questions about his own past. I don't think that'll change, but I do think he'll find a new peace now."

"And you?" Dad asks me quietly. "I know your mum's death was so hard on you. I know this year has been difficult. Have *you* found a way to make meaning from what we've been through in losing her?"

"I started this year feeling so angry. Cheated. Maybe I'll always feel that way, but now...I also feel so grateful," I say, my throat tight, and I'm struck by the simplicity and the truth that word contains. "I'll never stop missing Mum and I'll always regret the way that she died. But I got to *know* her—to really know her, warts and all. I got to grow up with her. When I think about it like that, I can't help but feel like the luckiest woman on earth."

Maybe history is powerful not just for the lessons it can teach us, but for the perspective it can bring.

Epilogue

CHARLOTTE
Manchester
1972

"I think we were meant to find one another," Theo says. We've collapsed side by side onto a sofa in our new living room, both exhausted from a long day moving into our new flat. I turn to look at him in surprise. This awkward history buff has stolen every inch of my heart over the past two years, but he's not prone to romantic outbursts. He leans across to kiss me gently. "You have to admit, we make a spectacular team."

He's right about that, and that's exactly why I'll be marrying him in a few days. I'm not so sure about pre-ordained destinies but falling in love with Theo unlocked a happiness in me that I never imagined I would feel, especially after Mum died.

One of the first things we did when we got the keys to the flat today was to hang a series of photographs on the hallway wall. Those mismatched frames chart the story of our family, starting long before we even born. There's a photo of Theo with his adoptive parents, Mariel and Evan. One of my mum and dad on their wedding day. The last photo we have of Mum, a shot of her with Wrigley at Poppy's first birthday. One of Archie and Carys, with Poppy and their new baby, Owen. And

mixed in amongst it is everything Theo finally has of his first
family. He and Helen spent weeks searching through the boxes
from Turner's flat and his office, and eventually they found a
little wooden box, the Eiffel tower carved on top, a series of
precious gifts inside. Notes from Giles to Eloise, from Eloise to
Theo himself—side by side now on our wall in a hinged frame.
There's the photo of a pregnant Eloise and Giles framed along
with Giles's rosary beads and medal. Beneath that, there's the
photo of Theo as a child at that fair, and finally, the gifts Helen
gave him on his birthday last year—enlarged copies of file photographs from Eloise and Giles's military records.

"Last one," Dad announces. He sits one final box down on
top of a stack of others, then motions toward Wrigley and his
new rescue greyhound, Spot, who are snuggled up on a rug
near my new dining room. Both dogs look at Dad, then drop
their heads back down onto the rug. "Come on, you two!" he
says, playfully impatient as he gestures toward the dogs. "We
better give these lovebirds some privacy."

Dad has gradually recorded an extensive oral history with
Professor Read's team over the past two years, turning to face
his own past fully for the first time. I choose to believe my
mother's intentions were good in hiding those letters from Professor Read to Dad over the years, but as difficult it has been
for my father to delve into those memories, it's all also been
restorative.

A few months ago, he finally retired—properly, this time.
He now volunteers at an animal shelter three days a week. I
can't help but wonder if there's space in my father's future for
a third great love of his life, because he and the shelter's director Catriona seem to be awfully fond of one another. We visit
Drusilla and Quinn for a roast dinner every Sunday, and lately
Dad has been bringing Catriona along.

It's an odd kind of family, but that's exactly what this group
of strangers has become over the past two years. We share a

secret knowledge of uniquely powerful legacies and that has bonded us in a way that's hard to describe.

"Thanks, Dad," I say, standing to hug my father. He wraps his arms around me and squeezes gently, then releases me as he clears his throat. My eyes are misting over, and I can see from the way he's blinking that his are too. "For *everything.*"

"You'll only be forty minutes away," he says stiffly. "I expect to see you once a week. If not more. You too, Theo. My door is open anytime."

"Yes, sir," Theo says. Dad extends his hand as if to shake Theo's, but Theo throws his arms around Dad anyway, and Dad chuckles as he returns the embrace. "And we'll see you Saturday, of course."

I'll drive back to Liverpool Friday night so that I can dress for the wedding at home. Theo will get ready with some of his friends here at our flat. It won't be a big wedding—just our closest friends and family gathered in Dad's beautiful garden while a celebrant officiates.

Dad nods curtly and whistles. This sound tells the dogs he means business and they both run to his side, and Theo and I follow them all to the front door. As Dad steps over the threshold, he turns back to look at us one last time.

"I'm proud of you," he says unevenly, then he glances at Theo. "I'm proud of you both. It means something to me that I've been able to watch you both blossom together over these past few years." He pauses, then adds gruffly, "Actually, it means everything."

"I love you, Dad," I say.

"I love you too, Lottie," he murmurs.

Theo slides his arm around my shoulders. Dad helps the dogs up into the body of the truck he borrowed to help us move. He reverses from our driveway, and we watch until the taillights disappear around a corner. Theo turns me gently to face him. We stare at one another in the fading purple-pink light of dusk.

"Time to start our new life together," he whispers, smiling softly.

Our future stretches out before us, full of unknowns, but also full of promise, built on a foundation of freedom we will never take for granted. We can thank people like my dad for that, and Eloise and Giles Watkins, and Jocelyn Miller.

And whatever we do with the freedom we have been gifted, whether our achievements and our struggles are big or small, we will do it in honor of those who gave so much so that we could live in a better world.

★ ★ ★ ★ ★

ACKNOWLEDGMENTS

Firstly, thanks to Susan Swinwood and the team at Graydon House for publishing this book in North America. Thanks to Rebecca Saunders and the team at Hachette Australia, and to Kate Byrne, Anna Boatman, and the team at Piatkus Fiction UK. Thanks to Amy Tannenbaum and the team at Jane Rotrosen Agency. It is a pleasure and an honor to have my books in the hands of such remarkable teams.

Thanks to Mindy Hollamby and Demelza Pringle for the "sanity read" when I finished a round of edits, and to Lisa Ireland, for helping me make sense of tricky plot problems. And as always, thanks to my family and friends for support and love as I worked on this book.

I found the following resources useful in the writing of this story:

- *Her Finest Hour, The Heroic Life of Diana Rowden, Wartime Secret Agent* by Gabrielle McDonald-Rothwell
- *Violette, The Missions of SOE Agent Violette Szabo GC* by Tania Szabo
- *Carve Her Name with Pride* by RJ Minney
- *Violette Szabo, The Life That I Have* by Susan Ottaway
- *How to Become a Spy, The World War II SOE Training Manual* published by Skyhorse Publishing

- *SOE In France 1941-1945* by Major Robert Bourne-Patterson
- *Mission France, The True History of the Women of SOE* by Kate Vigurs
- *I Heard My Country Calling: Elaine Madden, SOE Agent* by Sue Elliott
- *The Women Who Lived for Danger: The Agents of the Special Operations Executive* by Marcus Binney
- *The Heroines of SOE: F Section: Britain's Secret Women in France* by Squadron Leader Beryl E. Escott
- *SOE in France, An Account of the Work of the British Special Operations Executive in France 1940-1944* by M. R. D. Foot

It should be noted that any errors are entirely my own.

Author Letter

This novel is set around historical events, but some changes have been made to timelines and details to simplify the narrative. So, what's true, and what's fiction?

Eloise and Josie could both be considered composite characters. I have drawn small aspects of their stories from many of the 39 female agents who served in the SOE's French Section during the war, but much of Eloise's story, particularly the early parts of the book, are inspired by true events from the life of Violette Szabo, and much of Josie's story, particularly her final days, has been drawn from what we know of the life of Dianna Rowden.

Violette Szabo was a young widow and mother who had some limited military experience with the Auxiliary Territorial Service when she was recruited by the SOE. She was sent into occupied France after just a few months of training and traveled alone to a restricted zone around Rouen to investigate the potential compromise of an SOE circuit there. She was arrested several times (including for failing to procure a *permis de sejour*) and talked her way out of trouble each time. She gathered crucial data about the compromised resistance circuits in the Normandy region, as well as the German V1/V2 rocket launch sites. Just as Eloise does in my story, Violette went shopping while in Paris and, using forged currency provided to her by the SOE, purchased a brooch for an official (in reality, an intelligence officer named Vera Atkins).

Violette returned to France for a second mission just after D-Day, and she and other agents drew the attention of German forces outside of Salon-La-Tour. Some accounts have Violette single-handedly holding off German troops with a sten gun, just as Eloise does in my story. Other accounts say this is the stuff of legend and that it did not actually happen. What is certain is that Violette was captured that day at Salon-La-Tour and subsequently imprisoned and interrogated. As the Allies advanced and prisoners of war were taken back into Germany, she briefly escaped a box car to fetch water for critically dehydrated POWs in an adjoining carriage.

Ultimately, Violette was taken to Ravensbrück and was executed there at just 23 years old on or before 5 February 1945. She was survived by a young daughter, Tania, who was raised by her grandparents. The story of Hugh/Theo in my book is entirely fictional.

The character of Jocelyn was inspired by SOE agent Dianna Rowden, a British woman who had lived in France at various points throughout her life. Separated from her beloved mother and stuck in France as the occupation began, Dianna became involved with the Red Cross and ultimately escaped to England via Spain and Portugal. As with Violette, Dianna had just a few months' training with the SOE before she was sent into France on her first mission.

Dianna was involved in the SOE operation to destroy the Peugeot factory near Sochaux (she was particularly active in retrieving air drops of explosives to fields around Montbéliard). The RAF had attempted the destruction of this factory by air and misjudged the location, causing hundreds of civilian deaths. An SOE agent named Harry Rée liaised with the factory director and facilitated the safe destruction operation from the ground.

As a courier, Dianna Rowden courageously ferried messages all over France—travelling as far afield as Lyon, Besançon, and of course Montbéliard and Paris. She was ultimately betrayed by a double agent and captured, and after enduring interrogation and torture at the notorious Avenue Foch *Sicherheitsdienst* headquarters, was moved to the civilian prison at Karlsruhe. She was then transported by passenger train with 3 other young SOE agents (Andree Borrell, Vera Leigh, and Sonya Olschanezky) to the Natzweiler-Struthof camp.

These agents were told they were receiving a typhus inoculation just a few hours after their arrival at the camp. In reality they were injected with phenol, although the dosage was not likely enough to kill them. Several eyewitness accounts confirmed that the final woman was still conscious when she was placed into the furnace. Witnesses also reported that she shouted *"vive la France!"* just before her death. An attendant involved in the murders had gouges on his face—the result of her last-ditch efforts to save herself.

The story of Jocelyn's personal life is entirely fictional, including her romance with Noah, her health challenges and her relationship with her mother and Aunt Quinn.

It is unfortunately true that Dianna Rowden's mother was not informed of her daughter's death for some time after it occurred, and even then, she was told nothing about Dianna's heroic wartime missions. For more than 12 years after the end of the war, Mrs. Rowden mistakenly believed her daughter had failed to achieve anything worthwhile in the field. In the end, it was not any government official who explained the truth, but rather the author Elisabeth Nichols, who tracked Mrs. Rowden down while researching a non-fiction book, *Death Not Be Proud*.

The character of Gerard Turner was inspired by (although is not closely based on) Henri Déricourt. Déricourt was friends with Nicolas Bodington, the real second-in-command to the SOE's French section. Concerns regarding Déricourt's trustworthiness and security had been raised by agents in the field, but these concerns were dismissed by officials at Baker Street and he was allowed to continue working with the agency.

After the war, Déricourt was tried for having "intelligence with the enemy," however Bodington testified on his behalf and Déricourt was acquitted—a result which infuriated other high-ranking SOE officials. It is now widely believed that Déricourt was complicit in the arrest of many other SOE agents, and possibly hundreds of French resistors.

The character of Helen Elwood is loosely inspired by Vera Atkins. After a wartime career with the SOE as an intelligence official heavily involved in the recruitment and training of women agents, Atkins launched a relentless investigation into the SOE's missing agents after the war, devoting her own time and even money into finding answers for families left behind.

The career of the character of Professor Harry Read is inspired by the Professor M. R. D. Foot, official SOE historian to the British government. In my story, Professor Read is attempting to have a book about the SOE published in 1970, however Professor Foot was permitted to publish his first account (*SOE in France*) in 1966.

Is it true that there was a fire in the SOE records in 1946, although most of the records lost in the fire related to the Belgium section of the SOE, not the French section. It is also unfortunately true that many essential records were destroyed accidentally or intentionally in the days after the war.

I found it heartbreaking, inspiring and challenging to immerse myself in research around the women of the SOE as I wrote this story, and I so hope that you've enjoyed reading it.

If you'd like to get in touch with me, you can find all of my contact details on my website at kellyrimmer.com.

THE
PARIS
AGENT

KELLY RIMMER

Reader's Guide

GRAYDON
HOUSE

1. Were you aware of the Special Operations Executive before you read this book?

2. SOE agents were often recruited as civilians and sent into occupied territory with only a few months' immersive training. Do you think you could be trained to survive and succeed under such conditions, in such a short space of time? What do you think you might do if you were approached for such a role at a time when the world was in such chaos?

3. Josie is a young woman with a chronic illness, managing her health at a time when that illness was poorly understood. Had you ever considered what life might have been like for the chronically ill during wartime?

4. Eloise makes the choice to leave her young son behind, first in the care of her mother, but later in the care of strangers. She's motivated by a desire for revenge and later, by a desire to do what she could to ensure her son grew up in a world at peace. Did she make the right choice to leave Hughie?

5. Geraldine hid Professor Read's attempts to contact Noah for decades. What was her ultimate motivation for this? Do you agree with Charlotte that had she survived, Geraldine would eventually have made peace with Noah's need to better understand his own past?

6. Josie has a fraught relationship with Drusilla. What was at the heart of that tension? Did it seem a realistic dynamic to you?

7. Gerard makes terrible decisions throughout the war but perceives himself to be helplessly trapped. Even so, he does try to help Josie once she is arrested. Did you feel sympathy for him at all?

8. Which characters in this book did you like best? Which did you like least? Why?

9. Which scene in *The Paris Agent* affected you the most, and why? What emotions did that scene elicit?

10. Were you satisfied with the ending? What do you imagine happened next for Noah, and for Charlotte and Theo?

11. Was there an aspect of the history in this novel that surprised you?

12. What will you remember most about *The Paris Agent*? Who would you recommend this book to?

13. Was this your first Kelly Rimmer book? If you've read any of her other titles, which did you like the best?